I0779429

Susie Drake and the Stolen Memories

—A 44th Morning Adventure—

Jay Hall

44th Morning LLC

Cover Artist: Dan Drewes
Editing and Formatting: C&D Editing

Library of Congress Control Number (LCCN): 2023921966
ISBN: 979-8-218-42418-3

Dedication

To Rhonda Souder,
For the encouragement and inspiration

Chapter 1: Misty Susie's Detached Memories

August 17, 2050

Midnight in a cemetery on the outskirts of Tucson.

"ALL THESE DEAD PEOPLE," SUSIE said to no one. "I didn't kill any of them." Flashlight in hand, she aimed the beam toward one of the graveyard's older sections. "Scratch that. I see three headstones for guys I murdered. *Hmm*. I thought the caporegime had them buried in Phoenix. In fact … I know I have three dead guys there. Just not the same fellows."

Soon, the illumination carried across a tombstone bearing a more recent date. "Sacha Fitzpatrick Ahern. The last of my Earthling friends. Gone at ninety-one years of age. You lived a long, full life. Why'd you have to leave me?"

Did she expect an answer? There wasn't any other human around, living or deceased. Trilling insects, yes, and maybe a fox or coyote.

During the act of transferring the lantern from one hand to the other, the light weaved over something which made her perform a double-take. She held the torch firmly by the handle, scoffing as it poured across the anthropomorphic form.

"A full-sized granite angel. Wings, too. Nice." Spotting a bronze bench located in front of the statue, she eased down upon it. "Me in the presence of a carved occupant of heaven. Who'd've thunk it? Let me introduce myself. Oh, yeah, I do talk to myself and inanimate objects a lot. More than I do people." She quickly patted the figure's forever-praying hands. "Are you asking something from God or me? *Ha*! Not a lot I can give you. How about a fast rundown of who I am? Good, because it's all I got time for.

"I'm Susie Drake. I was born in 1902. Yep, I'm one hundred and forty-eight years old, and I don't look much older than twenty-one. My parents had powers. I inherited some myself. Besides being almost immortal, I'm practically impervious to harm, can manipulate people's will and memories by touching them, run short distances very fast, and am very strong. My pops was a nutcase. He killed my mom and almost done me in. In the aftermath, I had memory problems for a long time.

"What does someone with a face compared to a long-ago actresses do for a living? Model? Act? Not I! Assassin! It became my profession for half a decade or so before I met some people whose kind ways changed me. This led to my working for the government, doing greater good stuff.

"Later, I wander into a war between my friends and an army of alien wizards. It's a battle unknown by ninety-nine percent of the world at the time—the 1970s. Not long after the fighting ended, I became a soldier of fortune. Many times, I used my strength and speed to save people, tampering with their recall, as I don't want publicity. Make that … *didn't* want publicity."

Drake directed a shimmer at Ahern's resting spot. "My late friend testified before Congress about the secret war after being the first to publish a book on the subject. The Joint Chiefs reluctantly backed her story, and then all hell broke loose. Uh, sorry, all *heck* broke loose. By then, all but a few of my friends' children survived, except for some exceptional off-world pals and myself. The press hounded me, made me a superstar. Poor me, yeah.

"Tiring of the attention, I traveled incognito into most every country before receiving an invite from Sacha. She and her hubby have a guesthouse, and would I like to stay? Indeed, I did for seven years … until she passed six months after him."

Rising, she paced the ground between her and the sculpture. "What do I do now? On her deathbed, Sacha recited the same ol' lecture. Make new friends. Understanding others, she insisted, will make me understand myself better. Sweet old gal she was, but I already know me as best as I ever will. I. Don't. Make. New. Friends. Very. Well. Too much trouble." Susie halted, moving her face close to the stone object. "You're stuck in mid-prayer. Pray me an answer. I need one."

Drake scanned the night sky. A shooting star streaked diagonally before burning out above the angel's head. Rather than admit grief overwhelmed her, Susie interpreted the meteor's movement as a sign.

Nose to nose with the stone spirit, she attempted communication. "You got an answer to the prayer, didn't cha? Tell me. What do I do now?"

Silence … until something clicks.

"E'tatanya! Of course. She's an Exile. I've been in exile from living for years. I know another Exile whose name is Angel. It all fits!"

PEANUT BUTTER CRACKERS, BEEF JERKY, and vanilla cream soda, Susie had stocked her cooler with these snacks. Seated at a picnic table on the outskirts of Lambly Lake, twenty-two miles northwest of Kelowna, British Columbia, she finished a package of beef links. The sun's reflection on the water added a halo around a green-haired woman who sparkled from the ether into reality.

Susie burped after sipping the soft drink. "'Bout damn time you showed. Why didn't you meet me at Bunyan's Flapjack Restaurant like we agreed? Y'know, I worked there for a short time back in the 1960s."

Both hands rested firmly on the newcomer's hips. "Everyone in town, including the tourists, *knows* you worked there. There're photos of you plastered on the wall. Journalists and opportunists scour the forests searching for Lointain. They harass older Kelowna families rumored to be the Exiles' allies and trample the protected forests looking for a world they can't possibly see. Sacha's confessional books altered all of our lives."

In the early 1800s, the Exiles had begun inhabiting a magically manufactured floating world above the woodlands outside Kelowna, invisible to the eyes of Earthlings. These once prosperous inhabitants of a farther-away realm had provoked its ruling class by seeking eternal life (only partially achieved) and revealing their planet's existence to Earth (accomplished centuries later via Sacha's testimony). To keep the forced expatriates mum on where they had originated from and other cult secrets, a spiritual patriarch had placed a curse on the Lointainians. Every few years, demons and unimaginable creatures attacked the colony as a reminder to the citizenry to maintain secrecy. These skirmishes had produced injuries and property damage, but seldom any deaths. Both the atmosphere inside the fabricated globe and the elixir for near-immortality instilled a variety of powers in its residents, providing an edge over the bizarre invaders.

"You know there's no longer a curse on Lointain. My long-dead friends ended it for you. Don't worry about the news media and other thrill-seekers; they'll never get past the false entrances and other wussified decoys." She bared her teeth then eased up on the bitterness. "Sacha passed away. She won't cause you any more harm."

Relaxing her arms, E'tatanya cocked her head. "I'm sorry about Sacha. She was your final mortal connection with a bygone age. You do still have others who care about you. Forgive me my petty concern about annoying outsiders. I'm not accustomed yet to the changes in my people's outsider status."

Drake patted the wooden plank on which she sat, long legs stretched outside the table. "Come sit. I have two favors to ask."

After tying her emerald hair into a wavy ponytail, E'tatanya positioned herself a half-foot from Susie. "I hope you request my transporting you into Lointain. There are many who long for your company again."

"Listen to me." Drake leaned an elbow on the table, adding a civilized, "Please." After a pause, she continued,

"Tell everyone … I said *hello*. It'll have to do. First favor: I want you to send me to another world, dimension—whatever. Somewhere not very populated. A place in dire need of help. A job which'll take a long time finishing. You know all the sorcery stuff. Should be easy, right?"

"I'm not a sorceress. I'm a healer, a shamaness. I don't dabble in the dark arts. Contradictory as it may sound, I do what I do in the name of Jesus Christ." Serious-eyed, she added, "I can do as you ask. I know the perfect place. Let me explain it."

E'tatanya resituated her body on crossed legs. "Nearly three million persons currently dwell on the old planet. Over a hundred times, many died when a spaceberg collided with the world. I'm alluding to a living galaxy-iceberg, or Galacteeq. Normally, these creatures splat on a globe and birth one frozen tundra. Here, after decimating a majority of the population, it created two living polar shelves; a huge one in the north, a smaller one just above the equator. Alive, yes, and both create a thick, unbroken ring around the sphere. Baby Berg is moving ever so slightly north to join its buddy. Unfortunately, the human survivors are stuck in the dry plains between the monsters and will end up squashed no matter where they venture."

"Teleport the people over the ice. There's your solution. You Exiles exceed at it."

"Only certain powers work on this world. Teleportation is not one of them."

"How do you plan on taking me there if teleporting doesn't work?"

"A three-seat spaceship, given to Lointain by a world in another dimension. I worked there as an exchange shamaness."

"Okay. Can't they use explosives and blow a hole through Baby Berg? How wide is it?"

"At its narrowest point, thirty-five miles. That section is also the most jagged with high- velocity winds. Even if munitions worked, I couldn't do it. These shelves are living beings. They aren't hostile. They seek survival like all of us. Another reason is just as important. To strike against them, separate or together, they would release a toxic gas for defensive purposes. The poison would wipe out thousands of natives. I can communicate with Baby Berg telepathically, gaining its trust—Galacteeqs are peaceful when not provoked. What I propose you do is lead parties over its flattest region, a length of forty-four miles."

"If you can speak with it, tell it to stop moving or have one or both shelves back up. They'll meet eventually."

"I tried negotiating those points and failed. The smaller piece will slow its pace if it detects us transporting people."

Susie snorted. "If the Baby burps, it'll swallow us, right? Okay, seriously, how will we travel? We'll need traction cleats, ice axes, special harnesses, yada, yada, yada. You got all that prepared?"

"The human leader will provide everything you need. You and those crossing with you will ride inside procophants. They're like a combination kangaroo and elephant. Each can tote four people and adequate supplies inside their pouch. Resistant to cold, they have cleated feet, can detect ice cracks miles away, and leap onto safe formations. On the downside, only ten of these intelligent animals have given their cooperation for the transport. They only jump when necessary, so don't force them. I mention this because they travel slowly. Forty people, including yourself, out of a few million at thirty-five miles one way. You said you wanted a job 'long-time finishing.' This is it."

"Intelligent ice, intelligent procophants. I like bossing around dummies. Who are the dummies on planet … whatchacallit?"

"Planet Ouspenskrankyla. Breathable air. Nice people, not dummies. When you show up, Susie, they will be in awe of you. The Ouspenskrankylaians have only one race, one culture. Each person is amber-skinned and white-haired. One look at you, and they'll beg to obey."

Tapping her foot, Susie exhaled. "I don't want fans. Guess I'll have to whip 'em into shape. I'm definitely in, no matter how long it takes." Hiding a grin, she said, "Ouspenskrankyla, huh? You chose a world with the word 'kranky' in it. Did you pick it on purpose as a reference to my personality or was it merely a Freudian slip?"

The near-immortal blinked, never certain how to deal with her friend's always off-kilter disposition. "It's 'kranky' with a 'k'. You needn't search for hidden implications that don't exist. I'll write it off as part of your grief. So, what's the second favor you ask?"

Hesitation mounted a skirmish across Susie's face before she found the words. "I want certain memories severed. Not eliminated, just stored away. I know you can do it. You've told me so yourself. If I could do it correctly with the memory adjustment part of my suggestive power, I would. But it's too tricky using it on myself."

E'tatanya turned her head in the lake's direction, biting her lip, wishing she hadn't been open with Drake regarding her skills. Then, facing her companion, she said, "I know what you're asking pertains to the deaths of your friends. The simpler, easier approach would be making new ones. Like it or not, people feel drawn to you."

"New friends who'll live and die while I won't age an iota. I know I gotta face those facts and start over. First, I need a break from the grief." The former assassin stood, kicking at the ground. "It won't be forever. Remove remembrances of specific people while I'm away. You gotta admit, it's not everybody who's forced to live beyond the lives of their friends and their friends' children."

"Withdrawing recollections can alter your personality. You were once a very violent person. I don't want you reverting back to her."

"I'll keep the proper reminders so that it won't happen. I've made a list of who stays, which is everyone I've murdered, and who goes, namely all my friends." From a satchel on her motorbike, she removed a pad of paper, handing it to the Exile. "I've thought this over for months now. I'm not changing my mind."

The healer read the names to herself. She knew Susie well enough to know arguing represented a waste of breath. "I'm very much indebted for your agreeing to help the Ouspenskrankylaians. I had no other option regarding their relocation. Assisting them across the berg *and* remaining long enough for their resettlement will pay for the second favor. I'll check in on you now and then. When you're ready again for Earth, I insist on restoring your memories."

"No problem. Where will you store them?"

"There exists a universe which, when first formed, projected massive-sized cliffs alongside a steep, congruous galaxy. Quite unique. The planets within are very small, all uninhabited, each orbiting its miniature sun with a singular bluff. I've claimed one for a storage facility and a place to practice any magic I shouldn't attempt on Lointain. I'll keep your remembrances there, inside one of the enchanted pouches I always carry with me."

"All you had to say was somewhere far away. When will you remove the memories and when do we leave for Ouspenskrankyla?"

"Now and immediately after. Have a seat. It won't take long. Though I must warn you about something."

I'M DITCHING MY ORIGINAL PLAN of asking Susie for help. She'd probably turn me down, anyway. After hearing her and the green-haired witch chat, I've formed a new scheme.

A light breeze blew a pine needle beneath the Lambly Lake picnic table. Unobserved, the leaf transformed into an ant. The insect made its way onto E'tatanya's yellow shoe and morphed into a tiny dot of fast-bonding glue on the outer heel. Former Exile Ren Pith, an expert at shapeshifting into living creatures (for no longer than ten minutes) and inanimate objects (no set time limit), knew this moment to be his best opportunity at hitching a ride on the sneaker of the woman he despised.

On Wednesdays, Pith enjoyed ruminating on his unhappy life. Today being a Wednesday, he happily commenced his mental tale, imagining himself relating it to a movie producer.

Life was fine up until I was seven years old. I lived with my parents and two brothers on the outskirts of Lointain's main city. Halcyon days. In 1974, the curse hit. Monarch bees were part of a horde of prehistoric bats and insects infiltrating the planet. During a curse attack, the adults herded most youngsters out of town, toward shelters installed in the mountains. My folks and siblings were on an Earth vacation. Left in the care of my grandparents, we were seconds away from teleporting to a sanctuary when I felt a sting on my arm.

Inside the safety cave, Grandpa examined the bee sting and waved it off as 'just a little puncture' and 'Rennie will recover nicely.'

'One stung me, too,' he said. 'I'm a-okay.'

But I wasn't. I passed out a couple times.

My so-called protectors showed no concern, telling anyone who asked how I was merely tired. When we returned to the city, I asked Grandma to please send for E'tatanya.

'No,' she replied. 'She's already healed those who truly suffered. Now she's on Earth, helping a needy group.'

What was I— garbage?

Because the sting mark faded and I displayed no physical side effects, my parents heeded the grand idiots' advice and kept me out of the healer's sight.

Age twelve, the seizures started.

Here, the producer would ask, *'What about your powers? Don't all Lointainians have super-gifts?'*

Yeah, I would tell her, *all of us can teleport. Everyone has at least one primary power. I can shapeshift into any inanimate object and most living creatures up to ten minutes.*

After I had the seizures for seven years, I became able to whip up geomagnetic storms, one releasable every fifty years. Remember the 2035 massive blackout in Russia and China? It was mine.

'Cool! Makes for great special effects. Did you get in trouble? I predict magnificent dramatic scenes!'

Those two countries wanted me prosecuted. Jack Boudreaux, Lointain's leader, said no, not until there was a full-scale investigation, even though I admitted what I had done. It wasn't intentional, and no one was hurt.

There's a bigshot Exile landowner, Luther Fontenot, who wanted me banished. He argued how my reputation scarred our world, but the truth was he had business dealings in both those nations, and they were pressuring him ... I guess.

'These convulsions,' the film coordinator would begin, 'any way we can jazz them up on screen?'

What I experience is no ordinary bout of epilepsy, no grand mal seizures. When I tremble, blue lightning surrounds my body, lifting me up. I never remember what happens next. My Dad told me I screamed like he imagined a banshee would wail before my skin turned a dark black. My older brother would joke afterward, "No wonder you like soul and funk music!" Of course, my skin changes back to white when the seizure ends. I've always thought that if I had remained black, then maybe I would've felt connected to a community. I sure never fit in with the Exiles or Caucasian Earthlings.

Finally, my parents requested E'tatanya. Do you know what she said after witnessing a spasm? 'Why didn't you contact me immediately after the bee sting?'

Not responding, 'stupid grandparents,' took every bit of restraint.

E'tatanya couldn't help me. She required a living or recently dead monarch bee to extract its DNA or 'spiritual blueprint,' as the healer called it. They're extinct. Too bad, Renaldo. I was given a pill which decreased the number of spells by a fraction. Big damn deal.

About now, the producer would stare at her watch, wanting me to hurry the story up. 'I need a director of epic-type movies for this project,' the organizer would state.

A few months pass. I start performing rituals, habits. Tapping fingers x number of times. Not walking certain streets because they might bring me bad luck (even if it meant taking a much longer route). Leaving my apartment only when my digital watch read certain times in the minute column (never leave on a 3, 8, or 9—again, bad luck). I have Obsessive Compulsive Disorder (OCD). I counted (since I'm obsessed with counting) one hundred and seventy routines and fanatical thoughts. I added seven more only to make it one hundred and seventy-seven, which is a 'lucky' number, although it doesn't make sense being 'lucky' to have massive OCD.

Seemingly unimpressed, the production overseer would ask, *'Any Oscar-worthy moments with the OCD?'*

Isn't it enough that the disorder debilitated me? Most common sense thinking gets overruled by what I call the OCD voice. I lost out on experiencing all the important social skills because my friends shunned me! All I've known is unrequited love. I keep telling myself Isabella loves me, but I think I'm nothing more than her pity boyfriend.

Guess what? E'tatanya couldn't help me this time, either. 'Both your ailments are curable, but I still need a single monarch bee. I've made inquiries to my many sources. They must exist somewhere.'

Yeah! In the past, you green-haired witch! No one's invented time traveling yet. Really? Seems I recall hearing campfire tales about a guy, last name Rodanthe, who traveled back from an alternate timeline to 1960s Earth and caused a helluva lotta trouble. This fellow owned an obsession for Susie and interfered in her life.

What's that, producer? My story not interesting enough for a film? How about this ... I'm hitching a ride on E'tatanya's shoe into a pocket dimension and will steal Drake's memories. Somewhere in those recalls lies information on contacting Rodanthe. Find him. Get me a monarch bee, or steal my younger self the heck away from the heartless grump-parents. Destroy anything which gets in my way! I'd call the film a blockbuster, wouldn't you?

"IT SOUNDS LIKE YOU HAD a good time." E'tatanya piloted the spaceship on its fifteen-hour journey from Ouspenskrankyla to Lointain before teleporting onto Earth. "By the size of the reception and outpouring of thanks, you're a hero on two worlds now."

"The people there are amazing. I'm glad you gave me extra time. There was persistent bitterness between some factions I managed to sort out." Susie rested her feet upon the recliner's lift. "I've blabbed too long about how I spent my hundred years off Earth. Tell me what's happened since I've been away. It's 2150. Do they have flying cars yet?"

"About 2150." A nervous exhale passed. "There exists a huge time difference between the two worlds. When you arrived on Ouspenskrankyla, by their calendar, it was 1950 Earth time. The fifteen-hour trip there and back costs you, not me, seven years. I know magic charms which work in my favor timewise."

"Hurrah for you. It feels like a hundred years for me, and it's okay. I haven't aged any. So, do they still have gas cars?"

The healer altered her rehearsed speech. "You mentioned flying cars. The Thrusk brothers developed them a few years ago, based on a blueprint drawn by an old friend of yours. The government awarded first usage to parcel delivery firms like UPFX. In the last year, someone started sabotaging the aerofreight vehicles, or Zeps, as they're known by. Four aeropilots died in the explosions, so did five people on the ground. There's been an arrest, a man who was once part of the Amish. The evidence against him is pretty flimsy. A friend of ours wants your help in clearing his name."

Susie's eyes paced all over the pilot. It wasn't the information which set off an alarm; it was the tone used. "You know what you sound like? Like a TV newswoman reading about a murder, and the victims were members of her family. I can tell there's more significance going on here. These friends of mine … I've no idea who they are and probably won't recognize their names until I get my memories back. How's about you put the ship on autopilot, zap off to your cliff universe, grab my recollections, and whip 'em back in my head?"

Weakly, E'tatanya said, "Susie, I can't—"

"Y'see, there's this song stuck in my head, and I desperately need to figure out who sings it before I start killing people! Just kiddin' about offing folks."

Starting over, E'tatanya told her, "Susie, I *can't*! Someone stole your memories. I am so sorry."

"You're shittin' me, right? C'mon!" The side of her mouth became small, fighting anger. "What was the place … uh … 'congruous galaxy,' you called it? Uninhabited planet? A place where people can't rip you off because there're no damned people. Right?"

The sea of silence engulfed the celebrated heroine of Earth and Ouspenskrankyla, drowning her in the unfathomable reality of the situation.

"You stored 'em in a pouch and said some magic words, rendering them touchable only by your hands. They gotta be there. Hit the autopilot, and let's go looking."

A rare sweat bead lingered on her forehead when the words she spoke made matters worse. "I also placed a trackable hex on the packet. Every six Earth months, I planned on looking in on the sack. It was gone after the first check. The tracking spell led me to an empty container on a nearby planet. Memories gone. I applied every trick I know to find them and called in assistance from Lointain as well as other dimensions. The results were always the same. Now—"

"Argh!"

At that moment, she expected Susie's interruption would either precede loud profanity or extreme violence. Through E'tatanya's breath, a cool mist escaped, floating toward Drake. Within the unseen cloud, a calming complex of molecules. The vapor worked fast. Her confrere behaved rationally.

"Someone knew the magic words you spoke and followed you to the hiding place. Who else could do this except another Exile? Correct?"

"Yes. It's where I was leading. One of our most sensitive trackers discovered an essence near the Lambly Lake picnic table where you and I met. This unique substance was also on the shoes I wore at the time. The extraction was not present on the uninhabited world, due to its unusual atmospheric conditions. Renaldo Pith is the owner of said ethos." She initiated a short background on the man, one a movie producer might relish. "Before you say, 'let's go get him,' I must tell you he could be hiding anywhere among thousands of galaxies and dimensions, if he even lives.

"Five years ago, Pith, whose powers include the manufacturing of geomagnetic storms, forged one so devastating that it destroyed electric grids on Earth, including the entire internet. Only two years ago did the planet fully recover, although much information never returned to what's now called the GNet."

"And Pith?"

"He bragged about causing the calamity. Because he originally hailed from Lointain, our leader, Jack Bordeaux, commissioned a task force to capture Pith. He naturally resisted and escaped by both shapeshifting and teleportation."

"Why would he want my memories?"

"I don't know. I spoke with his parents and friends. They didn't know. We checked all the spots he frequently visited. His reasoning remains a mystery."

"Maybe he sold them. I was a badass criminal once. Those days, especially my killings, are about all I can recall." Frowning, she said, "I don't remember much of my life. Even less than when I left Earth."

"I warned you about it before I made the snip. Any singular memory lends itself to hanging onto strings of other remembrances. Once those threads remain untethered, they can dissipate, fade. Restoring what I removed would reseal the strands. Recollections never become extinct."

"How certain are you about Pith?"

"That he swiped the bag? Ninety percent. Finding him? Forty percent."

"Who wins the ten percent as a suspect?"

"Does the name Hugh Rodanthe mean anything to you?"

Susie rubbed her chin. "Gee, how come I can't place it? Oh yeah! Some scumbag leaped on your bod and swiped what doesn't belong to him."

"He is, or was, a time traveler. In the 1970s, he sent you several letters. Their purpose being to goad you into remaining, uh … a criminal badass. You resisted. There was much more to his scheme. Rodanthe may be back. I'll explain it in detail later." She allowed the information to sink in.

"When we reach Earth, I have a friend who will present you a treasure trove of documented data on yourself. It's not meant for replacing what's temporarily lost." The quality of her voice wavered. "We Exiles are no longer welcome on Earth. The havoc Pith caused brought the ire of nations upon us. There are pockets of allies who risk jailtime to speak with us. We'll visit a special one. Memories or not, I believe you can help the ex-Amish man."

The earlier calming spell erupted yawns from Susie. "I'm gonna doze off. When I awake, tell me this crap about my memories being gone was a joke. Nobody would wanna have what I went through in their head. I know it was bad stuff. Really bad." Into a deep sleep, she sunk.

E'tatanya radioed a psychic message. *Susie and I will arrive at your house, Liam, seven p.m. on May 13th. I have yet to tell you about the problem with her memories, and I haven't told her about the pandemic. There is still plenty of hope for Matt and his brother.*

Intermission (April 2022 and May 2057)

SUSIE CALLS OUT MY NAME, "Jay! Hey! I gotta beef with you."

I don't immediately answer because I'm surprised she's already learned my name. What else does she know? Only one way of finding out.

"Hello, Susie. I can see you sleeping in a brown recliner. Dreaming about me, are you?"

"A nightmare is more like it!" she growls. "*Somehow …* maybe because of a graveyard angel, maybe not, but I know you're writing a book about me. I read some of it before it mysteriously vanished. You wrote a short recap of who I am, what I've done, my deal with E'tatanya, and her telling me my memories are missing. There was a blank spot over a page between my going to and coming back from Ouspenskrankyla. It's where someone, likely the Pith guy, swiped my recollections, right?"

"I really, um … can't say."

"Sure you can. Just tell me where I can retrieve my recall, and we'll go our separate ways, okay?" Stuffed inside her "okay" was the threat of annihilation if I don't comply.

"Listen, it wouldn't be fair to the readers—if there are any—if I gave away information regarding one character to another. You and me … we're tied together, and I don't know all the rules, let alone the why of it."

"I am *not* a made-up character! I'm flesh and blood, bones, and muscle … enough strength for flattening you like a pancake!"

Highly doubtful even if she were real and powerful. She and I exist in different worlds and timelines. There's no way to bridge the gap.

Breaking what I know is a law of fiction, I inform the protagonist about my lack of knowledge regarding her memories' whereabouts, which is true. I don't mention Pith's name or anything on the page introducing him. Discovering such info is her job.

Instead of exploding when I tell her this, she acts nonchalantly.

"Fine. I don't need the help of a psychotic voice, anyway."

From inside Susie's head, I can hear her thoughts. *Hmm. There's gotta be a way for reading everything he writes before I lose access and it vanishes.* By "vanishes," she's referring to my saving the document onto the cloud. I can't allow it. Too much breaking down the fourth wall will dilute the plot!

I try for a truce of sorts. "Susie, I'll try giving you a few spoilers now and then, contingent upon how they affect the pace of the story. Okay?"

"Depends. I don't like the notion of a 'story.' Makes it sound like things are gonna drag on too long." Sneering, she spits, "This isn't a series you're writing, is it?"

"No way! The book will be self-contained."

"Movie deal?"

"I hope. I have no idea who'd play you. It's not exactly a role that would fetch an award nomination."

"Ha, ha! Then who'd you cast as [MULTIPLE NAMES DELETED]?"

"I had to remove your friends' names. They're not integral to the story."

In response, Susie sticks out her tongue at me. "Forget the book. Sell Hollywood a manuscript and then—"

"Then you hope the movie can somehow transcend time and space, allowing you to see it and figure out where your memories are without working for it. Forget it!"

Out her mouth flies an onslaught of obscenities and when finished, insults. "Coward! No agent will want your crappily written novel, nor could you sell it to a movie studio or even the most pitiful streaming service. I hope, when I find my recollections, that you're nowhere in sight 'cause you haven't the imagination for solving the theft yourself!"

"Stop fishing for clues," I snarl assertively. "You're asleep on the spacecraft. Return to your dream. Over and out."

"Moron!"

Chapter 2: Messy History and Sloppy Joes

May 12, 2057

PERFORMING AEROBICS IN THE LIVING room, as instructed via the multi-colored, 3-D holograph, Imene Hogan Karas addressed her husband exiting the kitchen. "Who was that at the back door, honey?"

"Matt Allgyer, asking if I'd heard from E'tatanya yet."

A finger snap paused the instructional course. "I'm warning you, Liam. Associating with the Exile woman will get you into trouble. You should tell Matt to apply for a lawyer loan. It's the only way he'll get his brother a reduced sentence. Poor guy, shunned by his Amish family."

"I'm gonna wait a couple weeks; see if E'tatanya appears. And if not, then I'll sign as backer on the loan. Matt's still new to his ex-Amish life and hasn't mastered the GNet yet." He sighed. "I can't abandon my support of the Exiles. The government's wrong for blaming an entire race for the terrorism of one of its members. It's only a misdemeanor if someone reports me talking with her."

"Oh, *only*. Well, that makes all the difference! Let's see … you're the radical detective who collected evidence against the neo-Nazi mayor of ultra-conservative Mason which, of course, is your hometown. Your neighbors not only shun you but me, as well, since I'm a radical Black Muslim journalist. But go ahead; speak with E'tatanya. I'm sure they'll be happy hanging us both from the strange fruit tree."

When he laughed, he waved a hand across his face, as if apologizing. "First off, I'm not radical; I'm liberal. Mason is less conservative than you think. I know because I speak with people here all the time, whereas you avoid them. No, no, don't argue. Next, you're light-skinned black, like your great-grandfather. You're no more radical than I am, and nobody but me in Mason knows you're a Muslim. Besides, you're a cultural Muslim, not a practicing one."

She scooped a slipper off the floor and tossed it at him in fun. "I won't bail you out when they arrest you."

"No one will know I've spoken with her. She'll teleport into the garage … like last time."

"Uh-huh. Anyway, you know she can't use her powers to help Matt. Any evidence discovered through Exile magic is inadmissible in court unless you can prove it on your own. The D.A. would see through you and figure out E'tatanya's role."

"It's not *her* whose assistance Matt wants and needs. It's someone else's." He allowed a dramatic pause. "It's Susie Drake."

Imene opened her mouth, withdrew the words itching to escape, and pondered for a few minutes on the rich history Drake had played in the lives of her and Liam's family three generations removed.

"She, uh … Susie's been missing for seven years. Some say she's hiding in a cave in the Arctic. Even if E'tatanya found her, what good could she possibly do, Matt?" Slowly, she edged toward Liam, rubbing a hand on his shoulder. "Susie's the personification of redemption. She represents the link between our families in a manner almost spiritual. But … she's not a private investigator. We should respect her wish for privacy until she decides to reemerge."

"It's not like that." His hand slipped onto hers, and he guided her toward a chair back inside the kitchen. Leaning against the touch-screen stove, he clarified, "I'll tell you now, even though E'tatanya asked I keep it secret until she returned.

"Seven years ago, she transported Susie to another planet. There, she helped an endangered population move from one location to another. That time is up. Both women will return here anytime now. Susie will help Matt because she has many connections and much experience dealing with authoritative figures. No one's going to bullshit Susie Drake. No one."

After a brief silence, Imene said, "The healer always liked you best. I guess it's why she kept me out of the loop. I see your point. I still don't want anyone seeing you associate with the Exile, okay? But Susie … goodness! What she has stored in her head is bound to be good enough to help Matt and his brother."

"YOU SHOULD'VE TOLD ME ABOUT the lost memories." Liam leaned against the workbench in the garage, arms crossed over his chest. "Knowing what was at stake, I would have created a better assortment of videos and documentary clips on Susie."

"You're right," E'tatanya conceded. "At the time, my motive revolved around your and Imene's loyalty."

Susie slurped a straw inside a chocolate milkshake. "I do remember these, though I prefer strawberry … I think. I don't recall anyone you guys showed me on the computer. Well, except for the celebrities and a few politicians."

Liam sighed. "My family and my wife's family were close to you. We have a rich history." He lifted a stapled sheet of papers from the bench. "I'll read off names of those in the powered community from back in the 60s and 70s and give you some background on how they figured in your life."

"No, no, don't mention any names. Jay will have a conniption fit. I'll read through it later."

"Who's Jay?" E'tatanya asked.

"You don't wanna know." *Slurp, slurp.* "What do we do now?"

A fair amount of silence followed.

"Okay. Do you have anything for me to look at or read on Pith?"

"Smell that? Dinner's almost ready. Imene's cooking tonight. I traded her my night as chef so that we could talk. After we eat, I'll give you my dossier on Pith and show you the videos online I saved of him. But, please, do look over these documents." He handed them to her. "You couldn't have had everyone listed here removed from your mind."

Standing, Drake tossed the empty cup into a trash container and inserted the pages into a shoulder bag. Then she wrapped a hand around the healer's arm, pulling her toward Karas. Uncharacteristically affectionate, Susie hugged them together, whispering, "Thank you, guys, for all the help. I intend on returning the favor by doing whatever I can for Matt and his brother— both of whom I want to meet." Breaking the embrace, she snapped a finger. "Oh yeah. E'tty, you never did fill me in on this Rodanthe character. You said he was a time traveler. What business did he have with me?"

E'tty. The green-haired Exile stifled a giggle at the nickname. "In the late 1960s, he began sending you letters, signing them 'a friend.' These notes contained provoking lines, designed to make you break your redemptive ways and return to a life of crime. You didn't revert. What you did do was follow a falsely planted lead, meeting a man in Uruguay who rendered you in a coma for a while. I treated you off and on during that time."

"Rodanthe had limited contact with persons in the community." Liam picked up the narrative. "There are events involving him we're unclear about. While you catch up on your history and Pith's background, I'll compile some info on what we do know about him. You see, witnesses claim they saw Pith break into a museum dedicated to the powered community. The only things missing were documents pertaining to Rodanthe."

"Yeah, okay, whatever." Drake moved her head in a circle, sniffing toward a wooden door. "I *know* what's cooking. Sloppy Joes! Didn't you say your wife's a Muslim, Liam? I didn't think she could eat such stuff."

"She'll cook most meats, but she's a veggie. You should try her killer salad."

Susie made a face. "No, thanks. How's about you, E'tty? Just 'cause you got green hair don't mean you gotta eat green food, right?"

Amid a bout of quiet, Liam scratched his neck and E'tatanya stared straight ahead.

"*Ew*! Is saying 'green hair' politically incorrect? Lemme guess … 'uniquely hued tresses?' Well then, what's wrong with you guys?"

The shamaness side-glanced Karas, regretting what she would say. "Imene prefers I maintain a distance from her. It's all part of the ban on Exiles … because of Pith, I'm sorry to say."

"To be fair," Liam objected, "my wife does enjoy your company. She's always believed you had something against her. The distance she prefers has more to do with the townspeople who might see you in the house. Sorry."

Deep, theatrical groaning exited Drake. "Enough with the sorrys already! Pith brought down the internet and eventually Earth nerds rebuilt it … At least, that's the version I got. Why the ban on the Exiles? My memory of them is pretty much gone, but I know they're good people. Besides, I do remember how petty social media was. Good riddance to the trolls and haters."

"When the crash came," Karas explained, "the geomagnetic storms were so powerful they fried all computers. Pith must have known wizardry because mixed within his abilities was a tracking spell for the elimination of all electronic data on memory sticks and any type of disc unattached from a laptop or desktop. Yeah, the 'Earth nerds' do have their methods for retrieving information thought lost. But it was too late. A month before the collapse, a pandemic, one much worse than COVID-19, began spreading across the world. Scientists, researchers, and doctors lost all the materials they'd gathered for coming up with a vaccine and a cure. This was 2052. By 2055, when the GNet was up and running, three point three billion people had died of RES-51.

The return of the net coincided with a steep leveling off of deaths. Spring of last year, Thrusk Inc. developed a serum for preventing and curing the virus."

Not a sound could be heard while Susie contemplated a response.

"Thrusk, eh? Same bunch who built the flying cars. Interesting. Guess I understand the resentment toward all Exiles. Earth people do tend to be small-minded about such things. So, E'tty, I'll bet you tried coming up with a cure on your own, right?"

"There's hope for your recollections yet," She smiled. "The son of an old friend of yours, [NAME DELETED], set up a lab for me in Nova Scotia. Work had to take place on Earth or else it could have wiped out the entire Lointain population if released into the atmosphere. We made headway, all in secret … or so we thought."

Liam resumed the account. "A downed internet didn't stop snoopy newshounds. They learned what was going on and aired it on TV. A nutcase group broke inside the lab one night and destroyed it. The UN General Assembly condemned the Exiles, not the radical group. Sanctions against Canada almost ruined the country."

"Three point three billion. Shit." Drake opened her mouth, closed it, and reopened to speak. "Pith's the number one suspect for stealing my memories. E'tty, you said he bragged about taking down the internet and other power sources. Is it possible he lied? Could anyone else but him be responsible?"

The question wasn't an unforeseen one. "Once he admitted involvement, neither Earth nor Lointain suspected anyone else or considered an accomplice."

"What about Rodanthe? I don't remember him but anyone, let alone a time traveler, who'd mess with me is undeniably suspect. I'll bet the Thrusk brothers made a lotta money off their serum. Did they help create the GNet thing?"

"No one really knows if Rodanthe returned," Liam expressed. "You can read Sacha's notes on him taken from interviews with [NAMES EDITED OUT]. The Thrusks had an important hand in reviving the net. They're very respected and considered too nerdy for anything devious unless you're on their competitors' board of directors." Anticipating a remark from Drake, he rapidly added, "The comment about the Thrusks' rivals was meant in humor."

Susie wasn't in a humorous mood. "Still worth checking out if it hasn't already been. Consider it more homework for you, brainy. Find any links the Thrusks and their opposition might have with Pith, Rodanthe, and the Exiles. Are there any others out there with powers?"

"There're a couple hundred Remnants. Last year, Congress forced them to either register their abilities or else be denied certain privileges, like voting, owning guns, etc."

"What's a Remnant?" Another lost fact for Drake.

"Someone who gains powers by an exchange of body fluids with another Remnant. You, Susie, you're credited with creating the first one back in the 1950s."

"Well, yay me. Hope they enjoyed themselves while taking my fluids. Wish I could remember who it was. Could any of these Remnants separate or together be responsible for the geomagnetic storms?"

"Not likely," Karas responded. "There's a website which lists their powers. Assuming it's correct—and I do since I know the webmaster—there's no way all of them combined could pull such a stunt."

"Unless there's an unregistered Remnant with immense powers you don't know about." Susie winked.

The sound of Imene calling, "Dinner," ended the conversation.

E'tatanya faced the others. "I'll return here … inside the garage … tomorrow at the same time. I don't want to draw undue attention to this house or the project. When I come back, let me know what I can do to help within those guidelines."

A strong hand gripped the Exile's arm. "You're having supper with us." Susie dead-eyed both of them. "You tell me I found redemption, E'tty. Well, Liam, Imene's gonna have to forgive her for something she didn't do, or I'm gonna kick the shit out of her. And if I do kick the shit out of her, I'll make sure she goes flying out your front room window headfirst. There're no village hicks watching the house. If there were, I'd have kicked their asses by now. Any objections from either of you? Good. Let's chow down sloppy Joes and killer salad!"

Chapter 3: Who's After Who

SUSIE PULLED APART THE IVORY-COLORED drapes and lifted the cord on the beige blinds. Sunshine scattered straight ahead, licking the eyes of a sleeping man on a sofa.

Grumble, grumble. "What? What time is it?"

"7:30. I let you oversleep. Imene left earlier. Said she'd have breakfast in town. I can fix you eggs and stuff."

Liam squinted, held a hand over an eye, staring at the speaker. "Oh God, Susie! Are you only wearing a T-shirt?! Cl-close the blinds! Hurry!"

"Relax. There's underwear 'neath the shirt. And I'm sorry for gettin' you in the doghouse with the old lady over E'tty. You … forced to sleep on the couch … it's such a cliché. I should tell Jay to change it."

"Who is this—"

"Don't ask," she wisely interrupted. "After you shower and dress, I wanna show you what I found on the GNet. Hey, hey, don't close the drapes. I'm still sunshine-deprived. My last month and a half on planet Ouspenskrankyla was filled with clouds, no sun. Don't worry. No one's gonna see me or think I'm your mistress. I mean, I chased away a half dozen teens from your yard this morning and threatened them if they told anyone about me." She laughed when he didn't. "Good Lord, you can't take a joke! You and your wife both!"

SCRAMBLED EGGS, BACON, AND A PANCAKE embraced Liam's nostrils even before he had entered the kitchen. "You made me breakfast. Thank you!" Seeing she had slipped into blue jeans also pleased him.

She poured coffee into two cups. "I figured I owe you for last night. I'm a good cook. I do remember that much."

Wrongly dismissing her culinary skills, he commented, "Very delicious."

"I see you're surprised. Hey, try living for a hundred and fifty-five years and not picking up some talents here and there. Okay, I cooked; you clean up. We good?"

Scrape, scrape, proclaimed the wooden chair across the tile floor as Liam collected plates and cups.

Susie said, "I know you didn't have time to get on the GNet and find the links I asked you about. Before you do the research, let's talk about the Amish dude involved in the explosions."

At the sink, Liam waited until the garbage disposal finished its roar. "The *ex*-Amish dude*s* are Matthew Allgyer, who's seeking help for his incarcerated brother, Samuel. I have a file on the case already printed for you. You'll want to read a few commentaries on the charges I downloaded as well." Dishes cleaned, he started on the utensils. "The research you asked for is done. I worked on it in the garage after the dinner drama."

"I didn't see a desktop or laptop out there. Oh, lemme guess; it's whatever portable GNet connecting device is hipster cool now."

Ever since her return from Ouspenskrankyla, she had exhibited a nostalgic fondness for 20th-century technology, championing antique relics such as phone booths, 8-track players, and overhead projectors. E'tatanya had explained the fascination as a memory surgery side effect.

"There's an L-shaped gizmo inside the garage's wall cabinet. It's called an OmniScoop. Most people mistake it for an unusually thick, carpenter square. It's actually a computer, one which displays holographs and connects through an advanced set of headphones with a planet that's basically made up of accumulated knowledge. The machine taps into this giant cloud world and returns any data you'd want to know, provided it's already been documented somewhere on a myriad of planets." Liam laughed. "My great-grandfather invented it back in 1972. You knew him."

Drake held up a finger. "Whisper his name in my ear. I don't wanna give cranky Jay the benefit of another deletion." The relative's identity failed to have an impact. "Okay, now you can continue."

"A crystal found on Ouspenskrankyla acts as the brains for the OmniScoop. It's a common gem, and it lasts for decades."

She frowned. "How easy is it to manufacture a bunch of the machines?"

"Very easy."

"Then why didn't people use it when the internet crashed? Wouldn't it have helped save lives during the pandemic?"

"Yes, it would have. It's run on a technology developed not only by my great-gramps but also by an Exile. E'tatanya showed the President how it worked. Anti-Exile fever ended any chance of it becoming even a temporary replacement for the net. Rumors of the OmniScoop's existence resulted in the breaking-in and burning of some tech buildings. Imene and I wouldn't be alive today if word got out that I owned the most workable model."

She snapped brusquely, "Stupid shithead dumbass Earth people! Now I regret going to Ouspenskrankyla. If I'd stayed, I would've whooped President Brain Dead's ass, and any other leader who turned down using the OmniScoop! Nobody could've stopped me from bringing the fancy computer to the scientists working on a cure!" Out her mouth came more vulgarities and combinations of swear words which would've made an Army sergeant blush.

Liam wiped his hands on a towel, stared downward, nervous about the anger boiling in the fist-clenched woman. "Susie, please, calm … down. No matter if you'd been here, people were so worked up in a frenzy it's doubtful many would've trusted a cure developed on a machine with the help of Exiles. In case you've forgotten, *everybody* knows of your deep connections with Lointain. You helped save over three million people on Ouspenskrankyla. Not even half that amount would've taken the cure, no matter how strongly you vouched for its safety."

"Okay. Whatever. What suspicious connections did you find?"

"None with Pith or Rodanthe. They would've hidden it deep if there were any. Pre-pandemic, Thrusk and their competitors sought out any Exile who might publicly back their projects or products. Boudreaux nixed it from the get-go. A Lointainian named Luther Fontenot did do business with the Thrusks. He owns land and industries on Earth. But as one of the Exiles, he was denied making any endorsements unless all the profits benefited the children of his home world. Luther would have none of that. Other than the Boudreaux-Fontenot bickering, I couldn't find any resentment over the Thrusk brothers. It's not like influential people didn't champion their stuff. There's always a legion of pseudo-celebrities itching to make a lotta bread by supporting the fad of the day."

"Gee, hasn't it always been so?" Standing so fast it frightened her host, she rubbed her hands together. "I wanna read up on the Allgyer boys, but first … since you apparently forgot … I found something on the GNet you should see." *I'll let cranky Jay tell the readers how and what I found. Let's see if he gets it right …*

Doubtful.

Before the previous night's dinner, Liam had trained the houseguest on how best to make her way around the GNet. Snoopy Susie had repaid his kindness by rifling through the desk drawers beneath the laptop, discovering a handwritten cheat sheet listing passwords for sites the detective frequented, along with the GChat names of other investigators and colleagues whom Karas relied on for help, and vice versa. It didn't bother the meddling intruder at all when she had invaded his privacy, nor did she feel remorse at pretending to be Liam when sending out emails and GChatting. Those deceived by her actions, believing they communicated with a trusted comrade, had supplied pertinent data and wondered at the odd behavior of their chum who had failed to ask such polite questions as "How are you and your family?" or dispensing a simple thank you for their contribution to an enigmatic inquiry. *Hmm. I'd rather be "cranky" than rude like someone I know!* The account had irked Drake, and she extended her middle finger, waving it back and forth in front of her head. *Like I said, rude.*

Ignoring Susie's strange conduct, Liam immediately caught on to her intrusiveness with a glance at the laptop screen. "You broke into my desk and stole my passwords, didn't you? It's the only way you could've accessed this site on storage facilities." Cold eyes beheld her. "Maybe … maybe you should stay at a motel instead."

She blew a raspberry. "You *knew* what you were getting into when you invited me. At least let me explain before your undies get all bunched up and you kick me out."

Thirty seconds of exaggerated motions with his arms later, Liam relented to her kissy-kissy blue eyes.

Susie pulled up a second chair, patting the seat cushion, a gesture for him to sit. "You told me the Feds discovered Pith had seen a shrink in New York in the early-mid 2040s. The man died before the big geomagnetic storm thingy and … and … all his records on Pith vanished. I think the creep stole them not long after he quit seeing the psychiatrist. That's what I would do—do it the moment a scheme popped in my head— and I'll betcha he decided to take down the net and power grids years before he did it … assuming he did."

Smarting from her "breach of security," Liam grunted in a monotone. "There's no proof Ren Pith stole the transcripts. Other clients had their records missing."

"Well, yeah-ah! You know it's how thieves operate. Make it look like no one in particular gets targeted." She knew how pissed Karas was and avoided a debate. "We also know from the Feds, via a bartender Rennie befriended, that he broke into homes and apartments in the ritzy areas of New York while the occupants were away. Mostly, he raided the fridges and the liquor cabinets. But he also stole an odd array of goods." She lifted a printout from beneath the laptop. "A guitar once owned by Robert Johnson. Three souvenir plates from America's Bicentennial. The entire series of *Wings* on DVD. An autographed photo of Princess Diana. From every place he burgled, he swiped two AA batteries."

"The batteries," a ticked-off Liam said, "come from what Pith told the bartender, a man who went missing when 'Rennie' unleashed his fury against the Earth … like I wish I could do against you."

Sigh, sigh. "I'm sor-r-r-r-y!" Her voice dropped. "You don't really care what I saw about the passwords. You're mad 'cause I read a female's name with a heart by her phone number. Are you cheating on—"

"It's not like that! Okay … I found comfort in talking to her when Imene and I went through a rough spot. I didn't mark out her name because … because Imene can do much better than me." He sweated a little. "After last night, well, we're not exactly solid."

"Bullshit. Last night was on me. My swiping the not-so-well-hidden list is a sign you gotta mark out her name before your wife finds it. I'm surprised she hasn't by now." Drake waited while he dabbed at the sweat beads before continuing, "I won't read the rest of the items Pith stole. The cops never recovered any of them. None. The batteries, I chalk up to the guy's OCD. Right? Right. He must've stored the goods somewhere, like a rental storage shed."

Cool and collected now, Liam countered, "The Feds, police, and hired P.I.s checked all storage units in the New York-Newark area by the owner's or renter's name and opened many. Pith—according to his parents—hated using aliases. And, no, he never returned to Lointain. The Exiles have ways of knowing who gets in and out."

Loudly—really loud—she cracked her knuckles. "The guy's not gonna hide his shit in New York or nearby. He'll be clever and let his ego and OCD dictate a hiding place. In your write-up on him, it says before he went bonkers when the monarch bee stung him, he showed interest in the Pilgrims who landed at Plymouth Rock. Too bad he didn't remain a history geek, eh? So, near Plymouth, North Carolina, not Massachusetts, there's a little speck-in-the-road named Ren. The only blink-and-you'll-miss-it named that in the USA. Your source in Raleigh confirmed there's a storage facility in Plymouth owned by someone named H Tip—backward for Pith. Coincidence? I. Think. Not. Tip bought three units in 2047. On a scanned bill of sale, someone wrote, 'one facility for owner, he will rent other two.' Those two units remain unrented. I say we take a flight to Plymouth and check 'em out. You in, partner?"

"Well—"

"Gotta check with the little lady, huh?" she cut him off and threw in an assumption. "No balls on you, P.I."

"I was going to say you did a pretty good job of investigating. Might be a bust, but definitely worth checking out."

"See? I'm not all boobs, butt, and legs." She curtsied and watched him search through a glass canister behind the laptop. "What now?"

"Magic Marker. Blot out the name on the paper."

With their melodramatic war behind them, they focused on priorities.

"What's first, Susie—meeting with Matt Allgyer or going to North Carolina?"

"Plymouth. Bring all the research, files, reports, and whatnot. I'll read 'em on the plane. Oh, and I'll need a brunette wig."

Excerpts from the journal of Liam Karas, May 2057:

IMENE AND I MADE UP OVER the phone. She was in Bloomington, getting ready to interview an Indiana University professor who claims he's discovered a way of recycling time. The past, so goes his hypothesis, aligns with the planet's orbital period. One year ends and the next begins, right? Wrong, he says. For example, 2056, at 11:59:59 PM on December 31, moved ever so slightly into a never-ending time loop. "It's always there in the timestream," the physicist related in a press conference. "Entering any given timeframe takes highly skilled Thought Projection or TP." The learned scientist teaches a course on TP for $500 a semester at his house. No guarantees, no refunds. "Once you're situated in the year of your choice—a specified period which I recommend you're very familiar with—your mastery of Thought Projection then shifts aside the amount of time you need for *whatever reason brought you back. Reserve only the smallest timespan, as you can constantly reuse it. Earmarking more than two weeks can lead to cracks in reality. You don't want that!"*

From me, "I can imagine what Jack Boudreaux would say about the professor. The Exiles act like they have a monopoly on time travel theories, even though they've never achieved it."

And her, "Boudreaux's a jerk. Be careful in North Carolina. Does Susie truly think a brown wig will disguise her famous face?"

"Seven years is a long time out of the public eye. Plus, she performed some makeup hoodoo. She kinda reminds me of a punk mime."

"Liam, I trust you to say 'no' if she gets frisky."

To this, I thought about replying, "She'd rape me if said 'no.'" Instead, I copped out. "I'm not her type. She's not mine. You are. You be careful home alone. I should be back before tomorrow afternoon, depending on what, if anything, we turn up."

"Has she said anything about knowing us from before? It bothers me how she never asked if we were close friends, mere acquaintances, or strangers."

"Susie hasn't said word one about it. Neither did E'tatanya. I'll say something

when we're on the plane. I hope her recollections aren't even more limited."

OF THE THREE UNITS RENTED by H. Tip, two echoed loudly when Susie banged hard on the lift door. Hearing the noise, the manager, busy showing unrented facilities to prospective customers, stepped around a corner alley and eyed us suspiciously.

"Let's return at night," Susie suggested, "when the doofus has gone home."

I knew she intended to destroy the shed's lock, and it's not like the manager would allow us the key to Unit 44. We booked our (separate) motel rooms and ate dinner at a steak house.

Flashlights in hand under a starless sky, we creeped back down the thinly paved path between the rental units. My partner exerted no effort in yanking off the outbuilding's (somewhat rusted) lock and breaking the combination latch. So much for subtlety and putting things back the way we found them. Inside, a goldmine. All the items Pith had stolen from the swanky apartments of the New York elite, plus a vast collection of conspiracy-minded books regarding the assassinations and deaths of the Kennedy brothers and Princess Diana, and the validity of Anna Anderson as Anastasia Romanov.

Susie found the Holy Grail ... the stolen transcripts (on CD and paper) from Pith's psychiatrist. "There's a CD player and headphones here, too. I can buy new batteries on the way back to the motel. The written stuff is yours. Let's go."

"Wait. The manager can ID us, and it's likely there's security camera footage. With the sophisticated facial programs that the cops' computers have, they'll easily come up with our names. I have a cop friend in Raleigh. I'll tip him off to what we found, minus the shrink's records. He can keep our identities out of this."

"O-o-okay. So, what am I waiting on?"

I made sure my sigh reeked of irritability. "Things can go down smoother when you refrain from destroying property, such as crushing locks. I could have picked it without much hassle."

She said nothing but did pay for a new padlock and helped make the smashed combination lock at least look presentable.

From her purse, she showed me an array of credit cards under different names. "I checked them out last night on the GNet. Can you believe they're still valid after all these years?"

"Sure. You left your cards with E'tatanya before you went to Ouspenskrankyla. She placed a spell on them and your many bank accounts. Your credit is outstanding. What's the mailing address of the one you're gonna use the most?"

"Uh, someplace in Philadelphia. Do I have a history there?"

"Yeah, I'd say so. I won't go into depth. That creepy Jay character will object."

WHAT WE LEARNED FROM THE therapist's written and recorded summations of the sessions with Pith:

Susie was wrong. The two different forms of records (CDs and handwritten) were from different days, not just separate versions.

Pith conveyed extreme hatred for his grandparents and E'tatanya, blaming them for his seizures and OCD.

No mention of Rodanthe, the Thrusks, or Susie. He admitted causing the 2035 Russia-China blackouts but by accident and came across as sincere.

The CDs included not only the psychiatrist's viewpoints, but five of them contained full sessions. Pith sounded controlled and relaxed, nothing like I imagined. Other than his resentments expressed above, he didn't voice anger toward anyone else.

He had a girlfriend in New York, something previously unknown. Isabella Raven. She never came forward when Pith was all over the news.

Around 10:30, my phone rang. "That was my police contact," I told Susie. "He's on his way to the shed. Once he 'authenticates' the stolen goods from my 'anonymous' tip, he'll reach out to the Feds."

"Fine. Now, you best get to your room and call your old lady. Tell her we're going to New York tomorrow."

I picked up my phone and laptop. "I'll do some research on Miss Raven before morning." Nodding at the discs and texts. "We'd have to hurry to get those back to the rental unit."

"We're not returning them. Not until after the whole ex-Amish case is over. Ya never know when they might come in handy."

KNOCK, KNOCK. THE DOOR OPENED. Isabella wore her hair in a shag style, dyed purple. An assortment of tattoos decorated both arms. One proclaimed, *"Try Me!"* while another shouted, *"Back Off!* If these skin illustrations weren't contradictory enough, one wall of her apartment featured posters of 80's heavy metal bands while hand-drawn artwork flaunting 70's soft pop female singers and television program characters resided on the other. Chocolate stains marked her T-shirt, above the custom-designed illustration of a winged-dinosaur perched upon the famed Hollywood sign.

"Whaddaya want?" Raven asked, pulling up her loose-fitting boxer shorts. "You from my boss's lawyer's office?"

"We're from *Ladies' Home Journal.*" Susie smiled. "Gee, aren't you the snappy trendsetter!"

Liam spoke after a round of swear words fled from the offended apartment renter. "Please ignore my assistant. I called this afternoon. About helping you with your complaint …"

"Oh yeah. Lemme turn off the Buffer Beams."

Later, Karas would explain to Susie the concept of the dual lasers bordering the doorway, invented by the Thrusk brothers while she had been off the planet. At three and six feet off the floor, the beams served not only as a home defense alarm but, depending on the intensity of the color, could sear through a person's clothes and skin. For all its scorching power, Isabella's dark red security system wouldn't have left a scratch on Drake's near-invincible hide. It would, however, have burned a cutting line on her attire, leaving her almost in her birthday suit.

"Have a seat," she offered, pointing at two beanie bags.

"Uh, we'll stand." Liam cleared his throat, ready to spill the truth behind their visit when Raven spoke first.

"My boss … ex-boss … said either I put out or get out. So cliché, don'tcha think? So very twentieth century, and I *love* that century … but not sexual harassment or racial discrimination. I'm three-quarters American Indian.

Cherokee!" She fiddled with a 1966 Holiday Inn ashtray she had purchased on the GNet, even though she didn't smoke. "When are you guys gonna charge my boss and get me my unemployment money? I can't afford me no lawyer loan. I really enjoyed my work at Hayalche Incorporated. They even let me work freelance with their computer programs just as long as they received a small share. Man, oh man, what I'm working on now is—"

Susie's held-up hand overruled Raven and Karas's open mouths. "You give me your boss's name, and I promise you that *I* will personally take care of him. Gilligan and me … Er, Liam and me, we're not from your human resources. We're here about Ren Pith, your current or ex-boyfriend."

Plopping down on a bean bag, defeat stamped Isabella's face. "Shit fire and hell water! Did the jerk tell you about me? Are you guys the frickin' Feds?"

Drake decided she liked the girl, who reminded her of someone from her past, just don't expect Jay to say who. "We wanna find him. And no, we're not cops. Beanpole there is a private dick."

"Well, lady, I don't 'wanna find him.' Who do you think *you* are with that attitude? Susie Drake or somethin'?"

Susie happily removed her wig and layers of tacky emo-skater makeup. Call it a picture-perfect Moment—Drake did, in her mind.

Raven staggered upward. Out her mouth came a sound like, "*Ahgh!*" ten times! Behind watery eyes and a few, "Oh my God!" exclamations, she bent down, kissed Susie's shoes, and then lifted her weepy face. "You … you've always been my hero! I've read … all … all about you … and I saw you when I attended … the Washington D.C. Sacha Ahern hearings! I was a little girl then."

Susie helped her rabid fan up from the floor, tears dripping on her hands while Isabella continued.

"You … when you told the Senator from North Carolina, 'You interrupt my friend talkin' once more, and I'm gonna rip your head off and shove it up your ass,' I knew you'd be my idol! Oh God! Susie Drake … in the flesh! Today is the pinnacle of my life! Where's my phone? I wanna selfie!"

THE TRIO SAT AROUND THE small kitchen table. Isabella served her guests lukewarm coffee and semi-stale doughnuts. "I'd have fresher stuff to give you, but it's been three weeks since my last paycheck. My dad and brothers give me money, much as I hate takin' handouts. So, like, I wait until the fridge begins smelling before I go to the grocery."

"I can smell it from here." Susie tossed in a smile for her admirer.

Weakly, Isabella said, "Yeah. Guess I got used to it."

Liam pushed his coffee cup aside. "I really need to get our interview going, Isabella. When was the last time you saw Ren?"

Elbow resting on the table and chin in palm, she eyed the ceiling, as if searching for the answer. "'51. The summer. He left without saying a word. Dumbass! Good riddance!"

"Why's that?"

"Well, Mr. Beanpole, it was the OCD. It drove me crazy! For instance, we had an old digital clock next to the bed. He could never walk out of the room or the apartment if the minute ended in a 3, 8, or 9. Ever! Once, I tossed out the clock … and he bought another one. I says, 'Let me be in charge of the time; you needn't look at the damn thing.' Nope! And he was always straightening things, didn't like food touching other food on his plate. He'd flip the light switch a certain number of times. And when driving, there were certain streets he could never, ever take, and if he hit a bump, oh Lord, he'd think he might've run over someone, no matter what I said, and he'd insist on driving back around just to make sure. If I even cleared my throat … well, it meant I was deathly sick to him, and he'd either demand I take medicine or see the doctor!"

"That's a lotta concern for a guy who destroyed power grids and the internet, resulting in three point three billion deaths," Susie said.

Raven leaned back in her chair, eyes displaying hurt. "I never believed that shit. Ren was a lotta things—obsessive and paranoid and hated his grandparents and was grumpy too often—but he also loved me, and he loved kids and animals and sunshine, and he wanted to be happy. I just … I just couldn't love him back that much. I know it's why he left. I was the bad guy, not him."

To this, Liam inquired, "Why didn't you come forward with this information? No one spoke on his behalf."

She slammed both hands on the table. "You *know* what the press and the government did to the Exiles! They woulda literally crucified me and my family. Ren's mistake was runnin' after the grids blew up."

"Who then," Susie started, "do you think is guilty?"

"I dunno. Not a clue."

"Did he ever mention the name Hugh Rodanthe?" Karas asked.

"Yeah, yeah. Time traveler." Blows raspberry. "I've read the name in Ahern's book. Susie knows all about him … though you never met, right?"

She shrugged. "Someone stole many of my memories, so …" Out came a brief recap of the case she and Liam worked on. "Do you think Pith might be the thief?"

"Maybe." The word came out turtle slow, putting substance into her next response, "It's why you mentioned the time traveler, I betcha. Rennie talked constantly about how he wanted to change the past. Not *if* he could do it, but how and when. He knew the complete history of Rodanthe's interactions with the powered community. Who could contact the guy whenever they wanted? No-frickin-one! Yeah, if he thought Susie had Rodanthe's number, he'd steal her memories."

Drake's eye movements triggered Karas's encyclopedic knowledge. "You're right about no-frickin-one being able to contact Rodanthe. Only [NAME REMOVED] and [NAME DELETED] ever entered the time traveler's aerocube, and he did confide in a therapist, but that's ancient history."

"Aerocube?"

Liam laughed. "Invisible spaceship, Susie. The inside, legend says, is decorated like a nerdy bachelor pad. Plenty of futuristic gizmos." He chewed and swallowed what he could from the doughnut. "I'm not even sure how Pith would access the memories. We know he became pals with a bartender who suddenly vanished during the police investigation. Was Ren the scientific type, or did he have connections in the technical field?"

"The barkeep wasn't a *pal*. He buddied up to Rennie 'cause he was an Exile. Then he narked on Ren to the FBI for stealing from rich people. Definitely not a friend! I'm glad he didn't give my name to the Feds." Leaving her chair, she began collecting empty cups and leftover food from the table. "Sh-eeee-t no, he wasn't into science. All he had was *me*. You can look around the room and see how un-sciencey I am!"

"Was there anyone else he ever mentioned who could have befriended him or approached him with an offer that meant using his powers?" Karas added, "Could be a person he mentioned just once, maybe only by their first or last name."

Around the table, she continued walking, stopping in front of the kitchen sink. "Well, now that you mention it, he did say something about a dude who somehow knew him. They'd met down the street at—"

Susie saw it. The red laser beam pouring through the window, landing on Raven's forehead. Propelled off the seat, Drake screamed at Isabella while in mid-air, "Get down! Get down!"

Too late. The bullet burst through the small windowpane, striking the young woman in the temple. Had she moved a couple of inches sooner when Susie had shouted, the shot would have taken out an oven mitt hanging below a cabinet and bearing the likeness of an infamous mid-20th century politician.

Karas crawled quickly on the floor. No pulse registered on Isabella's arms.

"Call the cops," Drake ordered, nostrils flared. "I'm going across the street to hunt down the shitbag who did this."

LUTHER FONTENOT SCHEDULED THE MEETING for mid-afternoon, in the desert, not too far west of Zawiyat Dahshur. He wanted the man he'd bargain with sweating from the sweltering heat. *I'll arrive late. His vehicle won't have air conditioning, not after I tampered with it late last night.* Adjusting a mirror on the reverse side of the sun visor, he licked three fingers and patted down either side of his head, approving of his recent haircut.

The temperature hovered around ninety-eight degrees Fahrenheit when Fontenot parked his cool-inside white van next to the Jeep Warrior.

Mamdouh El-Banna aired himself with one hand, holding a battery-operated fan with the other. His forehead and face dripped sweat, and the white shirt he wore was soaking wet from perspiration.

"I don't understand it." El-Banna swung an open hand at the chilly air exiting the van when Luther stepped out from it, batting the coolness toward his face. "The A/C worked fine in my Jeep yesterday. I had the truck maintained three weeks ago. They said the freon level was fine."

Fontenot's feet didn't touch the sandy ground. They hovered above it. "Please, Mamdouh, have a seat in my wagon." He laughed. "You might need a jacket after a spell!"

Bada bing, bada boom! I landed a need-to-be-grateful sucker! Let's see what a rapid change of temperature does for this particular fool.

The Lointainian only waited a minute before getting down to business. Leaning an elbow on the steering wheel, he inquired, "Have you thoroughly looked over the proposal I gave you?"

The Egyptian wiped the dampness from his face, head, and arms onto a wipe he yanked out a paper box on the front seat floor. "Yessir." Mamdouh sneezed into another tissue, holding onto it. "Sorry. Sudden cold air always does it." He smoothed his hands over his shirt, hoping he'd appear more professional. "It's a good offer. Unfortunately, you being an Exile voids the entire deal. I'd be under arrest. Worse—maybe executed."

Almost a century of wheeling and dealing with mortals had prepared Luther for any excuse. "First of all, no one will know you've signed a contract with an Exile. I have many Earth aliases. Secondly, the magic I'm giving you, while concocted by my people, can easily fall into your grasp by means both non-suspicious and giving credit to your government, now at a time when it most needs a morale boost."

The younger-looking (much, much older age-wise) guy had him there!

The older appearing (much, much younger age-wise) fellow wanted to know, "Just how do I come by the miraculous method?"

"For someone educated at the University of California Berkley, you sure don't have much imagination, do you?" Fontenot gazed intently at the passenger seat occupant. *He's too cooled off. Better turn down the air, or maybe brainstorming isn't his forte.*

"I no can guess at the moment. Please, tell me how."

Time to move matters along before he becomes overly tired.

"Your country has tourism teams near Qena within a thirteen-mile radius of the Sunset Pyramid. It's all because of

Sacha Ahern and the posthumously published book on the tomb's role in the war between Earth and the Wizards, back in the 1970s. People want to see the legendary monument, and it's a goldmine for travel agencies. You should head down there, not on official business, but say, visiting your brother, Neper."

Hearing the name surprised El-Banna. "How do you know about him?"

"Never mind how I know. Go. Open the glove compartment. There. See the folded yellow paper? Spread it out. It's a map, yes. Tonight, I will place a gold box inside a secret room within the pyramid. Open the container, and you'll find a scroll and … the precious elixir. You're well-versed in hieroglyphics. Shouldn't be a problem understanding the directions. One drop of the potion, accompanied by the incantation, will change however many square miles of desert you want into fertile farmland, complete with wells and suitable for growing corn, fruit trees, keeping livestock—whatever you need. It'll be as we've previously discussed—a goldmine." Fontenot enjoyed luring Earthlings into a promised land filled with trapdoors. "Take your brother and nephew into the Sunset. Pretend you're lost and 'accidentally' hit the shadowed latch. I aged the scroll during a special trip years ago. What? What is it? You look scared."

The Irrigated-Agriculture Advisor was most certainly afraid. "Because of Ren Pith, people hate the Exiles. There is no way anyone will believe what I find is anything but Lointain magic. No way! It doesn't matter what the elixir can do. Egyptians will destroy the results and blame me *and* your kind. Jack Boudreaux will—"

"Boudreaux will object to the use of the potion," Luther interrupted, "denying the scroll's existence or claim it's fake. And it is fake! That, my friend, is when you rally your government cronies and public opinion against him. '*I* found it in *our* nation,' you counter. 'It was there before Pith and, therefore, we have a right to use it as we wish.' Remind them how hard the pandemic struck Egypt and how the economy hasn't recovered anywhere close to its leaders' expectations. You can be the man who brings the cradle of civilization back from the brink before the recession slides into permanent chaos."

A little doubt remained pasted on the other man's face.

"Be real! No one's going to destroy a cornfield where once a desolate desert stood! People have to eat, Mamdouh. Children need fed. Some*one* must tend the crops and such work means a paycheck. No one will pay attention to Boudreaux's whining. Leave him to me. I have a plan in the works for Mr. Self-Appointed Leader."

El-Banna stared out the window at the old, old world, wishing he'd never accepted Fontenot's original invite two months prior. "You should present the magic to President Kamel. Tell him how you found it in the pyramid. It wouldn't be dangerous for you, someone who can teleport and shapeshift."

Cooly, the Exile responded, "If I did, there'd go the fame you'd receive and the opportunity not only for a high-priced advance to pen your memoirs but also the chance at being the agriculture minister, instead of a mere advisor. Plus, I'm of European descent. There's no profit for me handing over the priceless treasure."

"Your company will reap major profits, sir. You told me so."

"Absolutely. Throsk Industries. Not to be confused with Thrusk. Similarly enough named for a puzzlement which I hope promotes my dealings." His laugh was not contagious. "*Hmm.* Okay. Throsk can handle all the details surrounding employment, planting, livestock, exporting—you name it. The government will naturally investigate the company and find it a hundred percent run by Egyptians. A necessary fabrication. You and another fellow planted higher in the bureaucracy will vouch for my reputation. Luther Fontenot as Bassem Saad owns an impeccable background. I have my people in place—family, friends, Lointainians all on my payroll, all temporary citizens of this country."

The advisor opened the door ever so slightly, dreading a return to his hot Jeep. "May the scheme have no setbacks. I don't want to pull up stakes for Sudan."

Starting the engine and turning up the A/C, Fontenot wanted the final word. "I never fail. Never."

Intermission (August 2022)

"HEY, JAY! I WANNA TALK TO you … *now!*"
Four months later, she's still bossy.
"What is it, Susie?"
"Why did you kill off Isabella? Huh? Why?"
I can see her seated on a plane, dozing, wearing her brunette wig and heavy goth makeup, all the while standing up in her mind, giving me a dirty look.

Plane? Hmm. Seems like a part of a chapter's missing.

"I didn't shoot her. I wrote what happened. Hey, when did you board the—"

"You *created* what happened," she interrupts.

Ah-ha. She's testing me, unsure who controls the narrative.

"It took the cops four days to decide we could go back to Indiana. I should've given them *your* name. They blame Pith for the murder, although we know he couldn't have had anything to do with it."

"Back up, Susie. Last thing I wrote was you telling Liam you were heading across the street, hunting for the assassin. Nothing happened afterward. Not yet."

Eerie silence.

"Ha, ha! You're not managing the story, are you, jackass? Guess it shows I'm more substantial than I thought."

"I still have some power over you. Tell me, briefly, what's gone down since the shooting?"

She feels my willpower press down on her, and to annoy me, she speaks slowly, often repeating sentences in a singsong, childish voice, taking half an hour to tell me a few minutes of news. She didn't find, see, or confiscate any clue regarding the killer or their identity. Liam, however, discovered two hidden mics in the apartment. Appears the assassin didn't want his/her name mentioned.

Once the police arrived and learned the legendary Susie Drake was on the premises, chaos erupted. Someone phoned the paparazzi (she believes it was an officer whom she turned down for a date), and an army of news photographers surrounded her and Liam when the cops escorted them outside and down to the precinct. Despite their story and alibis, they couldn't leave town until cleared (she says it was more for publicity and favors owed to the network which owns the police department). On instructions from Susie, Liam only admitted finding one bug (it's because he claims the mic is very, very high-tech, unlike any he's seen, and he wants to check it out further).

"You really didn't see this stuff happen, did you?"

"No," I tell her.

"Good! Who the hell are you … really?"

She can't see me shrug. "I thought I made you up. You figured me a voice in your head. We're both wrong."

Susie begins walking toward the back of her head. "I'm gonna join myself sleeping. I have a case I'm working on, and you have yours—discovering who we are and how we got into this mess. Now leave me alone. Moron!"

Chapter 4: Comings and Goings

Excerpts from the journal of Liam Karas, June 2057:

BEEN OVER THREE WEEKS SINCE I wrote. Isabella's murder hit me hard. I've investigated killings, never been there when it happened. I was prepared for the intense police questioning but not for the insane media coverage. My God, they never stopped with the questions. "Are you and Susie lovers?" "What power do you have after having sex with Susie?" "Does your wife know? Does she approve?" "Where's the kinkiest place you and Susie ... did it?" One gossip rag featured a photo of Susie and me on the cover with the caption, "World's Sexiest Woman Prefers Skinny Nerd!"

Imene and I spoke several times by phone from New York. As both a journalist and wife pissed at many of her peers, she penned an exposé on the poor treatment Susie and I received, and how Isabella's slaying became a footnote to the return of the most famous woman on Earth. Sadly, the article did nothing to quell the news coverage. Time owned that responsibility.

"I'm not hurt or jealous," my better half related. "I do think it best that Susie stays elsewhere for a few weeks until things cool down. Maybe your green-haired Exile friend can help."

The police insisted we not leave the city until they cleared us, during which time talk show hosts and columnists inundated Susie with interview offers. I wish she would have accepted at least one request. Then people might stop harassing Imene and me with false tales of infidelity! She agreed with my wife's temporary change of residence suggestion without slinging insults and used whatever power she operates to contact E'tty.

When we finally made it to the Indianapolis airport, the circus awaited, tailing us down to Mason. Photographers and camerapersons documented Susie's entrance into my home, where Imene gave her a subdued welcome. In the garage, E'tatanya waited, along with a cool Harley.

"Make sure the press sees you leave," E'tty suggested. "The paparazzi will follow, but you can get away. Go deep into the Hoosier National Forest. I'll find you. From there, it's your choice of two hidden mini-worlds, each protected by portals unseen by

human eyes; one in Brooklyn, the other in France."

Before leaving, Susie said, "Take a break from the case. Allgyer's trial ain't till next year, anyway. Oh, and tell your chick if she wants an interview with me, she's got it, but not until we're done with the case. Ciao!"

SUSIE RETURNED TODAY, LOOKING a whole lot relaxed. Not a photographer in sight! Plenty of important things are going on in the world for them to cover. One of those "things" involved the mayor of Chicago wanting his city and all of Lake County to secede from Illinois, allying with Wisconsin. Imene traveled to the Windy City, covering the hot topic.

"How was France? The portal's somewhere on the border between it and Switzerland, right?"

"Didn't go there. I picked Brooklyn instead."

I'd been there before. Two invisible portals; one on Cozine Avenue, the other on Flatlands. Sandwiched in-between them stood a house showcasing very unusual architecture amid a gigantic forest, all this unnoticeable by anyone without powers. She doesn't recall it, but when Imene and I were seven, Susie brought us and our grandparents into the hidden world. We spent a few days in the appropriately named "Old House," listening to Susie's adventurous tales and exploring the woods. I can pinpoint the exact moment I knew I'd one day marry Imene—she and I sitting by a bonfire, roasting marshmallows and digging the heroic odysseys of the legendary Susie Drake.

Why Brooklyn? Typical her ... She tracked down the cop she believed "ratted us out to the paparazzi scum." He claimed he didn't, said he wasn't small-minded enough for pulling such a trick because she wouldn't go on a date. Another officer, who had overheard the romantic evening request, had made the call. Thus went the story Susie now believed, her being a better-than-average judge of character.

She and her new pal exchanged info on Isabelle and Pith, omitting the therapist's records and the mic I kept. Placing the blame for the hit on Pith came from "someone higher up the pay scale." Susie's buddy thinks Pith could've been scared that the dude his ex was about to name could either reveal his whereabouts or have physical evidence linking him to the geomagnetic storms. This sounds reasonable, but more likely, the unidentified "dude" is the assassin. Why would her ex use a rifle when he possesses powers untraceable to a murder?

"Will your policeman help us if anything new breaks in the case?"

She hesitated. "Doubtful. He's pissed at me. Before I left, he told me he's a Remnant now. Hey, it was him who wanted to sleep with me!"

"Police chiefs don't like Remnant cops. What power does he have?"

"He can levitate anything up to five hundred pounds, so far."

"Either he keeps mum about it or registers with the Remnant Bureau. I have a couple friends at different precincts. If you like, I can contact them. They're not Remnants, but they're pro-Exile and should help your friend if he needs it."

"I'll ask him." She stared out the front room window. "Y'know, I thought you lived in the sticks until I spent all those days near Winchester Street. Have you ever been there?"

I sighed. "It's a talk for later. Oh, and I had tech nerd friends of mine check out the mic from Isabella's apartment. They'd never seen anything like it. It self-records into a tiny chip and can broadcast for miles with a little tweaking. We're talking futuristic or from another planet—take your pick."

SHUNNED BY HIS AMISH FAMILY, Matthew Allgyer rented a small house in Paoli, fifty miles south of Mason. On Drake's second day back from Brooklyn, she and Liam drove the backroads for an afternoon chat with the brother of the man accused of murdering four aerofreight pilots.

"Let me see if I got this down pat," Susie said, her bare feet resting on the rolled-down car window. "Matt and his bro—or bruder, as they say in Amish speak—Sam, got drunk during Rumspringa. A wiseass redneck from a nearby town took advantage of their condition. The three of them destroyed the barn owned by a black man. Topping it off, the bruders had sex with two women, both of whom are married."

Behind the wheel, Liam amended the account. "The local yokel admitted spiking the boys' soft drinks with some kind of drug. It was him, not the Allgyers, who burned the barn, and he paid the women to sleep with the brothers, knowing it'd lead to an automatic shunning. It didn't matter that the sex occurred while they were unwittingly stoned or that the ladies were separated from their husbands. They broke the unwritten set of Amish laws, the Ordnung. Matt handled the banishment much better than Sam."

"Imene told me how Sam asked for reinstatement. Why was he refused?"

"The bishop accepted Sam's confession and change of behavior. But a vote in the church body had to be unanimous when ending excommunication. It wasn't. All of this was in the file I gave you. I know you read it on the plane to New York."

"Yeah! A month ago! Anyway, this avoidance stuff happens on the verge of the pandemic, 2052. Remind me … what got Sammy all stirred up?"

"When the RES-51 was under control, businesses had a major workplace shortage due to all the deaths. The percentage of fatalities among the Amish was low, owing to their isolation. Businessmen wanted to recruit from them and other strict religious sects. Normally, the Amish schooling ends at the eighth grade. Intense lobbying changed that. Congress passed laws making it mandatory that all teens attend high school, no matter their religious beliefs. The government hired a cruder brand of truant officers to make sure the kids stayed in school an extra four years or else the parents went to jail. Factories, firms, and other institutions began sending reps to high schools for future recruitment. Who wouldn't want to employ a hard-working ex-Amish?"

Susie smirked. "How many moms and dads wound up behind bars?"

"Enough. Donors began pitching in for lawyer loans. One major contributor was the Thrusk Brothers. In their press release, they said they don't appreciate folks' rights gettin' trampled on."

"Bet they didn't mind that the kids learned about operating the GNet and wanted their own computer, huh?"

"Don't go there. I think the bruders are cool." Liam honked the horn at two deer crossing the road. "Sam, who worked in a grocery store not far from where he used to live, became angry when he heard his younger siblings had no choice but to show up at the local public high school. Amish ninth through twelfth grades weren't set up in time for the first freshman class and, because of Congress, would never meet the guidelines their laws established. In front of his co-workers—none of whom had ever been Amish—he ranted against the government, going as far as to promote violent consequences. Matt said it was typical big talk, how he'd heard it a lot from Samuel. But when an experimental, remote-controlled Zep accidentally crashed into a Mennonite bakery in Delaware, oh boy, the kid's rhetoric turned radical."

"Was anyone killed?"

"No, a few minor injuries. The Thrusks paid for the damages and doctor fees and wanted to do more, but the Mennonites refused. Th publicity brought in more customers than the bakery ever had. Everyone put the accident behind them except Sam. What's odd is how in protecting the people who kicked him out of their culture, he did more things to disobey the Ordnung, like running for Congress, suing the Thrusks, and even physically attacking a high school teacher who taught against Amish beliefs. His campaign never got off the ground. He couldn't afford a lawyer loan and the teacher pressed charges. Afterward, no one saw Sam for months, not even Matt.

"The Zep explosions happened last fall and winter over Cincinnati, Indianapolis, and Louisville, where two people claimed they saw Sam in the vicinity of the crash, and this was before the Feds named him as a suspect. Once they searched his house, his journal poured out pure hate for the Thrusks and their invention. However, there was no evidence of bombs or signs of any materials used for homemade explosives. Security was very tight around the aerofreight testing, and it included surveillance video cameras. Nowhere in the crystal-clear images could anyone find our boy. After the first bombing, Thrusk's people thoroughly examined the flying cars an hour before the tests began. So, how'd he do it?"

"He didn't! What a flimsy ass case. Now Rodanthe or Pith could've done it. Quick-o change-o from a small bug without a camera catching Pith."

"Except"—Liam held up a finger—"no one has seen him. We have no photos of him, just written, physical descriptions. We wouldn't have any interest in him if it weren't for Pith's erratic actions. Yes, Pith could be involved. What's his motive?"

"The thrill of the kill. Same as when he nuked the grids."

Karas drove his electric car across a highway, onto more backroads. "We'll ask Matt if Sam ever mentioned Pith or Rodanthe."

"Hey, you never told me. What's my connection with the Amish?"

"No wonder you can't remember. You were on your way to visit my dad in the early 2010s when the accident happened, meaning you had E'tatanya cut out the memory." Out came a tale he enjoyed retelling. "You were riding your Harley north on Highway 37, between Paoli and Orleans. Ahead of you, in the southbound lane, a Chevelle begins passing a line of vehicles. The driver doesn't accelerate fast enough, you believe, and it looks like he won't be able to merge back into his lane because of what you called 'other shithead asshole conceited drivers.' The guy in the Chevelle doesn't see the Amish buggy in your lane, not far from where you are, and even though the buggy driver pulls over to the roadside as far as he can, the Chevelle can't stop fast enough. You speed ahead, leap off the cycle, and with your *hands,* knocked the offending vehicle off the road. However, the spooked horse takes off like a bat outta hell, and nothing the Amish dude does slows or stops it. Applying your short-distance super speed, you hustled upside the carriage, leaped upon the horse, and brought it to a stop. Nobody was hurt … although you gave the driver of the Chevelle an earful and made him pee his pants when he realized who you were."

"*Hmm*. Matt wasn't born then. Why would the Amish even mention how an outsider helped them, especially so many years ago?"

"The people in the buggy, they were Matt's grandparents. The police told them about you … *all* about you. You changing your life meant a lot. Yeah, you became a household legend. Matt said his folks forbid talking about you outside the immediate family. I guess one could say that you—"

"Don't say it!" she yelled, her anger more playful than mean.

"—helped shape Matt's and Sam's rebellious spirit before they were even spit in their daddy's eyes! And now you're helping to get them outta a jam which people could argue that you're somewhat responsible for!"

"Argh!"

The Generous Helping Restaurant, Mitchell, Indiana

REN PITH WORE A CINCINNATI Reds baseball cap although he knew nothing about the game. Small American towns tugged at his heart. Could be a result of his grandparents' dislike of anything associated with the United States and consequently Ren's disgust of his elder relatives.

Seated in a comfortable booth, the Exile wore a blue striped T-shirt and blue jeans, removing the cap only when conversing with the dark-haired waitress who didn't wear a ring of any kind.

"I'd ask her out," he mumbled to himself between bites of scrambled eggs, "if I lived here. She's pretty and knows who Clifford D. Simak was. She prefers his *City* novel while my favorite from him is *The Goblin Reservation*. How would we work out as a couple?"

The fantasy weaved through his head until he noticed how a piece of hash brown had collided with the maple syrup of his pancake. "Yuck!" Scraping the golden-brown potato refugee into a napkin, its destination would be a trash can, not his mouth. In Ren Pith-ville, nearly all foods resided under strict segregation rules—no touching!

Nah, I doubt she and I would be a good match. She knows the regulars by name and what they've been up to. I think she'd want to keep living here, not move away with me and explore the world. Daydream dissolved, his focus fell upon a dreary detail. *All that trouble, scrounging up the Vetiti20 in order to break open Susie's memories ... and she knew nothing which interested me or Winthrop. It'd take me a lifetime figuring out how to transcend time and space, finding Hugh Rodanthe.*

"Would you like more orange juice, sugar?"

Staring up at the waitress, he removed his cap. "Yes, please."

"Be right back with you." Walking away, she smiled, reasoning the customer was extra polite.

No, the hat-lifting reflected Pith's OCD, totally unconnected with having refined manners. On her way back with the drink, the raven-haired server stopped at the booth in front of Pith's, participating in a brief chat with its occupant, the topic of which solicited three "oh my goodness" reactions from the bringer of the OJ.

"Here you go. Will there be anything else?"

"Uh, no." While not possessing the keenest social skills, to say the least, he lingered a few steps above being uncouth, understanding how the woman barely kept exciting news, gossip, or trivia at bay. "It might be none of my business, but did you just now hear something amazing?"

The moment she slid into the seat opposite him, Pith's heart executed double flips, pulled her close, and kissed her wet lips. His heart did … not *him*.

"The man in the next booth," she said, hand cupped over her mouth as if disclosing a secret so sensitive lives depended on it remaining unspoken, "told me that he heard on the radio how Susie Drake is staying at some folks' house up in Mason! Isn't that *fan-tastic*! I'd heard about her having an adventure in New York where—"

"Excuse me," he broke into her enthusiasm, gulped down the fruit juice, removed his wallet, and handed her a twenty-dollar bill for the ten-dollar-and-fifty-seven-cent meal. "Keep the change."

She stared at the customer scuttling out the door, a strange man who would never enter her life again but who remained a brain-lodged curiosity until she passed from this world into the next. "I wonder if he's read Simak's *Time and Again*?" she mused under her breath. "He reminds me of the book's main character. What'm I saying? I don't even know the guy!"

In the alley behind the café, Pith considered the coincidence, or not. "No, no such thing! Fate brought me here to Mitchell, in the booth tended by the woman who'd bring me the news I needed. Mason! Meaning the Karases ... where I'll easily eavesdrop and follow Susie as she hunts for her memories. She's bound to lead me to a cure for my auras, which I feel one coming on soon, and the OCD. 7-2-17-6-22-2-77 ... Now I can teleport away!"

LUTHER'S SIX-FOOT-TWO FRAME slowly phased inside his luxurious house in central Lointain due to the fact quick teleports made his wife a nervous wreck. Posturing before a hallway mirror, he studied his dark brown hair. *All the gray colored out. Dumb humans had no idea they dealt with a man nearly four hundred years old. Doesn't matter. The land I purchased will sell for thirty times what I paid. Time for a salad, a little platypus-duckbill wine, and resting out in—*

"About damn time you got back!" Edna's red face matched the color of her shiny dress. "Did you forget the banquet at the St. Clair's?"

Comically, his hands slapped either side of his head. "Oh, how I tried! Boring philanthropist chatter. Environmentalist nutcases. Headed by a woman who can't speak five sentences without mentioning 'the future of our children.'" A lack of sympathetic laughter left him frustrated. "You should have gone on your own."

Obeying her mental command, the couchchilla (part sofa, part overgrown chinchilla servant) plopped down between her and Luther. "I had to remain. When you hear the news, you'll understand why. Exactly *why* I stay with you, I don't understand. Please sit."

GOOD TIDINGS, IT WAS NOT. Fontenot's primary Egyptian business partner, Mamdouh El-Banna, died after receiving multiple gunshot wounds during a riot with dedicated nationalists. The superpatriots hadn't accepted El-Banna's explanation of how he came in possession of an Exile elixir and ancient scroll instructions for converting the desert into rich farmland. Rumors of a Lointain businessman forging deals throughout Earth had lit the loyalists' ire. Jack Boudreaux's condemnation of the potion and its authenticity mattered not to the demonstrators, despite Luther's beliefs to the contrary.

"I heard what happened from Angel Renaud," Edna stated. They both stood now, as the future somehow didn't seem so glum when standing. "I asked her why she was telling me all this. Because, she said, a few of Lointain's supporters in Egypt spotted Luther with El-Banna." She made a fist and hit her husband square in the chest. "You … you stupid asshole! You have shapeshifting powers! Why the hell didn't you change into someone unrecognizable?"

Stumbling for an excuse, he stuttered, "I-I, uh, um, I'm not g-good at coming, um, up with—"

"Liar!" This time, she slapped him. "Vanity! You think you're so damn good-looking that you don't want to alter your face even to save your ass! All these centuries I've put up with your mirror gazing. Well, it's finally got you in trouble."

Luther shook his head several times before words escaped his mouth. "No, no, no! No trouble. It's time for presenting the document, my dear. Boudreaux can't expel me if he's no longer in charge. He couldn't do it anyway."

All she could do at hearing his plan was drop back upon the couchchilla, laughing. "So, you're finally getting the balls to do what you should've done after we came back from that exhausting trip into the past! There's a big stumbling obstacle you've forgotten. Ousting Boudreaux won't stop the council from kicking you off this world. Jack will still be a member, and you can't change who sits in the group until after the new year."

From a table along the wall between the foyer and dining room, he poured platypus-duckbill wine into a glass, along with a pinch of pepper. Upset at his wife's mood, Fontenot remained upright, not wanting a place beside her on the sofa. "You paid no attention when I said, 'he couldn't do it anyway.' I made a transaction for the betterment of an Earth nation deeply rooted in our people's history. There doesn't exist any paper detailing the contract I made with El-Banna. It's on a holograph, a point unaware by anyone other than the dead man and myself, and the access point is well-hidden. I allowed the Irrigated-Agriculture Advisor to find the elixir and scroll. That the radicals didn't believe him isn't my fault. As for the supporters who ratted me out, well, why didn't they go straight to Boudreaux at the time? A quicker reaction on their part would've prevented El-Banna from entering the pyramid and making the discovery. No, not disguising myself as anyone else helps my case. I wasn't involved in a devious venture. Improving impoverished Egypt and relations between them and us was my goal. The council will agree. I'm sure."

Edna knew he considered himself beyond scandal, but it wasn't the case. Boudreaux was clever. So were E'tatanya, Angel, and others who aligned their allegiance with Jack. Could the document save his rear end?

She asked, "When are you going to turn over the deed?"

"Tomorrow. There will be legitimacy tests and interviews with the people who not only witnessed the signature but heard the promise made to me. Your whereabouts and mine at the time are going to be under scrutiny. It's all taken care of, as you know. We perfected our alibis when we went back into the past. Nothing can stop us now." Hearing no negative feedback, he inquired if she'd like a glass of wine.

She brightened. "Guess I was wrong to doubt you. Yes, wine sounds nice."

Not a mouth muscle fell out of place. "Get it yourself. I'm not your servant. I'm the next leader of Lointain."

"WHY WAS MEETING WITH MATT a 'bust?'" E'tatanya quoted the descriptive word back to Liam.

"He didn't tell us anything we didn't already know, other than Sam never said anything good or bad about Pith or Rodanthe. In fact, Matt doubts Sam even heard of either man. He was too obsessed with the Thrusks." Karas turned his head, aiming an ear in the direction of the bathroom. "Does it sound like she's talking to someone in there?"

"It does. Is she showering with a man?"

"She'd better not be! I told Susie if she picks up men that she has to have them take her to their place." Exhaling sharply, he turned in his chair, facing the Exile across the dining room table. "Matt seemed distant. Don't know why. Maybe he had a run-in with someone in his former community. The bad news we got was that we can't visit Sam at the federal prison in Terre Haute. Well, I can. Susie can't. She's too high profile. I'll have her jot down some questions for Sam."

Laughter amplified from behind the bathroom door. When it opened, Susie stepped out wearing a large black towel, her hair wet beneath a white cloth. She didn't mind walking on the Karas' carpet with dripping feet and scowled when Liam pointed it out.

"Hey E'tty, glad you're here. There's a favor I need."

The healer stared into the opened bathroom. "I never knew you talked to yourself. Must be a side effect of the memory slice."

"No, no, no. I was chatting with Jay. He can be a nuisance, dropping in at the worst time."

Glances swapped between E'tty and Liam.

Drake huffed. "He wasn't in the shower physically! Good Lord! I can tell by his voice that he's old and disgusting. No, he's like a mental visitor from the past. He's writing a book about me."

"In the past?" Liam questioned. "What's his last name? I can find the book on the GNet."

"I never learned his last name. Moron, probably." She cackled. "He lives in 2022 and says the literary agents aren't biting for what he's written so far. The guy argues with me so much … he's not a people person. I doubt he'll ever be published."

Skepticism flooded the green-haired healer's sigh. "Can we stick with reality and the present? What favor are you asking?"

"After I get dressed, I want you to take us to see Jack Boudreaux. Jay says he owes me a favor."

Fatigue engulfed the emerald-haired shaman's sigh. "Maybe what you need is a priest who can exorcise this Jay demon. Forget about Jack. He has too many troubles right now. I meant to tell you both. He's no longer the Exile leader." Anticipating their "what happened," she explained, "Apparently, back in the 1850s, Jack signed a document whereby he would relinquish top management of Lointain, and the Exile community, should he still be in that position after two hundred more years. For reasons he chalked up to stress, remembering the extremely important paper completely slipped his mind. The Fontenot family, noted for the proficiency of their business skills, will soon choose a replacement. Most likely, the reins of power will fall upon Luther Fontenot, the current head of the Fontenot clan. It was the late Gerard Fontenot who obtained Jack's signature two centuries ago. We don't know the reason behind Jack authorizing the paper or why he would hand it over to that particular family. The secret also died with Old Gerard."

"Won't life in your world go on as usual?" Liam asked.

"Probably. For now, the council will remain as is. The Fontenots have been in the background since Lointain's creation. Whoever they pick will certainly need Jack's advice on many matters."

Susie tapped her feet impatiently against the rug. "I don't recall much about Boudreaux other than he's a stickler for obeying the rules. That oughta change with him being bitterly unemployed. I wanna talk to him, and I won't take no for an answer."

Off she marched, dressing herself and leaving behind two companions who wondered how she came to be so audacious.

COMMUNICATING TELEPATHICALLY WITH Boudreaux from Liam's garage, E'tatanya relayed the request for a meeting. *"No, Susie isn't interested in a reunion with anyone. There's a favor she seeks. And no, I don't know what it entails. Shall we come to Lointain or—"*

"I will be there soon."

"Jack, please teleport into the living room, not outside. We can never be certain who's watching."

A short time later …

"I saw a photo of you online," a confused Susie welcomed the ex-Exile leader. "You looked older and had red hair."

"It must've been a mislabeled picture of my son. I hope you'll return with me. There're quite a few people anxious to see you." Boudreaux shook hands with Liam. "I hope my presence in your home doesn't result in trouble for you and your wife." Juggling conversations like a politician, he nodded at Drake. "Tell me about the favor you seek."

"It's one you *owe* me. C'mere; I'll whisper the circumstances behind why you owe it. You may not want others listening."

Soon …

"What you told me is true. But I thought E'tatanya removed much of your memories which involved the powered community."

"What I told you didn't come from a recollection. Jay told it to me."

Jack's eyebrows danced. "Jay? Who's Jay?"

Into his ear, E'tatanya breathed, "Jay is the name of her mental illness. Play along. I'm working on a potion to cure her of Jay."

Once upon a time, Jack would have considered the current scenario beneath him. Not so now. Stripped of his untitled position, he felt loose and open to the kind of changes he always avoided. He appreciated how, so far, no one questioned him on the document which ended a two-hundred-year-old lifestyle.

"Very well, Susie. What favor can I do for you?"

"Time travel. Into the alternate future year of 2210. Find Hugh Rodanthe, question him, maybe beat the crap outta him."

Jack initiated a dismissive glance. "We don't have the power for traversing time. Even with your memory sliced, you should know that."

"Not so fast, slick." Drake elbowed Liam. "Tell him what you found."

The presence of the man with the gray temples was imposing for Karas. "Um, okay. A week ago, E'tatanya updated my OmniScoop. Searching for 'time travel,' up popped a whole lot of factual information, along with the usual multitudes of theories. Several races on other planets have perfected it. Most of these worlds only authorize journeying into the past when there's a justifiable motivation.

One exception is known in English as the Trade Federation. They will happily turn over their method for time excursions in exchange for something of equal value."

The Exile's former leader cocked his head. "What could you possibly have to trade for something so unique?"

"Recycling time through Thought Projection." Susie explained all she knew from Imene's interview with the college professor. "You and E'tty sign up for the classes. You guys will know if it works or not. If not, I'll think of something else. Oh, it costs five hundred dollars a head. But you Lointainians have riches out your asses, so no biggie."

The healer twirled her green hair. "The instructor's hypothesis sounds ludicrous! You should think of something else. Besides, the Trade Federation is known for selling junk and hyping scams."

"*Mmm*," Boudreaux hummed with a tone of enjoyment. "I approve of Susie's idea and the hypothesis is not as preposterous as it may sound. I heard a variation on the theory during the Renaissance. I doubt you would recall it, E'tatanya, for you tended to Emperor Charles V in Brussels when he came down with a bad virus. I assure you the notion has much merit, and I mean to hear out the professor. The money's no issue, of course, and I have friends who will create disguises for us." This meant brunette hair for a certain greenhead. "Susie, Liam, I charge you two with providing us the proper documents for enrolling in the class. My people will hand you false identification papers with fabricated names." He enjoyed handing out orders again. "Should you need anything else, E'tatanya will handle it."

Excerpts from the journal of Liam Karas, July 2057:

BEEN BUSY THESE FEW WEEKS. I'll start with a Samuel Allgyer update. He never would've qualified for a lawyer loan if an anonymous person hadn't donated 2.3 mil to the fund. Said philanthropist specified their contribution was valid only if I remained on the case as an investigator. Who would establish such a stipulation? I'm betting Susie, although she neither confirms nor denies it.

Sam's lawyer wasn't thrilled having me around due to my link with Susie and rumors about how I'm an "Exile lover." Twice, the attorney questioned my being too involved with the "legal action" due to "Drake's connection to the Exiles" and how the news media might interpret my investigations as a "backdoor argument for vindicating Ren Pith." I turned down the 50 thou to resign my research position. In retaliation, the defense team got a court order barring me from meeting with Sam without their permission! They argued that the New York fiasco displayed me as a "loose cannon exhibiting poor judgment" and "falling under the influence of a powered person who, while once a certified hero, now showed signs of mental fatigue and a damaged character."

What nonsense! Then again, if the lawyer learned about Jay, a judge might order Susie examined by a team of psychiatrists!

I submitted questions for the paralegals to ask Sam. Apparently, he's brooding because he can't speak with Susie. The responses I received back gave me nothing new to go on. I told Susie how she should've told me about the 2.3 mil before making the contribution. I know of several payment prerequisites which would've allowed her and me a wider range of privileges in dealing with the attorney. Too late now, and she still didn't own up to her monetary involvement.

Boudreaux and E'tatanya's enrollment in the Thought Projection/Time-Capturing class fared much better. Sporting different faces and hairstyles, they met with the professor. From the outset, Jack didn't like the idea of paying now and waiting until the fall semester to take the class. He offered five times the admission fee for each of them if taught the course over a two-week time slot. The instructor was happy to unload the five grand from a man he had no idea could've paid millions.

Jack surprised us by asking if they could stay with Imene and me for the duration of the class. It didn't astound me that he had an ulterior motive— he sought a reason for staying away from Lointain and explaining the daily duties of leadership to one Luther Fontenot.

"I'm not shirking any responsibilities," was his excuse. "No one taught me my role. Let Luther learn on his own."

Good knowing even Boudreaux can be petty!

Imene was livid at first, having the Exiles as guests. She insisted they not walk outside unless they whisked their false faces on. Three days into their stay, she began to cozy up to Jack! The same person she constantly trashed for his pomposity, she now revered for the firsthand historical anecdotes he recounted each evening in the living room after dinner. I could tell she longed for an interview with him. In Europe's and Asia's colorful past, the Exiles had roamed gypsy-like, albeit also as mysterious dignitaries, forbidden to divulge too much about their history. Boudreaux's tales didn't conflict with anything related to Lointain's curse, which is far less the threat it once was.

How did the class go? Jack explained on the eve of the final three days, "Thought Projection involves one part mind exercises taught during 17th century Sumatra, a second part self-hypnosis, and a third involving a strange potion. E'tatanya claims the concoction is native to a micro-planet in a galaxism arrived at only by warp-speed astral flight. How the professor came across it, he won't say."

The healer groused, "He's no ordinary teacher. I have a feeling he has deep Exile connections." Does she trust him? "I don't approve of what he teaches. What he's instructing amounts to straight-line backward travel. Time is circular, not linear. Anyone practicing his methods could seriously damage the framework of existence."

"How easy is it for a layman to secure the tonic?" I asked.

"Fortunately," she replied, "very difficult. The professor should know better than to offer his mixture for any price."

Susie clicked her teeth. "I can use my persuasive power on him so he never does. Just tell me his name, and I'll do it."

Imene and I later commented how shocked we were when E'tty provided Susie with the info on the teacher. It's very much against her character yet demonstrates the level of concern she must have regarding the formula.

How does any of this help us travel into Rodanthe's alternate future? "The TP process," Jack told us, "provides what one needs to keep the body fit for surviving the journey into the past and back. All we require now is a spaceship specifically designed for time travel and the blueprints for the actual modifications involved for such a journey. These things, we can pick up on the Trader Federation. Making such a deal entails E'tatanya and I bargaining as unsophisticated, naïve merchants. Maybe, Liam, you can help me with such a role."

Ha, ha! Jack told a joke, and Imene thought it was hilarious, laughing a little too loud and long. I'm not jealous. Not of some old guy who can't recall signing away his leadership role!

Won't the TP be a dangerous thing on a world visited by people/creatures from (I correctly assumed) all over the galaxy? "Not to worry," E'tty responded. "Very few shoppers on Trade Federation would ever consider making the journey through a galaxism. Unless you're immune to countless hexes protecting the subatomic universe or can easily shrink your body, it's not a place you'd seek out. I'll have no problem getting the potion."

What approximate date are we looking at for leaving to Rodanthe's timeline, and you're coming along, aren't you, Jack and E'tty? She said, "First week of your August, if we're lucky. No, I can't join you, sorry. I've moved events forward on my calendar to help with this mission. I will teach you and Susie how to fly the ship. Training will take place on Lointain, of course."

(I thought Imene would faint, hearing this. I did receive a thorough lecture later. She suggested Susie go alone. It is my case. I gotta follow through, I told her. Naturally, I slept on the couch again. Cliché much?)

Jack confirmed he couldn't join us. "I've been away long enough. I'll need a few days in Lointain before traveling to the Trade Federation."

Once again, I'm paired with Susie. Oh ... and unfortunately, Jay.

Chapter 5: Into the Susie Universe

Partial transcript of New York City Police Lieutenant James Flannagan's interrogation of detainee Susie Drake, Tuesday, July 12, 2310, on Alternate-Earth.

JF: CORRECT ME WHERE I'M wrong. You claim that you and Liam Karas came here from Prime Universe Earth in a spaceship, searching for Hugh Rodanthe. We can talk about the science behind the trip later. You piloted the craft, landing it in the courtyard of the Rodanthe Museum of Time Travel History. At approximately 9:40 PM, you and Karas break into the museum, confronting and frightening the curator, who stayed late working on an exhibit. Have I said anything inaccurate so far?

SD: Yeah. The spaceship is a used piece of shit! We didn't break into the museum. The door handles in this alternate world are backassward. I yanked too hard. We wanted outta the rain. So sue us.

JF: Any lawsuit depends on the Rodanthe estate. Seeing as how you're the original Susie Drake, I doubt they will sue. What happened after you scared the curator?

SD: I said, "Take us to your leader, Hugh Rodanthe." He laughed, asked why we were dressed funny. I laughed back, saying, "You're the oddball in the toga." We didn't understand how some of you 24th-century people wear togas and other thin garments. I thought maybe we interrupted a costume party.

JF: The temperature scale on this Earth changed dramatically over many decades. Dressing light from the constant heat is the accepted norm. Continue, please.

SD: Talking with the curator got us nowhere. He called for the manager and a guard. They didn't believe our story. I had them go check out the spaceship through the window. Now they were interested. Liam found a flier with a date on it. The year 2310, not the 2210 we aimed for. We entered the wrong year into our Thought Projection mindset. Uh, it's like a mental control panel ... sort of.

JF: Let's pause here. Once you discovered you over-traveled, why didn't you hop back in your ship and go there?

SD: The curator called me a "third-rate Susie Drake imitator with poorly dyed blonde hair." I felt compelled to prove my identity. I wasn't sure how until the manager said that since 2032, no person on this crazy alt-Earth could buy anything without showing a card bearing their fingerprints and/or passing a retina recognition scan. Neither Liam nor I had prints or eye data in the computer. Ha! Once the curator realized I was the real deal, he nearly shit his pants!

JF: Okay. You won the satisfaction of proving who you are. Why not then leave for 2210?

SD: You're not a historian or Prime Universe fan boy, are you? I didn't think so. The manager and the curator asked me a bunch of questions about things I did in the 1960s and 70s. I told 'em I had big portions of my memories cut out and stolen. Long story ... So, I recommended that they ask Liam what they wanted to know. While they did, I caught the ten o'clock news on the floating, 3-D holo-vision thing. One report caught my attention. Winthrop Rodanthe, heir to the family fortune. Wanted for theft, forgery, and extortion in Romantica. He's why we didn't leave. Just the guy I wanna talk with. And by the way, where's Romantica? Sounds like a European country the size of a butt-crack.

JF (cracks knuckles and laughs): Winthrop Rodanthe. Rich kid pain in the ass. I personally busted him for vandalizing a statue of his great-great-great-grandfather,

Hugh Rodanthe. Sad thing, him being the last of the clan. Only he survived the family massacre during the 2298 Remnant Uprising. Don't get your hopes up about speaking with him. He lives and flies around in Hugh's famed aerocube. Plus, he's a Remnant, believe it or not. He can turn invisible. Oh, Romantica? It's a large-ass country. Collects what used to be Spain, France, and Italy.

SD: Aerocube, huh? I've read where it can turn invisible. Since his great-great-grandpappy used it when he traveled back to the 1960s Prime Universe, what's stopping Winnie from doing the same, except to Prime 21st century and causing a lotta trouble?

JF: Supposing he did, what would you do if you found him?

SD: Like you're doing to me—question him. I'd use my emotion control and force the truth from him. If he admits to or participated in any one of three crimes back in my timeline, I'd haul his ass there with me. (whispers seductively) Please, Officer, don't tell me I'd need to wade through volumes of red tape extradition papers. Pweeeze?

JF (laughs): No such paperwork exists, and don't even think about such paperwork, or some jerk-ass will start printing 'em up. (drums fingers on table) There are no laws forbidding heroic folks from the Prime Universe from bounty hunting on alt-Earth.

Of course, it's never happened before. (chair creaks) I'm gonna talk to the captain about you. Get you and your pal outta here. Then, uh, over say, dinner, you and me, we talk about your options, y'know, gettin' you guys set up with a reputable detective agency, for starters.

SD: Dinner. Hmm. You're single, right? I don't break up marriages.

JF: Divorced. Occupational hazard. One kid. He's with her this weekend. I know Jamie'd love you.

SD (sound of her feet setting atop the table): Well, whaddaya waiting on? Go ask. I'm hungry.

LT. FLANNAGAN BORE A GLUM countenance reentering the interrogation room. One quick eye contact with the dream date of the millennium and he sighed furiously. "Sorry times infinity. I don't like what's goin' down."

"You mean it won't be a cheeseburger oozing down my throat?" Susie caught on it was something worse when he didn't laugh. "I'm a big girl; tell me."

When he sat on the table, facing Susie, something about him reminded her of a famous Hollywood film actor from the 1960s and 1970s. *Some actor I saw in cop shows. Why am I only referencing celebrities? I know I had Hispanic friends. Wish I could remember their names. Flannagan is an Irish name, right? Funny, he doesn't look Irish.*

"Okay. Even though Winthrop is the legal sole heir of the Rodanthe fortune, he didn't obtain it without a fight. His parents were revamping the will during the time the Remnants struck. A copy of the first will named his older sister as the designated beneficiary, followed by his second-born brother. Since the document listed the chief recipients from oldest to youngest, it seemed natural for Winnie to win out. The kid had already been in trouble. His maternal aunt hired a lawyer and disputed the will, claiming the boy mentally unfit. Shrinks for either side couldn't agree on Rodanthe's mental state, and neither could a court-appointed therapist make up his mind. The case kept getting moved up through the courts and still hasn't been settled, although the punk is the legal heir until the Supreme Court rules."

"I'm even hungrier, Jimmy. Wrap it up."

He enjoyed how she said his name but didn't like what he had to say next. "Auntie What's-Her-Face heard about the ruckus tonight. She's on the museum's board of directors, and she's pals with the police commissioner. Because you're the real Susie, she sees you as a threat, considering how Hugh harassed you. She's asked the commish to charge you and Karas with trespassing and breaking and entering."

Susie stood, snarling, "We didn't break—"

"Yes, I know. Sorry for interrupting. Let me finish, okay? Okay. Those aren't big deal charges, especially since you're not from this timeline. However, because you're from Prime Earth"—Jim sighed and shook his head—"the idiot aunt argued that you're a flight risk. She convinced the commish you might destroy the museum and other Rodanthe property unless you were locked up, pending the initial hearing."

So angry was Susie that when she gripped the table, a good-sized chunk broke off. "A few minutes ago, you referred to me as heroic folk. Does the shithead commish lump me in with Rodanthe?"

Flannagan slid off the table, holding up both hands. "The guy's a jerk, but … but he hasn't talked with *you.* Let me handle this. Please cooperate. I'm gonna set him up to speak with you. He gets star-struck easily."

She whispered with a conspiratorial voice, "You want me to touch him and alter his mind, set Liam and me free, don'tcha? I can do it. I normally wouldn't, but seeing as how some lady I never met railroaded me … I can also have him give you a raise, or would it cross an ethical line with you?"

"You won't be able to use your super-abilities for a while." The lieutenant moved closer. "Once you leave this room, a sergeant will place a power restrictive bracelet on your arm. You have those in your world, don't you?"

She shook her head.

"They became necessary here after all the Remnant uprisings and can shut down powers even in Exiles. What I was getting at earlier, you can use your personality skills on the commish. Please, for your own sake and Karas's, go peacefully."

"I've been in worse situations. How long do you expect me to be locked up?"

"The hearing will be tomorrow or the next day. I'm gonna leave soon, have a chat with the aunt and convince her that you're on her side." Flannagan eased an arm behind her. "Come on; might as well get the unpleasantness over with."

"Why are you doing this, Jim? You know nothing permanent can happen between us. You might get in trouble with the boss, or fired, or whatever happens to rogue cops."

"Why you gotta ask for? Can't you just go along for the ride and enjoy a mystery?"

A kiss on the cheek symbolized her response. "Whatever. Bring me dinner. You owe me. I don't want crappy prison food. Oh, and bring something for Liam. I'm sure he's super-pissed."

POP, POP! BANANA-FLAVORED BUBBLEGUM reverted into a fully grown man.

Renaldo Pith only pondered his unfulfilled life on Wednesdays, which was why he eyed and sighed at his wristwatch and waited for Tuesday night's transformation into the next day. He knew a lot about metamorphosis. It was his premier power.

Not long ago, one too early and dark morning before the sun yawned, he had entered the spaceship meant to transport Drake and Karas to an alternate universe. Inside the craft, he had stuck his hand on the bottom of the navigator's seat and altered his body into a chewed-up piece of gum. Not only did the alteration allow him passage into 2310 Alt-Earth, but it also allowed his proximity to Susie's rear end!

"Amazing this shitty ship made the journey without coming apart. *Hmm.* Is it Wednesday yet? Not yet. A minute and a half. Ninety seconds. Don't like nines. Not yet eighty-three seconds. Better."

Midnight, finally, and for the best possible meditation on either his unhappiness or recent days, he imagined himself speaking with someone, real or made up. In this instance, he chose a radio talk show host from 1960s Prime Earth, Frank O'Brien.

"Glad you can join us tonight, Ren," Frank began. *"You are an audience favorite."*

Yes, I know. I can't stay long, Frank. I'm on a mission.

"Can you bring us up to speed?"

While transformed as a coaster on an end table in Liam Karas's house, I overheard his and Susie Drake's plans. They're here now on Alt-Earth in 2310.

"Wow! Their only reason for going there would be to find Hugh Rodanthe. But wait ... his time was the previous century, correct?"

Yes, you're spot on, Frank. At 10:57 p.m., Tuesday, I spoke with a man who works at the Rodanthe Museum of Time Travel History. I told him I was looking for Susie Drake. He reported that the police hauled off Drake and Karas for breaking and entering. And ... she's changed her agenda—it's Winthrop Rodanthe she seeks now.

"Big news, indeed! Has this latest detail modified your own plans, Ren?"

Definitely. Soon as we're done talking, I'm heading for the police station and will learn what's become of the Prime Earth twosome. I can't have them snoopin' around 2310 Alt-Earth. Can't have them snooping around 2310 Alt-Earth. Can't have them snooping 'round 2310 Alt-Earth. Dammit! Say it right! Can't have 'em snooping around 2310 Alt-Earth. Argh! Can't have them snooping around 2310 Alt-Earf. Earf?

Can't have them snooping around 2310 Alt-Earth! There! Perfect. (exhaustive sigh) Sorry, Frank.

"*No need apologizing, Ren. I know you're a colossally busy man, but do you have time to stay and speak with one of your many, many fans whose calls have swamped our phone lines?*"

Okay, just one.

"*Hi there, Tammy! You're live on the Frank O'Brien Show! Do you have a question for our guest?*"

"*Well ... I'm just about Ren's biggest fan. I live not far from the Rodanthe Museum. I'm twenty-two years old, slim-figured with large breasts, and long brown hair. If you like old-fashioned women who like a dominant male, I'm it. So, how's about meeting me anytime tonight?*"

Except for the hair color, you could be Susie Drake. Are you serious about hooking up?

Click. Dial tone.

Dammit! I can't even control my own fantasies! Enough of my Wednesday contemplations. It's time I found out what Drake is up to.

ONE STEP AWAY FROM EXITING the spacecraft, Pith felt the floor become wobbly, and he held onto whatever would keep him upright. He raised his head just a crack above the window line, not wanting anyone to see him but just enough for him to see what the heck was going on. A police officer supervising four forklift drivers, directing each into their best possible position, whereby lifting the flying saucer gently up and onto a flatbed truck.

"We shoulda waited on a crane," one driver shouted. "Be easier, don'tcha think?"

"Old lady Rodanthe wants it off the museum's property," the cop told him. "Don't damage it. It's gotta take a couple clowns back where they came from."

Me, too! Pith thought. *The last time I was here, I barely got back to the Prime Universe. I'm not making that mistake again.* Wishing to remain unseen, he resumed his place as a piece of chewed gum beneath the pilot's chair. *They're no doubt taking this hunk of junk to the impound lot. From there, I'll change into a dragonfly and head toward the precinct closest to the museum. I must do something ... anything that'll take Drake and Karas's minds off Rodanthe. I best think fast because it sounds like the cops are chaining the ship down on the truck!*

AN EPILEPTIC, OCD-RIDDLED EXILE outlaw walks into a bar ... Not a joke, it happened when Ren stepped inside a tavern, desiring directions to the nearest police station. A response came not from the bartender or a patron, but from the tele-tube gliding around the large room. Since late was the hour, no games of noseball, leapball, or CrowNickle would air until the next afternoon. Only news, commentaries, and reruns of *Bailiff Billy Bob* aired. And disclosed during the *Almost Midnight Report* was this major dispatch:

"*Prime Earth Susie Drake landed on Alt-Earth this evening!*" The computer-generated newscaster spoke so excitedly that glitches threatened to crack the CGI of his DNA. "*Accompanied by a yet unnamed male, Drake broke* *into the Rodanthe Museum on East 70th Street. Police have since detained the famed celebrity and superheroine. The spokesman for the East 67th Street Underground Precinct declined an interview, nor would he disclose what, if any, legal action they plan on charging against Miss Drake and her companion. In upcoming* Reports, *we will speak with noted Remnants and Exiles on this amazing development."*

Leaving the bar, Pith overheard someone say, "We're Prime Earth! I never believed me no-nonsense 'bout different Earths. This Susie broad … she's part of a conspiracy by the Science Elite. They just wanna make us feel like second-class Earthlings. 'Alt-Earth' … phooey! No such a-thing!"

Braindead redneck, Pith contemplated, strutting down the sidewalk. *The Science Elite Foundation would rather have Alt-Earth be Prime than not. I forget the name of the professor … the one who traveled here from the original Earth, thereby creating the first parallel universe. Whatever motivated him had something to do with Susie Drake. Wish I could recall his name.*

DURING THE PAST TWO CENTURIES, most of the Remnant rioters had focused their aggression against the police who they claimed had failed in protecting them from non-powered persons. In the aftermath of the rebellions, newly constructed precincts had found a stronger home underground, beneath a layer of fortified cosmic material, donated by the Exiles of Alt-Lointain, a society which looked down their noses at Earth's insignificantly equipped, super-skilled populace.

The 67th Street station represented one of the first headquarters relocated below street level. If you asked Lt. James Flannagan about the security of the place, he might say, "Well, the roof is solid as they come. But down here, especially in the tombs where we lock up the criminals, a flea hittin' the wall might make it crumble apart."

Ren Pith didn't seek Flannagan's or anyone else's opinion. A simple reconnaissance mission as a horsefly informed him how the 67th stood in dire need of refortification or it might not stand for too many more years.

Cruising through the upper corridors, Pith happened upon a conversation which would captivate his scheming OCD mind.

Flannagan: Yes, Captain, I know it may be futile talkin' with old lady Rodanthe, but I wanna try.

Captain: Heh, heh. That blonde really has you whupped, don't she?

Flannagan (sighing): Whatever you say, boss. I'll be back in a couple hours.

Captain: You're doing this on your own time. Remember that, Jim.

Flannagan: Sure. Oh, and don't let that boot with the crewcut anywhere near Drake's cell, okay? He hates powered people, and if he starts shakin' the cage door, who knows, the place might collapse.

Captain: Yeah, yeah. I did request some instant concrete to patch up the cells, but y'know how it goes. Someone above our pay grade probably won't approve it.

"The place might collapse," Pith rejoiced. *The very words. Place your bets. Might makes right. Collapse on schedule. Yes! Three words each x four equals twelve words.*

Twelve is one and two. One is for me. Two stands for her, whoever the "her" is in my life, which right now is Isabella. She'll be proud of me when I clear up all the nonsense surrounding the pandemic. We can get married once I'm rid of the OCD.

Later…

FLANNAGAN RAN TOWARD THE SIGHT of ambulances outside the 67th Street precinct. The first person he recognized, the captain, blocked him from entering the station.

"Don't go in there, Jim. The medics are still haulin' out the injured. We're lucky nobody died. Several jail walls collapsed. Shit, what a mess! We had to move prisoners down a few floors. This might be it for the 67th. I've said many times, we need a new—"

"Susie Drake, Liam Karas … did their cells get damaged?"

"Yep. We hadda take them star prisoners down to the vault." Laughing, he patted his pal on the back. "Your girlfriend will be safe there. Those bottom floors are rock solid compared to what's piled on 'em."

The lieutenant gritted his teeth. "Man, I asked you not to let that redneck boot near her!"

"It wasn't him!" The captain spat on Jim's shoes. "Don'tcha get uppity with me! From what I heard, a moose— an honest-to-goodness moose—head-butted the hallway walls on four different levels. Three reliable detectives saw it, chased it, and lost it in a restroom. You *know* what it really was, don't ya?"

"A shape-shifting Remnant!" Flannagan cradled his head between both hands. "But, uh, you're keeping it under wraps, right?"

"You bet your ass I am. We can't prove it was a Remmie … not now. The press will accuse us of anti-Remnant mongering, and the politicians will want our precinct shut down. No, Jimmy, this stays between you and me. I've already warned the three knucklehead detectives to zip it or else. Anyhow, how'd it go with rich bitch, Rodanthe?"

"She's gonna talk with her lawyer and have him interview Drake and Karas. She'll drop charges if her guy likes what he hears."

"Jeepers! How'd ya get her to soften up? Did you jump in the sack with her?"

"Nah, I dazzled her with common sense." Flannagan snorted. "I'm gonna walk around … too keyed up, y'know? Two hours; will that be time enough for me to check on Susie?"

"Sure. Have yourself a horny little conjugal visit."

FROM ATOP A NEARBY APARTMENT building, Pith watched the captain and lieutenant converse through binoculars he had swiped from the police station. More than adequate at lip reading, he learned he had two hours to come up with a plan regarding Drake before the lovesick Flannagan developed his scheme.

"The cop will get her released. Nope, can't have that."

Time elapsed. Pacing the roof, he recalled ogling Drake through moose eyes. "She sat on a cot. Peaceful in her cell. Wearing those idiotic power restrictive bracelets. Why was she doing that? Impressing Flannagan by not resisting." *Scratch, scratch.* He clawed along the side of his mind, hoping to dig out what didn't make sense in the jail scene. *It wasn't something I read. It was a weird fact someone told me ... who and what? Winthrop. Had to be. Those bracelets. They what?* Scratch, scratch, scratch. *They only work on Remnants. Susie's not a Remnant. Her background is* [FACTS DELETED].

What the ...? Something just spun through my mind, removing what I was thinking about! What was I thinking about? Oh, please Lord, don't let this be a heightened form of OCD! Maybe I messed up a routine or didn't think the correct numbers. 7-12-17-26-27-43-67-71! I banish all ye previous bad numbers I thought when I shouldn't have thunk them!

Pith breathed in and out several times and even smiled happily. *I don't know what train of thought I lost. It doesn't matter. I know what I need to do. Put Susie in danger, not for her life, but for Karas's. That should get her out of those bracelets.*

"WHAT IS IT WITH YOU and cops?" Liam asked. "You wrapped both the Brooklyn detective and Lt. Flannagan around your finger. Neither one accomplished anything worth mentioning as far as the case goes."

"Be quiet." Susie was not in a good mood. "I promised Jim I'd be peaceful, and I think you're wrong about the moose. It was Pith, not Rodanthe or a ticked off Remnant." Her voice echoed through the lowest floor of the 67th.

Only she and Liam occupied cells in the vault, approximately four hundred and ten feet below ground level. One could consider the reassignment a hazard of their celebrity status or the need to keep the champion pin-up girl of all time away from the rest of the male population.

"*Now* you decide to be a pacifist!"

"I can't very well go ape-shit with these power inhibitors on me!"

"You should've thought of that before you agreed to put 'em on!"

"You're the one who got us into this by agreeing to help your 16th-century pals, Sam and Matt!"

"'16th century pals' … what an insult! Those bracelets have also numbed your formerly sharp mind. Or maybe it's Lt. Jimmy Sweetness who got to you! And besides, comin' to the alt-future was your idea, you blonde bimbo!"

Drake bent her head, gazing in the corner. "Did you piss by the wall? The far-right corner?"

"No! What kind of—Oh hell, we got water comin' in."

Forgetting their argument, they stepped close to the spreading puddle. Susie tapped a foot along the water's edge. "Must be a busted pipe behind the wall, y'know, for the restrooms and whatever water hook-ups are down here."

"You're right. It'd have to be a hurricane up there for rain to get down here … I guess." Yet, the water spread further and deeper.

Karas grabbed two bars of the old cell door. "Guard! Someone out there! We have water coming through the walls!"

Soon, the clear liquid entered their shoes. Susie beheld panic increasing in her companion. *There's nobody else down here. This cell was the only one with a door, which is why they threw us in together. We'll drown long before Flannagan gets here.*

Pacing the squishy floor, she lifted her arms. *I never did feel powered down when they put these things on me. My hands and head throbbed. Maybe I can break them.*

"Stand back, Liam, away from the door."

His mouth formed a circle, but before he could produce a question, Drake lowered her hands, backed up to the far wall, and with her wrists bent, bracelets leaning forward, she bolted at the metal plate on the door. *Crack, crack!* The cuffs broke, falling into three inches of water. Susie's left elbow said hello to the ancient entrance, and it said goodbye to the jail.

"The stairwell's to the left," she said, walking through water in the corridor.

"What's the plan? Walk upstairs and ask a cop for a mop and bucket?"

"No, smartass. When Flannagan interrogated me, I saw the emergency exit diagram on the wall. On the seventh stairway landing up from the vault, there's a door leading to an escaladder. I think it's part ladder, part escalator. It leads into the underground parking garage. Even if it's out of order, we can climb it."

"What if the ladder thing is broken?"

"Then we'll shimmy up, or maybe I'll toss you up now that I have full use of my powers. Let's get goin'." She engaged big steps, reaching the stairs first.

Behind Liam, a thin red streak snaked through the six-inch flood.

"You didn't cut yourself, did you?"

Turning his head, Liam exclaimed, "Good Lord! There's … there's yellow in the water! The wall pisses and bleeds! This is one screwed-up world!"

A FEW SCANT HOURS INTO a Wednesday, Renaldo Pith sat atop a short concrete wall lining an alley between the 67th Precinct's underground garage and a bail bonding agency. The outcast Exile, having viewed Drake and Karas sprint fast from the city block following their escape out of a watery jail, plunged headlong into his second fantasy as a celebrity guest on an imaginary talk show, one that he had decided would air during Prime Earth's Golden Age of Television.

The host, Robert Rob Robertson, announces, "Please welcome the interplanetary, intergalactic purveyor of fun and adventure, Ren Pith!"

Pith walks out from behind multi-colored curtains, pretending a fumble and drawing laughter and wild applause from the studio audience. After shaking hands with the host, he salutes the sidekick, who stands in-between the set where Robertson sits and the show's orchestra.

The subordinate, Freddy Fred Frederickson, upon receiving the gesture, performs his trademark series of handstand flips across the stage before resuming his normal position.

The audience applauds Frederickson's stunts, as does Pith, who attempts his own flips, falling flat on his face.

The studio viewers and Robertson love it!

Skip to the reason for Ren's appearance.

"I understand," Robert says, munching on peanuts as he speaks, "that you got the goods on Susie Drake. How ...? Ha, how'd you do it?"

"Well, Robert, I learned the police had moved Susie and her pal from the second-floor jails down to the vault, over four hundred feet below the ground surface."

"This was antler ... Er, I mean after you changed back from a moose, right?"

Audience laughter and a handstand flip from Freddy.

"Yeah, real punny, Robbie. You're right. I transformed into a bee, flew down to the vault, and developed my plan. My goal was for Drake to break out of the power inhibitors, escape from jail, and become a wanted fugitive. I landed on the back wall of her cell and shapeshifted ... taking the form of the wall itself. Then—and oh, you'll like this, Rob, —I performed a rare, second transformation. Part of the concrete became water. Lots and lots of water!"

Robertson laughs. The audience, too.

"Restraining the solid part of me while mutating sections into water was not easy."

"Ren, what you're describing is a stand-up comics nightie ... nightly nightmare!"

Robert, Frederick, and the audience laugh, so does bandleader Alan Allen Allene.

"Did I say 'nightie?' My brain has turned to perverted water! Ha, ha! Please, go on, Ren."

"As I was saying ... Really, Rob, can I finish, or shall we bring out your next guest now, the incredible new singing sensation, Mary MaryAnn Merrymaker?"

Big audience oohs and aahs.

"No, no. Remember, the lovely Miss Merrymaker is your current girlfriend and basking in your limelight is her biggest claim to fame."

"True, Rob, very true," the conceited guest spoke.

"Do continue with you fascinating story, Ren."

"Okay, so the water in the jail is a few inches high. Susie busts out of the shackles and the cell, taking her buddy with her. Before they leave, I get so happy succeeding that my right foot accidentally changes back into flesh and scraps itself against ... I don't know ... a nail on the floor and starts bleeding."

Audience gasps.

"Seeing the blood, well, I pee myself."

Uproarious laughter.

"Drake's pal, Liam Karas, he sees yellow and red in the water, and says to Susie, 'Good Lord! There's ... there's yellow in the water! The wall pisses and bleeds! This is one screwed-up world!.'"

Robbie paraphrases the last line, "Yes, Alt-Earth is one messed-up world! You can fix it, can't you, Ren? Inside your OCD-riddled mind lies the solution. Tell us the answer! Fix the problem! Fix it!"

Over and over again, the audience shouts in unison, "Fix the problem! Fix it!"

In his chair, Pith trembles and shakes, straining to avoid having a seizure on national television. "Yes ... I will fix it. I will fix it. Fix it ... fix it ..."

Numbers bounce through Rennie's mind. *6-7-12-16-17-22! So messed up, but not as messed up as Ren Pith.* Upon the concrete surface, his fingernail outlined Isabella's name. *Can't wait to see her when I get back to Prime Earth.*

Inside his head, a blanket pulled back over a remembrance note. *The spaceship! I better claim my seat. It won't take long for Susie to find out the cops impounded it. Stupid daydream. I can't fix this world, but I can repair my life. I think."*

Off the little wall, he leaped, wishing he had come up with a viable solution for Alt-Earth's many problems, instead of disappointing Robertson, the excited viewers, and his would-be date, Miss Merrymaker who, in his fantasy, resembled Susie Drake.

THE SPACECRAFT WAS NOT WITHIN the confines of the Manhattan confiscation yard. Shapeshifting into a falcon, Pith flew to the impounds in Staten Island, Brooklyn, Bronx, and Queens. To his dismay, none of the facilities served as a temporary home for the ship.

Susie had attempted a different tactic, despite bitter and often foul language from Liam. Pushing him inside an unoccupied, all-night laundromat, she served an ultimatum.

"Look … Flannagan is our only hope. He'll know where the cops hauled off the vehicle. I'll use my emotion control power on him if I must. You and I can't go huntin' for it without being spotted."

On a cracked rubber chair, he sat, aghast at how crummy furniture still existed. "Why don't you ask your buddy Jay where it's at? While you're at it, ask him why he didn't warn us about coming to the wrong time … and not breaking into the museum … and Pith trying to drown us."

Her smile rang phony. "Nah, leave the moron out of this."

"Ask him!" Karas shouted. "Or else … or else I'll go outside and scream that we're in here!"

She knew he was tired, drained, and worried he'd never see his wife again. "All right. Stay here. I'll talk to him outside, around back. I might have to punch myself in the head if he starts blabbing nonsense."

Intermission (November 2022)

IT'S A COLD AUTUMN NIGHT, sleep beckons. *Throb, throb.* Yes, it's her again.

Susie screeches my name.

Why couldn't I have a supernatural connection with an easygoing, polite character who says, "Hello, sorry to bother you, but can we chat?" I'm only sixty percent certain I constructed Susie back in the 1980s, molding her from various images and giving her a surname from a long-forgotten neighborhood legend my middle brother conceived. In any case, it's how I think she came to be.

"Jay! Stop avoidin' me! You owe me answers, jerk!"

There she is, pacing in a steamy alleyway. Looks warm where she's at.

"What's up, Susie?"

Straight to the point, no foul language. "Where's the spaceship?"

"I don't know. That chapter is yet to come."

She picks up a trashcan lid and slams it against her head. "Didja feel that, ya moron? Hope so. Hope it shook some sense into you."

"Heard it, seen it, and can almost smell the puke inside the can. Didn't feel a thing. Now, Susie, I don't know what to tell you about the ship. The police hauled it away. Pith is looking for it, too. Far as I know, he hasn't found it."

She wipes a trashcan lid stain off her forehead and calms down approx. twenty percent. "Pith. It was him who changed into a moose and later tried to drown Liam and me, right?"

"Yep. I typed it in the Word document after it happened."

"Time out." She snaps her fingers a couple of times. "Last time we talked, I told you to discover who exactly we are and how we got into this mess. You don't see things in my life as they happen. How do you even know anything that does happen to me?"

The words come out crisp. "I don't know how I know. When I sit and write about you, the scene appears, or maybe I hear you thinking about stuff. Earlier—well, days ago for me—I heard Pith's thoughts. He was on top of a building, watching Lt. Flannagan during the chaos at the 67th Street precinct and formulating a plan about you. This must be when he came up with the flood scheme." I bet she perks up hearing this tidbit. "You see, Winthrop Rodanthe told him how you came to have powers."

"Pith and Rodanthe … working together! It makes sense. Do you know where either of them is now?"

What'd I tell you—perky!

"Like I said, Pith is looking for the spaceship. Either he'll find it, or he won't. Rodanthe, I have no idea."

"You heard Pith's thoughts. What else was on his mind?"

Before responding, I make sure she hears me inhale and exhale expressively. "No, I can't tell you. It'd be cheating. Should anyone read my account of your adventure, they'd cry foul at me giving you spoilers. You have to dig up whatever info you want to know on your own."

"Are you [EXPLETIVES DELETED] me? I'm no Sherlock Holmes, and I'll bet you're no Conan Doyle. You've already told me Pith and Rodanthe are in cahoots. What difference can a few more nuggets hurt?"

"C'mon, Susie, didn't you already suspect they were in league with one another?"

Cutely, she puts a finger on her lips and wiggles while standing on one foot. "Now that you mention it … no! Yes! But only when you said so. You *are* changing the narrative by altering my mind!"

"Hey, babe, you've done the same thing with your manipulative emotion control power for decades. How's it feel having it done back to you?"

"Don't call me 'babe' and don't write or think notions into my mind."

My voice carries lots of indifference when I say, "I'll keep on doin' what I'm doin'. I suggest you talk with Flannagan. And—"

"—Be aware how Pith may be watching, especially if he hasn't already found the ship. Don't tell me … he snuck aboard back on Prime Earth. He needs a ride back unless he can fly it himself. Right?"

"Sounds reasonable, but I really wouldn't know."

She begins heading toward the laundromat's rear door. "You better find out how we're connected. I say this for your own good, Jay. Me—mean as I am and hard to get rid of—I could be a brain tumor or the beginning of schizophrenia. I'll leave ya with that happy thought, creep."

Meanwhile, back on Prime Lointain…

ON THE WESTERN EDGE OF the city, a long, cobblestone lane wound through an orange grove and ended at a gatepost above which hung a sign reading, "*Mundo de Lutero.*" Translation: "*Luther World.*" Most folks never ventured beyond this point. Only invited guests and employees traveled via a levitating golf cart contraption toward The Fontenot Complex.

Modeled on the ancient Talud-Tablero Temple of Guatemala, its inward-sloping surface, the long pyramid step-style was not meant for ascending by foot. One entered through side doors and rode orb-a-lifts to the floor of their destination.

Jack Boudreaux had always considered the structure, and the off-putting nature of the entire Fontenot Industry, a contradiction to what Lointain stood for. Other than the Citadel, which contained valuable relics of the Exiles' past and present, no other building on the planet came equipped with a security system. Even he, the world's former leader, must carry an identification badge when entering the facility.

Seated in Luther's bare bones office—a desk with nothing atop it, three chairs, no wall art—he did appreciate the man's ability for organization and getting things done.

"Glad you could make it, Jack!" Teleporting in, the industrialist shook hands with his predecessor who hadn't stood. "I know this place puts you on edge, so let's get down to it." Into a clear vinyl chair, he dropped. "I'm aware you conducted a thorough investigation into the document, interviewing witnesses and all which goes with a peaceful transition. What are your conclusions? Am I or am I not the new commander of Lointain?"

He mentally counted out one hundred and eighty seconds, hoping the silence annoyed his host. It did.

"Hmm. 'Commander.' I never bought into titles. Even 'leader' didn't seem appropriate."

"You were always too modest. Now … please, the results of your inquiries."

Sighing, he said, "I found nothing objectionable other than your father, Gerard, conning me into signing a document when I was very ill."

In his reply, there was no sound of offense taken to the remark about his parent. "You or your son could've told my dad how it'd be better waiting until you were well. You didn't. As I heard the story from him later, he felt bad cornering you. He never viewed it as a con."

"Of course not. Forgive my brash assumption. Luther, you said the document went missing for many years." Jack spread his arms. "Such an important paper. And why would your father pick the two-hundred-year span?"

Luther crossed his legs beneath the desk. "I have no idea. Our world was still new. I suppose he wanted to give you ample time to rule. Oh, sorry. Not rule. Whatever it was you did."

The cutting statement eked out a smile. "Curious, though. Not long after the two-hundred-year deadline, the document magically appears."

"Magically *reappears* fits the truth. Knowing Dad, he must've enchanted the paper into hiding. I always wondered why in his will he specified for his house remaining in the family and not for me to ever sell it. It's where he hid the document. The thing found me, not the other way around." Laughing, he stared at the ceiling as if recalling a treasured moment. "Yes, I kept the old haunt. Rarely entered it. Imagine my surprise when I saw the certificate atop a table. I checked into its genuineness for several years." Luther interlocked both hands upon the desk. "I could've come forward with it earlier. However, Earth's pandemic hit, and everyone suffered because of Ren Pith. I hesitated, not wanting people to think me a villain for ousting you during a crisis. Truthfully, I would've destroyed the transcript if you and I weren't at loggerheads on many issues facing Lointain. Face it; you represent maintaining the status quo, and I seek change, bringing our world out of the nineteenth century … or earlier."

Boudreaux, used to this criticism, wasted no time responding. "You exaggerate. Lointain has adopted more change in the last seventy years than any Earth nation. Speaking of which, let's talk Egypt. You came out of the disaster with your freedom and head intact. Somewhere, there's a holograph contract of the deal you established with El-Banna. He didn't unearth the formula and scroll. You planted them and told him where they were."

"So says you." Still, he couldn't perpetuate eye contact.

On a roll, Jack pressed on, "The Egyptian's death saved you a lotta trouble. Did it ever occur to you that food grown from the particular branch of magic you sold would go bad rather quickly?"

A dumbfounded, partially-opened mouth constituted a *no*.

"Were fertile ground suddenly covering the former deserts," spoke the man who denied being a leader, "there'd be a lack of basic nutrients needed for any good farmland. Only enough decent alchemy exists for less than a week's worth of produce before a diseased decay begins. Animals who feed on such grass will turn very ill, and the same goes for anyone who has eaten the very fast-growing vegetables. The land itself may look green and healthy, but within four weeks, all back to desert. And the result: Earth's nations standing behind Egypt and despising Lointain. Had this scenario developed, you can guess your fate—permanent banishment." A fake cough killed his satisfied grin. "You came out very lucky, Luther, much better than your business companion.

"I retrieved the substance and its instructions from my contact in Cairo. They're locked away in the Citadel. You might show gratitude for what I didn't do—give Earth leaders the names of all your aliases and corporations. Since I'm unaware of what, if any, illegal or improper actions you brought on, I kept quiet."

Luther's perspiration shone lightly. Embarrassed, he dreaded being in anyone's debt, let alone the man he considered an executive dinosaur. "Lesson learned, Jack, and thank you for your discretion. It might please you to know that Throsk Industries paid for El-Banna's funeral and donated over a million dollars to his family. In all honesty, I didn't believe the riots would happen. In light of what I learned today, I will never offer Exile magic for use on Earth ever again."

Unless you can completely get away with it, Boudreaux contemplated as he stood.

"If there's nothing else, I must be on my way." Beating the other man to the handshake only infuriated the leader all the more.

"Always a pleasure, sir." Doubtlessly, he didn't mean it and desperately wished for an excuse to banish the older man.

COLOR LIAM RED FOR GRUMPY and unhappy. Had he brought his laptop with him, maybe he'd write in his journal, or perhaps it'd turn out like what's presented below, assuming he could connect to the Internet, GNet, or whatever-net this Earth offered. Or not.

Why did I picture this Alt-Earth as sunny and relaxing? It's anything but. Susie's brains seem to be between her legs. Jimmy this and Jimmy that. Bad enough that her Jay delusion suggested she speak with Flannagan, but when I vote against it, what does she do? First, she spots a 67th Street precinct detective on a smoking break (even though smoking cigarettes is illegal on this Earth). Running full speed before the cop can react at recognizing the jail escapee, she works a finger to his neck, gets him to reveal where Flannagan lives, then tells him to forget he ever saw her and to never smoke bootleg cigs again.

THE UNLAWFUL ACTS CONTINUE when she hotwires a car. I hesitate to climb in, despite her insistence otherwise. "Either you get in or you stay at the laundromat while I talk to Jimmy. Just remember, the police know what you look like. Jim's the only cop we stand a chance bargaining with."

I laugh in her face. "You mean you can bargain with—a night in his bed, you two-bit slut!"

Okay, I laughed and spoke in my head, not aloud. I give in. The police will catch us sometime, anyway. I'll never see Imene again.

IT'S ALMOST THREE A.M. WHEN a shocked Flannagan ushers us inside, tells us we're nuts for coming here, and serves us cookies and a thick, warm green liquid made from some fruit I never heard of, but it tasted good and didn't kill me ... so far.

"You shouldn't have run. Going upstairs, telling someone—anyone—what happened would've looked good for you." He yawned. "Sorry. Tryin' to wake up. Here's the good news. The captain is more concerned

with catching the rogue Remnant responsible for damaging the building and causing the flood than capturing you guys. You heard me right. The flood. I was bringing food down to you, accompanied by old lady Rodanthe's lawyer, when we saw a face appear on the far wall of your vault cell. It didn't see us. It changed into a bumblebee and flew off. The captain won the commish's ear and said we oughtn't waste manpower on Drake and Karas." His eyes roamed to the blue hologram clock. "I gotta be at the station in four hours to start interviewing bigwigs in the Remnant community. Lucky me."

Neither Susie nor I mentioned the Remnant's name because we don't want to bring up Jay.

She said, "We'll be on our way as soon as you tell us where we can find our spaceship."

Flannagan cleared his throat. "HOWse. Contact the 67th. Enter 1-2-1#. Provide my badge number. Ask for the location of the Prime Earth spacecraft. All." We heard a sha-woo *sound repeat three times. "While we wait for the response, tell me, are you heading back to your timeline?"*

Very cool this HOWse thing! Maybe I can take technology back and make millions ... if I ever get back to my time.

"Pith is here. I gotta bring him back. Maybe Rodanthe, too."

"Susie, who told you this?"

"There's no time to explain. If we stay for a few days, should we disguise ourselves?"

He stifled a yawn. "Yeah, really good disguises. I'm betting the commish will want at least two detectives huntin' for you. The Rodanthe lawyer promised me he'd convince the old woman to drop the charges. You're the victim of Remnant pranksters, and Mrs. R hates them."

"We'll fly outta the city. Find a good hiding place in the country." She gave a thumbs-up. "This world's gotta have some cool motorcycles, right?"

"About the countryside. You see, it's not—"

A female voice, sounding like it came from the walls, interrupted the lieutenant. "HOWse reporting. Reply from 67th 1-2-1#. Prime Earth spacecraft taken to Manhattan impound. Reported stolen. Impound fence destroyed. No injuries to humans. Investigation will commence at 10:15 a.m. Thursday next week, 105th Rhinelander Underground precinct. All."

AN ERUPTION OF ANGER AND frustration. I vented at Susie, calling her all sorts of names based on her sex, hair color, and former career, and toward Flannagan, centering my disdain on his profession, planet, and popularity with Susie. The cop did answer my questions.

"How could someone steal a spaceship in Manhattan without a single eyewitness?"

"Probably Remnants. They have ways of shrinking or making anything invisible."

"It has to be a Remnant?"

"Your question answered your question, Liam. There'd be witnesses otherwise. Regardless if someone piloted the ship, our radar would've picked 'em up."

"Where would the Remnants likely take the ship?"

"Far from the city. That's what I was tryin' to explain earlier."

The United States of America from seventy years ago no longer existed. Segregation happened in a big way. State lines were redrawn for the benefit of politicians and the wealthy. For example, Congress designated Pennsylvania, Maryland, Virginia, and Delaware as East Coast Farmland. All the meat, vegetables, and fruit consumed along the Atlantic and inland for a couple hundred miles originate in those four former states. Cities and towns no longer exist within E.C.F. No Philadelphia or Baltimore. Just the farmers, their help, and the families live in this restricted zone.

"What about supplies?" I asked. "Doctors, schools, gasoline?"

"They order supplies through the HOWse system, like I have. Drones, helicopters, and aerofreight vehicles, aka Zeps, deliver very quickly."

Susie beat me to it. "Zeps, huh? How long have you had them and who invented them?"

"Oh, they've been around for fifty years or more. Ulrich Rodanthe drew up the plans and started the first factory. Why?"

"No reason. Was there ever any sabotage during the Zeps' early days?"

"Not that I remember. Again, why?"

"It has to do with why we came here in the first place." She slurped down the green drink. "You were saying ... the Farmland is a restricted area."

"Unless you have business—personal or work-related—with Farmland residents, you cannot enter. The exceptions are people bringing supplies which can't transport by air, emergency personnel, repair staff, and contractors, or anyone with a special permit. There are police-medical stations conveniently located throughout the region. Those persons who don't work on a farm but

work and/or reside in the area undergo extensive vetting before they can claim a job."

"What kind of person lands a special permit?"

"Bigwigs, their family, and/or dates. Inspectors, dispute negotiators, cops, firemen, first responders. Just folks who come in for a few hours, less than a day ... and ... oh, I get it! You want me to forge two passes for you and Liam! No way!"

She made a kissy face. "No, Mr. Thinks-He-Knows-Me. First of all, I want you to tell me where I can find this Earth's version of the Exiles and how I go about contacting them."

"They live in Lointain, a planet situated above Nova Scotia. They have an embassy in Halifax. It's your best bet. You wantin' to go there, are ya?"

"Eventually. Embassy ... wait till I tell that to my Lointain's Boudreaux. Was your Lointain ever above British Columbia, like mine?"

"Yeah. The Exiles moved their world when the place drew more attention to Kelowna below than the local cops could handle. This happened seventy years ago, the same time as when the USA map got redrawn. Lotsa folks relocated to Lointain and the Canadian province. All the chaos got the attention of the emperor, who told Boudreaux

his country could only host the Exiles' homeland if they moved East."

"Emperor?" This was my question.

"Emperor Doug Douglas, or Doug-Doug. Very popular guy. He was a stand-up comedian and, rumor has it, a Remnant, which likely explains how he convinced the country he should be emperor." He leaned an arm atop his chair. "Whaddaya want with the Exiles, if I may ask?"

"Help from their trackers finding Pith and maybe Rodanthe. I'm not sure they can do it with non-originals, in Pith's case. Whether they're able or not won't affect the other reason I asked about the special permit. Some Exiles can fly. I'm hoping they can find the spaceship before the 105th precinct does. Whaddaya think, Jim-Bob?"

I think she oughta knock off the nicknames.

"Well, I know the 105 pretty well. Got a cousin there. Today's Wednesday. Their investigation starts next Thursday. Given who piloted the ship ... you and your notoriety ... and assuming you're still a fugitive by then, they're gonna want full press coverage. They love the stuff. Count on interviews with their captain and your face everywhere. You best be hidin' good, both of yuns. The week after, they'll examine the tips they've received. It won't be until Friday—

two weeks from this Friday—that they send up the drones and copters hunting for the ship. It's a lotta land to cover, and they're gonna milk publicity as long as they can before they beef up the hunt." Flannagan ended with a loud exhale. "Now, what's your aim?"

"Depends. Can you get Liam and me all the necessary paperwork for traveling to Halifax? We'll come up with disguises no matter how we go, by car or plane."

Flannagan left his chair and paced. "Neither of you can fly or take the elevated train system because the Retina Recognition Registry wouldn't verify you. I do have an idea." His pacing increased until he bumped against a cabinet. "Uh, lack of sleep. Hold on a sec. HOWse, contact the 67th. Enter 1-2-1#. Provide my badge number. Leave message for my captain, give his badge number. Tell him I'm not feeling good. Say I'll either be in or call at thirteen hundred hours." The lieutenant sat back down, rubbing his face. "Here's what we'll do. I haven't had a vaca in a long time. I'm taking it now. I got at least six weeks comin', and I won't need ... better not need all of it. There's gonna be a lotta repair work at the station, and I'll say I'd just be in the way. Let the haters hunt the Remnants. I'll tell the captain I want a nice, leisurely drive through the Farmland, north through the Umbrelands ... I'll explain it later. He should go for it 'cause New York precincts usually send a cop into those lands a few times a year for a surprise inspection on what we call the Hinterland Stations. Y'know, checkin' on the rural police. I won't be doing any reviews, so don't worry."

Susie and I exchanged raised eyebrows. She said, "This could end your career, should something go wrong. What about Jaime? Don't you have custody soon?"

"I'll contact the ex. Letting Jaime stay with her longer means she'll be nicer to me later on. I'm counting on us finding the ship and maybe Rodanthe. Either one will get me a win. Anyway, the department's too understaffed to let me go. Are you good with my plan?"

I said I had no problem with it. Neither did Susie. Flannagan said he'd drop by a friend's place, bring us false IDs and disguises. We'd leave the next morning once he squared his vaca with the captain.

"I'm gettin' some shut-eye. There's a couch and recliner for you guys. I won't wake yuns before I go out. Stay inside and away from the windows. There's plenty of food. Am I forgetting anything?"

Being sarcastic, I replied, "No, and if you did, Jay would tell us. And no, don't ask."

Chapter 6: Inside *The Imene-A-Bago*

LATE AFTERNOON, LT. FLANNAGAN, AKA Jim-Bob, returned home, but not driving his own Float-A-Ford. Old-fashioned cars, such as the one Susie hotwired, were rare. Gasoline scarcer. Float-A-Cars run on Cloudonine, a hybrid mix of hydrothermal ice crystals, helium and, some folks claim, a quart of Dr. Pepper. The advantages of a FAC: drift over potholes, ice, and snow, and longer-lasting tires when motoring on pavement. The disadvantages: not enough Cloudonine stations and separate lanes for FAC and electric cars. No, he left his FAC at the rental agency, choosing a hybrid Float-A-Camper/electric RV. Why a crossbreed? Well, roads through East Coast Farmland could often be in a state of disrepair, and there were an adequate number of battery charging centers.

Jim-Bob's friend accompanied him home. The man snapped photos of her and Karas for the false IDs and brought along an assortment of wigs, facial disguises, and easily applied makeup for the deception of law officers and reward hunters. Knowing he abetted escaped prisoners didn't bother him, but he showed signs of being star-struck in the presence of the authentic Susie.

"How about you cut your hair, Miss Drake?" the friend suggested. "You can slip it beneath the wig of your choice."

"It grows back very, very fast. I mean, lightning-fast." She evaluated the merchandise for veiling her identity. "I'll try the long, straight black wig with bangs, a false nose, and one of these protruding chins. How about you, Liam? Got a curly gray hairpiece here. Ha, ha."

"Since this isn't my world, and I may be stuck here for God knows how long, I'm gonna shave my head. I will take the phony sideburns. Are these glasses the prescription kind?"

"Nope," the friend answered. "Just glass. I suggest you choose a temporary tattoo. Members of the British Royal Family are popular."

"England's still a monarchy?" Karas inquired.

"Uh, no. France went to war with England a long time ago. Scotland is as it always was. Birmingham south, including London, is Olde England. The northern part is Normengland. They're both democracies … now. Anyway, there's an Englandland theme park in what used to be Hawaii. Every four years, visitors vote for a queen and king. A Princess Di lookalike always wins as queen."

"So, who usually wins the king's title?"

"Guy Fawkes," the friend continued. "Go figure."

"THING'S A MONSTER, JIM-BOB. Look at the length of it." Black-haired Susie peeked inside the hybrid Float-A-Camper/electric RV. "We oughta name it."

Bald Liam suggested, *"The Susie-Beth.* Y'know, a play on Jim-Bob. Make sure Jay writes the title in italics."

"When are you guys gonna tell me who Jay is? If he's Susie's musclebound boyfriend, I best watch my mouth."

"Don't make me puke!" Drake didn't care whose feelings she hurt. "*The Susie-Beth.* Thank you for not callin' it *The Susie-Bitch.* How about *The Imene-A-Bago?* Your wife and Winnebago. 'Cause I know you're homesick."

"Okay. I was gonna suggest something to do with Imene, but I couldn't think of anything good."

Flannagan recommended they carry the supplies he and his friend had chosen for the trip into the vehicle, stepping out of sight of anyone in the neighborhood who might be watching. Susie halted the progress, announcing she had questions and drawing ire from the men for the delay.

"At absolutely nowhere along our journey will anyone ask us for proof of identity beyond the fake IDs your friend made. Is this right?"

Jim didn't like being outside in the open for too long, especially with the temperature so warm this early in the day. The humidity and Susie made him sweat. "Long as you don't act erratic and we do nothing to attract the wrong kind of attention, yeah, that's right."

Tight-nosed and sneered-lipped, she responded, "I don't 'act erratic' unless someone pushes me in an 'erratic' direction. What about Halifax? Are we gonna need retina checks before entering the Lointain embassy or speaking with Boudreaux or E'tatanya?"

Scowling eyes insisted, "Let's talk inside *The Imene-A-Bago.*"

Loading materials while entering, Liam lay across the second back seat section, and Susie rode shotgun. Flannagan adjusted the automatic mirrors.

"I'll be the one pitching at the embassy 'cause yep, you gotta have your retina scans on file. Before we arrive, think of the best remark I can give which would summon the Exile you wanna speak with."

"Is Boudreaux the leader? He lost the job in my universe."

The lieutenant scoffed at Drake's query. "'Course he is. Darn good at it. Better than any Earth leader while I've been alive."

While Susie contemplated the marked difference in the Exile hierarchy, Karas voiced a question. "You mentioned Umbrelands earlier. What is it …'? A state which manufactures gear for staying dry when it rains?"

Pweet-pweet! The engine switched on and sounded like a young bird ready for flight. *Pweer-pweer!* The motor purred when gears atmospherically and electronically unlocked and shifted. Jim-Bob eased the long van through the alley and expertly turned the sharp corner onto a two-lane street. No parked cars were harmed in the making of his exit onto Sutter Avenue.

"Umbrelands, huh?"

The yellow-tinted sunglasses on his face always relaxed him. He needed a calming agent now more than ever. *What was I thinking, transporting these fugitives across state lines? There's not a chance of somethin' happenin' between Susie and me. The line I gave about finding the spaceship or Rodanthe winnin' me points was pure bull. If word gets out that I had Drake and Karas with me on vacation, it won't matter what I find or who I catch, unless it'd be the reanimated corpse of Hitler!*

"Umbrelands," finally recalling the question, he continued, "is what used to be a good chunk of New England. Nobody likes the name. Most folks call it the Siphon State.

Some parts of the country—just as they always have—get too much or not enough rain. There's good weather—sunny and mild—and bad—tornadoes, hurricanes, all kindsa storms. Thanks to the Exiles, we have ways of siphoning too much rain away from those places and dropping what's needed in the drought areas. Vacuum spells, known as Vertiti11 among the Lointainians, suck up however much precipitation land leaders say they need when tropical storms emerge. The Vertiti11 can also stop the bad weather before it begins. Just like you gotta empty a regular vacuum cleaner, the hurricanes and other whatnot gotta go somewhere. In the Siphon State, they get recycled. Water, wind, hail … you name it, somebody has a use for it, in various sized portions."

"We could use the spells on my Earth. But why does the Siphon State take up such a big region?"

"The section of old New England not included in Umbrelands, such as major portions of the Eastern Seaboard from Connecticut northward, joined with the rest of New York State, becoming East Coast VacationLand. Redesigning the country meant people needed retrained for different occupations, according to where they lived, unless they were cool with moving. Sadly, yes, forced relocation occurred a lot. There are four Vacationlands across America, and they draw in lotsa people and money. You'll find old-time suburbia more often in those lands than anywhere else. Theme parks dominate all the VLs. It's how the Rodanthes made all their money. Their corporation still owns major shares in the VLs."

Latching onto the conversation, Susie speculated, "Could be the perfect hiding place for Winthrop. Depending on how things turn out with the Exiles, we might stop there."

From the corner of her eye, Liam leveled attention toward Jim.

Drake sighed at the hint. "I mean, stop if we have the time."

"We'll see." Flannagan knew there wouldn't be time. *Because I'm a cop, no one's gonna scan the ID barcodes in this country. They will at the Canada border. It won't take the Mounties long figurin' out two of the three scans are for dead people. They won't want an incident in the homeland, not with Doug-Doug in control. They'll alert the U.S. Border Patrol, who'll arrest us. Then we'll spend a long time in a VacationLand known as jail, unless Susie finds us a way outta that big mess or until I can remember the number of my contact in Winnipeg.*

SMOOTH SAILING DEFINED THEIR CROSSING the G.W. Bridge. Over the Hudson, farms rich with an abundant variety of healthy crops painted the landscape on either side of the two-lane highway.

"What a difference it makes on this side of the river," Liam observed. "The sprawling metropolis ended right at the shores. There's no sign of the old New Jersey. Concrete and steel … all gone."

"Thank God!" Susie exclaimed. "Bet this a healthier world than ours."

"How about all the people? Are they crammed together in what … TenementLand?"

Jim didn't laugh at the snide remark. "Many of them died during a pandemic. It was a virus at first believed transmittable only between Remnants. Non-powereds avoided, shunned, and victimized the Remnants until scientists claimed the group immune. Then, those with powers were sought out, paid top dollar for sex. The so-called experts were wrong. Heightened skills or not, anyone could catch the disease. Millions died." Driving down a long, straight road, lined by thousands of tall corn stalks, he said, "That happened sixty years ago, making the redrawing of America easier."

Both Drake and Karas expressed "sorry" for their comments. Jim-Bob waved it away like he did a barely noticeable fly out the window of *The Imene-A-Bago*. Except, in this case, the insect was none other than Renaldo Pith. *Buzz, buzz!*

ON THURSDAYS, PITH PREFERRED ANALYZING the state of his affairs in the form of a mental, numbered list. Today, the fifth day of the week, sent him back into his familiar habit.

Lt. Flannagan. Susie couldn't have been more obvious on where she'd hide out. I realized there wasn't anyone else she knew in this world, but there was a lot to be said for being creative—seeking out the leaders within the Remnant community, for example. They'd have powers to help her and would likely cooperate with someone of her caliber.

Dumb cop. If he hadn't shown up at the 67th precinct while I was keeping a vigil nearby, I might never have known where he lived. I thought he'd spotted me climbing into the camper while he was in the process of renting it. Nope. I didn't change into bubblegum again because I'd done it twice, and doing it a third time was bad luck unless I knew for certain I could do it a fourth time during the same day. A cobweb in the middle of a top pantry shelf, it was me. No one ever looked or dusted there.

The Imene-A-Bago. Lame-o! *The Renno-Bago* sounds closer to Winnebago. 2-6-7-16-17= *The Ren-A-Bago*, making it even more perfect. Of course, no one's going to name it after Rodanthe, then it *would* be the Winnebago.

Farmland, Umbrelands, Vacationlands. It didn't sound like America was a democracy anymore. Neither Susie nor Liam mentioned this unless I wasn't around at the time. "Forced relocation." Made even me angry, and I didn't live on this screwed-up planet! Prime USA probably wouldn't stoop to such tactics. Even so, I expected outrage from the Americans. Good knowing I wasn't the only one with flaws!

The Alt-Lointain Exiles contributed much to Alt-Earth, and they were looked upon most favorably. Winthrop never mentioned this interesting fact. I kept wondering if I should visit my alt-version. He hadn't done anything spectacularly criminal or else people would recognize me. Had he gone through the same nonsense with his grandparents that I had, or had he had a happy life? I could find out, and if the lucky scenario rang true, killing him and taking his place would help me out of my current miserable existence.

And 7, because I can't do a 6 and leave a 7 behind! I was flying away, as a fly, and would eventually switch into a faster airborne creature. I didn't want to travel with them all the way to Halifax. I'd teleport here and there and come back and check on their progress. While they had chatted in Flannagan's driveway, I'd stolen a gander at his TravPad and copied the planned routes of travel in my TravPad. Unless they encountered trouble, they shouldn't veer off course.

I had gone over this already!

HOT. IT WAS REALLY WARM outside. She had rolled down her window for the quickest minute before pushing the button, sending the glass upward and enjoying the air conditioning. Weather conditions never bothered Drake. The winds, however, pushed a foul odor at her. Flannagan explained the smell derived from the chemicals used for growing crops out of season and at a size twice the norm. Farmers, their families, and workhands dabbed an Exile-made salve at the base of their noses, which turned the stink into several fragrances, cinnamon donut being the most popular.

"Crops, animals, barns, tractors, silos … are we ever gonna see anything different?" Susie tired of the scenery. "There aren't many woods out here. Why's that?"

"You can't see them from in here. Most woodlands grow at the far edge of property borders. Would you wanna have a forest in the middle of your cornfield?"

"Don't be a smart-Jay. Uh, I mean smartass. Where are we at now when this used to be Jersey?"

"We're nearing the former New Jersey/New York State border. As you noticed, there aren't a lotta roads. The planning of E.C.F. called for a precise amount of country roads and highways cuttin' through the land designated for farming. Wherever possible, the newly paved paths were perfectly straight, set the same number of miles apart, and an equal amount of north-south and east-west roadways. It made travel by wheel faster with fewer curves and hills to negotiate."

"Also, more boring." She stuck her tongue out a little. "I like curves and hills when I ride my Harley."

"Well then," Jim said with a jagged smile, "you'll enjoy the road we're taking from the coast into Canada. First, we take a side trip cross the Jack Boudreaux Bridge, then—"

"What?" Drake interrupted. "They named an American bridge after an Exile?"

"Yes," the officer related, "a gang of Remnants destroyed the original crossing. One of them dated a banished Exile woman. Boudreaux felt accountable for her actions and decided to front the cost of a new bridge. After some debate, the new bridge was named after him."

"Good," she commented. "He sounds like a genial kind of fellow."

"Don't let a random act of kindness make you form an opinion of him. He can be a pain in the butt from what I've heard. Okay, so, we cross the Boudreaux, and we're back in New York State. From there, we head toward what used to be New Haven. The interstate will take us into Halifax. It comes with multiple bends and steep inclines. You'll never guess its name. Go ahead. Guess."

Susie rolled her eyes. "I'm not going to guess. For a cop, you can sure be childish."

"I'll take a crack at it," Liam announced. "The Susie Drake Inconsiderate Freeway. Drive at your own risk."

"Close," Flannagan responded. "It's called The Elevated Genevieve Marin Interstate. Cool, huh?"

"Who the hell is that?" Susie inquired.

The men exchanged glances, which resulted in Karas's explanation.

"You read it in the report that I made for you … of your background. It's your real name. Genevieve Marin. Have you forgotten already?"

"All right already! You threw a lotta info at me. So, why didn't they name it the Elevated Susie Drake Interstate? I doubt anyone refers to me as Genevieve Marin. It sounds French."

"Politics," Jim clarified. "Liberals believe Susie Drake has too much negative connotation, what with your assassin past. Conservatives counter about how you kicked butt during the war with the alien wizards. There're bridges, roads, and schools named after you across the country. Whether it's called Drake or Marin depends on the Land's ideology leanings. Of course, technically, it's your counterpart from this timeline that they're named for."

She blew a loud raspberry. "Bridges, roads, and schools, huh? I think I can speak for my counterpart when I say we'd both prefer a brand of Harley named after us."

Meanwhile, back on Prime Lointain…

THE POLAR CAP IN THE northernmost section of the floating world served as not only a home for those animals who depended on a cold environment in which to exist but also as the residences of Exiles dissatisfied with the warmer climate dominating the majority of the planet. *Brrr … brrr …* not!

Yes, frigid defined the temperature where one found snow and ice. Frozen precipitation did not abound everywhere on this large continent. At the birth of the manufactured realm, its creators carved out a community, along with roads leading in and out, protected by semi-sealed force field domes. The magical core of the planet provided fresh air—life-extending oxygen—and through small holes in the roofs, winter weather seeped through, lowering thermometers and maybe covering lawns with white wetness, more during purposely produced blizzards. Residents enjoyed having a little mix of multiple seasons year-round.

Not everyone hailed the glacial lid. One misanthropic Grinch sought the relocation of all the Exiles in the pleasant Exile-ville.

The lookout towers ranked as the cap's tallest structures, each ending at a height of three thousand four hundred and forty-three feet and protected by a dome.

In the executive lounge on the 277th floor, Luther barked at the green-haired woman entering the room, "You're an hour late, E'tatanya! Jack may have put up with your tardiness, but I expect promptness."

"Hello to you, too, and remember, I don't work for you, and this world is not an authoritarian state." She strolled past him, toward the window, and stared through a high-powered pair of binoculars. "Such a beautiful sight. Look … a tamed Rhigosaurus. They harm *no one*. Wish I could say the same for all of God's creatures."

Instead of joining her, he rapped a knuckle on a metal table. "Come. Sit. We both have other places to be." He spoke true, and she graciously sat. "In a way, you do work for me. I head the council. For as long as you're a member, you're also essentially my employee. Remember that, okay?"

The corners of her mouth tightened. "I agree. We both have other places to be. What did you want to talk about here that you couldn't in the city?"

In his chair, he leaned back, crossing his legs. "Fine. You were there in the beginning at the heart of everything, much more than I was. The council already existed before Lointain. In the center of this world, Jessop and those helping him placed the magic mechanisms, or Mechanigic. You assisted in the birth. This amazing planet was the result. What I want—need—to know is how does one readjusts the size, either its length or width or both?"

Of all the questions she had prepared for which he might ask, the information he sought was never among the first billion. "Seriously?"

"Sure. Why not?"

"For one thing"—she stared downward at the table—"Jessop forged the magic, and he's dead. No one can repeat what he did, not even a consenting descendant who might know the spells. Fiddling with the mechanisms without the incantations could spin Lointain off its floating axis or make it implode." Lifting her eyes in his direction, she interrogated, "Why would you want to expand the planet's size?"

"Lointain has grown stale from a lack of progress. Jack disagrees, and he is wrong." During the speech, his hands became illustrators for his comments. "I'm not referring to changes in our religious practices, relaxation of rules, or the brief inventive craze of the early 00s. With a few exceptions, we're an all-white world and our numbers aren't growing. The cultural aspect stagnates. We need diversity. In my dealings on Earth, I've met many people of various races and ethnicities whose contributions to their societies border on fantastic, yet they're excluded due to their skin color or a certain belief. The minds of these persons contain fresh ideas, just the kind for bringing our community into a new age of creativity. Arts, business, sports, science, medicine …" This last factor, he let hang, hoping it would impress the healer. "Frankly, we need new blood. I propose these one hundred-some families I've screened will contribute more than your average Lointainian does. They will need homes, which is why I hoped for an expansion of the planet."

Not long ago, Jack had informed her of his meeting with Fontenot, wondering what controversial internal adjustments he might seek. Now she knew.

"I applaud your yearning to make our culture more eclectic. Population growth and ethnic change are not, nor have ever been, factors in the components of our society. Since the 1970s, when we collaborated with Earth's powered community, only a few people have joined our way of living. These hundred families you propose move here … you know it will never happen. The council would never agree, even a committee of your choosing."

Luther represented the kind of person who almost always came with a prepared response to most questions. "As Lointain's leader, I have veto power over the council. I doubt very much they would risk a coup over expanding the betterment of the planet. The hundred families I want joining our populace are not risks in any fashion for our way of life. Just the opposite. They are led by men and women I've worked with in business, and all have high moral principles."

"How nice, a world reimagined in your viewpoint."

"Stop!" His laugh was cute, intended to make her comment be one without merit. "Once you've met with these people, you will like them and appreciate the diverseness of their mindset, worldview, and ideas."

E'tatanya considered the possibility of the coup he mentioned as highly likely. Fontenot had his confederates, she knew, yet she doubted any would wager an unwinnable battle against the many defending Jack's philosophy. Was there a middle-ground alternative?

"Are there Remnants in any of these families?" she asked.

"Three are comprised completely of powered people." He performed a quick count on his fingers. "Another ten are spread out within other units. Why?"

"Your best chance for approval without stirring an angry pot is to submit one of those three per year. Based on how each subsequent family blends in, you've either made your argument or lost it." Also, she contemplated, it bought time for those opposed to Fontenot's policy. "You're aware I communicate with planets across a multitude of universes and astral planes. I propose allowing the immigration of a family or individual from one of these realms into Lointain once a year, alternating with those Remnants for whom you vouch. Of course, an independent bureau must vet all candidates."

A low growl accompanied his frown. "Subverting my original notion won't work. Remnants or not, all those I favor for citizenship will become legal residents. The only question remaining is where they'll live." He stood. "Let's walk toward the windows."

Before joining him, she transmitted a telepathic alert, asking Boudreaux to meet her in an hour at her home.

"Luther, Earthlings without heightened abilities won't have the special immunities needed for living here. Only those persons not suffering from any pre-existing conditions own a chance of making it past the third year. This is especially true since only natural-born Lointainians qualify for the life extension elixir if they so choose."

Exerting the utmost calm at what he perceived as her unsubstantiated negative opinions, he offered, "Then protecting them from diseases and whatever will be your responsibility. Now, step up and look outdoors."

Stupefied by the man's callous audacity, she decided to remain instead of obeying the temptation to teleport away. "What is it?"

"In my opinion, the polar cap is a waste of prime real estate." His fingers flicked against the glass window. "The creatures out there don't need such a large living space. They can survive in a quarter of the land size. Drain the snow elsewhere and install more domes … ones for better suiting Earthlings. It's where they will live."

"Not a chance! You … You're not thinking clearly, Luther."

"*Hmm.*" He stepped away from her fast, nearing the table where they had sat. "My thoughts are lucid and sharp. Our talk is over. Go, run to Jack. Unless you can find a way of physically expanding the planet, my people will live wherever I decide, and you know where that is."

Not a word more did he speak. Fontenot teleported inside Mundo de Lutero.

E'tatanya's left hand massaged her face. "Ugh. I wish I had joined Susie and Liam on their time travel trip. I bet they're having loads of fun!"

AIR CONDITIONING AND THE RHYTHM of the road lulled Liam into slumber, stretched out across a long, flat sofa in the rear of *The Imene-A-Bago*. Dreaming, he and his wife strolled through Mason, arm-and-arm, below an angry purple sky, amid vendors of sassafras ice cream, serenaded by buskers singing songs whose lyrics dealt with time while at a make-shift booth in the town square, Susie sold kisses for a dollar forty-four each. An idyllic setting ruined when water began seeping out from beneath local buildings, its origin being none other than a disgruntled ex-Exile who also peed in the water. Peed and peed, emptying an unimaginably enormous bladder. Instead of awakening at the smell of urine in the nightscape, Karas slipped into a dreamless sleep.

Susie rested her bare feet upon the dashboard, careful, not letting her toes push any buttons to the left of the glove compartment, their function a mystery, and she had other questions of higher priority.

"You never told me," she addressed the driver, "whatever happened to Alt-Earth's version of me."

"No one's seen her for over three hundred years." Great care he used in picking his words. "There was a secret war between Earth and alien wizards back in the 1970s. I suppose you experienced it as well in your time."

Drake remained silent.

"Here, anyway, the death toll of her friends was staggering. She was never the same. Reports during the thirty years after the war placed her in Ellesmere Island, Northernmost Canada, living in a cave. Or, instead of the

North Pole, some folks swear she hid out in Iran's Lut Desert. One weather extreme or the other."

"*Hmm.*" She wiggled her toes. "Judging by what little I know she went through, if it was me, I'd absolutely want a change of scenery … which is exactly what I did after the last of my 1970s' friends died.

"Could you have remained in one location for over three hundred years?"

"Nope. I love adventure and motorcycles too much. I think your Susie feels the same. Just because no one's seen her doesn't mean she hasn't hidden in plain sight during her missing years or that she hasn't altered the minds of people who did see her. I've done it many times."

Her viewpoint interested him. "There's a college professor who proposed a theory like what you just said. In the time my Susie's been missing, he claims she's responsible for unexplained savings of lives, some of which Remnants have said it was them but couldn't offer any proof. The dude's an expert on you … her."

She clicked her tongue, releasing a chortle-filled sigh. "You said 'my Susie' about the other." Cutely licking her lips, she said, "Jeepers, Jim-Bob, I thought I was 'your Susie.'"

His face turned toward her, desperate to display an unreadable expression. "Depends on the benefits of you being 'my Susie' versus someone who ain't here."

"Touché! We'll discuss it later."

"Why not now?"

"'Cause it might bring Jay around, and we don't *ever* want that."

"Stop with the excuses!" Jim exclaimed.

"I. Am. Not. Ready. For. The. Discussion. Do. It. Later."

"I know you well enough that somethin' will come up, postponing or canceling 'later.'"

"I promise." She crossed her heart and hoped to die if she went back on her word. Naturally, it'd take much more than "hope" for her to die. Jim gave in, not egging the issue on. Plus, he had other questions for her.

But first …

Out the windshield, on either side of the road, were six-foot-two statues of Jack Boudreaux, heralding his bridge across the Hudson, back into New York State. The faces showed signs of someone having chipped away the nose and mouth. Spray-painted obscenities decorated the bodies and the bases of the images.

"Remnants in this area are huge Exile fans," Jim explained. "However, farmer kids and other locals still blame them for the downing of the old bridge, and they take their frustration out on Boudreaux's likenesses. They're a small faction. Most people who live and work around here don't want a showdown with anyone who has powers. They respect the Remmies' territory, much as they'd rather not have them living hereabouts."

"These powered folk … are they members of the farmers' families or squatters? By what you told us earlier, I thought only people checked, double-checked, and triple-checked by the FBI or the CIA could live in Farmland. Not sure you know about those agencies."

A short snort. "The CIA still exists. The FBI became the Bureau for Undermining Mischief-Makers, or BUM. The change afforded them more authority, which us cops don't like. We do like calling them 'bums,' while they insist on remaining 'Feds.'"

"How do you know all this?" she asked.

"I studied Antiquated Acronyms in college."

"'Antiquated Acronyms.'" If her pout was phony, he couldn't tell. "Thanks for making me feel ancient. And you're a typical cop, not answering my question."

"Sorry."

On the New York side of the bridge, different sets of crops grew. The occupants of *The Imene-A-Bago* paid no notice.

"They're not farmers or their families. Sometimes, they're hired hands. They can land a job as long as they keep their powers a secret from other landowners. Once they're outed, they're out on their own. The way they get past all the red tape is through their abilities and help from others of their kind. Rural Remnants live in the woods and caves. Usually, one member of the group has camouflaging skills. This enables them to make it look like there's nothing strange goin' on in the woods, no people hidin'. If no one in the clan has a masking or mimicking power, then they try recruiting one from the urban Remnants. A masker or mimicker can haul down a lotta money or a high position in the tribe."

"I can't do either. I can make the clodhoppers believe they're seeing trees and leaves instead of people."

"Clodhoppers! Ouch!" He jiggled both hands. "My maternal grandpappy was a farmer. The guy worked the land from sunrise to sundown. He was pretty smart, too, and had lotsa common sense. My mom hated farm life. She married a fellow from Cuba. My dad *loved* Grandpappy's farm and since Mom adored him, she decided the fields, barn, and planting wasn't so bad. Now you know why a bloke with an Irish name looks like he's from the Caribbean! Oh, and none of my folks are clodhoppers."

She rubbed his arm. "Sorry! I meant no offense. I lived on a farm for a while, according to the file Liam made about me."

Here it was, Flannagan's grand opening for the question he'd been dying to ask. "Other than movie, TV, and music trivia, what do you remember from your past?"

Chapter 7: Blast from the Past

"ARE YOU SURE YOU WANNA open a door you can't shut?" Susie removed her feet from the panel and gauged him with lazy eyes. "You may not like what you hear."

"I already know a lot about the history of Alt-Universe Susie," Flannagan claimed. "Yours and her timelines don't separate until the early 1950s, according to the textbooks I've studied."

There came a few fast glances at her, not swift enough to disguise the story his face hid, a tale Susie found easily interpretable. *He had a schoolboy crush on the other me. I wonder if it's why he became a policeman. Hunting down a lady fugitive, changing her evil ways. The joke's on him if he thinks any woman could be like me, and I was no lady, that much I recall.*

"Not knowing her and never having read your history books, I can't comment. What memories I have aren't always associated with a specific year. The further back I recall, I can narrow the times down to a decade, maybe." Drake's posture soothed against the seat. "Looking back … those feel like not-so-bad days. Yeah, I killed a lotta people. Wrong as it is, I get nostalgic for the thrill of permanently ridding the world of murderers, knowing I'm one, too."

Certitude pervaded his tone. "You *were* one. Even without your memories, you know you atoned."

"Not past tense, buster. I'll always be atoning, forever seeking redemption but never achieving it. Not in this lifetime." She shrugged. "You asked what I remember. The most vivid recollections are the hits I made as an assassin. I didn't want my killings removed by E'tatanya. It keeps me grounded knowing the bad stuff I did."

Jim-Bob steered with one hand, the road being long and flat. "Are you telling me that you hadn't killed anyone when you hired on as an assassin?"

"My first murder happened sometime, I think, between the end of WWI and the beginning of WWII. Mom and I lived in a big city. I don't know which. One night, a guy followed me home from gettin' groceries. I crossed a vacant lot and walked in an alley between two abandoned buildings. He rushed up, threw me against the ground, and put a switchblade along my throat. I could feel his free hand go beneath my blouse.

"Not recognizing my own strength from the panic I was in, I thrust the hand with the knife up toward his chin. *Hmm.* Dude had a long chin." Susie's fingers rubbed the skin of her jaw. "Yep, the blade cut into his chin. I shoved it in as far as it could go, slicing off part of his tongue and up through the roof of his mouth. All the blood … ruined my pretty blouse! The cops told the newspapers a large, muscular man slayed the creep. I'd also broken his neck when I saw him wiggle around, suffering. Guess I had a little bit of a conscious when I started out."

"What was his name?"

"[NAME OMITTED]. Pretty common, eh? He didn't have much of a criminal record. I suppose he got away with a lot of stuff, or else he was picky. Believe it or not, I attended his burial rites. Small crowd. Mother and close family were there, no friends. I know this 'cause I asked the priest. My story was—and I hated lying to a man of the cloth—I'd met the deceased in a tavern where I was a barmaid. The minister told me that he had pals, all bad, and the ones who weren't dead from their lives of crime, they'd reformed. Not [DEAD MAN'S NAME]. Even in front of the padre, he'd brag on his exploits. Apparently, he thought he could keep his lucky streak of illegal acts goin' to the bitter end. Too bad nobody reached him like they did me. It doesn't excuse him from doing what he did, and I'm glad I did what I did."

Slapping at the space between them in mock annoyance, he grinned. "You attended the funeral and talked to the priest because you felt guilty. I bet killin' him gave you nightmares. Acting tough all the time … give it a rest."

"Ha!" A glassy stare punctuated her mood. "You don't know me. I wanted an in-depth look at his character. There are circumstances I don't recall without my memories, but I sense a feeling … Mom and I were on the run; why and from whom remains a mystery. So does her face. At the time, I wondered if [DEAD GUY'S] attack on me was planned or coincidental. I'm pretty sure he picked me at random. Oh, and I had no nightmares. Not then. If I ever did, I can't recall."

"Fair enough." In the rearview mirror, he noted Karas fast asleep. "I forgot to mention this earlier. The Marin Interstate has several exits, each connected to the highway above Farmland, and they all have restaurants, fuel and recharging stations, and motels. We'll stop and eat. Liam should be awake when we arrive."

When he said "motels," she heard an added, hopeful emphasis.

"I prefer eating and sleeping in the camper. Liam checked out the Alt-Earth's version of the GNet while you were out yesterday. Too many average people carry outlawed facial recognition software on their phones. I don't want him and me spotted."

Jim-Bob blew a raspberry. "Did Liam login to the A-Grid or M-Work? Oh, and I'm not bothered that he used my password."

"Do I look like a computer nerd to you?" she screeched. "He did all the research. All I seen on the screen was a silly wiggly lightning bolt and a 3-D image of a desk pop from it."

"It's the M-Work browser home page. You can rest easy. The M stands for machination. Its software specifically selects questionable and outright fabricated information for all searches. Only the very paranoid accept its sites as valid. Some corporations and many politicians plant false data to dupe customers and voters. Bad as it may seem, the app is protected by free speech."

The popping sounds her mouth made were meant for dismissing his world's technology. "Then why did you install it on your computer? Liam laughed at your PC. He said he was shocked anyone in this century still owned a desktop machine, let alone a working one."

Face tightened, lips shut, the poor guy felt bullied by these Prime Earth prima donnas! "FYI, desktops are making a comeback. As for M-Work, I use it when investigating crimes, gettin' into the mind of a potential perp. It's very helpful like that. The facial recognition stuff Karas read … all nonsense. Phone scanning is very limited for the public anymore, and only cops have authorization for facial identification software." Seeing her shiny, toothy smile, he knew she'd been goading him on. "I wanna hear more memories. Good times, bad times … enlighten me."

SUSIE DIDN'T IMMEDIATELY RESPOND. Reliving the only past she knew didn't hurt despite the intense levels of violence. No, it provided her with a warmth people couldn't offer. Was this only an opinion, what with her memories stolen? *Other than E'tatanya, I had everyone I ever cared about deleted until I could pull myself together. I'm nearly immortal. They grew old, ill, and died while I remained young. My looks, not my personality, brought me lovers and friends, Yet I wouldn't have changed my path if the kindheartedness I received was based on false pretenses. Remembrances or not, I don't think anyone truly understood me. They couldn't. Not when I had a previous memory loss at an important time in my life. The darkness knew me. It kept me nourished and satisfied. Why should I look upon it like it was a curse?*

"Okay. How about one of the earliest hits? This happened when I was part of a crime syndicate in Cleveland during the early 1960s."

He frowned. "More murder escapades? Don't you have any happy times floatin' inside your noggin?"

Air blew out her mouth, puffing her bangs upward. "Damn, you're impatient! There might be a cutesy ending just for you if you'd keep your undies from crunchin' up inside your butthole, you asshole!" She didn't laugh using her voice but with her eyes.

Jay, if you're readin' my mind, and I know you are, then give the readers an accurate account of the story I'm about to tell Jim. The memories I have are gettin' sketchier all the time. I don't wanna make stuff up to cover what I can't recall, but you know the real facts. Should a miracle happen, and a publishing house print your book, I'd like the truth told, not the fictional version. Besides, you owe me.

(Author's note: Not sure how I "owe" her, but okay. We'll return to the future Alt-Earth after the seventh-page break.)

1961, Toledo, Ohio, Prime Earth

CALIFORNIA HAD LOST ITS LUSTER in Susie's brilliant blue eyes during the early days of Camelot. She didn't vote, and she couldn't care less about the New Frontier. New business, now there was where the action was. Money, murder, a Harley, and a Chevy truck. That was what the little assassin girl was made of. Strictly speaking, she was still green as a hit woman. A Chicago goon was notch #8 and we were not counting the fellows Drake had killed to relieve herself from bad situations.

Those days, working freelance, brought Drake under the scrutiny of Cleveland's premier crime syndicate. The consigliere had heard rumors of "outta dis world super-duper powers" from a New York caporegime who'd badly wanted Susie full-time in his family. Our girl was a wanderer and wouldn't settle down in one place for a few years until the name Fitzpatrick tickled her ear.

While she dined in a greasy spoon, street soldiers handed her a "request" for a meeting. Intrigued, she accepted, meeting the prospective boss at a downtown hotel. The offer of an assassin's job crossed between the parties.

"I'll work for ya until I get the urge for pushing on," she told the consigliere.

"I wanna see powers first."

She grabbed his holster gun faster than he could breathe, turned off the safety, and shot four bullets down her throat.

While he pissed his pants, she contributed a wide grin and a John Wayne imitation. "I'll be shittin' lead come sundown, pardner. How's that for powers, ya greenhorn you?"

Notch #9. An Akron wise guy who (so the story went) was too cozy with a fed who happened to be his girlfriend's stepbrother. The trouble wasn't the friendship with the FBI man; no, as he was on the take. The love interest happened to be the niece of Cleveland's underboss and notch #9 had beat her black and blue. Defender of abused women, Susie enjoyed tearing the deviant's face off, literally.

July 3.

"You ain't met our usual assassin, Susie," the consigliere stated. He sat on his desk, admiring her legs and everything above them. Aware of how she hated married philanderers with a violent passion, he kept his hands to himself. "Guy's off for a few days. Big Independence Day fanatic. Takes the wife and kids to Cedar Point for the fireworks and parades. Real patriotic fella. One of these days, I'll tell ya what he did to some schmuck who let the Stars and Stripes accidentally touch the ground. *Ooo-eee*! Was not pleasant. You gonna take his place in Toledo tomorrow. We got this guy …"

They had this guy who, a few years ago, had secured a huge loan from a Texas mobster and never paid it back. Changing states and names, a Minnesota gangster hired the dude to do his bookkeeping for a couple of months. You guessed it. The guy embezzled a crap load of dough. Once again, changed locales and IDs, he became a (rich) solid (rich) citizen in Toledo. The fraudster and swindler had a sweet tooth for cocaine, buying the snow from a much too overly curious Southern-born drug dealer with a memory for faces and a fondness for the underworld mob scene. Said supplier alerted Texas and Minnesota, who hired Cleveland, and wherein Susie went for notch #10.

July 4.

TO HER DISMAY, THE GUY (TG) threw a family get-together at their residence on Indian Town Road. In the new development, years from completion, TG's house stood alone amid a backdrop of trees, brown grass, and a small lake. Set back off the road at the end of a winding drive, oaks and maples and snarly ranges of hills blocked the view of anyone driving the lonely street, even when all the lights inside the three-story, split-level neo-mansion were alight. Mrs. TG complained how the mini mountains made her seasick. But Boys and Girl TG loved the curvaceous landscape, playing war, spies, and keep-away from Snotty Snooty Cousin TG inside the ferocious forest.

Tonight, TG's flock flocked around a bonfire, lighting sparklers and Roman candles, marshmallows and s'mores, and generally boring the poop outta poor Susie, dressed all in black, including a black scarf, kneeling behind a thick oak tree and beneath a black, starless canvas.

"I don't kill women and children … much as I'd like to make an exception with this extremely cheerful bunch. I hope the family goes to bed soon enough and the guy sneaks outside for a smoke."

Not ten minutes later, a woman (the maid) stepped outside, summoning Mrs. TG to the phone.

"Somethin's up," the assassin narrated, staring through an eyeglass. "Wifey looks panicked. Her and the hubby are talking away from the brats. He's holdin' her in a sympathetic way. Now she's gathering the kids and leading them inside. Pops is putting out the bonfire."

Drake's tree stood a few feet from the edge of the hill line nearest the house. Sneaking backward and down the incline, she scurried in a half-circle, seeking a better viewpoint after TG opened a basement door and disappeared into the darkness. Soon, the missus and the young'uns carried small bags out the main entrance, heading for a station wagon.

"I'll be right behind you, dear." This was the husband not quite shouting. "I gotta cancel three meetings and have one of the VPs delay the Cincinnati contract for a few days. Say hi to everyone for me, and don't worry, hon; your dad's a tough one."

Slam! Slam! went the car doors, and off they went, headlights of hope beaming prayers for a father-in-law.

"How lucky can I get!" Susie whispered. "If there's a patron saint of assassins, then she's lookin' after me tonight!"

SNEAKING THROUGH THE HOUSE ON plush carpet, not a single board creaked under Susie's feet. Up the winding staircase she glided, hearing TG's voice from a room down the hall. *He's bossing around a poor slob on a national holiday. The guy's stinkin' rich; why does he even bother working? Sell the business and retire, for shit's sake.*

Only half her attention tuned into the man she had come to kill. The other section wondered where the maid had gone. *If he's planning on screwing her, I'm gonna cut his thing off and shove it in his ear!* She didn't know why she hated adulterers as badly as she did. Here in the past, she faced the first wave of memory problems.

Nearing the only lit room on the top floor, she heard the orders TG grumbled into the phone.

"No, don't show the Cincinnati contract to the trustees yet. I gotta smooth over a couple concessions. The deal must receive the votes of seventy-five of the board or else those Queen City kooks will sense we're not united behind our offer. I'll pitch the deal because I know how those bastards think and I speak their language, not you. You understand me?" Receiver hung up, he fumed. "Idiots. I run a corporation chockful of morons."

"If you weren't up shit creek, pal, I'd give 'em all the axe … literally." Susie enjoyed a fun entrance.

"W-W-Who are you?" His eyes bugged cartoonish-like. "Why are you dressed all in black? You're not one of my wife's friends, are you? You … you're a model, right?"

"Yeah, and tonight, I'm modeling death. Before we go any further, where's the maid? I wouldn't want her interrupting … us."

Us. He loved the sound of the danger of the thrill of the erotica of the passion of this Hollywood actress-like, of this supermodel-like, of this chance of a lifetime.

Pointing at the window, where the blinds stood raised and the curtains opened, he answered, "She's in the cottage behind the house. You can see it from here. It's a housekeeping job. We don't like the term 'maid.'"

Drake sashayed across the white carpet, knowing full well he consumed every movement of her body. "*Mmm.* Pretty fancy digs for a housekeeper. You sleeping with her?"

"No." TG hated false accusations, even if he would have enjoyed bedding the hired help. "Now, are you gonna tell me why you broke into my house? I'd rather you leave without my phoning the police because my father-in-law is ill and I'm due in Mansfield."

She plopped backward on the firm but soft mattress of the hand-carved, Medieval-style canopy bed. Flipping off the elastic clasp, her hair fanned out, and she moved both arms up and down along the bedspread. "*Ooo* … this is nice! I don't think I'll ever leave."

Bloatedly loud was his sigh. "Fine. I'm calling the cops. I thought you came to seduce me. Glad I didn't walk into that trap. I have enough problems at work without a scandal."

"You betcha you have problems." She leaped off the mattress. "Stealing from mobsters in Texas and Minnesota. Those guys got long memories, pal. *Hmm.* Wish I had a long memory. Oh, I can see by the goofy look on your face that you didn't expect me to know about your past. Well, guess what? I'm here to kill you."

"NO, YOU'RE NOT GOING TO kill anyone." TG opened a dresser drawer. "There's no revolver on you; otherwise, I would've seen the gun's outline through your skintight clothes. Blackmail is what you're after. You know I'm worth millions. See? I'm not going to argue Texas and Minnesota with you. I have places to be." Producing a checkbook, he asked, "Name a reasonable figure and promise me I'll never see you again. By and by, I have friends who would cut off your pretty head in an instant."

Man, oh man, was she enjoying this assignment!

"Well, slick, you won yourself a painless death, whatever way I decide is best for murdering you. Some guys I've offed have drawn serious weapons on me—guns, knives, a machete, a sword. Money's your arsenal, and I like it. Sadly, because I'm new in the organization, I gotta bring back proof of your death. Now, the usual fellow, bribing him would probably work from what little I know about him. He doesn't have to bring back proof. They *trust* him." Both hands went behind her head. She pouted and performed a little poor-me dance. "Oh, and just 'cause you don't see a gun doesn't mean I'm not extremely lethal. I am. Trust me."

TG exhaled sharply. "Okay, I'll pick the figure. Four million to leave. I'm positive you can find your way into a morgue, chop off a hand, and tell whoever it's mine."

"*Errgh!*" She batted her lip up and down, making a burbling sound. "You don't believe I'm dangerous, do you?"

He shook his head and glanced impatiently at a clock on an end table. "Who do I make the check out to? Don't worry. You won't get harassed at the bank. I'll call them in the morning and tell them that you're family."

"Looks like I'm gonna have to prove my strength to you."

Drake hummed an early 1960's song about running scared while checking out the room for a heavy object. Nothing caught her fancy. She recalled a tall sculpture in the corridor and went to retrieve it.

"What the—" TG couldn't decide whether to cuss or gasp at the sight of the slender woman carrying a life-sized, brownish-yellow marble statue by its neck.

The floor shook a little when she set it down near the bathroom door. "Now will you believe that I'm super-strong?"

"Uh, impressive but maybe you know a way of drawing up extra adrenaline. I read something about it in *The Enquirer*."

Frustrated, she motioned him closer. "Who is this ugly thing supposed to be?"

"Rutherford B. Hayes. My wife's related to him." His finger wiped the dust off of the President's head.

Up went her pinky. "You think I could smash him with this little finger from the skull on down?"

Laugh, laugh! "It took three hefty guys to carry it upstairs. Adrenaline aside, no. Not even one of them karate judo kinda guys could harm this baby."

"Stand back."

"What?"

"Stand back, dammit!" she screamed.

As TG walked backward toward the bed, down went her pinky, and Rutherford B. Hayes, too. Dust and brownish-yellow fragments of various shapes and sizes covered Susie's shoes, clothes, and the once-clean carpet.

"Jumpin' Jiminy! My wife's gonna go batshit when she sees what you've done!" Chuckling nervously, he reconciled the situation. "You *do* have powers!" The bed seemed to offer a place of comfort, so he sat.

Shaking off the dust with her hands, she stepped out of the mess. "C'mon. You didn't really believe that nonsense about adrenaline, did you?"

The man's knees shook, and he tapped his feet wildly. He was in a pickle all right. "I just … I mean … I wanted a fast explanation because I'm under pressure with my father-in-law being ill, and I should have been on the road by now, and they're gonna wonder why I'm late …"

"More like, they'll wonder why you never made it." Dust marked her footprints stepping toward a chair next to the bed. "I told you. I'm here to kill you."

TG COLLECTED HIMSELF, STEPPED AROUND the shattered president, entered the bathroom, and threw cold water on his face. This wasn't the end, so he believed. It couldn't be, for he'd been in dire situations many times before.

Walking calmly back to the furniture designed for sleeping, he sat on it. "You're young. The things you can do with millions of dollars are staggering. As I proposed earlier, I'll write a check for whatever amount you want. Take a hand or ear from a corpse at the morgue as proof you killed me. No—better yet, after you have the money, tomorrow night, you kill a hobo, bring him here, chop off his hand, and burn down the house. You live happily ever after, I'll start over somewhere, and no one else will be the wiser. Agreed?"

"Wait." She budged the chair closer to the bed, throwing her legs across. "One minute, you're all"—begins whining—"'Oh, my poor father-in-law, my wife's gonna be so worried about me, blah, blah, blah,' and now you're peachy with destroying the house and never seeing the family again? I. Think. That. You've. Done. This. Before." Susie wrinkled her nose. "You've skipped out on the loved ones a few times, ain'tcha?"

"Texas, Minnesota, and many places in-between." His arms stretched wide when he said "many." "Now, how about the deal I'm offering? Are we okay with it?"

"It sets a bad precedent. I'm sworn to carry out this job."

The man's eyes rolled upward. "An assassin with an ethical code. Great! By the way, how many people have you murdered?"

"Not counting the fun killings, you'll be my tenth as a professional. All men. All responsible, one way or another, for the death of innocents. You're the first who's not attacked me … so far."

"I'm not responsible for anyone's death." TG sat tall in the saddle. "I'm a good guy. The loot I ripped off … I've donated a lot to charities. Much of the money went into business investments, creating jobs, and putting food on families' tables. I'm different from your other nine. Please, give me a chance. Yeah, I'm willing to abandon my current loved ones. They'll mourn me and move on. I still grieve over the other wives, sons, and daughters I left behind. It goes with the territory. The past gets close … I'm on my way. Better me always hurting on the inside than those I care about somehow getting caught in a violent crossfire." Sending an eyeful of snub in her direction, he added, "You're gonna learn what I've discovered the longer you stay in the business, young missy. The heart will become your Achilles' heel if you remain in one place too long. Count on it."

"I'm not as young as you think I am. Despite my faulty memory, I know I've learned more and seen things you could never imagine. I'm not given to stereotypes or classifications, either. Don't throw a label at me. I'll purposely be its opposite. Count on it."

TG applauded. "I think I may be falling in love with you! We understand one another. Can we please agree on a deal?"

She didn't accept his statement, him being different from her other hits. For now, she let the comment slide, focusing instead on the man's empathy arousing efforts by playing the "kindred spirits" card.

"You do talk a good talk, mister. I could phone the boss and tell him you weren't home. I'd fake being sick, have him send the main assassin, and you'd for sure have better luck getting him to take the money, the thing—"

"Great!" he broke in. "Then it's settled. I'll still pay you something for your trouble."

"Well, not so fast, slick. You said, 'you're gonna learn what I've discovered the longer you stay in the business.' I'm confused. You did borrow money from the Texas mob. You did *not* work for them. In Minnesota, you did work for a local mafia family, bookkeeping. This was several years later and not for very long. How is it that you 'discovered' anything I might 'learn' from such a short span of time?"

"You've taken my words much too seriously. I was only attempting to dispense fatherly advice."

Deciding the truth—she was born in 1902, old enough to be his mother, despite having the face and body of an eighteen-year-old—was too much information for TG to absorb, Susie began questioning his past.

"How old are you?"

"Forty-two."

"How many wives and families have you had?"

"Counting the current crop, six wives and more kids than I can count. Maybe twenty-two."

"In each case, where you hit the highway, did someone find out you'd cheated the gangsters?"

TG leaned back across the bed. "I was eighteen when I swindled the Texan gangster. The guy should've known better than to trust a teenager! He deserved me ripping him off. Thirteen years passed before the Minnesota embezzlement. Three families before the Twin Cities affair, three since. What did I tell you about the heart, huh? I said it'll 'become your Achilles' heel if you remain in one place too long.' No one ever caught up with me. Not even close. Not until now. Besides, leaving Toledo was already in the planning stages for next year. Honolulu. It's where I hope I'll be, come next fall."

"Abandoning your families means you're not a good guy. What you do with your money doesn't make up for the hurt you leave behind. The more I learn about you, the less I like you."

Ouch, ouch! She needn't pull any physical punches to hurt him.

Though his body remained calm, his words did not. "Who are *you* to judge 'good' or 'bad?' You said the men you murdered as an assassin were accountable 'for the death of innocents.' Yet, by your acts of violence, you inflicted broken lives on innocents—the wives and children left behind. And these are only the men the mob hired you to eliminate. What about the fellows you executed for fun? Fun! I admit being far from perfect but … whacked guys for fun! *You*, lady, you're a monster! If I did own a gun, I'd do the world a favor and shoot you."

Drake reveled in TG's rant, almost laughing at the saliva building at the side of his mouth. "Point number one, bullets won't kill me. Two, I don't know if anything will. Three, I'm me, and I'll judge if I damn well wanna judge. Four, sometimes the bosses provide for widows and orphans. It's not my responsibility. Five, you don't wanna ever see me go full-blown monster. Six, when I said I killed for fun, those guys were monsters harming innocents. Finally, seven, I stick by what I said 'bout you … unless you wanna defend yourself."

One exhaustive sigh later, the man set both feet on the floor, patted a rhythm on his knees, and swore a few times when checking his wristwatch. Most folks wouldn't have paid his hairstyle much attention. Parted on the left side, the bulk of his light brown hair remained remarkably thick for a forty-two-year-old who'd dyed and reshaped it many times, distinctively for each new life change. A swoop of his hand through the mane shook it up, rocked 'n' rolled it, jazzed it just right and completely toward the left, subtracting years from his face.

"Lon Chaney Sr. was my film idol growing up, even though he died when I was a baby. His movies still showed in theaters when my family lived in New York. Out in Hollywood, I had an uncle who worked lighting on the Universal movie sets. He'd befriended Chaney, watched him apply the makeup. I moved to L.A. in my teens, wanting to be an actor. By then, I had my own bag of 'facial illusions,' as I called them. I practiced a lot of face movements in the mirror." Pausing, he treated Drake with a quick show of different visages, which impressed her. "Sadly, my acting skills were poor and horror movies were on the decline. The mob, luckily, wasn't.

"My entrance into the life of a Texan racketeer, I viewed as a one-off role. Fake name, phony face, Massachusetts accent. The money he loaned me was for financing a movie studio outside Dallas. Man, you shoulda seen his eyes light up, thinking he might become a Hollywood mogul!"

Now Susie eyed her watch, bored. "What does any of this have to do with what we talked about?"

"I'm tryin' to give you a glimpse of who I am!" TG's voice carried loud, so much so that he peeked out the window at the housekeeper's cottage, afraid she'd hear him and venture forth, checking on the master's safety. She didn't. "Makeup, disguises, both in films which never made celluloid and in a life which has been continuously stuck in an identity crisis. I'm not bad. I'm too murky for the evil side of existence. I've never known who I really am. Not really."

"*Whaaaaaaaat!* You sure are one entertaining, screwed-up, bullshittin' sonuvabitch!"

"You're one hundred percent right!" Arching his back, he hunkered like an old professor might, explaining a far-fetched theory no amount of experiments could corroborate. "No one has *ever* known the real me. They can't! He doesn't exist! My wives … I was always who they wanted and needed, but not me. Same with the kids, the employers, friends. I became a chameleon, adapting to emotional and social mores, habits, culture, likes, and dislikes of whomever I associated with. Anytime … oh, anytime I felt myself facing a conflict of opinion or taste, well, I shoved it away. Blending meant surviving. I was so much one of *them* that blending also meant being bland. In cases where there were a variety of personalities, I favored the majority. This way, no one would ever suspect I was on the run from one gangster and then another."

Mellowly, Drake asked, "Why didn't you pay the Texan back? You seem like the kinda schmuck who hasn't trouble getting a cash flow."

"I didn't wanna! I still don't wanna! Had I done that, I'd have compromised my need for constantly being an imposter. Once I embraced the wanderlust of the counterfeit personality, I feared the real me might someday emerge. What if I hated the real me? It could shatter my neatly built façade. No, I went with illusions. When I left my families, it was out of the goodness of my heart. Those were hard times, maintaining a false image. Their safety rested on my shoulders. Understand, if I were found out by the mob, it would be due to a slip of my tongue."

Onward he ranted. *No wonder he wanted to be an actor. The guy's the most immature adult I ever met!*

"Hey, lemme get a word in. It wasn't your tongue that gotcha caught. It was your nose. Your coke dealer turned you in. *Hmph.* All this talk about identity crisis and all along it's drugs that's messin' you up."

TG leaned toward her. "No, sweetie, it wasn't for me. My banker is the addict. I caught him in the act one afternoon when I entered his office without knocking. At the time, he'd been scoring off a street dealer who charged him out the nose, pun intended." The betrayal settled in, and he punched a fist against the bedpost. "He … my dealer … I checked him out. A French Canadian with no connections to my past."

"I heard a different story. The man's no Canadian. He's from Louisiana." Oh, how her eyebrows wiggled! "Guess he's like you—an actor, assuming a role, using makeup and a phony accent. Ya think maybe he conquered his identity crisis and knows who he is since he sure as shit learned who you are?"

The quip hurt TG's pride.

"Why would you even consider helping your junkie banker?"

"Leverage, blackmail if necessary. He doesn't know my background, but he knows I'm no perfect citizen. When I told you cashing a check at the bank would be a breeze, he's the reason why." TG stared at Susie's set jaw, noting how beautifully stable, chiseled, and precise it was, meaning he was getting nowhere with his speeches. "You and I are so alike while also different. People judge us as one-dimensional. The guy who goes along with the crowd, never complaining. The tough female whose occupation and powers won't permit her to have a family life. We're much more than that. You've said so yourself. You don't really want to kill me. Make it look like you did, and then let's team up. I'm not talking sex or romance … not unless you want. We pull our resources and our talents, travel around the world for a few years, and then go our separate ways. It'd be educational, learning from one another. I promise I won't ever marry again and leave the wife and kids behind, even after we split up. What do you say?"

She truly didn't want to kill him. Not now, not after he'd exhausted her with unbridled compliments, backhanded schemes, autobiographical quirks, and strange insights into her persona, which she had long denied. *Lesson learned tonight: don't engage in conversation with a target. Get it done, get it over with, and get out.*

"You know we can't leave together. I promise I'll make it painless. What I don't know yet is—"

Vomiting. With the realization his life would soon end, he upchucked. A hotdog, green beans, and grits. Not his idea for a last meal.

"Sorry." Wiping a handkerchief across a stained mouth, he eyed the bathroom. "Let me clean up, okay?"

"Sure." She walked with him.

"I wanna leave my wedding ring and billfold behind." TG switched on the lavatory light. At the sink, water splashed on his face. "Maybe you can make it look like a suicide."

"If it's what you want. Other than the puke, you're handling this very well."

He leaned on the counter, eyeing his face in the mirror. "How am I supposed to react? You tossed out all my ideas … the ones where I live another day."

In the doorway, her shoulders lifted in indifference. Drake's patience dissipated, like fog when daylight arrived. "You screwed up. I'm doing my job. Unfortunately, those ideas of yours collided with the wrong assassin. I'll say this, you outlasted every other guy I was sent to kill."

"*Whoop-de-do*. Can you at least bring me the pad of paper off the nightstand? I'll write my wife a goodbye note."

Susie gazed around the bathroom. There was no secret escape route. "Sure." Stopping halfway between the bed and the bathroom, she lightly thumped the notepad against her chin and called out, "Poison. Most painless suicide method. I didn't bring any with me. Do you have some? I know my toxins pretty well."

TG stood in the doorway, one arm behind his back. "What'd you say?"

"I said, I know—"

Here. In this instance. On this spot inches from the man whom she was supposed to have axed long before now, Susie the assassin lost all gullibility and (for a while) trust in anyone. Her mark hastily brought forward the hidden hand in which he held an aerosol for killing insects. Drake had already extended her hand, holding the writing paper, and didn't react fast enough. TG pushed hard upon the can's black button, spraying a stream of insecticide into her pupils. Drop went the tablet, up went her fingers, desperately wiping at her eyes. She pushed him aside, swore, and dashed for the water faucet, not noticing, of course, the beginning of his second act.

Mrs. TG loved telling tales of Rutherford B. Hayes and showing off items the nineteenth president owned, reciting anecdotes on memorabilia passed down through one generation after another. One such object was a forty-four-inch, double-pointed Kampilan sword, used by the Spanish Conquistadors and presented to Hayes in the late 1860s, when he had been the governor of Ohio. TG's wife preferred the item remain on display in her husband's study, but he often kept it sheathed behind the bathroom door. Why? The concealed actor loved playing with it, pretending he was a swashbuckling movie star of the 1930s, creating a drama for the wife as a method of foreplay.

Unsheathed, he rammed the sword's always-sharp blade into Susie's neck, pushing it through her throat.

"That'll teach you to turn down my brilliant concepts!"

Out of the bathroom, he ran like a cheetah. Downstairs, grabbing the keys to his car and nearly falling in the foyer, hurling the front door open and giddily giggling all the way to his Chrysler.

BY THE TIME TG REACHED the top of the staircase, Susie had pushed the sword's double-pointed end out her throat and neck. The weapon fell on the floor. *Clang, clang!* No blood squirted or dripped out her body, and the holes created by the blade healed up almost immediately. Such was a benefit of near immortality and rapid reparative powers. There was red body fluid on the steel.

Once she rinsed her eyes clear of bug spray, Drake wiped clean the Kampilan, wrapping the ensanguined towel around her arm.

"Can't have anyone puttin' my blood under a microscope, let alone touching it. Otherwise, strange things can happen."

(Author's note: That's a Susie story for another novel … *hint, hint.*)

When had she heard the entrance door burst open? A minute and a half ago? Two? Given that the bedroom window overlooked the backyard and the housekeeper's villa, she darted across the hallway and into one of the children's sleeping chambers.

"Spoiled kid has a bay window. I've never had one." Drake pushed away a Teddy bear and some toys and leaned a knee on the wooden, angled bay. "Ha! There he is … getting into his car! The guy should've been gone by now."

What Susie didn't know … TG, during his madcap merriment vamoosing from the house, had tripped over his youngest son's overturned Radio Flyer wagon. The accident had cost the escapee precious minutes, despite keeping a firm grip on the car keys.

On the second floor, Drake backed up toward the bedroom door, snarled and huffed, and bolted at the window, screaming, "*Arrrgggghhhh!*" She didn't cover her face with hands or arms as others might because mere broken pane glass wouldn't mar her lovely, angry features. Hamming it up, or maybe in an attempt to cover more distance during the leap, she performed two somersaults—the first a definite eight point five while the second should rate a ten, for it landed her in the standing position atop the overturned Radio Flyer wagon.

The black Chrysler Impala had already left skid marks in the grass, nearly smacked a tree, and rode sideways upon a small hill before pouncing on the curvy paved driveway. Laughing even now, TG steered the getaway vehicle toward the road, a quarter mile away.

The landowner's opponent maintained her advantage— super-speed for short distances, roughly up to a mile. Bounding off the wagon, Susie decided to make the contest interesting, grinning at the sight of a limestone birdbath a short jog away. The bowl section easily came loose. Dumping the water and bird poop, she ran extraordinarily fast, stone dish in hand.

Nearing the bottom of the drive, TG exhaled in relief. "Cincinnati, here I come!" Why didn't he check the rearview mirror? Well, why should he? All the time he had spent with the blonde assassin, and he never inquired for a full description of her unusual talents.

Cleared of the many obnoxious rolling hills, Susie skidded her shoes to a stop and commenced her tryout for the bird bowl throw at the 1964 Olympics … or the 1961 Toledo Assassin Olympics. Left arm pointed downward, she spun anticlockwise, built up momentum (kicking up dirt and wind), and released the bathing basin. *Whooooosh*, it flew at an incredible speed, smashing through the Impala's back window and obliterating TG's skull. Dead he was, and his foot eased off the gas. The car aimed for the mailbox until Drake sped ahead, yanked on the rear bumpers, and ended the Chrysler's flight.

Back on Alt-Earth…

"SO MUCH FOR THE CUTESY ending!" Jim-Bob exhaled. "I did enjoy the story and I can see the headlines—back in the day when there were still newspapers—'*Bird Bath Bashes Bad Boy's Brains*.' Was it your intent to kill him or stop the car?"

"Whatever it would take." She climbed into the back of *The Imene-A-Bago*, opened the cooler, and removed two bottles of a blue drink. The label read "*Memory-Cola*." Back up front, she handed Flannagan his drink. "What's this stuff taste like and why 'memory?'"

"It's meant to taste different per person. For me, it tastes like fried chicken livers. The manufacturer claims it helps prevent Alzheimer's. There's little proof to back it up. Don't leave me hanging. Did you leave after killing the guy or what?"

They both popped open the bottle lids at the same time. A fast sampling of the soda reminded her of a certain candy bar from the 1920s (whose named she couldn't place) known for its vanilla taffy and peanut butter flavors.

A quick clip played in Susie's mind—her walking through New York City's Murray Hill on a breezy, sunny day, the exact year unknown.

"Nope, I stuck around. I knew the consigliere would read about the guy's death in the papers and wouldn't appreciate the mess I made. The Impala was in good enough shape for me to drive it to Lake Erie and dispose of it. I took a cab back to the house, using my mind-altering power on the driver so that he'd never recall taking me there. Up into the bedroom, I carried the guy and what remained of the bird bowl and made a shambles of the entire floor. He never wrote the suicide note. I found samples of his writing and penned one. Basically, it said, *'dear wife, blah, blah, I'm tired of living, blah, blah. Tonight, I attempted various means of killing myself, smashing self with Hayes statue and bird bowl, dismembering a hand, finally drank poison. Boy, do I feel ill.'* Making it real-like, I poured drain unclogging liquid, herbicides I found in the shed, and other stuff down his throat. Of course, there wasn't much I could do about covering the head wound, other than bandaging it, making it look like he survived the impact, but it'd never fool a pathologist. I did cut off his hand for proof. Anyway, the papers pronounced it a suicide with 'questionable, unsolved details still under investigation.' My boss was happy, he paid me, and believe you me, I learned boatloads from the hit. I became a much better, thorough assassin, steering clear of my screw-ups and staying focused."

Jim's stomach churned. "You say it like you're proud of the fact."

"I can't change the past. Okay. The direction I embraced would later change me. Had I let the guy go free or teamed up with him, you and I wouldn't know one another, and any good I did wouldn't have happened. A bland, ill-defined me would have gone insane. No doubt about it." After a gulp of the wonderful drink, she asked, "Are we done with 1961 Prime-Earth?"

"One more question. What became of the bloody towel you wrapped around your arm?"

A fierce laugh! "Good question! I kept it with me on my Harley or whatever cycle I clung to for years as a reminder … try not screwing up as I did during the Blunder of '61!"

Chapter 8: The Suzii

AWAKE AND STARING OUT A side window, Liam confirmed, "I was really tired. Did I miss anything during the drive?"

"Nope. Just me telling a story."

"The camper must've floated a good part of the way," Karas assumed. "I didn't feel a single bump."

"I haven't turned on the float facet," Jim-Bob told him. "Surprisingly, the road crews did a fantastic job keeping the roads in shape. The main highways have A.I. repairs, in other words, computers know when potholes appear and A.I.R. fills them in. However, it won't be long before I gotta find a Cloudonine station."

Another Karas question. "Where are we? I see small buildings up ahead."

"This is the section of Connecticut set aside for servicing New York and travelers who begin their way up north. It's technically under Manhattan's jurisdiction but still a separate entity. Locals call it the Assistance Republic. The 'republic' part divided people. Workers and residents liked the idea of a territory managed apart from America. Politicians and business owners hate it. The A.R. stretches from here, along a thin territory, up to Canada and is ruled over by several districts."

"Didn't we take the long way arrivin' here?" Susie asked. "Why not straight up the coast?"

"Traffic." Lt. Flannagan spotted a large chuckhole ahead, cursed A.I.R.'s inefficiency, and pushed a button labeled "*F.F.*" (Float Facet). *The Imene-A-Bago* elevated off the road, floated beyond the crater, setting back down and automatically shifting into a smooth reunion with the road. "New Haven's a couple miles away. From Milford to Ossining and areas south is a thick, New York suburb. Traffic is nauseous." With his right arm, he reached backward, hand pointing at the cooler, fridge, and pantry. "None of us have eaten any snacks yet. I'd prefer exiting the Marin at the Olde Boston exit a couple hours away. They have better quality Assistance outlets."

Neither Prime Earthling objected.

"Good. If either of you wanna nap, now's a good time."

"Not me," Liam answered. "I want to see just how elevated the Marin Highway is. I'm feeling fine after nodding off."

Susie rarely napped and never in a moving vehicle. "I revealed a blast from my past, Jim. I wanna hear one of yours. Someone you've killed and how you dealt with it. You have killed, haven't you?"

"Way to get ultimate personal, Susie!" Karas exclaimed.

"No, she's fine." One could describe Flannagan's coy expression as "boyish." "I've never killed anyone. Severely injured, yeah, a few times. Those were the days before computerized A.I. guns equipped with biological bullets came along."

"I'm afraid to ask …" Liam began.

Jim's mood darkened. "Are you anti-cop? Why would you be negative against a weapon meant for saving civilians and police officers while never killing a perp unless absolutely necessary?"

"So, you're saying it's an actual smart gun, not the pseudo-smart guns which rarely work?" the private detective asked.

"It certainly is! I won't let you see my piece. It's against the rules." His lips smacked unhappily. "I shoulda had an A-Grid put in the camper. Then you could've seen a demonstration online. Anyway, computerized guns have been around for centuries. Too many of them are useless and lock up when one needs them the most. An artificial intelligence system eventually came along, and the sweet part after it was perfected several times was how it adjusted to both the shooter's mind and the potential victim.

"Being a cop, I have the authority to kill when the situation calls for it. Under normal situations, it doesn't often occur. These newer revolvers, called AIM—short for Artificial Intelligence Mindlock—do just that—they read my thoughts, assess the danger, and fire in a manner which won't kill the perp, provided he or she isn't able to shoot and kill back. For example, a guy exits a shop firing a gun. My AIM will figure out where best to shoot, disarming him. The biological bullet also has AI technology. It will never miss or strike a person where the AIM hadn't intended on hitting."

Liam challenged, "What if the 'perp' has an AIM? Whose AIM wins?"

"Only law enforcement officers have an AIM. It's automatic prison time of ten years for non-LEOs to possess this particular weapon and … the death penalty if they tamper with one, somehow fitting it to their mindlock and using it in during a crime … any crime."

"What about the public, Jimmy?" Susie sweetly said. "I'd want my friends, if I had any, being able to protect themselves. Why don't they get AIMs?"

Was he feeling ganged upon? Nope. Calm. "The citizenry has access to computerized guns if they so desire. Rifles are prevalent in the Farmlands. A lotta plain folks want AIMs. They claim it prevents kids from playing with guns and gettin' killed and cuts out the need for burdensome safety training. It's up to Congress, and they always veto it."

Karas wasn't satisfied. "You're a pretty decent guy, Jim. But what about a rogue cop who's tired of the justice system and decides it's best if he eliminates some criminal scum. The AI will read his thoughts and blow away the guys and girls. Correct?"

Lt. Flannagan tapped his head with a finger. "All persons issued an AIM must have at least one chip surgically inserted on their brain, near the prefrontal cortex. Don't ask me scientific medical questions, but the implant reduces violent impulse controls, negative thoughts, and antisocial behavior. I have the single, required chip. Other officers get a second one if an injury occurs which throws off the original or if the precinct shrink feels their mind has found a way around the TranquilChip."

Both men's eyes turned slowly at Susie.

Spittle foamed around her mouth. "I no longer have 'violent impulse controls, negative thoughts, and antisocial behavior.' I know you guys think I do, and if you keep lookin' at me that way, I'm gonna beat the shit outta the cop and leave you here on Alt-Earth all by yourself, baldie."

"Glad you have a sense of humor." Liam sighed around the point he would make. "Your situation is different. Let's say the TranquilChip existed on Prime Earth in the early 1950s. I don't think it would've worked for you. I'd tell you why, but Jay's probably listening, isn't he?"

"Yeah. I smell something awful in my head. Guess he farted. I know whatcha mean. It wouldn't've worked. Knowing me, I'd have head-butted a brick wall just to break the damn thing." She pointed ahead. "Hey, look, an elevated highway comin' up. Must be the Marin."

THE STRAIGHT-UP ANGLE OF the Marin on-ramp made Liam dizzy. Shouldn't he have expected a change in distance from the ground since the lieutenant kept describing the upcoming section as elevated? Yet Karas feigned surprise.

The ground on which four lanes of concrete lay, Jim explained, was made partially from destroyed city buildings throughout America and dirt which once composed the state of Florida, not long before it submerged under the ocean. At two hundred and seventy feet above the farthest point below, Morgan's highway made traveling the upper East Coast faster and safer.

"Safer?" Karas questioned. "What about heavy rains and snow? I wouldn't wanna go slidin' down the hillside, crashing into a house or business of the Assistance Republic or whatever the heck territory I'd wreck into."

"It's never happened," Flannagan stated, ripe with confidence. "Only vehicles with AI tracking, like *The Imene-A-Bago*, are allowed on the Marin and other roads like it. The

A.I.T. keeps the tires firm on the special pavement, and it prevents flat tires, blowouts, lost control of steering, and anything else which could go wrong with a car or truck."

"Don't tell me it battles Mother Nature's havocs?"

"No, Liam. Installed on either side of the hills are weather-resistant domes which automatically cover and protect the entire construct. Yes, the sides do deteriorate due to rain, but the Marin Brigade keeps it in tip-top shape, repairing any erosion."

Susie snickered. "A while back, you said this road would have 'multiple bends and steep inclines.' When's that gonna happen?"

"It does, and it will. Not dramatically nor alluva sudden. Try the Killar to Pangi road in India if you want excitement."

He sounded ticked. She picked up on it. "What's eating you?"

"Nothing. Never mind."

Not true. With each mile, Jim felt he'd do his companions right by turning the vehicle around and begging for the mercy of his captain. *I don't see how things'll turn out well. When we get off the interstate, I'll go where I can pray on the matter.*

INSTEAD OF CUTTING ACROSS THE land for a shorter journey, the Marin hugged the shoreline. Tall, concrete walls installed along either side of the road prevented motorists from viewing bodies of water, tourist traps, and whatever else lay below. When Jim tripped a switch on the vehicle's dashboard, a map of the highway appeared in 3-D, also displaying photos of upcoming Assistance shops, eateries, service businesses, and places promoting health, entertainment, and other forms of distraction.

Providence was Exit 2, the first being New Haven.

"They cater to teens," Jim-Bob announced. "There can be a heavy police presence. We're absolutely not stopping there."

Nor did they stop at Exit 3, Plymouth. "Not much variety there."

Exit 4. Olde Boston. "It's *the* premiere Assistance destination on the East Coast. In the early days, the shop owners wanted the city renamed New Boston. The developers and marketing teams chose 'Olde' with the 'e' at the end. They figured having storefronts resembling somethin' out of the 18th century would meet the travelers' fancy. It did. For better or worse, it means we'll park in a gigantic lot and take a bus or trolley into the town."

"Do people live there anymore?" Liam asked.

"The workers and their families live in Orient Heights and Revere. I have a cousin somewhere in Admirals Hill … a neighborhood inside the Chelsea District." Jim-Bob aimed the long vehicle at the turn-off. "We park by the waterfront and are taken to what once was the downtown area and Beacon Hill."

Another Karas question. "I guess nothing remains of Harvard, eh?"

Flannagan had dreaded any mention of the prestigious college. *I'm in enough trouble the way it is. Doesn't matter if they bite on what I tell 'em. How can things get worse?* "Several buildings still stand. One in particular is Austin Hall. It's a Remnant magnet."

Susie bit. "Hey, I wouldn't mind going there. Mingle with other powereds. Maybe they know something about Rodanthe, Pith, or the stolen spaceship ... remember it? *Hmm*?"

Ahead of them, cars, trucks, and campers formed a long line.

"Let's talk about it after we eat. And don't let this traffic make you think we're stuck here for a while. I can see the parking attendants not far away. They're sending drivers through multiple entrances."

"Let me hear it again, Jim-Bob. Liam and me are safe from anyone recognizing us."

"Yep. You with your stringy black hair, cleft chin, and big nose make you look like an almost pretty sight to someone with bad eyes. As for Liam ... bald guys his age have a notorious reputation for being, um, touchers."

"What's a 'toucher?'" the hairless passenger asked.

"They touch themselves in public. You can guess *what* they touch, can't you?"

"Why didn't you tell me this earlier? I could've gone with a different disguise. Jeez Louise!"

The lieutenant laughed. "I brought along an extra baseball cap. It's on the shelf above the fridge. Wear it. Your phony sideburns and glasses will make you appear less a toucher."

"What about cops and cameras?" Susie questioned. "There's bound to be upped security with the kinda crowds I'm bettin' we'll be surrounded by."

"Aw, c'mon, gimme a break, Miss Paranoid! Crowd control, yeah, private security personnel. They're gonna be watchin' out for shoplifters and purse-snatchers. Some things never change. If you notice trouble, Miss Hero, don't get yourself involved. All it'll do is get your face on camera, and the more severe the crime, the more likely a bored cop like me will see the footage, and *bam!* the facial recognition software has you caught."

BECAUSE MOST VACATIONERS LOADED ONTO buses, Susie and company hopped on a double-decker, non-airconditioned trolley. The majority of the passengers rode the top level, opting for the cool breeze and better appreciation of the shopping area. Just as Liam started complaining about the suffocating heat, the former assassin selected her first stop.

"Ye Olde Outfitters. C'mon, boys; let's have a look."

Drake readied for a jump off the streetcar. Jim halted her.

"Conductor," he called out. "Please stop for us."

On the sidewalk, Susie smiled so brightly it scared the policeman. "Ain'tcha just the politest thing, Mistah Flannagan! A country gal like me sho wouldsa got lost heres without'cha. Ah'm mighty gratefo' yous here wit' us."

"Knock it off, Susie-Beth, and yes, I try my darnedest to be polite. My grandpappy was a stickler for manners and kindness, and he would whip the tar out of me if I strayed off the path of graciousness and compassion. Well, by 'whip,' I mean it figuratively. He'd give me a look like I'd been to the woodshed."

Wondering why he'd freed the tidbit on his past, Jim-Bob waggled a finger at an open door. "There's your clothing shop. I'll wait out here. Hold on … you guys will need money. You can't spend Prime Earth bills here."

Drake cocked an eyebrow. "I have money. Your pal with the disguises gave me a couple hundred in small bills. Didn't he tell you?"

Teeth gritted, grinding … *grind, grind*! "It figures! Y'see, he and I became friends after I thought I'd reformed him from his thievery habits. But no, he's stealin' again."

"What makes you think the money's hot? He didn't give it for nothing. When he was on his way out, he asked if he could take my picture. Said he'd sell copies at a store called Sam Pleedo's and promised the money would go to charity. I used my manipulation power on him, made sure he told the truth. He did. And later, while you were out, he returned, and I signed over a hundred copies. That's when he paid me. I didn't wanna take it, but he said he could sell the prints for hundreds, autographed by—"

"The Prime and original Susie Drake," the cop interrupted. "Okay, I feel foolish. 'Sam Pleedo' … you heard wrong. It's San Pedro's, a mission where he works. The people who'd buy those endorsed photos are primarily high-stakes collectors. Most of them operate souvenir businesses five blocks from my friend's facility. He's done this kinda thing before. Believe it or not, he's sold autographed shots of the Rodanthes." Pause. "He didn't tell me 'cause he knew I'd object, what with you on the run."

"The police will associate him with you once they get word about the photos, won't they?" she asked.

"Yep. Don't worry about it now. Go shop."

Ten minutes later, she ambled out of the store wearing a floppy yellow hat and sunglasses with pink, heart-shaped lenses. No one could ever accuse her of being Susie Drake.

Behind her walked Liam, a shaggy black toupee beneath the baseball cap and a thick black mustache below his nose.

"It itches. Must be the spirit gum adhesive."

ALONG THE BOARDWALK, THEY MOSEYED. Window gazing at an antique emporium specializing in sports memorabilia, Liam and Jim bonded over their fascination with baseball. Susie, meanwhile, drifted along the concrete path, lured by the aroma of freshly cooked food. Inside her head, a wire tripped the word "café." Was this the genesis of a returned memory? *E'tty told me it couldn't happen. Said I might experience déjà vu but shouldn't become hopeful thinking what someone stole could magically restore itself. Café might mean anything. I won't ask Liam, and I certainly won't find out anything from Jay. I'll let it pass.*

Dropping the thought didn't change the mood she slipped into. *I'm nowhere near finding the spaceship, Rodanthe, or Pith, and I don't know how much longer I can remain patient. What I'd like to do is head out on my own. I have enough recall from the old days, which tells me that the info I need is in the heads of street goons. I crack those noggins open and out spills the locations of the who's and what's I'm lookin' for. It won't happen here in this tourist town. Jim said the closest actual city is Concord ... three times the population it used to have. We could head there from the Portsmouth exit. Why not? Nothin' substantial is gonna happen here.*

"AH … FOOD!" KARAS CROONED. HE and Jim had caught up with Drake. Invoking a tone of mock trepidation which needed more pastiche, he added, "Sure hope it tastes as good as it smells."

"Read carefully. The menu's taped on the restaurant windows," Flannagan informed both of them. "A good portion of meat these days derives from plants. Wherever you see a 'h/h' printed atop a menu, it means all their meats are half animal, half plant. I'm a veggie."

"So is Imene. She makes a killer salad."

Detecting the manifestation of sadness in her friend's voice, Susie smacked her hands together. "I want real meat and French fries. T-bone steak. I wanna pick my own cow, too. Wrestle it to the ground and rip off the loin with my teeth!"

Liam conducted a smile. "Double cheeseburger with bacon, mustard, and lettuce, a baked potato, and a strawberry shake for me. Can we get the authentic goods around here?"

"I see a sign for R-R-R from here. It stands for Rodanthe's Retro Restaurant. Old Hugh founded it, the flagship of the family empire. Compared with other eateries, it's relatively inexpensive and the food's excellent. The Rodanthes have contracts with the Farmlands' best suppliers. But …"

"But what?" Susie interjected. "Are the meals loaded with chemicals for turning folks into criminals like old Hugh and young Winthrop?"

"But … R-R-R faces multiple lawsuits claiming they bribed several farms into selling bad meat to their competitors. Nothing's been proven so far. A lotta people dining at the opposing restaurants have contracted food poisoning. Rodanthe says they had nothing to do with it."

Drake eyed Liam. "It's up to you. Where do you wanna eat?"

"Call me an unethical coward, but I *do not* want to wind up sick to my stomach … at least not until we're back home."

"No one's callin' you anything. Let's go eat." She stopped four steps later. "Aren't you comin', Jim?"

"You guys go on. I'll grab a bite at a veggie café." Pedestrians ambled around the conversing trio. "First, I'm going to drop in at the Christian church two blocks away."

Neither Prime Earthling commented with words, only surprised countenances.

"Yes, I consider myself a Christian. Not the best, but we all sin." Foot traffic increased. He guided his friends into a short alleyway. "My sister has always been a faithful believer, and she's the one who got me going back to church when she moved to the city. Having spiritual beliefs helps me with the job and the divorce. I was once very angry at the ex. Not anymore. I forgave her for cheating on me, and I asked for and received forgiveness for being more dedicated to my career than our marriage. I don't preach at people. If they ask, I'll explain my beliefs in detail."

"Imene's a Muslim. More like a cultural one than a practicing one. I didn't convert nor do I comment negatively on her religion." Karas's shoulders lifted and fell. "I haven't … I, uh … I've not yet devoted time on the topic as to my personal dogma."

The younger man's eyes placed Susie in the spotlight. "What? Me? If you wanna know my spiritual philosophy, wait till I get my memories back. I think …" She rubbed her belly. "Okay, we're gonna chow down. Jim's going to church, and then eating. The map on the trolley showed a large gazebo down by the river. How's about we meet there when everyone's done, say no later than an hour and a half?"

Everyone agreed to the terms and off they marched, pursuing two different agendas.

LIAM TACKLED THE TOPIC OF Susie's quiet mood. "You've fallen for him, ain'tcha? It was what he said about forgiveness that signed, sealed, and delivered Jim-Bob into your loner, black sheep, last of the independent's heart, right?"

"You're havin' fun at this, aren't ya? Imene has you so very whipped, wrapped around her pinky, lickin' her stinkin' toes. Because you lovingly wriggle in her shadow, now that you're centuries and miles from her, possibly forever, you gotta jab me with piss-poor observations which amount to a pile of Jay."

Karas stood rigid, face tight, fists curled, like he was going to cry … *boohoo, boohoo!* "*All* I stated is what's evident by how you act and look. What is *wrong* with you?"

"There's plenty wrong with me," she acknowledged matter-of-factly. "I can't stop you from seeing things which may or may not be based on fact, not without rippin' out your eyeballs. If you wanna be my friend or acquaintance, never, under any circumstances ever, speak what you consider is a definite fact about me without asking me first and not in public."

"I did ask! I asked two questions! If you don't believe me, ask Jay. I'll bet he heard me."

"Not gonna ask that shi—never mind. Just don't ask *in public!* Change the subject."

Had Liam posed his questions in a private setting, Drake wouldn't have answered truthfully. No, from out her mouth, she might say, "Jim has too much of a boy still left in him. He talks like a square salesman or a dry TV newscaster. I know his kind: two-story house, wife, three kids, and a white-picket fence. We're no match. I'm all woman; I prefer not sayin' much, and I can't be fenced in."

The truth was … she'd fallen for him back at the precinct. And ever since, Susie was at war with herself.

<hr>

A LONG LINE FORMED OUTSIDE the R-R-R. Fortunately, a woman wearing an earpiece and handing out menus to those unfamiliar with the set of food choices relayed orders to the crew behind the counter. Susie picked out the T-bone steak, very rare, French fries, and a cherry cola. Liam forwent the cheeseburger he craved, selecting fried catfish, a baked potato, and a chocolate shake. While they waited for their meals, the baseball fan pitched what he considered to be an unfathomable question.

"Alt-Earth came into existence due to a time-traveling 1950s Prime Earth physicist. History split on a different path for the two worlds because this planet knew and accepted something our world didn't for a long time—time travel and parallel realities. Not completely similar, of course. The scientist's involvement with other researchers and the government eventually altered the public's life, beginning small and ever increasing. People were born in Alt-Earth who didn't have a counterpart in the Prime, and vice versa. This wouldn't necessarily have stopped the continuance of doppelgängers throughout this century. A couple hundred years ago, I'll bet there was a Liam and Irene Karas on this planet."

Lifting and shaking her hands, fingers spread apart, Susie exclaimed, "Lord have mercy on the poor inhabitants of 21st century Alt-Earth Indiana! Hallelujah!"

He ignored her. "Let's believe as Jim does in God. You have two Earths. A lot of the same people. Is there one heaven or two? It doesn't seem to me that God would allow a second paradise just because a time traveler created another timeline. Two Sally Marie Ragsdills—to pick a fake name—same personalities, not much difference in their life stories. Can both end up in heaven?"

"Yeah, why not? God knew the physicist would do what he did because He knows everything. Maybe He even planned it that way. There's gotta be a contingency plan for all them doubles when they die."

Karas rubbed his hands. If it weren't for the baseball cap and facial disguises, he might resemble a mad scientist. "You know more about God than I expected."

"I'm. Not. Stupid!" She began wondering if Liam was related to the guy she had offed in Toledo, 1961. "Okay, smartass, what's your theory?"

"Free will … the Bible mentions it. The physicist's actions were his own, not God's. Unless a person believes in the mythological pantheons, only the one God can create life. Forming a parallel timeline generates life. The scientist wasn't God. Therefore, everyone ever born on Alt-Earth won't go to either afterlife because God didn't create them or give them souls."

Her smirk wasn't friendly. "Nonsense. Look at the kids in line, thrilled at how soon a Rodanthe burger will be crawling in their stomachs. Why, their over-excitement is so soulful it makes me nauseous. You can't tell me that Jim-Bob is soulless." Drake paused, wondering if Flannagan was the reason why Liam had brought up the topic. "Besides, you're likely not the first person questioning the relationship between God and Alt-Earth. I dunno what people on this planet believe where God and religion's concerned, and I don't care. From what I've seen so far, they're the same kinda people you find everywhere—good, bad, whatever."

The sigh Liam exhaled ran low on air before he responded. "I respectfully disagree. Alt-Earth is a planet of clones, more or less. No souls. They can play the humanity and sense of identity part very cleverly and convincingly. They're not the real deal."

Susie wondered if her brand of negativity had rubbed off on him. "I advise you not to tell anyone here that they're a soulless clone, 'not the real deal,' or else they might deal you a black eye and bloody nose."

CHURCH ATTENDED AND FOOD DEVOURED, the trio reconvened at the riverside gazebo. The men were eager to resume the journey. Drake had an opposing notion.

"Austin Hall." She held up a map torn from a souvenir shop guidebook. "I'm going. The Remnants living there might know something about the stolen ship. It's worth a try. You guys hang back. The journey will go smoother and faster when I run short distances at top speed."

Mingling with Remnants who harbored hostilities against non-powereds wasn't on either man's bucket list. All the same, didn't danger lurk if she went in alone?

"They might gang up on you," Jimmy warned. "We can watch from a distance and—"

"And what?" she broke in. "You gonna use your smart gun against someone who might fry you with lightning-conducting eyes? Listen … I can handle myself. Stay in the city, have fun. I'll be back when I'm back."

"What if you're not back by dark?" Liam asked.

"Consider me locked inside an interesting conversation. I'm a big girl. You're big guys. Figure something out."

<hr>

WHAT SERVED AS THE DIVIDING line between Olde Boston and the overgrowth of flora inside the long-gone residential and commercial districts south of the Charles River was the crooked journey of the Back Bay Fens parkland, ending at Jamaica Pond. Susie grumbled at the thickness of the brush which impeded her scurrying along at a timely pace. *I don't wanna arrive too late in the afternoon. More than that, I don't wanna stumble through this jungle in the dark on the way back.* Luckily, on the other side of the waterway, a quaintly trimmed, three-hundred-foot wide path welcomed her, and even luckier, it delivered her upon the lawn of Austin Hall. Off came the wig, phony facial façades, sunglasses, and floppy hat. She stored the items behind a shrub and advanced toward the classroom-like structure.

Sneaking quietly across the finely manicured grass, her ears failed to hear the slightest sound from outside the building. The hall had held up remarkably well over the decades of unuse. Walking toward an arched entrance, the steps and foyer were void of trash and weeds. The windows shone spotless. *The Remnants living here must have super-tidiness powers*, she reasoned through a sense of humor. *I'll bet the only weapons they have are brooms and mops*!

"Anybody home-ome-ome-ome-ome?" Her voice echoed throughout the corridor.

Electricity ran in the overhead light fixtures. Susie turned a knob on an old water fountain and dipped a finger when the liquid spouted upward. Not only was it clear, but when she licked her skin, it didn't taste putrid.

"Remnants, come out, come out, wherever you are! I'm an ally. You've really kept this place going … Kudos all around."

Opening a classroom door or two, empty chairs and vacant podiums chilled the air with ghosts from lectures past. The absence of people didn't disappoint her. Hadn't she already dealt with the phantoms who had allocated treasures and endearments upon her heart? Here in these halls of learning, Susie Drake felt lost. Was she involuntarily applying for a degree in the study of Burning Sorrow Deep Within One's Heart and Gut? Or could all she need was a bottle full of Tums?

E'tty removed unedited movies of good times and good lovin', so why is there still so much hurt remaining? I'm not thinkin' about my assassin life. That doesn't hurt. Don't tell me that I screwed up royally and now the absence of recalling love and happiness is causin' me grief! The best thing about this world is the impossibility of becoming close to anyone. Not even Jim. When I'm back on Prime Earth—and I will return—I think I'll do what this world's version of me is rumored to have done—hide out in an Ellesmere Island cave and the Lut Desert. I'll bid Liam and Imene goodbye and become a floating spirit, never indulging in relationships ever again. Close involvement with people does not mix well when you're almost immortal.

THE TICKED-OFF MAN STOMPED his left foot twice. *Stomp, stomp!* "Why are you in *here*? It's still light outside, for crying out loud! We need the Hastings Hall renovation completed before the others return. My, my … is there a problem with the materials? I thought we had an ample supply in case defectiveness became an issue."

She said nothing, thought much. *There goes my one chance at a nervous breakdown! Everyone else gets one, not me. Okay, it wasn't a "nervous breakdown" I was aiming for, more like a violent meltdown. I have had them before and, boy, can they ever be fun. Nobody else would say it's fun. But for me, it pushes the clogged-up shit right outta my ass and filters all the nasties through my veins and into my fists! I wouldn't hurt anyone, not since I'm reformed. But … the pathetic forest I stumbled through gettin' here … I'd rip it apart limb from tree from shrub! Too bad the gray-haired rodent had to ruin my tailspin into madness.*

"Are you gonna answer me, missy, or keep standin' there, looking like somebody stole your pudding?"

Mmm, the mere mention of pudding sounded good and kicked her out of the funk.

"You've mistaken me for someone else, coffin-dodger. Where are all the Remnants who're supposed to be here?"

"*Coffin-dodger* is it?" His wrinkled face inflamed. "I'll show you, blonde floozie! You'll wish you'd stayed at Hastings and continued working!"

Both his palms elevated while all fingers extended forward. A strong gale stormed from each hand. Everything in the corridor not securely nailed down went flying toward the foyer doors. This did include an unprepared blonde hussy, blown along on her rear end, cussing every inch of the way.

Outraged. Had her assailant been younger, stronger, an Exile, or a Rodanthe (on this point, she was as yet unsure), her infuriation might have reached the violent meltdown stage. Nonetheless, Drake, after skidding her butt against the wooden entryway, leaped to her feet and bounded back down the passageway, fulminating all the way. Both arms swept the senior citizen off the floor and close enough to her face where she might bite off his light brown nose. Instead of biting, she barked, permitting an excess of saliva the pleasure of dripping on his chin.

"Why'd you attack me? Over a silly nickname! You don't know me! But you sure as shit act like you do! Explain yourself, gramps!"

Tiny, hairy fingers touched her skin. "*Mmm.*" Amazement rang within his mutterings. "Lift me a little higher, please." It wasn't what Susie had expected or wanted as a reaction. She did as he asked. His brown eyes studied her hair and left ear. "Most unusual. I'm perplexed. Plastic surgery doesn't affect your face. Can't be done. How'd you do it?"

"Do *what?*"

"Remove the wrinkles and the ear gash. Certainly isn't makeup or else it'd have come off on my fingers." His nose twitched. "The chemicals you're using over in Hastings for the renovation ... might be the answer. The Remmies found them. One of them must have a power that can alter the atoms of certain matter, and when you came in contact with a specifically changed substance, it cleared your face to what it once was a couple hundred years ago."

Resisting laughter came hard. "All righty." She set him upright on the floor and patted his head. "I dunno what you been smokin', shootin' up, or injectin', but you have the wrong girl, pal. I've never had wrinkles or a cut on my ear."

Stepping backward a few inches, planting his feet in a broad posture, he thrust out his chest and firmly asked, "Who the hell are you then?"

"Susie Drake. And you?"

A voice carried from behind her. "We call him the Old Man. We don't use real names around here, kiddo, although everyone knows mine."

Turning one-hundred-and-eighty degrees, Susie's muscles tightened. Here was someone she might not defeat in hand-to-hand combat. Here was Alt-Earth's version of herself, another Susie Drake.

OVER TIME, THE HARVARD REMNANTS (they chose the designation, believing it made them sound intelligent) remodeled the classrooms of several buildings into bedrooms, libraries, entertainment centers, and kitchens. Old Man had chosen one lecture hall for his own space, allowing it to remain a small auditorium. It was here he brought the two Susies, or the Suzii, as he fancied calling them. Scooting the podium aside, he asked the Suzii to please haul in three recliners from the supply room behind the stage. Positioned at his approval, all the chairs faced row upon row of empty seats.

"We're all comfortable now, are we not?" Old Man acknowledged the quiet. "Fair enough. I'll be the moderator." Clears throat. "You"—he nodded at the obvious guest—"we don't know your story. You go first."

Shifting her body upward inside the plush leather recliner, Susie pulled up on the wooden side lever, lifting the footrest. Off went her shoes and on came an expression of stealthy alertness. In case a fool attempted an attack, her radar was on high alert.

"I'm Prime Earth Susie. Not a lookalike or a rambunctious Remnant."

Old Man licked his lips while Alt-Susie pondered thoughtfully.

"Let me tell you what brought me to this world." An abbreviated elucidation later, "I'd hoped the Harvard Remnants had insight into where I can find the spaceship. I'm guessing neither of you can help. If that's the case, then I should get outta your hair."

"I haven't heard or seen anything," Alt-Susie offered. "The Remnants who normally stay here are a quiet bunch … mostly. They've been gone to Olde Cleveland for the Remnant Olympics since before your ship disappeared. Had it passed by anywhere near here, Old Man's psychic alarms would've gone off."

"What about other Remnant groups, especially closer to New York?"

"It's possible. There's one gang I've heard about who likes stealing stuff even the major thieves shy away from. They sell the goods wherever they can and don't mind traveling outta their territory. Who's it I'm thinkin' about, Old Man?"

"The Staten Island Shysters. Their leader is a fellow who can regenerate body organs and skin tissue. No telling how old he is for a non-Exile. A few of them worked for the Rodanthe family as lawyers." He slapped the side of his chair. "I forgot to offer you ladies drinks. Gotta wide variety of alcohol and non-alcohol in the kitchen."

The Suzii said they were good.

"Okay, maybe later." Old Man contemplated Alt-Susie's consistently dour face, decided against a scathing comment, and instead focused on the visitor. "The cop you travel with has misled you. Leaving the States poses no problem 'cause he *is* a cop. When the Canadian border police scan you and your Prime Earth pal's IDs, the Mounties will have access to that info and all of you will be arrested once you reenter America. Your IDs probably belonged to people who've died over the last fifty years. It's cheaper than forging non-existent people."

Prime Susie didn't consider Jim's failure to mention a possible detainment as deceptive or a betrayal. "I'll ask him about it. Maybe he had a plan he never revealed. It's not like we're wanted for murder, just trespassing, breaking, and entering. Oh yeah, breaking outta jail, but we have a good excuse. Jim'll have the most explaining to do—hiding and taking us out of the city and country. Anyway, we're hoping for assistance from the Exiles. Regardless of whether they can help find the ship or not, they can at least teleport us across the border." Eyeing her counterpart, she asked, "What, if any, relationship do you have with the Exiles and the Rodanthes?"

Moving away from her usual wariness surrounding personal questions, the older Drake responded, "All the Rodanthes are conceited assholes. I know the barebone details of how Hugh affected your life. Even while I've been in seclusion, they've sought me for endorsements of their projects. No damn way. Every once in a blue moon, an Exile councilmember appears before me, encouraging me to seek a peaceful paradise in Lointain. There's no pressure from them. I still say no." Blankly, she added, "I can get you to Boudreaux without the embassy's red tape."

Hearing this proposal almost made Old Man fall out of his chair. "I'll be dipped in vomit and rolled in cracker crumbs! You still gotta make an appearance at the embassy, y'know? Alt-Susie in public after three hundred years! People gonna piss their britches in excitement!"

"Calm down. I've always sensed them watching me from their snooty world. I'm counting on them coming to me before she reaches the embassy."

"Well then, the Remmies here will piss their britches in excitement seeing the Exiles!"

In unison, the Suzii rolled their eyes.

One of whom queried, "I wanna call you somethin' besides 'Alt-Susie.' Any suggestions?"

"I've been going by Theresa Earth for three years. That's Theresa with an 'h.' Don't call me Terry or Resa; I hate nicknames."

"Gotcha, and thanks for agreeing to help us."

Old Man grabbed the next inquiry. "You came here investigating a triple murder. You overshot time, landed in the wrong century. Do you plan on back traveling to find Hugh or keep on Winthrop's and Pith's tails?"

"Four murders, including Isabella. I haven't written off Hugh, but he seems a less likely suspect. Pith is still my top candidate."

"What about Jay?" Theresa asked, her voice thick with hatred. "How do we know he can't appear in physical form and knock people off? The reason he's in your head may be to steer you away from the real murderer—him."

Susie disagreed. "You're givin' him too much credit. I think he's too simple-minded for plotting such an elaborate scheme."

"Have you tried putting a gun up to your ear and shooting as many magazines as it takes into your head?" the sadistic Alt-Susie suggested. "It won't hurt us. We'd just sneeze out the bullets, but it might rid you of the demon. I'd try it if it were me."

"I appreciate the recommendation. I might actually need him before the case is over."

(Author's Note: A compliment from the real Susie? Or maybe she's buttering me up for a future favor.)

OLD MAN AND EARTH PROBED Drake for non-recallable details from her past, those which she had discovered in Liam's files, especially how they pertained to her family and friends. (Author's Note: If you're expecting any juicy, heretofore undisclosed facts in these pages and a cavalcade of names which have no bearing on the story in *this* book, sorry. I suggest you readers email, text, phone, and annoy the publishers for a prequel. Please? To entice you further, I will allow one morsel of information below.)

"Y'know," Theresa commenced, "I figured the timelines of our lives would diverge in 1951. The creation of this alternative Earth hinged on one man's effort to save our mom."

"Liam told me about it. Obviously, I don't remember her. Let's try figuring out where our paths separated."

Ms. Earth sounded bored after an hour of dredging up events which corresponded with Susie's assassin career or happenings of a bland enough nature involving no one worth remembering. Truth was, surviving across four hundred years, always in good health, doesn't mean one's memory remains keen. Acting blasé was her method of dealing with her spotty remembrances. Eventually, the destination of their search landed square on a killing mentioned in the previous chapter.

"The guy in Toledo, 1961," Theresa sounded. "Failed to pay back a mobster. Seems like he did something else, too. Can't put a finger on it."

"Embezzled from a second gangster. Yep. Assassination by birdbath. Who's next?"

"Birdbath? No way! *That* never happened to me. I'm, uh … I'm drawin' blanks on the details on the setup for the hit and how I confronted him."

Susie filled in the gaps. "How'd you kill the guy?"

"To start with, kiddo, as in your case, his family left for an emergency. I went inside the house and shot his brains out. Maybe he started bullshitting me. I can't recall. If he did, it's why I popped him." Theresa's eyes proclaimed relief at finding the fork in the Suzii's road and amazement at the difference between them. "I can't believe you stuck around and listened to the guy! Sounds to me like you badly wanted to be a forgiving assassin. There's no such a thing."

"I wasn't as jaded as you at the time. That's all." Drake sensed a bout of intimidation arising in her older self and, well, she should—it was one of her favorite traits. "No, no. Let's not attack one another, okay? We gotta rise above our old habits."

Theresa's eye dance became so maliciously playful it scared Old Man.

"My younger me … do I detect an old soul inside you? Whatever made you wise?"

"We're both mavericks. Surviving with our sanity intact has made us wise. Right?" The lingering silence made her uneasy. "Has something I said upset you?"

"You know better than that. I'm merely impressed at how deeply you reformed."

"I don't understand. You seek redemption just as I do. What was different for you?"

She shifted uncomfortably in her chair. "The names you mentioned. Those people you can't recall because you had your memories removed. They must've aided you in ways I never experienced. In my life, they were nothing more but passing acquaintances."

"What?" Susie's eyebrows squeezed together. "Didn't you have adventures with them, capturing criminals? I'm sure they fought by your side in the war against alien wizards."

Unblinking, Earth replied, "Not 'adventures' in the camaraderie sense. It was a job. When we completed the task, I went my separate way. No hanging out with the gang. The war was very bloody. I saw many powered people, humans, and aliens fall by the wayside." She set a leg across the side of the chair. "I've always felt close to you, Susie. Reading Rodanthe's books on you made me wonder if he embellished way too much. The things you told us that you read in Karas's files confirmed just the opposite. Until now, I didn't realize how contrasting our lives have been.

"People didn't know much about me until after the war. The news media printed hyperbolized stories about a misunderstood woman whom men sexually desired and women wanted as their best friend. I was a pin-up girl, invited to parties of the rich, famous, corrupt, and cynical. Biographers of the powered community created a delusional world where I was beloved by all the key participants and a lover to [NAMES DELETED]. What pissed me off even more was how no one denied the exaggerations. Those so-called friends allowed writers and journalists to make them into my pals or lovers, never asking for my permission beforehand. The reason I didn't raise a fuss is that I avoid the press like the plague."

"You wouldn't have granted consent, would you?" Old Man asked.

"Not unless they made up for lost time and invited me into their life or their bed. Nobody rides the Susie Drake train for free." She emphasized those last six words for the sole purpose of provoking a Prime Susie response.

"You must've felt that way much more than me, Theresa. What I read on Zeke's computer made me sound like I was very acceptable to friendship and romance after a certain point."

"Yeah," she answered with a twisted mouth, "it's no wonder you wanted your memories cut out and sent to a planet where you could work off the emotional anguish. I would never have gone to such extremes for the Alt-Earth copies of the people we knew in the late 20th century."

Had Susie's sigh been any more weighted, it would've drained the room of oxygen. "How the hell did you rehabilitate if those 'copies' didn't help you?"

Theresa leaned forward, gripping the side of the recliner, resembling a lioness ready to pounce. "Simple, babe. My philosophy, except where it applies to letting people get too close to me, is … life's too short. The battlefield I stepped off of brought the point home in body bags. The people I killed— the people *you* killed—we own them. Yeah, they were scumbags. Hearing you talk about some of 'em today, I know that even though you're further along on your redemption quest, you still cling to the joy of killing, now and in the past. Now, now, lemme finish and don't point your finger at me! You may think you're done being a murderer, but you're not. Time is circular, not linear. I'm older … remember. I've dodged the shit storms bearing down on my psyche, urging me into knocking off crime syndicates and drug cartels for the pure pleasure of spilling blood. The storms I avoided, yeah, but not without first cuttin' the heads of a few snakes as sacrifices. I'm talkin' the big bosses. Help society and get my rocks off at the same time while sparing the underlings and lieutenants.

"If I hadn't done what I did, the dead would own me instead of the other way around. My advice is find yourself a great secluded place and hunker down when the urges creep inside you 'cause they will. First, they appear in your sleep dreams and then your waking ones. You'll thirst for blood like a vampire. Total isolation will be your saving grace. Oh, and, ha, ha, stock up on punchin' bags made out of thick steel and all the sleeping pills you can tote."

ARGUING WITH HER LOOKALIKE WASN'T something Drake wanted. *Let her believe I'm gonna go ballistic again someday. I can and will control my anger. If provoked by a worthy adversary, I'll defend myself. I won't be a soldier of fortune for any private or national army, not unless the purpose truly saves lives. The fact I'm here now, centuries later in another world, proves I've not deviated from my redemptive intention.*

"Okay, you're older, I'll grant you that. Have you lost any percentage of your powers and when did you first notice the wrinkles?"

The not-so-elegant Ms. Earth burped. "Dr. Pepper, kiddo. I live for the stuff. I downed a couple while I was working on the renovations. Oldie, be a dear and bring mo—er, me a Doc. You want one, Sus?"

"Sure. Whatever."

No one spoke until Old Man returned with two sixteen-ounce bottles of Dr. Pepper.

Theresa gulped down an ounce. "One of the Remmies has a Doc Pepper still in Dane Hall. We only use it when the Doc truck shows up late in Olde Boston." Another burp. "My powers do take three point four seconds to kick in. I work out a lot. Keeps the timing from gettin' slower. I still get the same results; nothin's been lost over time." A finger glided onto the most noticeable facial line below the right eye. "July 15, 2217. 3:13 AM. I walked by a mirror in the ladies' room of a

Jamaican bar and voilà—there it was. One of the few people I confided in back then said it came from hard living. The other line popped in ten years ago."

"Show her your ear," Old Man proposed.

Theresa pushed the hair back over her right ear and indicated a V-shaped gash in the upper helix. "My war wound. Nothing on Earth can damage our skin except time. Alien wizards are a different story. One of those nasties threw a hex at me. It clipped my ear. Later, I came across a book of their spells translated in English by one of their human spies. Damned if I couldn't find a way of adding skin or reversing the incantation. I still don't understand why the healing power didn't regrow the missing flesh." Her blonde hair recovered the damage. "Wish you could recall the war. I'd like to know how you escaped the hoodoo."

No signs of cheer lined her mouth. "Makes two of us, eh? What did you do after the war?"

"For the first twenty-some years, I island-hopped for the sole purpose of escaping the media circus. Islanders either don't keep up with the news or don't care. I did mercenary work off and on during the 21st century. I needed the excitement and something to do. On one particular mission, I got lost in a South Pacific jungle and wandered into a village of cannibals." Stretching her arms behind her head, an overhead light reflected a joyous tango in Earth's eyes. "They couldn't fathom why their teeth failed to bite my tasty-looking skin. It dawned in their head honcho's mind how I must be a goddess. What a life! Adorned by those people for something I *couldn't* do—be a meal.

"Boredom pressed me into leaving the tribe. The globetrotting Susie Drake years were upon me. In Ireland, I met a woman who taught me the trade of multiple disguises using almost any available item. There wasn't a country I didn't live in for at least a year. I learned a lotta languages but kept to myself. The places I remained the longest were a cave in Ellesmere Island, up in Canada, and a tent I'd relocate here and there in the Lut Desert of Iran. No one at any job I took ever knew it was really me. It wasn't until I came here that I removed the disguises. The Remmies protect my need for secrecy and privacy."

"Couple of hours ago," Susie said, "I promised myself I'd do the frozen island and desert hut thing, same as you. Not anymore. I don't wanna be a reclusive sad sack. Melancholy reeks off you, and it depresses the hell outta me. For someone whose motto is 'life's too short,' you've found a way of making near-immortality painfully long. The stuff about 'shit storms' is nothin' but you dealing with your own sadness or psychosis—whatever it is. You're wrong … predicting that I'll embrace madness just because you did. 'Secrecy and privacy;' why? What exactly are you hiding from?"

Standing, fuming, Theresa lifted the brown recliner and tossed it over Old Man's head at Susie, who caught it and gently set it down. Earth then jumped off the stage and stomped away, slamming doors behind her.

"Whoa boy," Old Man breathed. "Uh, give her five, and if she hasn't returned, I'll go talk to her."

"Are you her daddy? Let her get over it herself."

"No, and no. It ain't your place tellin' me what to do. You and Theresa may be cut from the same cloth, but she obviously has a sensitivity you haven't got." Between his wrinkles, a cocky smirk stuck out. "Oh, right, I forgot. You had E'tatanya remove all the good-time memories from your head. Why didn't you 'get over it' yourself or go out and make new friends and more happy remembrances?"

Tranquility moderated her voice. "I see it now. I didn't then. For once, I missed the big picture when it mattered most, and I paid a heavy price when Pith stole—"

"Can you ever accept complete responsibility for your actions without tossing blame on someone else?" Poison soaked his scorn. "I might've stolen 'em myself had I been there! Big damn deal! The fact you're taking accountability now is due to the differences you've noticed between yourself and Theresa. She has *helped* you. I'll wager the Jay demon has *helped* you, as well, and you're too stubborn to admit it."

Instead of being beset with deep remorse over Old Man's insult, Drake insisted he find and return Theresa to the forum. Without quarreling, he did what she'd told him to do, even if it wasn't her place.

Meanwhile, back on Prime Lointain…

EDNA FONTENOT CRAVED SOMEONE different. Due to their prolonged existence and spiritual faith, Lointainians most often veered away from divorce. Therefore, they married late, after finding the best possible mate. Marital affairs only struck couples experiencing tremendous changes in lifestyle and, given the slow evolution of the average Exile's routine, such adjustments were rare. A current exception was the Fontenots, one of whose sexual and emotional needs were not being satisfied.

Walking the family pet, Ursula, a Hawaiian poi-dog, through a small park of Saint Helena olive trees, she reflected on her situation.

Luther is faithful, she knew. *But he does have a mistress—his business. Since he became the planet's top dog, competing for his time has become next to impossible. The fool doesn't know it, but his crazy immigration plan may be what liberates me.*

Her husband sought the naturalization of a hundred Earth families as Lointainian citizens. The furor over the scheme had ignited quickly. Luther didn't need the council's approval, yet he didn't want an uprising over the controversial strategy. A handful of his friends supported the immigration policy, and those associates he'd reward with a seat on the council come the new year.

Not all these newcomers are traditional families, Edna had learned. *A half dozen are divorced male humans with a kid or two. Earth men are definitely more lustful than Exile men. I'm looking forward to their arrival next year. Even if none of them consider me their type, the prospect of becoming a Remnant will more than send them willingly into my arms. I won't leave Luther, not unless he does something very foolish.*

Thoughts of her daughter, who had recently given birth, plucked her strings of guilt. *The new family addition propelled us even more into the spotlight. I ... I can't let it deter me. The single men will live in the polar cap area ... former polar cap area. It'll be easy teleporting there, shapeshifting into a younger, sexier female, and meeting whomever I choose. I've earned the right, haven't I?*

Stepping onto a cobblestone sidewalk, she sighted her wedded partner entering their house, half a block away. *He's in early. There'll be news about something. I hope it's good.*

LUTHER DANCED A LITTLE JIG toward his wife, placed his arms around her waist, and whirled her around as he hummed a tune made famous by a beloved Earth crooner in the 1940s. Not even Lointain, circling high above British Columbia, was immune to suave vocal prowess and finely orchestrated music.

Uncertain of how she should react to her master's unusual behavior, Ursula articulated her own melody. *Woof! Woof! Arrrrf! Wooooof!*

"Okay, out with it," Edna spoke, pleased he held her while aware it had nothing to do with what lacked in their relationship. "I want to hear some good news."

Snapping his fingers to an upbeat rhythm, he guided her toward the couchchilla, on which they both sat. Grinning wildly, he excitedly announced, "The Cagnet deal is officially set!"

Perplexed yet happy for him, she inquired, "What deal is this? You have *so* many, Luther, I can't keep track."

His delight at the victory overshadowed what he considered as her "annoying ability to not distinguish between my projects." "Old man Cagnet's grandson bears a striking resemblance to Ren Pith. Just like his grandpa, young Cagnet can produce multiple doppelgängers. One of those clones— with the help of a few surgical alterations—will pose as Pith for the rest of his natural, very long life. As a Christmas gift for Earth, I will hand Cagnet/Pith over to the International Court of Justice. I'll inform the authorities how after capturing him, he willingly volunteered cooperation and wouldn't dream of escaping or using his powers against the jailers. Just in case they're skeptical, I'll hand them the DES formula for neutralizing his abilities. Cagnet will plead guilty and—"

"Wait," Edna butted in. "Why would he volunteer imprisonment? We all know Pith is a nutcase."

"We also all know he has OCD." Luther relished explaining this tidbit. "Abner and Ada have told us how their grandson hears what he named 'the OCD voice.' Cagnet will confess that the obsessive mouthpiece ordered him to offer no resistance to incarceration and trial after I ended his flight from the law. I'll use his own mind malady against him. The real Ren, wherever he is on Earth, will be grateful for his freedom. Through news accounts, he'll figure out I was instrumental in planting the clone. At some juncture, I hope he contacts me. I'm sure I'd have plenty uses for a rogue Exile. Clever, huh?"

"Yes, but what about his parents and other Exiles who'll recognize a phony Ren?"

Luther's shoulders straightened tall and strong. "As Commander of Lointain—my new soon-to-be title—I will forbid interference and visitation by any Lointainian in Earth's prosecution and imprisonment of the prisoner. What Ren did, I will reinforce to his parents, was a hideous crime, ending billions of lives. Not only do I not want them seeing him, but he … he, my dear Edna, will shout profanities about Exiles, making it clear he hates all of us. Cagnet will say he won't accept any non-Earth visitors. This step is part of a broader scheme.

"By condemning Lointain and its people, the boy will start changing attitudes toward us. Earthlings will despise him, of course. They will appreciate our sense of justice, not siding with one of our own. I have at my disposal several humans who will begin swaying public opinion on the planet below in our favor. What I anticipate is the industrial and more developed nations accepting us back and one at a time, opening embassies. Not just one major diplomatic center like we used to have in Washington. No, I want branches all over Earth."

Edna considered herself overwhelmed by the sheer size of his goal. *I'll fit myself in somewhere. I always do.*

She asked, "You have a full agenda, don't you? How will you fit in bringing the hundred families up from Earth?"

Her positive stance on and obvious interest in the immigration issue warmed his heart. "I may hand some of the responsibilities for it over to you … if you have the time away from your other duties. You serve on many committees. Dealing with these Earthlings can be mind-numbing. Their expectations on what life will resemble in Lointain … well, a lot of it reeks of unadulterated fantasy."

Speaking of fantasy, he had penetrated hers. "I'll take on the obligations! Banquets and fundraisers bore me. This is something worthwhile I can sink my teeth in." *Moreover, I can pick out the men I want way ahead of time!* "I was always very good at handling humans. Remember how they flocked to me for advice and comfort every time we were on the planet during one of their major wars?"

"Yes, you were continuously in demand and highly praised," he acknowledged. "You don't know how happy it makes me to have you onboard." Luther stood after kissing her cheek. "I'll bring you the files tomorrow, and we'll go over them together. Nothing can stop us now. Nothing!"

One thing can, she understood. *He has a lotta schemes flying at once and what I consider far too many loose ends. It only takes one unresolved issue to bring Luther crashing down, and me with him.*

Else-time…

EXPERIENCE THROUGH LONGEVITY HAS taught the Suzii how gracious amends can form after fights and arguments. Nevertheless, both needed practice at preventing physical and verbal clashes. They exchanged apologies and retook their places in the small auditorium.

"The Staten Island Shysters," Susie launched after a big sip of Dr. Pepper. "Let's say they stole the spaceship. It's nighttime, and they're sneaking it away from the impound. Flannagan said Remnants might have shrunk or made the ship invisible. Is that how the Shysters work when they grab large objects?"

"They've done it before," Old Man confirmed. "Shrinking is simpler and more profitable. Invisible runs the risk of damage."

"Who would be in the market for a spaceship? They're not common, so not anyone would know how to pilot one."

Theresa fielded the question. "When Hugh Rodanthe and his time-traveling buddies went on their missions over a hundred years ago, they flew aerocubes. It was much easier piloting one of those than any ship the Exiles could ever buy, steal, or trade for. The kind of spacecraft you described sounds like a prototype for the 'cubes. They're not easy to maneuver. I oughta know. I flew one."

"Don't tell me you tried out for a time traveler post?" Susie asked.

"Ha, ha! No way. Me and a fellow I traveled with at the time snuck into the airfield where they kept the ships. Knocked out the guards and had us fun learning the controls." A sad vibe caught her face for a second and drifted away. "Only reason we didn't crash was our familiarity with crappy planes during wars in Third World countries."

"What did you think when you heard about Rodanthe's objective of changing Prime Earth history, especially as it concerned me and those friends of mine whom I don't remember?"

"Honestly …" Earth paused. "The news media speculated about each time traveler's agenda. They never knew the specifics. Your community was the target, kiddo. Yeah, I knew it. Like I told ya … my world, my community … suffered horrendous losses. When the news came about Rodanthe's success, I cheered. Could someone please alter *my* history, I asked. Uh, no. They could, yep, but I'd never know it because, according to the brains runnin' the operation, if someone altered Alt-Earth's past, the result would be an Alt-Alt-Earth. Since there's a permanent connection to Prime Earth, the scientists can go to 1951 and keep printing parallel worlds while Real Time continues undisturbed." Again, she paused, scratching her chin. "Be pissed at old Hugh all you want right now, but when you get your noggin straightened out, you'll thank him, no matter the degree of personal pain he caused. You are much, much less screwed up than me. It was true long before the war. It was true by the fact you allowed the guy to live as long as you did and even considered lettin' him off the hook. Shit, if you weren't me, I'd kiss you for your compassion."

"And I'd bust your lip if you tried!" Susie, feeling a lump in her throat, threatened it away. "Don't devalue yourself. We're twins, y'know. I can *see* into your heart. You're on the right course. That's all I'm gonna say about it, older sis. Now, don't be a Lt. Flannagan and avoid answering direct questions: who would be in the market for a spaceship?"

Old Man spoke. "No one in their right mind would fly one, not these days, and no offense, Theresa. It'd make a good conversation piece. Something to charge admission for a look inside, maybe fix up a way to simulate a fake take-off. Some ex-Exiles might pay for one and sell it on other planets. Other countries with private armies might seek to use its parts for their own aircraft. I'm thinking … the Uganda National Coupsters. They bought two aerocube prototypes three years ago for such a purpose."

"Fine," Drake commented, adding a little sarcasm. "I'll keep my eyes peeled for odd backyard decorations, flea markets, and carnivals. Should we make it back to New York, how do I go about finding the Shysters?"

"They hang out in King Fisher Park in the Great Kills neighborhood. At least they do when they're not in trouble."

"Great Kills, eh? Sounds like my kinda place." Susie chuckled before becoming serious. "Theresa, what you said about the Canadian border earlier … if Jim doesn't have a plan for getting us across without arousing trouble, I'll use my suggestive power on whoever scans the ID codes. Make them scan their own barcodes. What? Why are you shaking your head?"

"The Mounties don't allow you out of your vehicle until after you're scanned. To enter their country, you put the IDs in a container and send them through a vacuum thing into their office. They check the codes and send 'em back. No worries, though, I have a scheme."

"What's that? Fight our way in?"

"No. I'm coming with you. I have a secret way of hiding so that the U.S. border team won't see me in the back of *The Imene-A-Bago*. Jim gets you and yours through, we wait in one of the many lanes of the Marin Bridge. Traffic's heavy between the nations. It's a mile between the countries. You guys hide in the back, using my invisibility technique, while I drive to the Canadian gate. I'll have a fake ID thingamajig for whoever my disguise represents. They'll let us through without any problems."

Prime Susie was totally slack-jawed. "I didn't hear a word you said after 'I'm coming with you.'"

BICKERING ASIDE, THE DECISION STOOD: Theresa Earth would accompany the three fugitives on their journey north. Susie pondered the reactions of Liam and Jim whereby a fourth passenger turned out to be her possibly psychotic doppelgänger. *Scratch the demented reference. She's okay. I'm okay. Uh, I guess I'm okay. Not really.*

Not enjoying the line of thought, she concentrated on someone else.

"Old Man, what's your story? Wish I could call you by a real name."

"Guess it's no harm tellin' you. My initials are O.M. Turn it around, you got Mo or Moe. That's me—Moe. I discarded my last name so long ago I don't recall it." Two fingers brushed down his bangs. "One of the Remmies styles my hair. Ha! For years, I had a Moe Howard haircut, y'know, of *The Three Stooges*. Mom didn't name me till I was a teen. She was a *Stooges* fan."

"Who isn't?" Susie asked. "How old are you?"

"Almost a hundred and forty. Must have a slow aging ability. I always bonded well with Remmies and the powerless. After college, I taught at Harvard. *History of Powered Persons. Remnants and Modern Society. Prime Earth: Before and After Rodanthe* was my most popular course. The redrawing of America during the Segregation Era ended Harvard as it was. I stayed. The Remmies flocked here in droves. Not particularly because of me, but from the university's reputation and the well-known fact that the administrators gave it to me. Educationlands are home to colleges anymore. Me? I still teach whoever asks. I will till I die, or they stop asking."

"No Mrs. Old Woman?" Drake prodded.

"Not unless you're willing!"

"You're too young for me." She laughed. Susie recalled Flannagan mentioning a college professor who had proposed a hypothesis concerning Alt-Susie and how she might hide in plain sight and alter the minds of people who see her. *This is probably the guy.*

"Are you comin' with us, Moe? Should you stay here, you might fall and break a hip."

If it wasn't already obvious that he despised the name, he made it clear by spitting a raspberry in Susie's direction. "That's Old Man to you! My hips are fine. Thank you for worrying. The work in Hastings Hall needs completed. Looks like I'm gonna have to do it myself since you're runnin' off with the help."

Theresa howled. "You're afraid of heights, you old windbag! No way you'd climb those ladders. Gimme three hours, and it's done."

"Make it an hour and a half," Susie contradicted. "The Suzii will cut the time in half." Leaving her chair, she pinched Old Man's cheek. "You be a good boy and have a decent meal waiting for us. Since it'll be dark soon, I'll stay here tonight. We'll leave at dawn."

"I'll have more than a decent meal ready for yuns. I'm happy as a tick on a fat dog that you'll be an overnight guest. Buuuuut, I'm still not comin' along tomorrow. The Remmies will be back early next week." He manufactured a tight smile. "I know you won't return before they do."

"*Hmm.* Suit yourself." Drake stared hard at him. "I betcha have an ulterior motive for not going."

"Let him be," Earth defended. "He doesn't travel well. Let's just say he has gastrological issues which fouls up the air whenever the means of transport or the people he's bottled up with upsets him."

"Good to know. I don't care for farts, either."

Chapter 9: The Trouble Maker

Intermission (March 2023)

WAY BEYOND MIDNIGHT, THE CRICKETS chirp, singing this'll be the day we serenade a barefoot Susie Drake, walking barefoot upon the Austin Hall lawn. A marble bench comes into view, and she takes a load off her feet and hopes to do the same with her mind.

"Jay! I know you're there. I gotta talk to you. Pronto!"

I'm watching *Inland Empire* on Blu-ray, enjoying the performances when the loud summons rattles my eardrums. *Hmm. How come I can put an entertaining movie on pause but not whining Susie?*

"Make it quick, Susie. I'm in the middle of a movie."

"This is more important. Has anything changed on your end? I don't mean has your ass gotten any bigger … probably has from sittin' around, watching movies. What I mean is, have you picked up any clues on why you're in my head and if I'm nothin' more than a literary character?"

Relaxing my feet on the hassock, I prepare myself mentally for a hassle. "No, nothing's changed since the last time we talked. Although maybe this movie might stir—"

"Forget the damn movie! I seem to either be forgettin' more events or else havin' a harder time recollecting them. Why aren't *you* helping?"

When I sigh really loud, I picture Susie holding both hands over her ears. "What is it that you want me to do? I don't know where your memories are. You will probably find them at the same time I'll write about it."

Her composure surprises me and, for an instant, I swear I detect something close to depression in her voice. "Do you remember when we first became aware of our situation? I don't. I do recall chewing you out because you claimed I was a 'character' you made up. How did I know? I can't read what you type. Understand, things which happened immediately after E'tty removed the memories have taken on a foggy feel."

For me to understand her question, I log into my PC and bring up the yet-untitled manuscript. "It's at the near end of chapter one. The Intermission of April 2022. Almost a year ago for me. Let's see … you wanted to know where your memories were … We talk about who might play you in a movie … you're swearing … figures … oh, you mention a blank spot in the book I'm writing. At the time, you had to have read what I wrote."

"There must have been rules in the beginning, guiding how we interacted. At one time, I musta thought you pulled the strings. Now, someone or something else is the puppet master."

Hearing this concerns me. Should I write only what I physically see or hear? When she and I conversed last August, I discovered events transpired in her ongoing story which I wasn't privy to viewing. If I transcribe action from my mind's eye, will it come to pass? Only one way to find out.

"Hold on, Susie. I'm gonna try an experiment."

"Gee," she responds, deep with sarcasm, "here I figured you were the Monster, not Doctor Frankenstein."

At the beginning of chapter nine, after Drake sits on the marble pew and before she calls my name, I type, *Old Man and Theresa bolted out from the entrance of Austin Hall. Laughing hysterically, they ran circles around Susie, seated on the bench, and each poured an open bottle of Dr. Pepper atop her blonde hair.*

I lean back in my chair, fixating on Susie. Soda pop does not drip from her head. She remains undisturbed or—as she might likely say—remains disturbed only by my presence. Returning to the book in progress, I delete the soft drink attack.

"The test failed," I begin. "I cannot change what happens to you by jotting it down on a computer document. Otherwise, you'd have your memories and be back on Prime Earth."

Grudgingly, she thanks me for the thought. "If you did, it'd make for a piss-poor, anticlimactic ending. Say, can you update me on any movements by Pith or Rodanthe?"

I want to get back to the film, so I concede a little nugget. "Before you crossed over the Boudreaux Bridge, I typed a list Pith conceived in his head. He was aboard *The Imene-A-Bago*, in the form of a cobweb. Instead of sticking around, he transformed into a fly with Halifax as his destination. He planned to come back and check on your progress. I never saw or heard him return."

Susie wants info on Pith's list. I deny her request.

"I cheated by giving you the morsel I did."

"Doesn't matter. I doubt Pith has found the spaceship. Knowing it's our only way off Alt-Earth, can I count on you to let me know if he pilots the ship to another world or the Prime Universe?"

"Yes, what you ask is reasonable." Her and Liam remaining on this planet could warrant … a sequel. No way!

"What's your take on Theresa and Old Man?" she inquires. "I've a hunch she'll be central in retrieving the spacecraft."

Locking the computer, I grumble. No doubt Susie hopes I'll slip and reveal a future fact I can't possibly know. "I've no opinion either way. But I'm guessing you do."

Instead of waiting for her usual end-of-chat insult, calling me "moron" or "creep," I disconnect her from my mind. Susie will chart her own story whether I view it as it happens or when a click in my head visually displays her experiences post-factum. That is, unless she plops into the head of an actual published writer!

DAWN SWEPT OVER THE STEPS of Austin Hall. Susie slung on the stringy wig, face pretenses, and the tacky hat and glasses. Nearby, Theresa packed Dr. Peppers and bags of peanuts into a backpack and placed her arms through the straps.

"Aren't you goin' to alter your face?" Drake asked.

Earth muttered words in a language once spoken by interplanetary wizards. *Presto chango!* Theresa's height lowered seven inches, her blonde hair became a retro-shaped, flaxen-colored hair style with streaks of gold, while her blue eyes now added sparkles of gray.

"Florence La Badie, darling. Well, as I remember her."

"Uh, I don't recall her at all. How do you know her?"

"Susie," Theresa asserted with dabs of frustration, "I know you don't have any memories of going to the theater with our mom, but you do remember movies, actors, and actresses, don't you?"

"Yes, but the films and stars you recall might just be different from those that stick in my mind. Now, who's Florence."

A sigh later. "She was a silent era actress. Since our histories are the same for the 1910s, I know you saw her in *The Million Dollar Mystery, Miss Robinson Crusoe, Saint, Devil, and Woman,* and my favorite, *The Trouble Maker.* Right?"

"It figures you'd like *The Trouble Maker* most of all." Susie couldn't tell if the woman understood the film title reference. "Yes, I know who you're talking about now. Anyway, it sure won't be any fun trekking through the thick brush and stickers. At least we're leaving early."

"What brush? Which way did you come here?" Theresa chuckled at the response. "No wonder it took you so long. We'll take the tunnel under old Broadway Street and cross over what remains of the Longfellow Bridge. Be prepared for big jumps on the overpass."

"Tunnel, huh? No such thing on my map. When I approached the Longfellow on the way here, there were big signs posted, saying it's condemned. It didn't look passable."

"The Remmies dug the tunnel, or more like used their powers for the construction. They built below-ground passageways all under Olde Boston in case the cops or Feds came after them." She clarified, "Making it over the Longfellow is relatively easy for the powered. It's *our* landmark. I'll show you the right places to jump or climb."

"You have pride in them. Are there close friendships and whatnot between you and the Remnants?"

Theresa comprehended the question's intent. "Yes. Without the prying news media and post-war egos bearing down on me, forming relationships gradually became easy. I'm not making excuses, if it's what you're thinkin'."

"Not at all. Just hopin' you're away from your buddies when next you have a ballistic fit."

"Me, too. Well, let's get a move on. It's not far until we reach the tunnel entrance."

EARTH STOPPED IN FRONT OF a store over which hung a sign that read, "*Seth's Shoe Repair*." Through the dusty window, one could see the tables where—presumably—Seth and his employees once worked diligently mending soles, stretching tennis shoes, patching holes, and whatever was needed to make the walking experience joyful. An overhead bell sounded *ding-a-ling* when she opened the door. Cobwebs galore greeted the Suzii.

"The floor doesn't look as dusty as the rest of the place," Drake observed. "The tunnel entrance is in here, right?"

"Yep. Nobody would ever think of lookin' for it here."

Susie surveyed the shop. "Plenty of tools still here. Why wouldn't people check it out?"

Chalk up the response delay to momentarily forgetting from whence her companion had traveled. "Oh yeah. See, shoes are made a hundred percent durable these days. One pair can last a lifetime. Of course, they're pretty expensive. Those damn Rodanthes … they must have a dozen pair they only wear at social gatherings!"

"*Hmm*. No wonder I haven't seen any discarded old sneakers tossed over phone or power lines."

Theresa laughed then coughed so hard she broke open a Dr. Pepper for relief. "I gotta visit your planet. I could make a fortune back here!" She pointed ahead. "See the wooden statue of a Dutch girl holding wooden shoes? Pull on her nose. It opens the tunnel door."

WHEREVER THEY WALKED, LED BULBS lit up the corridor then went dark when they had passed. Spray-paintings and graffiti documented stories of the Remnants: rising from sex or shared body fluids with so-called Originals, their quest for justice and equality, branching off into peaceful-minded activists or violence-inclined protestors, never organized under a single leader, not until hope arrived in the form of Theresa Earth. Beneath one of the many etched portraits of Alt-Earth's Susie Drake, her counterpart spied a sentiment.

"Theresa Earth Angel, I love you! There're all these musical notes drawn around you. Man, oh, man! How is it these Remmies know about doo-wop?"

"Yet another difference between our worlds. There was a huge doo-wop revival during the last twenty years. Remnants love the music 'cause they enjoy singing on street corners. It's the one cultural phenomenon which brought powered and non-powered folk closer … for a while."

"Why aren't there any sketches of Old Man on the walls? He's a legend."

"I don't know. You're right; there oughta be."

Coy-like, Susie asked, "How many people know he's your son?"

"What the [EXPLETIVES DELETED]?" She hadn't anticipated the question. "He's …" Nope, she knew there'd be no lying her way out of it. "How'd you know?"

"How can you *even* ask?" Her mouth formed a circle. "*Duh*! I saw how you physically corrected him at times, especially when he had dinner. Very untypical of a Susie Drake! The way you looked back and waved when we left. Not like a lover. Like a parent. I know enough parents to know what I'm talking about. One time, you nearly called yourself 'mom' or 'momma.' I'm guessin' he has his father's skin color, but he sure has your blue eyes."

Their pace slowed. Theresa stared straight ahead. *When, she wondered, was the last time I expounded the complete truth behind the birth of my pride and joy?* Never. Not even the Old Man knew his unabridged origin story.

"I met his father in Egypt. He joined the mercenary group I was attached to, fighting wars across Africa and the Middle East. We were in Lebanon. Fighting was fierce. Bombs going off all down this one street in Beirut." Her eyes skirted the ceiling. "Nah, can't recall the street name."

"What was *his* name? Don't worry about Jay. It's not like Old Man's pa is gonna be joining our expedition. Is he?"

Earth crossed her arms over her shoulders, as if hugging herself. The laugh leaving her mouth owned a sheepish quality, and her body language screamed the definition of unaggressive, to such an extent that it made Susie jealous.

"Wahed. Originally, he came from Afghanistan. Like I was saying, explosions all around us. It didn't bother me since it couldn't hurt me. He had some minor Remnant powers. There was this butcher shop, abandoned, and we ducked inside, not because we feared the blitz going on. No way. Bombs, blasts, and blood … *whew*! talk about an aphrodisiac. We dodged the fighting for reasons of horniness!" Theresa's fidgeting faded. "We were so hot for one another that we … I … he, well, no protection. Have you ever been pregnant?"

"Not that I'm aware of …"

"All through my pregnancy, Wahed remained with me. The guy begged me, 'Stop fighting until the child's born.' What'd I do? I mocked him, laughed disdainfully, and kept on as the war machine I was." Both her hands became fists and punched her head three times. "Idiot! I blamed him for my condition, taking none of the responsibility when I knew better and had the strength to stop it from going further. In that state of mind, I didn't listen much when he spoke. I figured I'd cool down when the kid popped out.

"Not far across the border in Yemen, a conflict breaks out. Someone shoots in my direction. Wahed jumps in front of me, takes the bullet." For almost ten minutes, silence. "He forgot I was bulletproof, said it among his last words. Can you imagine? What a thing not to remember. I was in Angola when Moe snuck outta me. It's not true—me not naming him till later. In the midwife's bungalow, there was a TV showing *The Three Stooges'* shorts. Later, he did wear a Moe-like haircut."

Susie hadn't expressed a "sorry for your loss" over Wahed. *I don't think she loved him or that he mattered much in her life.* "What was your plan while he was still alive? Not marriage and settling down. I don't need memories to know it isn't how we operate."

Sternly, Earth said, "I was gonna leave the kid with him." She moved her head in a circle, a habit Theresa exhibited when affirming a strategy which thankfully failed, no matter the sad circumstances behind the failure. "Y'know, I timed our travel with the utmost precision. Even his death didn't throw off my reaching Moçâmedes for the birth. One day, so went the scheme, I'd tell Wahed, 'Hey, look after the tot while I phone the commander.' We had a contact in Venezuela who provided our missions, and it was always me whom he spoke with and usually for half an hour or more. Instead of calling the chief, I'd have been in a Jeep heading for Benguela where a pre-arranged plane would fly me to Tasmania. I'd hide out first in Oceania and later up to Canada. Pop and spawn … they'd live happily ever after."

"You didn't put the baby up for adoption, not with him having powers. Because of who you were and what you did for a living, your enemies would target the kid. Did you use the wizard magic to alter your appearance while on the run?"

"'*On the run*?'" *Hiss, hiss!* "Have *you* ever retreated from a reckless undertaking?"

"Doubtful."

"Exactly! Why would you expect me to run with my tail between my legs? And don't answer that. We stayed in Moçâmedes for a couple months. Being in one place for very long meant I had to activate multiple disguises. On the phone to the commander, I requested and received a three-man team to replace Wahed. Not all men. The female assigned to me would watch over Junior, and if asked, would say she's the mama. Training the crew is what occupied most of my time."

Earth opened a bottle of Doc Pepper. The soft drink rewarded her with multiple burps. "Things moved smoothly for three years. The woman babysitting the kid decided she couldn't pass by the bounty on my head any longer. Lucky me, I discovered her betrayal early, ripped her lungs open, grabbed the brat, and left with the two fellows. Both died during conflicts in South America." Leaning against a concrete brace, her eyes gave the impression of dipping into another world. "I had only one viable option—Lointain."

"I wondered when the Exiles would put in an appearance. How about givin' me a swig of the Doc?"

Parting with the Pepper? Only for a Susie.

"Boudreaux was happy taking on the tike. The boy would receive an amazing education, and they'd hone his powers. In all honesty, there was no safer place for him. I told him I had 'leftover business to deal with' before I returned to Earth. Even now when we argue, if he goes sulking, he tells me has 'leftover business to deal with.' He cried buckets when I went away."

"What about you?"

The noise from her choking almost sounded like a pre-vomit cough. "I'm a terrible mother, aren't I?" No tears, just a scrunched-up face. "Aren't I?"

Asking this of Drake, the opportunity of a simulated, self-cross examination became a realization. Despite different pasts, Susie was Theresa and vice versa. An honest doppelgänger provided the sincerest personal reflection. Did it matter who was the shadow and who was the light, even if only one of them resembled a 1910s movie actress?

"If you are, then so am I because I would've done the same thing." On Earth's shoulder, she rested a hand. "You cleverly protected him. Weasel all around it, but the fact remains you love the guy." *Wish I had a son ... or daughter. I don't think I do. Nowhere in Liam's research did I read it. People take that shit for granted. Family.*

Stepping out from under a looming gloomy cloud and handing back the Pepper, she said, "Go on. What happened after the Exiles?"

"You didn't ask, but I'll tell you, anyway ... I visited Moe three times a year. Afterward? More of the same—fighting, hiding, assumed identities. A couple shit storms. We haven't enough time for me disclosing who I became and what I did."

Light up ahead indicated an exit.

"Old Man hasn't lived a long life because of any power he has. It's due to the air on Lointain, isn't it?"

"Yep. I never corrected him, but he knows. There are some things he doesn't know because I altered his recollections. Moe believes he and I traveled this world until he was old enough to be out on his own. It pissed off Boudreaux when he found out. I did what was necessary. If he had let it slip that he'd lived among the Exiles, not only would it have put him in danger for the association, it'd have stirred questions on his parentage."

"Why danger? I thought people on Alt-Earth adored the Exiles."

"Not always. Nowadays, yeah, ever since they laid down mind-boggling technology and magic in this world. Times were during the last century when humans and Remmies took turns despising them."

The smell of fresh air began greeting them from small holes in the street above. "Your son's old enough now for the truth, don'tcha think?"

"It depends. He's not a whole lot more mature than when he was eighteen. Just an old kid."

Susie laughed. "You and me are both old kids!"

Excerpts from the journal of Liam Karas (purchased in Olde Boston), July 2310:

I DIDN'T SLEEP WELL LAST night. Not only had Susie failed to return, but Jim stayed late at the poker game three rows of campers south of The Imene-A-Bago. *Money wasn't bet; the men and women wagered tickets for rides at any Vacationland. Flannagan carries a coupon book with him. One of the players was a retired NYC officer, which meant the two cops had plenty to talk about. The lieutenant slipped back in after 1 AM.*

Come 9 AM, we drank coffee. Best brew I ever drank in my life and the name of the café— Best Brew You Ever Drank—and triangular-shaped biscuits which I hear are the rage (I don't get it). We debated whether we wait or go search for our missing comrade.

Jim settled the discourse with his authoritarian policeman voice. "We commence the search party soon as we return to the Float-A-Camper. My poker pal gave me a map of the area. We'll face some sticker bushes on the way. I recommend we each buy a long-sleeved shirt before heading out."

The way he talked reminded me of a cousin who always adopted a stern mood when his girlfriend wasn't around. Jim-

Bob rarely spoke relaxed. Less so since Susie went traipsing off to Austin Hall.

Breakfast behind us, we bought the arm protective wear. I suggested we leave a note for Susie in case she returns while we're away.

"Could be she's back now." Jim indicated The Imene-A-Bago's *open door. "Or else we have an unwanted guest."*

"THIS IS THERESA EARTH. SHE'S joining us on our trip up north."

So went Susie's first words when we entered the electric RV. Next, she fed us a choppy dialogue about Harvard and an elderly fellow named Old Man. Who exactly was Miss/Ms./Mrs. Earth?

"Are you ReVoguist?" Jim asked. He explained the term: a man or woman who fancies a Golden Age movie star and copies their appearance, personality, and speech as best they can. "Let me guess ... you're imitating-."

"You'll never guess, cutie. Florence La Badie. She was a star before Golden Age and died tragically after a car accident. I wanted to pay tribute to her."

The ruse fell apart then. Theresa revealed herself as Alt-Earth's Susie. I enjoyed the comment Jim made after seeing the transformation from La Baddie to Drake. "Whoa! My great-great-great-great-grandfather met you once. It's one of those family legends passed down through many generations."

Immediately, Earth recited ominous-sounding clicks and reverted to La Badie. "You sure know how to make a girl feel her age, don'tcha, copper?"

Ever since I met Flannagan (seems like longer than a day ago), he's been like the apotheosis of a serious-minded, no-nonsense adult. Even when he played poker—so I heard around the camper site—he insisted on being a "moderator" and writing down all the rules in case there were "variations'" which rarely pop up according to geographic locations. But today, when Theresa unloaded her undivided attention on him, he grinned like a Cheshire cat, or a shy teenager placed in the spotlight by their ultimate crush.

"I meant no offense. My ancestor was most taken with you." Obviously, the "taken" part passed down through the family genes. "Where, if I may ask, have you kept yourself all this time?"

In answering, she seized his hand and led him to sit at the small table in the back. Okay, I felt offended, purposely avoided, and drifted toward Susie.

"Is it wise having her come along? I don't see the point."

A steely stare fired at me. "You wanna get home again? She's our best chance. Deal with it."

Dramatically, I tossed up my arms. "How about explaining why she's 'our best chance?' I didn't have to come along with you on this trip. You needed a co-pilot and someone to take over shifts flying the spaceship. You can't just say 'deal with it.' I won't be a silent partner."

"Well, aren't you a regular panty yanker?"

I didn't know what she meant, but I received a thorough explanation on Theresa. The Canada boundary detail sounded flimsy. I dealt with it ... for now. When Jim finally broke away from Miss Florence, Susie questioned him on a matter he never mentioned.

"If we went with your plan, the U.S. border cops would arrest us when we cross back over. Why didn't you bring this up?"

Nervously, he paced up and down the camper. "Because I don't believe the Exiles are going to help. Boudreaux prefers all legal matters to go through the proper channels. No matter who you are on Prime Earth, Susie, here you're an escaped suspect. Maybe if you'd landed your spaceship in Halifax or Lointain and requested an audience with the guy, then he'd listen to you. My hope was that by the time we reached the border for reentry, I'd phone ahead, see what if any progress the 105th Rhinelander Underground had been made on finding the ship, and go from there. We wouldn't—"

"I think I'll kick your ass outta this floating behemoth!" Susie shouted. "You'd send Liam and me—or at least Liam— back to jail! They'd never capture me. Traitor!"

Flannagan leaned forward, almost like he was gonna kiss her. "You didn't let me finish! As I was tryin' to say, we wouldn't cross borders like we first did. Yes, the Mounties would alert the Americans about us, especially considering the IDs you and Liam carry are for dead folks. I have a friend in Winnipeg who'd smuggle us across. Luckily, I remembered his number and phoned him, y'know, to make sure he's still living there. You two could get by on new IDs until you found a way home. I'm the one who'd be in jail after losing my badge and pension."

Now, Susie (not apologizing, of course) directed a tirade at her doppelgänger. "You never said one word about Boudreaux being a proper ass. Is it, or is it not, a waste of time going into Canada? Even if we get past the Mounties without them scanning our IDs, what's to stop it from happening elsewhere?"

Earth modeled a nonchalant pose. "Jack won't be a priss around me, kiddo. There's plenty of history between us, and I guarantee he won't chase you away. Once he hears a few Susie stories and news on his Prime Lointain counterpart, he'll be eager to help."

BACK ON THE ROAD. THERESA suggested we all take turns driving in case something unexpected abruptly occurred and the four of us separated. Naturally, Jim didn't care for the idea, but the three of us outvoted him, and his would-be girlfriend (Miss Earth, sounds like a beauty pageant winner) sweet-talked the notion into his hard noggin. Taking every Marin exit from here to Canada was another of her ideas.

"Let's enjoy this time we have together. It'll never happen again. Not we four."

Hearing her say this made me want to check her ID. It was extremely un-Susie-Drake-like. I think it was more the movie star speaking than the former assassin.

On the nearly sixty-mile drive toward Portsmouth, we departed the elevated interstate three times: Rockport, Plum Island, and Jenness Beach. Each of these destinations is an annex of the East Coast Vacationland and crawling with tourists this time of year.

Maybe I entered the wrong profession. Had I a degree in psychiatry, I wonder what my records would say on the kiddie-like behavior of Theresa; the normally stoic Jim-Bob cracking jokes and terrible puns; Susie dressing in a tiny bikini and purposely acting tempestuous around all vacationing men; and me enjoying this odd companionship of a road trip and not always fretting on how much I miss Imene. Each person in this quartet is a misfit. No wonder we seem to fit together like puzzle pieces.

Yes, I have my wife. I'm the only one here still married. Imene is also a freak. It's why we work. We have a unique blood connection to the world of Remnants and Originals. In a marriage with almost anyone else, we would feel lost. Neither she nor I was related to Sacha Ahern, but she was as much our kin as our parents. Same goes for Susie.

We stayed a few hours at Jenness Beach. Too long, really. Neither woman abandoned their phony appearance and both distributed outlandish performances for tourists and locals. The Suzii might as well call themselves Sisterzz or something similarly punk rock. They were amiable more often when together than apart. Their experiences in life traveled divergent paths at a certain point in time, yet they each rendered and suffered high degrees of hurt. It's the inner pain, I think, which draws them together ... magnetized misery, lessened when they're closer in proximity.

On the ramp leaving Jenness Beach for the Marin, Susie pointed at the sign indicating an exit bridge for travelers headed to Concord. "Yesterday, before meeting Theresa, I figured we'd go there. Once you guys were off somewhere, I was gonna head out on my own. I figured I'd find the spaceship faster if I was a solo act."

"Now whose ass oughta get kicked!" Jim rightly said. "Traitor!"

"Cool off, people." Theresa suggested we take the next exit at Portland and spend the night at a campground.

As it was my turn driving, I eyed the dashboard's 3-D map. "What about Concord? Say the word, and I'll steer its direction."

"No, no, no! No Concord." The objection belonged to Her Royal Highness, Earth. "It's become a haven for the artsy-fartsy crowd. Film critics, music snobs, lovers of experimental entertainment. We Stooges *fans aren't welcome there. The people who live and work there are ultra-liberal pretentious baboons. You'd think, with their supposed high intelligence and sympathetic funding of other disenfranchised groups, they'd support the Remnant causes, but no. Something about those of us with powers infuriates them. Jealousy, no less."*

I veered back onto the Marin. "Are you saying the main Concord industry is a writers' colony?"

"Dude, they film a lotta movies there. It's the indie version of Hollywood ... if Hollywood still existed. Hoity-toity though they are, they have no problem reproducing prints of famous art in hologram or black velvet form and literature on toilet paper. Almost all the country's film, literary, and music agents reside in Concord."

Susie's interest piqued. "Literary agents, huh? Too bad for Jay that he can't dictate my story. He'd have us stay in the city until someone published his book. By then, we'd all be long dead."

"No publishing advocate is gonna want a story about you, Susie," her "sister" claimed. "I don't say it to be mean. This journey of yours to reclaim your memories ... sorry. It won't contain deep thoughts, haunting character insight, or

life-effecting quotes. Will the readers find common ground with the personalities Jay writes about? Well, not us four, nor anyone else you've mentioned to me. It'll be a puff, summer reading at best. Unless ... he gets an AI site to author the novel. Maybe. I wonder what he plans on naming it?"

Jim offered, "Why not something obvious like Susie Drake and the Stolen Memories? Or The Suzii?"

"He could make a play on the title of a famous book," I *said.* "Like The Old Man and the Suzii.*"*

PORTLAND, ACCORDING TO JIM-BOB, fell under the rule of a miniature Assistance Republic loyal to Maine, or what re'Maine'd (pun intended) of the state after lawmakers divided parts of it into Vacationland, Educationland, and mostly Umbreland. Speaking of small-scale, the city reminded me of a tinier Olde Boston. It catered to older citizens who wanted their shopping and sightseeing escapades to cover a reduced size of land. To their credit, the stores were larger and well-stocked. We treated ourselves to a great meal (fish and potatoes for everyone). Near dusk, I parked The Imene-A-Bago *at East End Beach.*

Theresa insisted we commence a beach campfire before we hit the sack. Hand it to the lady, she can recite some of the best ghost stories I've ever heard.

"I picked up the tales from traveling the globe for hundreds of years. Pass them on to your kids, Liam. Consider it a cultural exchange between our Earths."

Sore point smacked!

"Imene and I don't have kids. We decided the world's too messed up a place to bring new life into."

"Well, adopt then, kiddo," she added. "Make happy the life of some boy and/or girl while they're living in your messed-up world."

"I dunno if either of us is ready for making career sacrifices. She's a journalist, I'm a detective."

"Those are careers?" Earth laughed. "They sound more like fillers until a real job comes along. Better decide soon, kiddo; you're not gettin' any younger."

"You're one to talk. Roaming the world, never settling down, always in disguise. At least I'm sure of myself and don't live behind false faces." I had forgotten how the person I spoke to and about could easily kill me with a flip of her little finger. It didn't stop me, for some suicidal reason. "You and Susie, you both had a hard early life and a downright dastardly time after your mom's murder. The finish line for redemption is up to the seeker. I doubt either of you believe you've reached it. Doesn't mean you can't be role models for those who are certain that you have redeemed yourselves. Like me. Like Jim. Such a waste. Children and adults of both worlds need symbols for good. Don't tell me how the news media and politicians ruin, distort, and take advantage of your celebrityhood. You guys can overcome such nonsense. Ya'll been around long enough to work the negative into positive."

The Suzii remained quiet too long for me. It was a cool night, and I was sweating. Then Susie tapped her equivalent on the shoulder. "How many times have you heard what he just said over the years?"

"Seventeen. You?"

"Seven. Any chance it'll change you?"

I can still hear their laughing ringing deep inside my ears.

DESPITE THERE BEING ENOUGH BUNKS in the camper, Susie met with concerned faces when she announced her intention to sleep beneath the stars inside a huge park, just off the main thoroughfare. "I need time alone. To think. Consider all our options before and after we make the border tomorrow." Wincing at Liam's half-smile, she added, "No, your tiny lecture didn't strike a mental chord. I operate in the here and now. But … keep up the pleasant thoughts."

Karas didn't need to say it for Drake to think it. *If I truly operated "in the here and now," there'd've been no point in having my memories removed.* Nor did her straggling off from the others have anything to do with tomorrow's possibilities. *Déjà vu has walloped me hard. I gotta sort it out.* The origin of the latest fancy rested with Drake's perception of her traveling companions and how they (or some semblance of them) fit in with her past.

Thanks to Jim-Bob's careful planning, she carried with her a sleeping bag, although nodding off on the hard ground would have been fine. Ascending a sandy hill, she arranged the bedroll in the middle of a three-tree triangle and set unbroken twigs in double circles around the napping spot in case anyone ventured close during the night.

"I can almost visualize the faces of the trio who remind me of Liam, Theresa, and Jim." Unwinding with bone-snapping calisthenics, she had read their names on Karas's computer and had ejected them out of her mind. "Maybe Jay's gotta point about names. Knowing what they looked like is enough. Two men, one woman. One guy was skinny, wore glasses, and nerdy. Like Liam. The other guy was brawny. A biker is my guess. Quiet, like Jim. The chick was a hippie. Had a thing about nature. Hard figuring her out. Sometimes those moody types make me feel joyful. Like Theresa."

The preciseness of the recall shocked her. "Déjà vu, my ass! I shouldn't've remembered so much! What the hell is going on—either my memory's comin' back on its own or E'tty doesn't know what she's doin' or talkin' about!"

What currently bothered her stretched beyond the absence of recollections yet also incorporated the dilemma. "I know what Pith is after, and why he's working with Rodanthe. He wants to change the past. No seizures, no OCD. No geomagnetic storms crashing the internet. Not a bad idea. He won't alter what was … he'll create another Alt-Earth. Unless … unless Rodanthe knows a way of amending history and traveling forward in the same world."

Wasn't it the ultimate dream—preventing her mother's murder and the subsequent foray into crime? "I'd still be on hand for my friends and the war with the wizards. Other assassins would take my place." What remained unknown was whether her mind would hold two sets of memories—from a life no one else could recall and the beginning of a clean slate. "No need pouring over it now. Everything depends on finding Rodanthe. He owes me for the sins of his great-great-great-grandfather. And Pith … I can change his past at the same time."

Did the former Exile assassinate his girlfriend? "I have more doubts about it than ever before. Winthrop doesn't seem a likely suspect, either. Who then? I gotta know before cuttin' a deal with either or both of those guys."

Birthing a plan generated a smile. "I'll iron out the details on the road tomorrow. Not a word to the others. Liam would shit bricks since what I'm planning will alter the lives of his and Imene's grand-folks. Once I retrieve my memories, I can draw up an intricate blueprint of what needs changed." Theresa's face navigated through her thoughts. "Okay, I'll consider sharing my scheme with her. She might wanna cut and paste her own history."

AT THE UNITED STATES BORDERLINE, Flannagan flashed his badge at the patrol guard. "How are ya? I'm a lieutenant with the New York—"

"Say no more, sir. I just need you to tell me who's traveling with you." The Asian woman was clearly bored.

"My wife and brother-in-law, ma'am."

"Fine. Go through. They'll scan your IDs at the other post."

In the back of the vacationer, a voice spoke from an indiscernible body. "Good plan o' mine, right? Now, Jimmy-Bob, pull over to the side by an empty picnic table."

Vehicles passed *The Imene-A-Bago*, carrying occupants eager for a good time in the neighboring country. No one paid attention to the parked camper or the changing of drivers within it. The muttering of a wizardry chant, which rendered three travelers invisible in the Float-A-Camper's kitchen, went unheard to all other ears.

"This makes me feel uncomfortable," Liam said. "I like being able to see my body."

"Believe me," Susie affirmed, "you're not missing anything special."

"I'd smack you, Drake, if I could see you. Your voice keeps moving around."

"How long will this spell last?"

"It'll last, Jimmy-Bob, until I speak the reverse charm." Theresa eyed the space where she figured he'd spoken from. "Hopefully, I won't forget the words. *Nyuk, nyuk, nyuk*! Now pipe down, Stooges, I'm driving on to the next post. In a sec." A mumbled sentence later, she shed the film actress persona. Turning her head, she exclaimed, "*Ta-da*! Do ya think they'll recognize me, kiddos, after all these many, many decades?"

Prime Susie objected. "You *said* you'd have a fake ID thingmajig when you entered Canada! They'll think you're *me* 'cause I've been all over the news. Are you aiming to get us in deeper trouble?"

"Let me handle it, okay? I know what I'm doing."

THE MARIN STRETCHED THREE-QUARTERS of a mile across at each border, allowing for vehicles to enter and exit the two nations. Between the massive rows of lanes meant for arriving or departing, lay a medium strip dotted with picnic tables, a building equipped with vending machines and restrooms, and several automated statues of Emperor Doug Douglas (aka Doug-Doug), each one furnished with the pre-recorded voice of the leader either saying, "welcome to

Canada," or "come back soon," or perhaps reciting a lame joke.

In order for the perimeter gates to lift, a driver placed the scannable IDs of all passengers into a metal tube, which whooshed the canister to an attendant inside a small post. ninety-nine point eight percent of the time, this watch person would verify the credentials, press a button, lift a gate (or more, depending on the length of the vehicle and all add-ons), and wave weakly as travelers passed onward, rarely waving back at the (usually) young person performing a thankless task.

Point two percent accounted for how many troublemakers (usually Remnants) spoiled the day of not only the attendant but also the armed guard who occupied the tiny post. Statisticians calculated the low percentage over a year, and it covered all the border points. Yet it only took one disruptive Remmie or criminal to stir up an international event. Employees within the plexiglass enclosures underwent extensive training on how to manage travelers who couldn't or wouldn't provide their IDs and/or have no entry in the Retina Recognition Registry. Figure the number of workers and stations from one end of the countries to the other, and it was unlikely for any man or woman showing up for their job to expect anything out of the ordinary.

Today would not be one of those ordinary days.

"MISS," CAME THE ANNOYED FEMALE voice over a loudspeaker, "once again, you can't be telling me the truth. Everyone has an ID. If you lost or misplaced it, we'll come out and perform a retina check. But you claim you've never had your retinas registered. Do you have an ocular disease or Remnant power located in your eye?"

"I am telling you the truth, and nope, and nope, to your question." Earth/Drake reveled in her teasing role. "Why don't you come out and see for yourself? Understanding will be immediate. I double damn guar-en-tee it."

A couple of loud groans resonated over the PA system. *Groan, groan!* Two people bearing unhappy faces emerged from the square cubicle. Theresa/Susie described them for the curiosity of the unseeable trio.

"The attendant is a black woman. Early twenties. Thin. Long black hair. Gorgeous … except … I can tell by her face she rarely smiles and is most likely a hardcase, to put it mildly. I mean, why else would a model-material chick work *here*, except for the probable fact she can't get along with people? The guard is a white dude. Early thirties. Curly blonde hair. Got a beer gut and very wrinkly uniform. Man has no self-confidence. He's carrying two orange cones because … yep, I see it in the side mirror, we have people behind us, and he's gonna send 'em to other lanes."

The attendant waited five feet in front of the camper while the guard paced fast behind it, laying down cones and shooing off other vehicles. He rejoined the pretty chick and, together, they neared the driver's side door.

A window rolled down. "Hi there! I betcha know who I am!"

The woman cried, "Please, don't hurt me, please!"

Reaching for his gun, the dude stopped, having realized the futility of it all. "Look, Miss Drake. You're wanted in the

States. Technically, you're no longer there. We got no beef with you."

"You guys are so cute! Come closer. I won't bite."

Dual hesitation.

"I promise to stay inside. C'mon."

Bug-eyed and scared, they inched closer.

The driver turned her head, facing them, and eased back the hair over her right ear. "See?" Her finger rotated over the V-shaped slash in the upper helix like it was a valuable diamond. "Every school child has seen a photo of this cut I received when fighting a wizard back in the 20th century. Prime Earth Susie remains unscarred. You've surely seen plenty of pics of her unblemished ear, too, thanks to Hugh Rodanthe. Go ahead. Touch it. It's real."

The guard's prior fear metamorphosed into horniness. Touching Susie Drake, any part of any version of the woman, would rocket him into the annals of history and surge his confidence problem soaring until it became … arrogance. In the back, imperceivable Prime Susie fought the urge to utter a drum roll as the dude's finger neared … slowly … and ultimately caressed the laceration of the legendary, mythical, four-hundred-and-some-year-old beauty queen.

"It's her! *Our* Susie! Oh God! Oh God!"

Into the arms of the shrieking attendant did he faint.

Ten minutes later…

THERESA PACED INSIDE THE OFFICE. *Much bigger than it looks from the outside. I'll bet someone with dimensional storage powers altered the size.* Near a makeshift kitchen, the attendant sat on a three-cushioned sofa. The formerly passed-out guard lay across the couch, his head on the black woman's lap. *I never figured them having a thing for each other. The way she's stroking his temples, and the evil eye she gave me when he touched my scar … guess it's true— opposites can attract one another.*

"Look … I'm sorry for what happened. He'll be okay." She had carried him into the post. "I gotta go. Things to do, places to be."

The vagueness snatched his attention. "Wait!" Suddenly, Mr. Guard didn't seem so out of it. Lifting his head, he secured all the earmarks of a bug-eyed Susie fanatic. "Revealing yourself just now. Is this a permanent change?" Briefly, his eyes bobbed at the co-worker. "Are we the first to see you … after centuries?"

"Yes, and yes. It's not such a big deal. Not like I've been encased in ice. I move about a lot and mostly hide in plain view. I'm ready for a change, I guess."

Raising, he stretched his arms and kissed the scowling clerk, who stated, "Good luck! We don't wanna keep you here since you're *so* busy."

Oh, she's jealous of me. I bet she's jealous of everyone in his life. "How kind of you to understand. *Um*, mind if I wash my hands? There's a sticky gunk on them from the door handle."

The girlfriend pointed down a tiny corridor. "Restroom is thataway. I cleaned the handle using an industrial liquid made by *your* pals, the Exiles. Yeah, you most def need to clean it off. Touching food with it … well, it might not affect *your* super-tummy, but it would anyone else's … anyone normal."

In the lavatory, Earth hurried her business. *"Super-tummy!" "Anyone normal!" Good thing I'm not super-sensitive. Neither of them thanked me for bringing him inside, or signing autographs, or takin' selfies. Maybe I shouldn't've resurfaced. I enjoyed the Florence disguise. It was—hey, what's this?* Taped to the wall behind her, a multi-colored flier caught her eye. Excitedly, she removed it, read it three times, stuffed the circular inside a pocket of her slacks, and rejoined the border boobs. *These two … I wonder if they contact the Mounties any time someone shouts "boo?"*

"Guys … change of plans." She submerged the thrill of discovery below the surface of her skin. "My camper … it's a rental. I need to take it through the gates and reenter the States, where my friends can pick it up. Then … before coming back here, I want to slip into a false body. I need to make Halifax as soon as possible. Guess I can call a cab from the nearest town."

Stunned, the young couple failed to comprehend her scheme.

"What 'friends?'" the envious guard voiced. "You said we're the first to know you're back."

"Remnants," she said, "they've helped keep my secret. Will you guys do the same and help me out?"

The notion of helping Susie Drake was almost too much for the guard. Almost, because the sharp fingernails of his lover dug deep into the man's arm. "Uh, we'll do what we can to make sure you get away unseen."

"He's right," the colleague expressed. "My sister works lane 17 on the opposite side, entering the shared nation zone.

I'll phone her. Let her know you're coming. Change into your disguise when you leave here, not anytime later. Her work partner will freak out if he sees you … much more than mine … if such a thing's possible."

Mildly, her vocation associate said, "I didn't act so bad. Anyway"—his tone strengthened—"don't hire a taxi to take you to Halifax. *My* sister lives five miles up the road. She can drive you there. If I can tell her who she's transporting and swear her to secrecy, she won't offer any objection to the request. The girl's one of your biggest fans. In junior high, she wrote a paper on you, how you're this incredible force for good and an inspiration to all young persons. You, Susie, you're the reason she volunteers helping in nursing homes and why she's studying to be a nurse."

Damn! I best not tell Liam about this; he'll rub it in my face.

"Go ahead, tell her it's me. I'm gonna wait in the camper. Come get me when it's time to vamoose."

In unison, they rejoiced, "Thank you, Susie!"

Chapter 10: Pith and the Redheaded Pendulum

A TIME EXISTED IN BYGONE years when the woman now calling herself Theresa Earth would not only never have felt excited about conveying news but instead, kept it to herself. *If this was them days, I'd have neutralized Liam and Jim in Olde Boston, the same place Susie and I would have battled until one of us either gave up or the Exiles came and hauled our asses away. They say having kids mellows a person. It wasn't until mine was in his sixties that I softened.*

The Suzii suffered the same memory loss in the early 1950s. Prime Susie had regained the lost times in the 1970s. Alt-Susie's partial amnesia continued until 2104, when the first "shit storm" coincided with a hurricane in the Bahamas, tossing her through concrete, metal, and wood until the Atlantic Ocean decided it could whoop her behind with a massive water paddle. Nope, her recollections didn't bounce back until she smacked her ears so hard, draining them of liquid, that somehow an eardrum pop released what she'd long forgotten.

Came a day when time travelers from Prime Earth penned books on the power community of the 1970s, with special added emphasis on its own Susie Drake. These other world accounts didn't chronologically match those of

Theresa's timeline, beginning in the early 1960s. The original and her doppelgänger traveled different paths, spewed contradictory ideologies, and each one's respective public evaluated them very dissimilarly.

Nevertheless, the new biographies of the reformed assassins skyrocketed each Susie's popularity, especially Alt-Earth's, where—as on all human-inhabited planets—its populations have short memories.

Skyrocketing sales of such memoirs and textbooks produced constant chatter and speculation about Theresa's psyche and personal life, luring her into depression and a severe case of identity crisis (had she suffered the guy's whining a century and a half earlier, maybe she would've recognized the warning signs). Even before melancholia had dug a root deep in her soul, waves of self-hatred and doubts concerning decision-making impaired her daily routines. Old Man would later speculate that OCD materialized at the same time her reminiscences had returned. She never spoke on these points to anyone other than her son and kept it concealed from her counterpart. Would anti-depressants work on her non-human, nearly immortal mind? She'd rather bury herself in sand than ask for medication.

In lieu of drugs, Earth—when faced with sorrowfulness—adopted what she called her "buoyant disposition." "Being joyful no matter how much it pains me," was the prescription she wrote herself. Naturally, the pharmacist amidst her mind wasn't always on duty to fulfill the treatment.

But, God love her, the one-of-a-kind Theresa had prevailed enough times, overcame mental and emotional adversaries, and had done so with awareness from the slimmest of audiences. When she reentered *The Imene-A-Bago*, she did so cheerfully and with a zing in her step.

"GUYS! LISTEN UP!" EARTH—ONCE more in her actress pretense—could only hope her Stooges remained in the back of the camper, for she saw nothing. The sound of sighs gave assuredness that she wasn't alone. "Here's what's going down. I'm gonna drive us through the gates and back around the other side, headed toward the States. I'll release you from the spell, and then you can drive to the Fair while I head toward Halifax. I have a ride waiting across the border."

"Fair? What Fair?" Susie bluntly asked.

"Uh-oh. Here come the border brats. I'll explain after I get us turned around."

The "brats" executed their part of the act to a T. She would later reward one of them with a lip kiss and thank the other by a handshake (and receive the middle finger for smooching someone's boyfriend).

Pulling away from lane 17, Earth halted the vehicle a half mile south. Speaking the reverse charm, her comrades reappeared in the flesh, each checking their clothes and various body parts, making sure no funny business had happened during the wizardry switcheroos.

"I found this flier in the post. There's a map inside. It's where I want you guys to go."

She handed the leaflet to Susie, who held it up for the reading sake of the males on either side of her. The first comment came from Liam.

"They spelled 'Renaissance' wrong. It only has one 'n' before the 'a.'"

"It's in code," Theresa explained. "Notice how the two n's are close together, almost like a 'm.' It's meant to be 'Rem'aissance.' 'Rem' being short for Remnant. The Remmies don't want uncool normals knowing they put on these events because it'd scare them away. But it's the best, legal way for them to earn an honest wage while making use of their powers. Most folks think the fair workers are former Exiles, and Lointain agreed not to give away the secret. Still, anyone in the know is aware of what's going on."

"Interesting," Jim said. "I thought they were currently Exile-owned and operated."

"That's cause you're not 'in the know,' darling."

"What's this got to do with us?" Susie asked.

"Check the schedule on the pamphlet. The fair left Olde Boston the day after your ship disappeared. Now they're near Chautauqua Lake, on the edge of East Coast Vacationland. It would make a lotta sense for the Staten Island Shysters to sell these people your ship … assuming they stole it." Earth's deductive reasoning sounded solid and stirred nods of approval. "You all go there. From here, the quickest way is back down the Marin. At New Haven, it'll be country highways through Vacationland's suburbs. You won't be able to avoid going through—"

"The Royal British Republic of Binghamton," Jim-Bob eked out in disgust. "Makes me wanna puke thinking about it. Mandatory tea breaks instead of stoplights and stop signs. It'll tack on an extra three or four hours at the very least."

Liam wondered aloud, "Do the British really have control over an American city?"

"Nobody knows how it happened," Flannagan expounded. "There was a long-forgotten clause George Washington signed which historians discovered right before the 2076 Tricentennial. Binghamton lost the lottery. So, it'll be a seventeen- or eighteen-hour trip, not counting stops." He studied the snarky facial reactions and questioned Theresa. "Why are you going to Halifax if you think the ship's near Olde Mayville?

"Well, I could be wrong. I'm not, but it's possible. If I am, then Boudreaux can help us after I reach the embassy. And since I'm probably right, we can count on Pith or Rodanthe or both hangin' around the fair. In either case, it'll help having an Exile or two on board."

"Unless they laugh you off." Drake smirked.

"They won't. Are we cool with my plan?"

"First," Jim breathed, "I want to know exactly who is driving you into Nova Scotia?"

"You're so cute when you're worried! The fainting guard's sister. About my plan …"

"About your plan," Susie interjected. "You showing up late with or without Boudreaux isn't gonna help if Pith and/or Rodanthe spot us and leave. Pith's the one I'm concerned with the most. One shapeshift into a fly, and he's good as gone."

"Enough fretting! Don't enter the fair until I arrive. There're hotels listed on the back of the flyer. Go to the Randolph Motor Inn and register under um … the Theresa Lamar party. I'll contact one or all of you through the HOWse. You do know what that is, don't you?"

"Yeah, yeah, yeah." Drake deemed the scheme lacking in balance but kept her opinion suppressed. "How are you planning on joining us? Is the guard's sister gonna be your full-time chauffeur?"

"Damn, you're negative! My hope is for Boudreaux teleporting us. Otherwise, well, I'll have to switch into my real self and let my celebrityhood win me a ride!"

Saying her goodbyes, Theresa left the camper and walked briskly to where her ride awaited at the Canadian border.

NEW AND IMPROVED ROADS FROM the dividing line at Calais, Maine, made the drive into Halifax smoother and quicker, just under four hours. What wasn't smooth and made time move turtle-slow were the constant questions, comments, and stories asked and spoken by the collapsing guard's sibling. Theresa mentally repeated a mantra, *I am patient. I have a buoyant disposition. I do not murder women who yack, yack, yack.* When the chant itself became annoying, she simply closed her eyes and attempted to decree herself into sleep. Sadly, this endeavor only reached fulfillment ten minutes from her destination.

"Let me off on Barrington. I'll walk to the embassy. It's on Brunswick, right?"

"Yep," the driver said. "Are you going to enter the place looking like the 40's movie star or Susie?"

"Before I go in, I'll change. I want all the security personnel going batshit. They'll think I'm Prime Earth Susie about to go on a rampage." She winked. "It'll make them earn their paycheck this week."

"Uh, in case things go bad or disappointing, I can wait. I don't mind driving you back to the States or wherever you'll meet those mysterious friends of yours." To Earth, the woman's eyeballs practically doubled their size during the hoped-for anticipation. "I never did tell you about my days on the underwater bowling league and how I met Doug-Doug's cousin when my blind date ditched me."

"No, no, don't wait! I know everything will turn out peachy. You tell your brother that he's a good kiddo, okay?"

Finally rid of the obsessive chatterer, Theresa stepped out of the electric car and began strolling on the Brunswick Street sidewalk toward the Canadian-Lointainian Embassy.

AT AN OPEN-AIR CAFÉ on the corner of Brunswick and Carmichael Streets, Ren Pith kept a vigilant eye on the embassy entrance across the way. Nursing a caffeine-free Lemola (a combination of lemonade and a cola), he bemoaned overturning his earlier decision to check on Susie's progress on the way to Halifax. Before taking a seat at the outdoor section of the eatery, the epileptic Exile conducted a rushed flyover above the Marin in hawk form. There it was, *The Imene-A-Bago*, heading south.

I should have followed them. I should have turned into an ant or something on the camper top. I should have known they wouldn't do the logical thing and come here. I should have stayed with them all the way, no matter how annoying they are. I should not have stolen Susie's memories; they weren't of any use. Uh, how many shoulds is that? Five? Okay, gotta do two more, or else I'll have bad luck. I should leave here now and track them again. I should not stare at the pretty waitress because Isabella awaits me back home.

This last thought bothered him. *She doesn't wait for me. I'm only fooling myself. The sole reason she spent time with me was due to my being an Exile. It's my fault she sent me packing. No, nix that. It's my lazy-ass grandparents' fault and E'tatanya's. They're all to blame for my OCD. I wouldn't have lost Isabella were it not for my habits.*

It was an endless obsessive pattern of pondering and tiptoeing into the unanswerable question: what would life be like now had the prehistoric bee never stung him, keeping him free of epilepsy and OCD? Pith knew it was pointless to dive into the wacky world of what if. He'd be there now, marching the streets of subjectivity, were it not for the cute, red-headed server who'd brought him his Spoke and a corned beef salad. Into his compulsive contemplations, he painted the pretty lass on whom he crushed.

I'm probably gonna ask her out on a date. Here's how it'll play out. The waitress and I will hit it off. I can tell by the way she smiled at me. I'll tell her, "I have no place to stay in this world." She'll reply, "You can stay with me." In a few years, we're married with babies. Our kids will have powers, and they'll have kids. I will not treat my grandkids in the same callous, uncaring manner that my wicked grandparents treated me. No way!

Drake, Karas, and me are stuck here. Susie hasn't yet, nor likely ever will, find the spaceship. Rodanthe has his agenda. I can't count on him taking me home. It's why I must begin charting my own destiny before it's too late. My future rests with the redhead!

A sharp wind blew along his hairline, tickled the skin, and darned if it didn't, for the briefest moment, clean away the grandeur off his delusions. *Who am I kidding? She's not going to go out with me. Yes, she smiled at me because I'm a paying customer! I've been sitting here for two hours, forty-seven minutes, and thirty-four seconds, taking tiny sips and tiny bites off the growing flat drink and increasingly stale food! The only reason she eyes me or comes close is she's waiting for me to leave so that she can collect her tip from not only me but from anyone else who takes this seat, and in the time I've been here, numerous other people could have had their lunch and left, leaving her more tips! If she were interested in me, she'd have come sit across from me during her break and asked me about myself. I saw her go inside and occupy a chair for fifteen minutes, laughing with her co-workers ... no doubt about me. "The creep won't leave," she told them. "He's stalking me. I know it. It wouldn't be so bad if he were handsome, but c'mon, why do the ugly losers always—always, I tell ya—sit in my section? Anyone know a weightlifter, boxer type who they can call and come chase this weirdo away?"*

That these thoughts became more grossly exaggerated as Pith gave them birth one could attribute to the voice of his motormouth OCD uncertainties. *She wants me to die. I mean, isn't it her only option? I planned on ordering dessert. What's to stop her from poisoning me? Of course, I'm nearly immortal, but I don't want a stomachache. I can't believe she hates me as much as she does!*

Locked in a whirlwind of despair, Ren didn't notice the arrival of the red-haired dream.

"Sir? Forgive me for not asking before now, but would you like a carry-out carton for your food and drink? I can transfer them into a clamshell box and plastic cups. They're very retro-looking!" Nostalgia was hip in Halifax!

In the real world, her eyes registered an error at having not attended him properly. In Pith's fanatical realm, she was really saying, "You must leave, cretin."

Standing and pushing his chair very hard below the table, Ren knew he mustn't cry. "I'm leaving! I'll go! Sorry for the trouble I caused you." Into her hand, he placed three times the appropriate tip.

"Wait … what? You didn't cause any trouble!" Ah, but she knew his type—alone, eating slow, trying not to gaze in her vicinity, and paying a huge tip. What made him different than the others? His clothes (authentic 21st century), atmosphere (scared of her, not anyone else), drama (definitely has an enigmatic past), and needs fixing (she excels at fixing men!). "I, uh, I get off work in an hour. You look like you need someone to talk to. I'm told I have two dynamic ears." Underscoring her listening skill, she moved red strands of hair behind both finely shaped hearing vessels.

Zap-wow-eee! Zap-wow-eee! Fantasy converted into reality. *Reagan and Rachel. I hope she likes those names for our kids. I am so in love!*

Didn't it always happen how real life fell flat when compared with the movies? For the shortest-lived moment, Renaldo Pith dangled on the scales of possibilities. Who knew where a conversation with the waitress could lead? Maybe nowhere, possibly somewhere. No precedent existed by which to judge the development. Yet … the type of woman he sought always vehemently steered clear of his stubbornly put-offish mannerisms. Isabella allowed him into her company because he was different at the right time when she needed someone unusual and opposite. The longer Pith's mouth fumbled over the most importantly correct words he ever needed to speak in his entire life, the more the green-eyed, red-haired beauty's heart pounded fonder.

Theresa Earth walked the sidewalk in front of the café where time stood still for a Prime Lointain man and an Alt-Earth woman. Dressed as Florence La Badie, lovely though she was, the near-duplicate held no sway in the OCD mind of a lovesick Exile. Foot and vehicle traffic on Brunswick and Carmichael waned at the most opportune second, allowing Earth's transformation into Susie go unnoticed … almost.

Susie! How … how can she be here? She's in the camper southbound on the Marin! She doesn't know magic. But she changed bodies midway across the street.

"Are … are you all right, sir?"

Renaldo Pith slipped, tripped, and held onto the scales of possibilities by a fingernail desperately needing trimming. *What to do? What to do? Heart or hearth?*

"Uh, dazzled by your request!" *God! How stupid was that!* "An hour, you say? I'll wait … here … if it's okay."

"Sure. I'll refill your Lemola." Starting away, she turned and said, "Please, sit. You look all tense."

Oh, honey, if you only knew!

JUST AS SHE PREDICTED, THE SECURITY personnel went "batshit" when they observed the legendary blonde enter the embassy. "It must be the fugitive from Prime Earth!" a receptionist said to her co-worker before they hightailed their butts out the back door. A bespeckled employee shuffling through passport requests thought to himself, *She'll kill me because I look official*, and slid beneath his desk. An assistant to the assistant to the Public Affairs Specialist shouted, "I quit!" and fell to the floor in a fetal position, weeping.

Theresa cottoned to the widespread panic. *Oh look*, she mentally transmitted to no one, *the tough-looking security supervisor is praying! Damn! Susie's accused of breaking, entering, and trespassing, not murder! It wasn't her fault that the jail flooded, and she had to leave.* Earth set two fingers between her lips and blew a loud whistle.

"Hey, kiddos! Cease fretting! It is I, Alt-Earth Susie Drake! Come see … I'll show you my damaged ear, the only one of its kind on any Susie!"

First, relief swept through the first-floor lobby, closely followed by abject shock. A shared surreal dizziness overcame those regaining their composure. Susie Drake … draped in heroic legend … a modern-day Hercules … too mythical, so fantastical for the clockwork world of today. In small groups of two or three, they dared approach her.

One woman, in her early sixties, crawled on her knees across a not-very-shiny tile, weeping. "Now I can … die … happy!" Tugging at Theresa's jeans, she explained, "I played you in high school and the local theatre ensemble. One of the Rodanthes wrote a play, *Susie's Heart Asunder*. A critic wrote of my performance"—tears flowed—"'*she epitomizes the fabled Drake, and may she ever be Susie until the real one reappears.*' You have reappeared. My time is over and done with."

"If you say so." Earth had had enough of butt-kissers back at the border. "I wanna speak with the Lointain ambassador. Someone go get him while I'm in a good mood."

News of the building's first-level ruckus reached the second floor's senior administrative offices at the same time confusion over Susie's identity ended. Managers, specialists, and assistants began piling down the stairwell, keeping their distance until "The Official Announcement" altered their conduct one way or another. The ambassador, a Lointainian, withdrew from his station, operating an indecipherable face until he could, for the benefit of his staff, make a decisive declaration. His employees graciously let him pass by, each one drunk on the intoxicating excitement.

"It's her, Mister Ambassador," the actress cried. "I've verified it for you."

Careful not to huff, he responded in a kind tone, "I'll perform the verifying. Have we not suffered enough Susie shams over the years? Please, move back a safe distance." Louder, he said, "Everyone, I advise caution. My powers will melt away any wizardry smokescreen."

The lobby security team finally moved into action, creating a wide circle around Theresa.

Amused, she remained wordless.

Arms lifted perpendicular to his head, the ambassador sang a short chant, the recital ending with sparks igniting from his fingertips like Independence Day sparklers. Once the flames self-extinguished, he whipped a finger across Earth's entertained face.

"No false face did drop! You've passed the first step in authenticity!"

Wild applause!

"You wanna lick my wounded ear? It oughta be the second step."

The ambassador laughed. "No. You want to know why I don't necessarily believe in your damaged upper helix? Because *you* suggested it. No, the final step is a password. You and I have met before. In the year 2072. The occasion was a peace treaty my father negotiated between the African Remnant Army and Lointain. At the post-signing party, you danced with me. I was, uh … quite inebriated. You took advantage of the situation, hoping to hack into my computer for whatever goods you thought I kept hidden. Using your suggestive power on me, you learned my password. What was it? You can say it aloud. I, of course, changed it after we danced."

"*Hmm.* It was a long time ago. Lemme see." Acting tongue-in-cheek, she dribbled a finger on her tongue. "Sugar toffee cookies!"

Here it came, "The Official Announcement."

"Ladies and gentlemen, I give you … *the* authentic Susie Drake!"

Massive applause!

Fronting a half-whisper, he flashed a condescending expression. "We should probably dance. It'll make for a wonderful photo. Most everyone who works here had a memory camera chip installed in their head."

"I'm in no mood for footing it. Plus, I never heard of a what? Memory …"

"Camera chip. Surgically implanted in the brain. All one has to do is focus on whatever they want a photo of, then blink twice with their right eye. Then they place the round, red glass of their EyePhone up to their left eye, blink three times, and the photos transfer from the brain." Sophisticated was this diplomat and his chin hung, disappointed at how backward he judged the woman before him. Still … "We really should dance or put on a little show. It would encourage competence in my workers."

"Look … I'm in a hurry and put up with 'The Official Announcement' nonsense for your benefit. Neither you nor any of your minions have asked me why I'm here."

Rocking his jaw back and forth, the ambassador sarcastically inquired, "*Why* are you here?"

She answered loudly for all who didn't hear the question. "I need to see Jack Boudreaux. Now!"

The emissary breathed out in a broken rhythm. "Susie … I can schedule … you an appointment … with Mr. Boudreaux. It won't come to pass until, *um* … next week … at the earliest."

"Not good enough." Her index finger flew beneath his chin and lifted him five feet off the floor.

The work team he had hoped to impress with finesse and diplomatic skills pushed back against the farthest wall, unsure if blood was about to spill. Prepared for the worst, the ground floor custodian grabbed a mop and bucket.

"Put me down! Who …? Who do you think you are? I'll tell you." Her strength and gritted teeth failed to intimidate him. "You *are* a celebrity. Nothing more. Okay, you have historical importance on your side, but your accomplishments ended a few hundred years ago. Where have you been since? In oblivion. What have you done since? Nothing, as far as anyone knows. Jack Boudreaux is the leader of an entire, self-sufficient world. You're a self-centered bully. I don't have your powers, yet I will not bend to your callous demands!"

Lointain's representative to Earth—the planet, not Theresa—had expected applause for what he considered as a "brave" speech and received none.

"I need Boudreaux now! Prime Earth Susie Drake, as you know, is in this timeline. She and a friend have kidnapped a New York City policeman. They're gonna kill him unless we do something."

Mixed reactions emanated from the spectators. Most didn't particularly care for the Big Apple or its residents. Sensing this, Theresa/Susie upped the phony ante.

"They're gonna bomb Vacationlands and Umbrelands because they don't like what happened to this world's version of America."

"Not our problem," the ambassador voiced, to a wave of boos as unrest began building within the crowd. These Canadians not only had relatives in America, but many of their countrymen and countrywomen labored at jobs which supplied the segregated lands of the modern U.S.A., from which revenue poured back into the provinces.

Identifying a thorn in the throng, she raised the false sensitivity stakes. "Once the explosions are over, it's assassination time for my Prime counterpart, beginning with Doug-Doug!"

Patriotism overload exploded in the embassy! Emperor Doug Douglas held a ninety-three percent favorable rating among his subjects (the remaining seven percent didn't like how the leader treated his ex-wife, the actress, Mary Marilyn).

The ambassador, no dummy he, grasped the fervor stirring about him. Instead of mocking it, he questioned the motive.

"What does Prime Susie have against Doug-Doug? Did he say or do anything to offend her?"

Backed against the proverbial wall, Earth thumbed through more fictional excuses. "She has nothing against Canada. She's a huge fan of Gordon Lightfoot, Triumph, and Rush. But … but …"—and here, she mined a real nugget—"during his comedic phase and a member of the cast of *SCTV Again*, he wrote and acted in a sketch making fun of me. Hey, I have a terrific sense of humor. I didn't mind. Somehow, Prime Susie saw the bit, and it launched Doug-Doug to the top of the hit list." Playing to the audience, she bellowed, "Are you gonna allow a non-Alt person to march into your nation and murder your beloved emperor?"

"No!" the resounding reply boomed.

"Shouldn't Mr. Dummy Diplomat send an S.O.S. immediately to Jack Boudreaux?"

"Yes!" even louder.

"If he doesn't, will you join me in tar and feathering him?"

"Yes, Susie, yes!"

Lowering the administrator, whose slumped shoulders signaled defeat, she followed him victoriously through a happy horde, up the stairwell and into his office, where a magical HOWse phone connected communication between Halifax and Lointain.

FORTY MINUTES LATER, JACK BOUDREAUX and E'tatanya materialized next to the envoy's desk, radically spooking him. They ignored the bureaucrat, fixating their attention on the woman they'd lost contact with after selflessly caring for and training her son.

"You look well, Susie."

"Ditto, Jack. Thank you for coming. You, too, missy."

Boudreaux addressed the ambassador. "Would you be kind enough to give us the room?"

Already upright, the diplomat smiled upon leaving the office, hoping the Lointain leader would smack the living daylights out of the woman whom he now considered an over-hyped has-been.

"I didn't want to ask when the diplomat was here," Jack began, "since, like most people, he's uninformed that you have an offspring. How is Moelwyn?" The Exiles despised the shortened yet official "Moe," preferring something a little mo' … classy.

"He's doing fine. He's a Harvard professor. Seriously … of Remnants. But you already know this, don't you? You or one of your spies pops in now and then."

"I was only being courteous. A pleasantry you should project … now and then." His raised finger meant she best be polite and allow him the floor. "To business. Prime Susie, as we've heard, has bombings and assassinations up her sleeve. I commend you on wanting to stop her. Please provide precise details."

Out spilled the truth. On dawned the unhappy faces. "You summoned us on false pretenses. The original Susie wants nothing more than to return home. We have no method for finding the spaceship."

"Trackers—"

"Our hunters cannot sense people from the main universe," Boudreaux cut her off. "The only way we could find the ship is if we knew someone from this timeline who has been inside it and used their essence for tracking purposes. I'm sorry."

Frustrated, Earth advocated another approach. "Come with me to the Rennaissance Fair. Rodanthe or Pith are bound to be there. Capturing the mortal is easy enough, provided he doesn't turn invisible, but it'll be harder seizing not the Prime Exile."

When he responded, "It's not our dilemma," it reminded her of the egotistical emissary and wondered if the men were cousins. The trip to Halifax might've failed there and then had not an alarm blared throughout the embassy. No ordinary warning system was this, for these ringing bells and flashing lights initiated a system which snatched away a powered person's super abilities.

REN DEMONSTRATED A CLASSIC NERVOUS wreck for an hour. Actually, for most of his life. His eyes often scrutinized the face of the waitress who swapped glances, all of them friendly, inviting, anxious. *It's like we've known each other for years. She looks over at me because she feels the same.*

Common sense voice kicked the OCD voice aside. *We don't know anything about one another. She only stares in my direction when she attends a table in this area.*

History had taught him how these bickering types of dialogue could go on for hours. Therefore, he concentrated on Susie.

She went to the embassy for help from the Exiles to find the ship. Why aren't Karas and Flannagan here? Where are they driving to in the opposite direction from Halifax? How did Susie even get here? Did she run short distances fast …? It is one of her powers. I can't believe she ran all that way and didn't attract the authorities' attention, even if they couldn't have stopped her. I need to know what she finds out from the Exiles.

The OCD voice powered on. *I have a chance for a happy life with the waitress. Why go back to the other Earth? I'm able to hide in plain sight there because the cops don't know what I look like, but the Exiles do. I'll still be on the run. Always.*

Make way for the C.S. voice. *"Happy life," my ass. I'll never have a happy life. Not with seizures and OCD. Miss Redhead will listen to my story and laugh while she runs off into her boyfriend's arms, forgetting all about me. The Exiles won't find me on Prime Earth. I'm a needle in a haystack.*

As promised, after an hour passed, Miss Redhead clocked out via a HOWse 3-D Timesheet. She had also changed out of her blue and white uniform into a blue blouse and white shorts, a retro 70's style, albeit not era-authentic. Carrying two Lemolas, she eased into the chair across from fidgety Ren.

"My name is [DELETED]," she began. "I've lived in Halifax all my life. I rent an apartment with my middle sister, [ALSO DELETED]. Briefly, I attended college at Dalhousie University and roomed with Doug-Doug's second cousin. I've worked here for three years but have applications at several hospitals and clinics in Nova Scotia. My dream is to get into the cardiology field, the same as my older sister and aunt.

Now … your turn. I *know* your story makes mine look like three straw hats on a slow steamer trying to circle Kelowna." She snorted at the end of the maxim, whose meaning eluded Pith.

Certain sections of her introduction hitched a ride in his mind while others he left stranded, confused. Listening was her strong point. His was mental debates.

Let's say I stay in this world. Do I even need to bother with Susie and the ship?

C.S. voice chimed in first. *I don't have the proper IDs for this timeline. On Prime Earth, I have money stashed in various banks under multiple aliases. The only money I have here I've stolen. I do not want to work for a living … but Miss Redhead doesn't seem the type who'd support me financially. She's a fixer, not a sugar mommy.*

The OCD voice wanted its opinion told. *Miss Redhead is waiting for me to speak! There's a good chance she's "the one" meant for me, after all these years. I'll give her a quick biography and head inside the embassy. I do need to find out the story on the spaceship in case things here don't work out.*

"Ren Pith, at your service." He thought it sounded too formal but didn't care. "I'm gonna tell you the truth. It's going to sound incredible. I ask please, hold off until I've finished to express doubts and fears."

"Fire away, Rennie!"

Was she too excitable and not worldly-wise enough for his story?

"I'm from Prime Earth. I'm an Exile." *Already her eyes light up! I was hoping for more sophistication, but I suppose she can't be blamed for hearing such things from a customer.*

"I'm wanted by all sorts of cops for crimes I didn't commit. I do admit to stealing the memories of Prime Susie Drake.

"You see, long ago, a prehistoric bee stung me and, as a result, and from not receiving proper treatment in time, I came down with epilepsy and OCD. By swiping those memories, I hoped to track down Hugh Rodanthe, asking him to help me either by changing my history or catching one of those bees. E'tatanya could cure me if she had a live one. When I accessed Susie's recollections through a power called Vetiti20, I realized she didn't know how to contact Hugh.

"I first came to your timeline when a bartender, of all people, introduced me to Winthrop Rodanthe, who'd been vacationing on Prime. I traded him the memories, but the deal we made fell through, and he brought me back to Earth, sans the recollections. Prime Susie and a private detective came to Alt Earth via a rickety spacecraft in search of her memories. I don't want her getting them back or meeting with Rodanthe because, once I retrieve them, I hope to make a better transaction with other members of his family.

"Unfortunately, Susie's ship went missing. Neither her nor I know where it's at. An hour ago, Susie entered the Lointain Embassy. She's gonna ask for the Exiles' help to track the spacecraft. I need to find out what she learns."

Miss Redhead sucked in a big gulp of air before squeezing it out slowly. "*Wowser*! I *knew* you were mysterious and had a history, but I'd never have guessed what you told me, not in a million years. I have a ton of questions. Do you mind?"

He hiked a thumb in the embassy's direction. "Please, ask them fast. I'm deciding on what action I take next."

"How often do you have seizures?"

"Once a month. Blue lightning surrounds my body. I scream like a wild man, and my skin temporarily turns black."

"Is there no medicine for it?"

"I wish!"

She drummed two fingers on her lips. "Why not ask our Exiles for help? One of them comes into the café every other month. He's very nice. Signs autographs. Gives away tour tickets into Lointain … provided, of course, one gets all the vaccine shots and pays for a teleporter. He doesn't have to do those things or show a great interest in us Earthlings, but he does."

"Who're you talking about?"

A dreaminess engulfed her face. "Luther Fontenot."

"Oh man, oh man, oh man!" Pith's neck bent forward. "In my world, Fontenot is not a nice person, no siree Bob. He's spearheaded a campaign to have me banned from Lointain. It's hard for me to believe he could be anything but an a-hole in any universe."

Her eyes winced when she enquired, "What crimes are you charged with?"

"Besides teleporting and specific shapeshifting, I can create geomagnetic storms. It's a side effect of the seizures. The first time I released the power was 1980 on one of Lointain's moons. Jack Boudreaux banished me for twenty years because of it. I learned from my energy levels how it takes fifty years for the storm ability to reboot. The next and *last* time I released an extreme disturbance was accidentally over Russia and China in 2035. No one died. I would have been devastated had there been a single fatality.

"Seventeen years later, another G-storm crashes the internet … at the same time, a killer pandemic strikes the

Earth. Stupid, stupid me—I bragged how I was responsible, but this was before word got out how scientists searching for a cure for the RES-51 killer virus lost all their data during the crash. I mean … why didn't they back it up on a drive, or cloud, or freakin' floppy disc! Boudreaux sent trackers after me. Luckily, there aren't any photographs of me. I hate cameras!" Pith repeated, "I hate cameras," fourteen times until he believed he pronounced the three words correctly. "What you just heard is part of my OCD."

She hid feeling "freaked out" really well. "Who else has the geo-whatever storm power?"

"No one I know of. It's not something that anyone with mimicry abilities can replicate. At least, not that I'm aware of. But someone *is* trying to frame me."

"Where is Winthrop Rodanthe? Reuniting Susie with her memories might be your saving grace."

"I don't know. Since he's wanted for theft, forgery, and extortion, can turn invisible, and has no doubt logged into Susie's recall, the man is wherever he wants to be. If Susie gets them back, no matter who gives them to her, it's not going to help me. Not with all of Prime Earth out to fry me."

"But … how are you gonna make a deal with any other Rodanthe without those memories?"

He spoke with a shaky voice. "I, uh … won't. Even though I didn't know Winthrop long, I know he's the salesman type. He won't keep the recollections. He's sold them by now."

Delicately, she voiced, "You're stuck here without the ship. Rodanthe could take you home if you could find him. You should transform into a fly and follow Susie around. She's bound to find the spacecraft eventually, right?"

"Maybe. Maybe not. It might not be fit to operate depending on what was done with or to it. There is another option."

"What?"

Rennie gulped on air, nearly choking until Miss Redhead slapped his back, recommending he not drink the Lemola so fast. The soft drink wasn't the source of gagging. Nervousness over declaring the alternative decision was. *I've never declared what I'm about to say with any woman. I'd set the odds against rejection at this moment at an even fifty percent which, for me, is pretty damn amazing.*

"An alternative is gladly staying"—here it comes—"should there be a reason for me remaining. A motivation for me not wanting to leave." Shrewdly, he ironed the OCD out of his voice with a courageousness he'd never before unbound. "Do you …? Do you know what I'm talking about?"

Indeed she did. Slinking her body down in the chair and stretching the stomach upward and out, Miss Redhead formed the solacing face Pith encountered whenever he dared be romantically inclined.

"Ren," her tone was one-hundred-proof saturated in pure consoling, "I'm very good at listening. It's why I'm here with you. I'm very sorry, but I'm not looking for a dating relationship. I don't want you missing out on finding your way home, thinking we might become a couple. I have no plans of getting seriously involved with anyone until after I land a job in the cardiology profession. When you return home and clear your name, I know, I *know* … you'll find a nice girl who'll love you and who you can settle down with."

"Clear my name?" I don't think she was even listening to what I said! All that shit about "nice girl," and "love," and

"settle down," it's nothing more than the Silver Medal Shoo-Away Award women have given me when what they're really saying is, "Ren, you're not good enough for a starlet like me!" I bet she'll tell her gal friends how a loser showed up at work, begging to date her. Here I thought the Exile part would impress her.

Frowning melodramatically, he stood. *The smartest thing Miss Redhead said was that I should follow Susie, but I won't do it as a fly.*

"Well, thanks for the chat." It didn't sound at all sincere. Out of his pocket, he threw down some bills, stolen earlier. "Keep the change."

"You're angry." The way she emptied the chair and lifted reminded him of a panther ready to devour what remained of a corpse whose heart it already devoured. "What I said … if you're dead set on staying, we can always be friends. You'll need friends. Alone on Alt-Earth. Living here all my life in Halifax … I know a lotta people. And …"

Don't say it! Please, don't say it!

"… and there're several cute, single girls …"

She said it! Oh God, why did she have to say it?

"Good for them. I'm off to find Susie."

"As a fly, right?"

I shouldn't answer, but I'm too weak in the presence of beauty.

"No," he snapped. "As me. Ren Pith. Alt-Lointain must have its own version of me. I'll be him. I've had much practice at it."

"But …"

"Goodbye, [NAME DELETED], have a nice life. At least one of us will."

"But ... Ren ..."

Pith turned his back on her, mumbling crude and offensive words about the red-haired female. Nevertheless, she yelled for him not to enter the embassy, not as himself. Pride and feelings deeply injured, he heeded her not and strolled casually toward his undoing.

<hr>

THE EMBASSY RARELY FOUND USE for its holding cell. This wasn't your ordinary square room, walls painted white except for the two-way mirror. Made from dark energy, what kept Ren Pith separated from others inside the consulate was essentially a force field.

Moping, he sat on an unmovable chair created from the same quantum particles and fidgeted. Oh, how he whined when entering the coop came two Exiles and Susie Drake.

"We were just talking about you," Boudreaux claimed, studying the detainee. "*Hmm*, in the face, you resemble our Ren."

"Except ours takes better care of his hair, keeping it styled." E'tatanya cocked her head. "I haven't seen Ren dress like this man does for a few hundred years."

Beginning to stand until Theresa shook her head discouragingly, Pith droned, "I don't understand. What happened to my powers? Why didn't anyone assume I was Alt-Pith?"

Casually would define how he had set foot inside the government building, his mind plastered with different thoughts of how best he should announce himself. Too bad! Amid loud bells and flickering beams, two guards rushed in his direction, cuffing him. Shapeshifting, teleporting … he couldn't muster his trusty abilities.

"It's called a Destabilizer," Jack explained. "The machine shuts down the powers of anyone not previously DNA-registered. Your genetic information is point zero, zero, one different from your Alt counterpart. While you're in the embassy, you'll remain powerless."

Pith, having been freed earlier from his wrist restraints, pointed at Earth. "What about her? Your contraption neutralized her strengths, too, didn't it? Don't let her take me back to our universe. I'm an Exile and should have rights under any Lointain."

"I'm not *your* Susie, baby-cakes. I live on this planet. They've had my DNA for a long time." Leaning an elbow on the table, she afforded him a menacing scowl. "I go by the name Theresa Earth. You, scum, you'll go by the name Corpse once Susie takes you home to pay for your crimes."

"I am innocent! I didn't kill anyone nor am I responsible for the death of anyone. Can you or your counterpart say the same thing?"

Boudreaux pushed Theresa away from the prisoner. "You do have rights. I intend on hearing evidence for and against you."

While those words didn't lift Ren's hopes, they did make him appreciate this Boudreaux much more than the Prime version. "I don't know what proof exists other than my word against others'."

"You can begin by telling us where we can find Prime Susie's memories," E'tatanya stated.

"I gave them to Winthrop Rodanthe. I thought he could help me with my medical issues through time travel. Once he heard where and when I wanted to go, he refused any help other than returning me to my time. The bum kept the memories."

The healer continued, "Let's talk about those 'issues' later. Where can we find Rodanthe?"

He'd lied to Miss Redhead about not knowing where to find Winthrop. *It's best not disclosing all of one's secrets. Had I told her, she would've phoned the cops to get the huge reward. Things are different now. I don't mind betraying the betrayer and thief, and ... I'm running out of options.*

"Remember, I didn't have to squeal on Win. I could say, 'I have no idea where he's at.' But ... if he did as he told me he'd do, then you'll find him at the Rennaissance Fair. It's run by Remnants. Where they're located, I truly have no idea."

"I do." Theresa disclosed what she had read on the flier. "I gotta phone Susie and let her know we have pathetic Pith. Other than him, we're all going to the fair, aren't we?"

The pitiful one spoke before the Alt Exiles opened their mouths. "I can point Win out to you. Somehow, he's obtained shapeshifting powers. You won't distinguish him, but a changed face and body can't hide physical characteristics. Categorizing and memorizing body language is a specialty of mine. Please, let me come along. I promise I won't escape."

This time, E'tatanya made the interjection. "We can do as you say. I'd give you an injection of DES-44 first. Don't know what that is? It's the Destabilizer in liquid injection form. One shot, and your powers are gone for forty-four days. I also keep a vial of DES-100 handy ... the one-hundred-day remover. Your choice."

"Well, how long will I be without my abilities otherwise?"

"Depends on what happens after we capture Rodanthe." Jack addressed the green-haired physician/enchantress/dimension wanderer, "You're better trained at tracking than I. What do you suggest?"

Snapping her fingers and whispering a spell, a seventy-inch screen materialized by the west wall. "The ambassador can watch over Mr. Pith, and they can view us as we search the fair for Rodanthe. Ren, I'll equip you and him with a temporary psychic headset. If you sight him before us, give the word. Your assistance will aid your defense. Now, Sus—er, Theresa, contact Susie and her friends. Obtain their room number and tell them we'll meet them in a few minutes. Jack, are you joining us?"

He moved his head around, thumped a finger on his ear, and blinked at the ceiling. "I just canceled my appearance at what I know would be a dull conference. Yes, I'd like an audience with Prime Susie. We know so little about her world since the time of Hugh Rodanthe's chronicles."

Theresa scampered off in search of a tamper-proof HOWse connector while E'tatanya teleported away, acquiring DES and any other medicines or portions she might need for the securing of Rodanthe. In the meantime, a melancholy Pith posed a question of Boudreaux.

"Sir, if you don't mind, what is my counterpart like?"

No version of this Lointain statesman could claim being coy as an attribute. "Alt Ren Pith holds a seat on the world council. He's known for his fair judgments and contributions to children, animals, and the environment. At least once a month, I have dinner with him and his family on the north side of the city."

The moan-nosediving from his lowered head embodied a stark sadness. "Figures. No prehistoric bee ever stung him, I bet, resulting in OCD and seizures."

"*Uh*, no."

"I dread asking. Who'd he marry?"

"Angel Renaud."

Ren bawled a deafening sob. "I ... She ... massive crush on her. My idiot grandparents ... hated ... hated her skin color. Didn't like ... black people."

Handing him a paper towel in place of a tissue, Jack realized his earlier fumble, building up Alt Pith's status. "Well, I applaud your anti-racist attitude. Angel is very kind and, um, she—"

"—is much older than me. Not that it matters. I wonder how they met and fell in love."

Something ticked in Jack's mind. "Your grandparents, did either—"

His query went unfinished as both women entered the room simultaneously.

"They're waiting for us," Theresa proclaimed. "Good thing you're staying behind, Pithie. Susie wants to break you in half like a twig."

A teenage Exile stood quietly next to the healer. "This is my very shy cousin, Shy. His name is Shy. His power allows him to see through shapeshifting disguises. He won't be joining us. Crowds deplete his ability. Instead, he'll stay here and watch the screen with Ren and the ambassador and telepathically let us know if he identifies Rodanthe, whose photo he's memorized."

A psychic message from the Lointain leader brought the diplomat zipping into the detention coop. Neither he nor the suspected criminal needed training on operating the psychic headsets.

"What you'll see on the screen transmits from an ocular broadcasting power inside Jack and my eyes once we recite an incantation and switch on the ability. Meaning, you'll see what we choose for you to view, probably only at the fair."

E'tatanya nodded at Jack, who promptly teleported the search party to Suite 127 of the Randolph Motor Inn, twenty-five miles from the Rennaissance Fair.

FLANNAGAN BRUSHED OFF THE STARSTRUCK sensation when the two Exiles zapped into the room, flanking the divine Miss Earth between them. Astounded at the scope of Drake's lack of recollection retention, Boudreaux handed Karas his requests for information on the Prime worlds.

Fatigued from waiting, Susie directed the call for action. "Guys, you'll have plenty of time for the history lesson. I wanna catch Rodanthe while I can still remember why I'm pursuing the bastard! Oh yeah! Memories! C'mon; the place closes in a few hours."

"Yes, I suppose we should," Boudreaux stated. "At some point, I do want more information on Prime Lointain. I don't understand why the other me isn't in charge these days."

E'tatanya proposed disguising everyone so that Rodanthe wouldn't recognize them and flee. "This includes Liam and the lieutenant. I don't want to second-guess what our target knows or doesn't know about them."

No one protested the notion of a physical redecoration, and all of them (except Jack) raised suggestions on their temporary appearances. Come a mumbo-jumbo, foreign-word-sounding series of incantations, the sextet retained a small sampling of their birth bodies. The remaining features, E'tatanya exaggerated but remained sensitive to not indulge in too liberal of alterations.

"Neat," Susie voiced. "I always wondered what I'd look like with an olive complexion. Can I keep it, E'tty?"

"No. It would fade within a day if I left it on. Oh, and don't call me E'tty. Sounds imbecilic and immature."

Chapter 11: The Rennaissance Fair

AH, THE MEDIEVAL ATMOSPHERE, THICK with colorful costumes, vibrant theatrical performers, an array of olde world handicrafts (Remnant made, not from China or what-used-to-be-China), and the delicious aroma of pig on a spit (unless you're a vegetarian). By the looks of things— smiles, music, dancing, eating … abundant food, good cheer—the festival represented a fairly good day during the 16th century. No famine, war, disease, or empiric cruelty in sight. Why, even the jousting knights in extremely shining armor didn't die during the (staged) challenges.

Only Liam and perhaps Susie … for she couldn't recall … had never experienced one of these attempts at recreating a historical atmosphere.

Karas voiced his determination for returning home with a souvenir for Imene. His Prime Earth companion just wanted to get back home, preferably with memories regained.

"Shouldn't we split up?" Theresa asked. "We'll cover more ground that way."

"Good idea." Boudreaux's posse included Liam and Earth.

"Jack and I will receive contact from my cousin or Pith if they identify Rodanthe. He might not have altered his face too much. From what I read, he's egotistical on the issue of his physical appearance." E'tatanya nodded at Susie and Jim-

Bob. "Let's check out the fire-eater, juggler, and other one-person acts. Our man could enjoy putting on a show."

AT THE FAR END OF the grounds stood a marvelous castle.

Liam scoffed, "It must've taken them a long time setting up that monster. It sure looks real enough. They're only here a couple days; why go to all the trouble?"

"It is real, kiddo," Theresa said. "These are some of the most talented Remmies you'll find. The centaur and the winged woman dressed like a fairy that you saw along the way, all done by either mass illusion or shapeshifting." She slipped an arm around his. "So, Romeo, whatcha gonna buy for your lady back home?"

"Well, I know she'd like a set of those hand-carved stone vases for our backyard. Regrettably, they're too expensive and heavy. The spaceship has a weight limit. I'll find something smaller."

"*Mmm*, let me work on it."

Eventually, Jack—uncomfortable in his transformed skin of a heftier man—felt discouraged. "I haven't heard a peep out of Pith or Shy, and we've covered a good distance. I'm thinking we should investigate the tents. Rodanthe may be a ringmaster, or magician, or playing the part of a king."

Something shiny around a dirt trail's bend caught Liam's eye. "Looks like a boat. Or a—"

"Pirate's ship." Earth halted the trio. "It's floating in the raised pool. Kinda dinky-looking for Remmies." They moved closer. "Ah, I see now. It's for the little tikes. Ha! The phony pirates make the kids walk the plank. When they fall, a mermaid leaps up, grabs them, and puts them safely on the ground." She confessed, "I used to work one of these festivals years ago as the busty bar wench, getting my ass pinched. This kiddy ride is new. Pretty cool, eh?"

Liam broke away from his companions and studied the exterior of the buccaneer's vessel. "It's new all right. Look here." His arm reached down into the water. "See these thin lines on the metal? It's the outline of a hatch. The hull of the pirate ship is the stolen spacecraft!"

INTO JACK AND E'TATANYA'S EARS, Ren exclaimed, "It's him! Rodanthe is a pirate!"

Calmly, like the leader he is, Jack inquired, "Which pirate? There are three."

"The one with blue makeup, a light brown mustache, a long gray beard, and a dark green bandana over his head," Shy responded, incurring Pith's pissed wrath at stealing his supposed spotlight.

"I can tell by where he's standing," Pith pleasurably pronounced, "that he's the operator of the pirate vessel. Note how he's giving orders to the others and counting money. It's him all right. The scratching of his nose … it's Win's habit, and I know *all* about obsessive routines."

A jolly-faced Boudreaux led his excited team toward a display directly across from the swashbuckler pool. Inside a large glass container, a Remnant mermaid swam circles and dived up, out, and back around the miniature replica of Atlantis. Via peripheral vision, Jack noticed Long John

Rodanthe eagerly at work, unaware of his blown cover, and telepathed E'tatanya a note.

"I'm going to get his attention. You walk up from behind and jab him with a DES syringe."

"We're on our way," the healer answered, her hair temporarily colored red.

JACK'S SMILE EPITOMIZED THE SINCERITY every actor wished they could unveil. "Excuse me, sir. May I have a word with you down here?"

The trio reminded Pirate Rodanthe of the two overweight brothers and one hag sister who had once worked for the family enterprise as house cleaners. *They were very efficient despite their frightening faces. This cannot be them. Not unless they're ghosts or zombies. Wonder what they want. I don't see any children around them.*

Stepping gingerly with the fake pegleg, he neared the railing at the top of a small pile of wooden steps. "Aye, matey, how's may I be of service to ye gents and lady?"

"Well," Boudreaux began the bogus babble, "my nephew and niece, who are around here somewhere, they want to try out your ship, but both are afraid of heights and water. Their father wants to break them from these phobias. I'm wondering … when they reach this point, can you do something for us which would help immensely?"

"*Aaarrr*! Is we runnin' a rig? A joke, I means."

"More like tricking them into getting on the plank and pushed off into the pool. Let the mermaid save them once they hit the water. It oughta cure them, don't you think?"

"Blimey! You're for turnin' me reputation into the scourge o' the seven seas, ain'tcha? How old be this lad and lass?"

"The boy is eleven and the girl is ten." In the distance, he spied E'tatanya nearing at a decent pace. "Will you help and how?"

BlackRodantheBeard tugged at his phony mustache and scratched his nose. "I'll have me mates blindfold them, I will. First, they accuse the buggers of dirtying the deck after we had swabbed it good. Tell 'em, 'you're shark bait now.' How's that, Capt'n?"

"Very good! Be sure you and your mates keep the blindfolds hidden. These kids are clever, and if they get a whiff of what you're planning …"

"Blow me down … they'll try a mutiny!"

Henry "Rodanthe" Morgan began dancing, barely keeping his balance on the pegleg and singing a sea shanty, *The John B. Sails*. Liam and Theresa marveled at the man's entertainment talents while Jack preferred the disguised criminal stand still, making the DES injection from the approaching healer a simpler job. With his back to Boudreaux, the boogying buccaneer sighted the odd transformation as it occurred on the dirt path twenty feet north of the pirate vessel. Others participating in or spectating a Medieval dance-a-thon witnessed and pointed at Susie as her suggestive power began rejecting E'tatanya's face and body spell. Chants of "Susie Drake!" began choking all other noise in the summer air.

In the minds of most present, Alt Susie walked in their presence. Winthrop, not a disciple of coincidence, reasoned otherwise. *I better transform into something and get the hell outta here!* Into what? Had he even practiced shapeshifting into an animal or insect? *How hard can it be? A bee? No, a bird. I must concentrate on which bird and then do it. Hurry before Drake gets here! A robin? Blue jay? Hawk? Yes, a—*

Amidst Rodanthe's sluggish decision-making process, Prime Susie cussed beneath her breath, discerning the ruination of a once probable capture. In her frustration, she shouted, "E'tty, Jack, catch him now before he changes! Grab the weasel!"

Pride be the downfall of the egotistical and pirates. Captain William "Rodanthe" Kidd hooked his brain on the word "weasel." The insulting description caught his self-esteem and latched sharply through his mind like a trout who'd swam after a worm, oblivious to how it was bait. There was no letting go.

Black Sam "Winthrop" Bellamy transformed himself into a weasel.

RODANTHE KNEW NEXT TO NOTHING about weasels. While in Central Europe a few years ago, he had happened upon a member of the Mustelidae family while escaping authorities in the wild. The steppe polecat dashed off but not before judging the wealthy thief and yelping, seemingly informed of the young man's social misconduct and laughing about it. This memory formed his first animal transformation. Very sleek, a yellow and brown body and dark gray tail, the nearly foot-and-a-half long *Mustela eversmanii* with brown masked eyes and a human brain struggled in the heat of the moment, unsure how he should escape.

I can run off and change into a hawk once I calm myself down! Weasels ... don't they burrow? Well, not me! Winnie's claustrophobia had carried over from his dude self. Even if he knew this current form could generate an odorous spray in its defense, lifelong upper-class breeding would forbid him from harnessing the stink at those who plotted his capture. *Running, it is. I know ... to the parking lot!*

By now, he'd again utilized too much time selecting a course of action. The Exiles engaged their own plot.

"How do we catch him?" Jack asked. "I can toss a force field around him?"

"I believe a jackal will do the trick," E'tatanya answered. "I can switch into one."

"Are you going to bite him?" Boudreaux wondered. "We don't want to kill him."

"I know. I'll change you into a large fox. Seems to me they're also predators of weasels."

On and on the high-ranking Lointainians debated. Weasel-throp Rodanthe initiated a departure by scurrying under Jack's feet, toward the parking lot's direction. Working together, the Suzii inaugurated a simple, coordinated apprehension strategy. Applying their brief, run-fast power, they formed circles around the polecat and synchronized the decreasing size of the intended corral. In place of one Susie leaping atop and seizing the varmint, they never decided who would engage the downward dive. Each Drake sprung at the same moment, bumping heads, falling, thus permitting the critter to slip away.

Flannagan requested help from Karas. The men yanked down a fishing net off the side of the buccaneer display. Holding one end of the five-by-ten-foot knotted nylon snare, they raced speedily around the collapsed Suzii, casting the decorative meshwork upon the small mammal.

"Flimsy, tattered material, but it did the job." Jim-Bob watched as the struggling polecat only became more tangled as it attempted an escape. For the teasing of certain ears, he raised his voice. "Amazing what good 'ol human, non-powered ingenuity can accomplish. Isn't that so, Liam?"

"If you say so." He knew better than to offend the Suzii and the Exiles.

Boudreaux dispatched a telepathic communique to the embassy. "Ambassador, the ocular broadcasting will cease in a moment. Please have everyone remove their psychic headsets."

Bounding at the net, E'tatanya chanted an incantation designed for the unmaking of metamorphosing Remnants. Lying on his back, hands turned upward from the previous position of the weasel's paws, Rodanthe, great wastrel of time that he was, couldn't immediately adjust to the body change. Honored with the momentum advantage, the healer poked the confused man with a DES syringe, nullifying his powers for a hundred days.

A few members of the congregating audience applauded, considering what they had seen as part of an act. Everyone else wept, cheered, and thanked God on His throne for the miraculous return of Susie Drake.

"Now you know how I felt at the embassy," Theresa whispered into Drake's ear. "Glad my disguise held!"

INSIDE THE RENNAISSANCE FAIR'S operational office, a chewing out was underway via the manager. "Why'd you have to be an internationally wanted criminal, dude? You made such a convincing pirate, and everyone adored you!"

Rodanthe said nothing. A rope tied his hands together in front of him.

The potbellied administrator twirled the left edge of his imperial mustache. "I will say this … when they release you from prison, the job is still yours no matter who I hire in the meantime. When we read through the customer assessment cards the last several months, one of the persons receiving the most compliments was you."

"How many months are we talking about?" the police lieutenant asked.

"Uh, seven. Why?"

"As you probably know, Romantica police organizations have warrants out for him. I suppose he shapeshifts into a bird, flies a long distance into Europe, and commits the crimes."

"I gave up the outlaw life and trained an American who robs, forges, and extorts in my name. I'm not above giving you his name." Open-mouthed and wide-eyed, he studied Jim-Bob's face. "Damn! I *know* you! You hauled my butt in for taking a pick to old Hugh's statue. You don't give up, do you, Mister Straight Arrow?"

Fists clenched, Susie growled. "We have your accomplice, Pith, in custody. Now, where are my memories, you [EXPLETIVES ROLLING BY SO FAST THEY BLUR TOGETHER AND SOUNDING SO NASTY IT MAKES JACK BLUSH]!"

The Exiles moved between Drake and the accused.

"I'll tell you! Pith stole them in the first place. He offered them to me in return for altering the past so that a monarch bee wouldn't sting him. I didn't have any use for your memories, not then. I told Pith, 'okay, it'd take me a while,' but I could get my hands on an aerocube worthy of time travel, and if we're lucky, we'd travel back into the past, change it, create a new timeline, and return to this one.

"No, no, he didn't want another alternate universe, no matter how better it'd be for his counterpart, nor did he plan on killing the doppelgänger and taking his place. Ren wanted to alter events on Prime Lointain whereby it changed his life without giving birth to a new reality. After laughing at his notion, I explained how the ramps old Hugh used in traversing the many worlds either no longer existed or required repair. Besides, there're closed time loops, opened causal loops, and a myriad of paradoxes one must contend with when altering a quantumly layered universe such as the Prime one. Not since Hugh mettled where he shouldn't have can anyone change the physics of his work with the Prime worlds, especially before the 1976 Earth-Wizard War."

This revelation derailed Susie's plans for remodeling her history. "You still haven't told me where my memories are!"

"I'm getting there! Hey, before we continue, I want to get this pegleg off. It's killing me!"

Flannagan helped him stand. Rodanthe's real leg was bent behind him, wisely covered by the length of the dark blue, steampunk-looking leather coat, especially tailored with a wide, back vent. Several belt straps and a Velcro kneepad maintained the fake leg's position.

Once removed, Win blew an intense scud of relief. Next, he asked if someone could wipe off his pirate makeup.

"I'll wipe his entire face off!" Susie threatened.

Instead, the healer snapped a fingernail three times, and off came the cosmetics, winding up who knew where.

"Much better! Ah, I can see by the eyes of those with powers that you were unaware of my black, caramel skin shade and angular eyes." Pleased at fooling their expectation of his facial features, he explained, "My father had an affair with his wife's secretary, who originally came from Phú Quốc, a Vietnamese island. My stepmom, being liberal, insisted I become part of the family. Her sister, a bigot, thought I should've been sent to Vietnam along with Mom. Only I survived the Remnant massacre. Auntie Asshole fought the will which left me the entire estate."

"I don't care if you're a green-skinned Martian with elephant ears!" Susie proclaimed. "Don't play the I'm-different card for sympathy. It won't work. You're a con man … a rich one. Now, what became of my memories?"

"Okay … learning his plan was in defeat, Pith left me with the jar of your recollections. Much later, I signed on as a pirate. I did so to escape my past and start anew. Early on, I heard how the twelve-year-old daughter of the woman who plays the fair queen had an incurable brain disease. A Remnant psychic surgeon within the fair told me the memories of any Exile, Original, or someone in-between could cure the girl. As I was already becoming close to the mother, a fondness grew for her child. I gave your memories to the doctor, and he inserted them in the girl's mind. She's completely cured." He levied a look of contempt at Drake. "Are you gonna remove them and condemn her to death? Your past saved her with only days left in her life. Ironic, huh? Your horrific former times means a wonderful future for someone."

"Let's not get hasty," E'tatanya commented. "Where exactly can I find this girl?"

"I know who she is," the manager spoke. A holographic map of the grounds popped up above his desk. "Here, mid-center is the palace. On its right side is a large playroom where the employees' pre-teen children hang out. I can take—"

She teleported away before he could finish.

Liam introduced himself to Rodanthe before stating, "You stole our spaceship and made it into the hull of the pirate ship. The instrument panels are no doubt ruined by the pool water. No thanks to you, we're stuck here on this Earth!"

"I didn't steal it. The Staten Island Shysters sold it to me before we left Olde Boston. It had parts on it which I needed for my aerocube. The old pirate vessel was in bad need of repair and after chopping off the top of the spacecraft, it was a perfect fit." Aware he sounded crass, Win rubbed his nose and added, "I can take you and Susie home in my ship."

Skeptic sighs packed the room.

"Okay, bring Flannagan and Alt Susie along. They can make sure I return. The crimes I committed in Romantica weren't as bad as the press reported. What's the big deal?"

Over the raised voices of the Suzii and Flannagan, the manager sought clarification on one of Rodanthe's assertions. "The pirate display was *not* 'in bad need of repair.' The Remnant mermaid wondered why you replaced the old hull. She said she could swim through it and saw no structural issues. The old section is still on the grounds, waiting for us to haul it away. Why don't we inspect it?"

"Good idea," Jim-Bob proclaimed. "Oh, and while we're at it, gimme the name of the American you taught the outlaw life. I'm gonna have it sent overseas. Let the European police catch him. And … once they get back with me, we'll compare crime times over there with your whereabouts here; see if they match. I'm sure management here keeps proper records."

"I sure do," the overseer said proudly.

Rodanthe's nostrils flared. "Hey! I saved the life of a little girl! It more than makes up for anything else I did!"

"What else did you do?" Theresa asked, inducing her buoyant disposition and stepping behind the prisoner. She creeped a finger along his neckline, dipping her suggestive juices into his blood. "C'mon; what *else* did you do? Confess."

The declarations of guilt commenced with misdemeanors before entering the dastardly land of felonies. The worst of these he began by admitting, "My butchering the spaceship had nothing to do with fixing the pirate vessel. My family owns the patent rights to all non-government-run aircraft designed for leaving Alt Earth's exosphere. Old Hugh bought the permits with the money he made from the sales of his books and other memorabilia after his historic adventures on Prime Earth. Great Uncle Ulrich created an industry of airborne machines. It's the livelihood of what remains of my family. I … I did what I had to. I also placed explosives in the aerofreight vehicles on Prime Earth. Believe me; I didn't intend on harming anyone. I'm no bomb expert, and I got the timing mechanisms wrong. The Zeps were supposed to blow up during the night when not in use."

Susie shot a smile at Liam. "We gotta get this jerk back pronto. He's just cleared Sam of any guilt." Scowling menacingly, she asked Rodanthe, "Did you pick Samuel Allgyer as a patsy?"

"No. I heard the cops accused him of the bombings. Better him than me."

"There'll likely be an extradition problem," Jim said. "However, I'll hold off alerting this Earth's authorities."

"Another problem," Liam announced, "is whether his confession under Theresa's power can be admissible as evidence."

"It will once I shake hands with the judge," Susie predicted, adding, "and hopefully, he won't know anything about my powers!"

E'TATANYA'S RETURN TERMINATED THE heated discussion on courtroom behavior, tampering with people's minds, and the extent to which one went to achieve justice. "I found the girl, spoke with her parents, and reached a way in which she and you, Susie, should find satisfaction."

Everyone in the room listened intently.

"The Remnant psychic surgeon performed a brilliant job. Inserting memories from a donor can turn out disastrous. The doctor ostensibly owned no notion of whose recollections he would attach into the child's brain."

"I thought it best not to tell him," fell another Rodanthe confession.

"Considering what I've since learned, it was probably the best course of action. Susie's times of violence haunted the girl. With relative ease, I removed the harmful sections and replaced them with magic-generated, generic, happy reminiscences. But not before I made a complete copy of Susie's background up until the time my Prime counterpart removed them." On the end of the healer's right hand, a round, green and orange light suddenly popped into reality, rolling along her knuckles. Within the illumination, blue and yellow gears turned every which way. "Step forward, Susie."

Not a word did she offer nor a discernable expression. A scant three inches separated the two women when the circular orb touched Drake's forehead. *Gasps! Gasps!* In the eyes of those assembled, Susie's hair and cranium vanished, leaving her brain in plain view.

"Watch now, peoples, as I reestablish the unconnected rememberings."

Sliding a finger above the patient's head, the healer guided psychic energy above and into the brain. A flash of deep white light—*flash! ...flash!*—and the onlookers' vision adjusted accordingly, blinking as green and orange sparkles lit up the complex organ. Another second passed, as did the visibleness of the gray matter.

Susie felt tickles dancing along her mind and scratched her scalp. "I could've sworn my hair disappeared."

"Just an illusion," E'tatanya confirmed. "Everything's there, especially your memories. Try them now."

Recollections were heavy things. Thumbing through the past too quickly could cause blisters on the mind and make one seek salve for the soul. Susie's eyelids fluttered dreamily. Sounding almost robotic, she openly defied an edict earlier proclaimed by a voice inside her head.

"Ah ... Jay, don't you dare delete these names ... Tom Connors ... Rebecca Russell ... Harold Hogan ... John Lunsford ... Lucy Griffin-Curtis ... Vaughan Rogers ... Roman Bresner. My very good friends!"

I won't cry, she demanded. *I mustn't cry.* The sight of her mother's precious face slammed hard against her heart. Fingernails dug deep into her palms. *They murdered you, Mom. I was there when it happened. Why didn't I stop them?* She remembered with ease, *Her killers shot me, too, and everyone considered me dead for a while.*

Accompanying the recall was a feeling of regret. *I treated Theresa badly back at Austin Hall.* When reviewing dozens of particular memories, she felt key sensations reemerge, emotions previously associated with those recollections—compassion, empathy, forgiveness, the craving for companionship, and the desire to love and be loved in return. *It was a mistake having those remembrances removed. The best thing about them being back is knowing who and what I took for granted and appreciating them in the present. I can't let myself act nonchalantly detached from my new friends.*

Drake's hands squeezed either side of her head. "It's too much for me to take in at once. I gotta get a grip on the here and now. But, uh, thank you, E'tatanya. The girl ... will she be okay?"

"She's in no danger. Susie, who's Jay and how could he delete the names you mentioned?"

Even the mention of *that* name couldn't dampen her mood of having old memories back in their rightful place, snuggling up with the new ones. "He's a long, disgusting story." Moving right along, she asked, "What's our plan now?"

The answer arrived in the form of a teleport back inside the embassy.

A disheartened sigh escaped from the manager. "The wife'll kill me. I didn't even get a single photo with my

EyePhone." Walking a circle around his desk, lips tight, an idea pounced inside his head. "Susie made a big impression here today. She wasn't alive during the 16th century. Doesn't mean we can't have a Susie display. Yes … I can see it now. Amazon warrioresses, all dressed in skimpy outfits, carrying swords, spears, and bows and arrows. I'll present them as a Greek tribe sent over to combat English knights! Yes … it will most definitely work!"

THE EMBASSY HOLDING CELL GREW crowded when seven people zapped into place, scaring Shy.

"Ten of us crammed together is nine too many. May I return to Lointain, sir?"

"You may," Jack said, "and thank you for your help." And quickly, there were nine.

"Much as I'd like to stay, I have responsibilities elsewhere," the envoy declared. He bid farewell to everyone except Susie, at whom he glared, believing her to be Theresa. And fast-like, there were eight.

Despite Lt. Flannagan preferring they place the two suspects in separate interrogating areas, Theresa led Rodanthe into a chair across the table from Pith. The one-time partners nodded at each other while E'tatanya withdrew the phony face and body concealments and dispensed with the computer screen.

"Two Susies," Pith breathed. When he said, "Great," it sounded dipped in a doom of his own making.

"Don't worry; where you'll end up, you won't be seeing us or any females for a long time, although you'll be fantasizing about us. Until then, call me Susie and her Theresa." Behind Ren, she strolled, deploying a finger on his shoulder. "Your pal's under the suggestive power of this world's version of me and now you're under mine. You can't help but tell the truth." Setting her rump atop the edge of the table, Drake addressed the men who couldn't fib. "Which one of you murdered or paid someone to kill Isabella Raven?"

Pith leaped upward, arms flailing and eyes bigger than pancakes. "Isabella … dead? No! It can't be! Why …? Why would anyone kill her?" The man who knew Raven best broke into tears.

Theresa handed him a paper towel, wondering why there weren't any softer tissues handy. An explanation of how the girlfriend had died slipped slowly from Susie's mouth, rousing a self-hatred commentary out of his quivering orifice.

"Shit! She died because I cared for her, and she dared to be my friend." In rapid succession, he slapped his face hard eighteen times. Attempts to stop the self-punishment were met with shouts, commanding him to cease. "Leave me alone! I must hit myself eighteen times without interruption or else do it all over again." Sniffing, wiping away tears, he offered, "I would never harm her. Never!" Entering Suspicion City, he steered his Ford Distrust around and turned the headlights on Rodanthe. "You! You killed her! The acquaintance we have in common, the bartender, he told me how you thought Isabella was a psycho! How could you even have an opinion about her? She never said anything about meeting you."

"Calm. Down. Okay? I'm sorry about your girlfriend. I had nothing to do with her death, and I never said she was a psycho. That viewpoint came from the barman. *He* knew her.

They used to go to the same high school. The guy buddied up to you because you're an Exile."

Clearing his throat for the insertion of a steady voice, Liam said, "The bartender vanished after the Feds spoke with him regarding thefts involving you, Pith. You do admit to those break-ins, don't you?"

"Yes. I enjoyed taking from the wealthy. I had no choice! My OCD voice told me to do it, or else it would remain with me for one hundred and eighteen more years. I became very good at thievery. Susie's memories, my shrink's transcripts, money here on Alt-Earth …" Ren wiped tears off his face. "Isabella … I-I still can't believe it."

Jim asked Pith, "Do you think the bartender could have killed her?"

"No. Considering the content of the conversation Liam and Susie had with her, no. The person I met down the street at the bar was Rodanthe, who was using an alias." Seven times his right hand pushed his hair up and over and afterward performed the same ritual seven times with his left hand. "Whenever we'd meet at the tavern, our talk concerned time travel and me changing my past."

"How about you, Rodanthe?" Flannagan inquired. "Could the mixologist be the murderer?"

"I knew the guy before Pith did. It was me who introduced them. His brother had worked for the Thrusks and died in an industrial accident at one of their factories. He helped me when I needed the explosives for the Zeps. That's why he disappeared. He wouldn't do anything stupid like assassinate a woman who had nothing on him." Suddenly, his pirate ship came aground in Suspicion City. Standing on the plank, raking his nose with a dirty finger, he eyed a shark circling the boat. The great white leaped out of the water, shouting, "Isabella was a psycho! She never told me her problems, so I had to tell her mine." How could he have forgotten? "I … I take it back. Pith's girlfriend would check up on him at the bar, asking who he'd met with. I guess she wanted to be sure he wasn't cheating on her. During those visits, she and the bar dude relaunched their old friendship. Just friends, nothing more, but he'd confess the work he'd done for me. It's a valid enough reason for a killing—knocking her off so he doesn't get blamed for the aerofreight explosions."

"Does this fellow have a name?" Theresa asked. "You guys keep calling him by his professional title."

Rodanthe laughed. "I never knew his real name, but he had it legally changed to Bar T. Ender. Should we call him Mr. Ender for you?"

"Wise ass," Miss Earth spat.

"I have the real name on my computer back home," Liam offered. "Not that I'll ever return, unless someone can fix the spaceship."

"There are ways of getting you home without a spacecraft," E'tatanya slyly volunteered.

SEVEN PEOPLE HAZARDED TO TALK at the same time, questioning the mighty mage's statement. Boudreaux's timbre sounded the most forceful.

"How exactly would you return anyone to Prime Earth?"

"Before I answer, are there more unresolved issues we should clear? I can think of two."

Theresa thumped a finger on Pith's shoulder. "This guy claimed he's not responsible for anyone's death. I didn't use my power on him, so I don't know if he was telling the truth." The same finger thumped against his head. "Let's hear it officially since you can't lie. Are you responsible for the geomagnetic storm which resulted in the deaths of a few billion people?"

Emphatically, he shouted, "No! I'd rather kill myself than hurt a single, innocent person. I admit I've been a thief, nothing worse."

"Any idea who might've caused the storm? A mimicker? Another Exile?" Theresa pursued.

"No. I would've said something a long time ago if I did."

Rodanthe sensed a bunch of eyes descending on him. "I didn't do it, nor do I know who did. I heard about it, though, and figured Ren was the culprit."

Dripping with sarcasm, Pith exhaled, "Thanks, pal." At the healer, he remarked, "When I mentioned my medical issues earlier, you said we'd talk about them later. How about now?"

She planted an opposite-facing chair in front of the table and next to the Prime Exile. "Let's hear it."

Much as the room's non-detainees couldn't offer sympathy for the powered thief, they did begin altering their attitude toward him once they'd heard a lengthy tirade about his past and current health matters. The consensus formed on how well the (relatively) young man had hidden his ailments, although no one present could testify to having experience with or knowing anyone who battled epilepsy or OCD.

"I'm surprised my Prime equivalent has no access to a living or dead monarch bee," E'tatanya announced. "I suppose the Alt version of other worlds can be very different. I shall return shortly with a specimen."

Ptoof! Ptoof! She dematerialized, leaving an open-mouthed Boudreaux with a question stuck on his tongue.

UPON HER RETURN, THE GREEN-HAIRED healer unfolded her left hand, uncovering a purple cube containing a large, immobile yellow and blue bee. "The violet color is a gas, keeping the dead insect in pristine, undecomposed condition and all the better for extracting its spiritual blueprint. By inserting the orange wax into Mr. Pith's bloodstream with a syringe, it removes all traces of the virus in the nervous system from the original stinger. A little magic helps, too." After a fast smile, she went on, "I will withdraw the wax with a different needle and apply an energy called Vetiti24 and with it, a healing incantation. The Vetiti will be what keeps the seizures from reoccurring and the mind from giving way to obsessive-compulsive thoughts and habits." Addressing her rapt audience, she asked, "Is there any reason why I shouldn't cure this man of what ails him?"

"How about for shits and giggles?" Susie quipped in order to achieve a laugh which never came. "Hey, he *did* steal my memories. Look at all the headaches it caused."

"You also undertook an incredible journey," Theresa countered, flexing her buoyant disposition, "met some interesting people—moi included—captured a killer ... even if he didn't mean to kill ... and got your memories back without a little girl losing her life. I'd say it caused some good times, too."

Jack stepped forward. "Go ahead and perform the procedure. When you're done, I want to hear all about getting the Primers home without the use of a spaceship."

Excerpts from the journal of Liam Karas, sometime in July:

ALT E'TTY HAD ASKED US ALL to leave the room while she tended her patient. Rodanthe remained, cuffed to the table. When she called for us back, I couldn't tell any noticeable difference in Pith, although he smiled more and acted less stiff.

"I feel lighter," he told us. "Like a weight's been lifted off my shoulders. I don't have the need to think anything in particular, especially not thinking a certain word or words over and over again until they all sound perfect. It could just be my mind playing tricks on me."

"Give it time," E'tty said. Dropping a hand on his head, she asked him to sit perfectly still. "Blink. Blink ... faster, slower, now normal." She snapped her finger, and a strobe light appeared in mid-air a few inches from his face. Bursts of bright flashes strobed, pulsating at various speeds of duration. Minutes went by. "Do you feel dizzy or sense a seizure or aura coming on?"

When he responded, "Nope," Ren joyfully popped the letter "p." "Normally, I'd have a seizure by now."

A green and orange cube abruptly manifested over Pith's head, circled the skull a dozen times, and thereafter floated toward the physician.

"It conducted a test equal to an EEG and an MRI scan. Your brain activity is normal. From what you related of my Prime self's assessment, there should have been a scar on the left temporal lobe. I saw none."

Jim asked, "What's gonna happen now?"

"My Lointainian companion is going to tell us her means for traveling to Prime Earth." Boudreaux formed a come-through hand signal.

"Jack." E'tty drew out the 'a' in his name in a you-should-know-better kind of way. "You're aware of how I journey through the universe in various forms. Not just our known space but micro-galaxies, near and distant dimensions, branches of multi-string worlds orbiting suns where time doesn't exist, and places for which our language contains no words on how to describe who or what resides there. With this in mind, do you really think it difficult for me whisking away to Prime Earth and Lointain?"

By his tightened lips, I'd say he wasn't thrilled with her keeping these facts secret. "You might have shared this important knowledge earlier. Think of all we could learn by contact with our other selves."

I barged into the conversation with a query. "Can Prime E'tty travel here? She helped with our obtaining the spaceship, but why even bother if she could've gotten us here in whatever way you'll take us back?"

"You need to ask her. Could be that they're stricter regarding space-time travel rules. Maybe she keeps it secret from her Jack, or perhaps she's never had the means of getting from here to there. Now," she said, louder for all to hear, "unless there's a reason not to, we can go there at this moment. Given what we've discovered from Mr. Pith and Mr. Rodanthe, I'd say the time for travel is upon us."

Returning to the room from the small foyer, Susie snapped her fingers at the Exile head honcho. "Hey, Jack, out in the corridor, there's a 3-D holograph chart showing the entire lineage of Lointain's first one hundred families. It matches the Prime version up to 1951, right?"

"Later. 1951 is when this Earth broke away from yours. My world didn't register any changes until early '53 through the design which, as you now can recall, was our

way of reading the timelines of specific mortals. Why do you ask?"

Already, her eyes shifted in a way I read as "a-ha!" The fashion in which confidence swarmed around her mannerisms raised goosebumps up my back.

"C'mere a sec. I wanna show you something." Soon afterward, she motioned for E'tty and Theresa and to haul the two prisoners along with them.

From the back of the holding cell, I could hear a vivid discussion at the hallway's entrance. Susie pointing here and there, voicing comments which (so it gave the impression) thrilled and infuriated Pith, also bringing out a very majestic deportment in Boudreaux.

Upon their return at the table, Susie addressed Flannagan and me. "We're heading to Prime Lointain, then Earth. Jim, I reckon you'll wanna come along since Rodanthe will be going. I expect the police in my world will charge him with involuntary manslaughter, among other crimes. As a representative of this planet, there'll be documents for you to sign and bring back here. I'm not sure how much red tape we'll face, but I'll make sure our Boudreaux helps, along with a New York Remnant cop I'm friends with."

Jim-Bob paced the floor. "It's gonna take more than document signing to smooth things out. It may require these Boudreauxs to speak with the commissioner and the prime minister of Romantica. Can you deal with that part of it?"

"Sure. I'm not gonna let you get into trouble."

"How long will we stay—" I didn't even finish my sentence before Drake halted me.

"You'll be back with Imene soon enough."

After a quick confer by Jack with the ambassador, E'tty made us huddle in a circle. "I'm transmitting an astrocelestimuclar greeting at Prime Lointain. We don't want one of the Lennixx attacking us when we transfer through the world's protective border." She awaited a reply while I wanted to ask about the astro-thingmajig. Too late. She had received a response. "We are go. Everyone breathe easy, relax, and please, no vomiting."

Green and orange bands of light circled the group, diminishing us a little bit at a time. The experience made me feel queasy, disoriented, and terribly homesick. Within minutes, I'd be closer to Mason, and off an Earth I could never call home.

Chapter 12: Trials & Taped

Tribulations

PERFECTLY, THEY TOUCHED DOWN UPON Prime Lointain soil. No one upchucked. Only the Exiles didn't stumble dizzily, struggling to stay upright. Laid out before them was the city which held the same name as the planet. Only one dazzling metropolis adorned the floating world, although a few small villages dotted the vast outlying countryside and jungles. Every one of the eight persons gathered had either lived in, visited, or seen photos of the community dispersed beyond the forest edge where they stood.

Built at the bottom of a massive mountain, the urban architecture, like its inhabitants, defied time. Rustic, Medieval, modern, and futuristic styles all congregated in a stew of agelessness. The shapes, sizes, and designs of homes, shops, and buildings presented a mishmash of structural planning, coordinated perhaps by the citizenry of Earth's nations and cultures. Yes, the once exiled peoples who lived in the colorful megacity owed much to the blue globe below, even if they rarely gave thanks to any Earthling.

Thirty feet behind the octet, inside a grassy clearing, a man and a woman suddenly manifested themselves from thin air.

"We are here," the female issued.

"I expect a very justifiable explanation for this unprecedented and unlawful breach of my world's boundaries," the male harshly voiced.

Jim-Bob chuckled. "First, we get two Susies, now two Boudreauxes and E'tatanyas!"

He and his company acted upon their better senses, not remarking how Alt Jack's temples were grayer than his equivalent, and Prime E'tatanya didn't have the single line below her eye as did her twin.

THE ALT HEALER (E'TTY2) COMPLETED a thorough account of the reasoning behind the odyssey from one universe into another, including Susie's last-minute discovery. "Helping us is also in your best interest, Jack." These words she directed at Prime Boudreaux (Jack1). "Perhaps relations between your world and Earth can heal once we sort out the treacherous mess."

"'Treasonous' is a better adjective," Jack1 stated, agreeing he'd help.

"Count me in, too," E'tty1 volunteered.

"You mages," Jack1 began, "I don't welcome the fact you kept the ability to time travel a secret. Something could have gone terribly wrong. Who knows what kind of disease *she* might've brought here and vice versa?"

"Hear, hear!" Jack2 voiced. "I'm thrilled we agree." The men shook hands.

Theresa spun her eyes. "Two Boudreauxes of a feather stick together!"

"What I wanna know," the one and only Liam Karas launched, "is why, uh, Prime E'tty, didn't you teleport us to the correct timeline of the Alt-verse in the first place? It would've saved us so much trouble."

She eyed the Earthling with patience and kindness. "As you just heard, Jack was unaware such transportation existed. Had I mentioned it right before your voyage or even years earlier, I imagine all sorts of red tape would've delayed the journey. Going forward, I anticipate the world council or an off-shoot committee will be in charge of approving universetrotting."

"I prefer we keep the knowledge of such passages under wraps," Jack1 declared. "A pilgrimage to present-time Alt universe for emergency reasons could be deemed reasonable in a council forum. However, since a correlation already exists with the future setting, it may be the only feasible travel destination. Entering their past and meddling with history can result in serious consequences."

Edging his way forward, Pith bestowed E'tty1 a hostile stare. "Etty2 came into possession of a Monarch bee and cured me of epilepsy and OCD. She did in minutes what you couldn't do in eighty-four years. How come?"

Once the E'ttys had traded contact information, E'tatanya1 replied, "I'm sorry. It never occurred to me to ask her about the bee and, obviously, she has access to medical and healing properties unavailable to me. I can skirt the blame, saying, 'You and I didn't associate much after you were stung.' I accept the responsibility for not doing everything I could. I ask for your forgiveness."

Surprising himself, he shook her hand. "I've been waiting eighty-four years for an apology. I'm seeing things differently already. I forgive you."

Sighing extra loud, Susie spoke up, "When do we get down to the current business? Hopefully, before eighty-four years go by."

"Patience," Jack1 said. "To achieve our goal once I call a council meeting, we're going to need more proof than just the word of Mr. Pith and Mr. Rodanthe. This will call for our Alt allies and their captive to return home, bringing back the information required. In the meantime, E'tatanya of this realm, I want you to access our suspect. Find out if he indeed possesses the dangerous ability before we make the accusation."

"What about us?" Liam formed a circle with his finger, indicating Theresa, Jim, and himself. "Do we stay here? I really wanna go home and let Imene know I'm okay."

"You can't do it yet." E'tty2 strode up to Karas. "From what I've learned of your trip, you have only been gone less than a week. In coming here, you've drifted back in time a week. On your Earth, you haven't left on your quest yet, and you certainly don't want to run into yourself."

E'tty1 added, "Lointain time runs slower than Earth. Stay here a few days. When you do go home, it'll all work out fine."

THREE LONG, LOINTAINIAN DAYS LATER, Susie and her motley crew had supplied the proof Jack1 required for inaugurating an objective with far-reaching consequences, should it succeed. No one else owned awareness of the presence of the octet who had journeyed from a different cosmos. When not collecting evidence, Jack2 and E'tty2 camped in a wilderness region east of the city. The Suzii watched over the handcuffed prisoners, who futilely debated against the wrist shackles, arguing they had nowhere to go and therefore wouldn't escape. Liam and Jim enjoyed the spare rooms of Jack1's downtown home, abundantly furnished with a massive variety of reading material.

All the Earthlings who hadn't already seen it concurred how the building housing the representatives' forum space reminded them of photos of long unused TV rabbit ears. On the morning of the hastily scheduled meeting, Jack1 reserved a lounge in the sideways construction for six guests, none of whose names appeared on the day's quickly printed agenda.

Entering the darkened chamber, Luther Fontenot turned around, posing a question. "I'm not happy coming here without first knowing why. You said it was important, Boudreaux. How so?"

"I'll tell you once everyone's here." He walked in front of the Exile leader. "There's no point in repeating myself."

The response irked the other man. "The point *is* I rule this world now, not you, not any longer, and I'm entitled to know what business comes before the council, which I head! And for God's sake, turn on the lights! I don't wanna trip in the dark."

"I'm heading for the light switch now."

The coordinated confinement came off like clockwork. Jack1 flipped the controls and on poured the lights. Unseen at the doorway, E'tty1 jabbed Luther with a hypodermic containing DES 10.

At the onset of a brighter room, something odd had drawn Fontenot's attention—a tall, four-sided object in the chamber's center, its edges painted light blue. These things happened almost simultaneously—he recognized the block as a force field cell, felt first the sharp needle enter his skin, followed by two hands pushing him into the jail. Sealing the cube telekinetically, Boudreaux1 also opened air vents at the top of the structure.

"What is the meaning of this?" Luther screamed. "Let me outta here right now!"

"Keep calm. Your freedom depends on how the council rules."

"I'll ban you from Lointain forever, Boudreaux! This is treason!" Squirming, he reached a hand toward his backside where the needle had penetrated the Exile's normally hardened skin. His peripheral vision seized the green-haired shamaness. "You … you've taken an oath to help people. What did you do to me?"

"Froze your powers for ten days. No shapeshifting or teleporting."

"You're banned, as well, E'tatanya." All attempts to rouse his super-skills were unsuccessful. "Such a waste of enormous talent. Both of you. My family will not sit by and let you detain me nor will the council."

"Aha." Jack1 pointed a finger directly in front of him, toward a metal sliding door. Again deploying his minor ability of telekinesis, his mind unlocked the gate and pushed it in each direction from the middle outward. Another cube, this one with pink-painted edges, came into view. "Your wife, Luther. Edna has been here for almost an hour, waiting. She, too, has had her powers nullified for ten days."

The married couple communicated vigorously between themselves over the fifteen-foot gap between force fields. "Don't worry, dear; once the council convenes, they'll free us and toss these traitors where we now stand. This is mutiny! A clear and present affront to the tight ship I run! These two weasels exist on borrowed time!"

Listening from another room, Jack2, Theresa, and Jim laughed at Luther's words. One of them recalled a time not long ago near a certain pirate vessel.

"Fontenot has it backward, kiddos," Theresa said. "It'll be him and the missus walking the plank."

SIX COUNCILMEMBERS AND FOUR alternates entered the chamber. Each one, earlier apprised of the situation, none of whom felt comfortable with the citizens' arrest of the planet's leader and his spouse. Jack1 and E'tty1 had replaced the traditional large, round table where the councilpersons sat with ten chair-attached platforms, complete with writing paper for the secretary and any notetakers.

"My friends," Luther at the assemblypersons bellowed, "you people are definitely sane! Please, free Edna and me from these cells. Madness has swelled the minds of Boudreaux and E'tatanya. They locked us in here for no reason. Surely, you won't allow it to continue."

In the middle of the legislative hall, the cocoa-skinned woman, dressed all in white, addressed the accusers. "Did neither of you inform the Fontenots of the charges?" Angel Renaud asked.

"No," Jack1 responded. "We wanted them informed once the hearing was well underway. Let the element of surprise bedazzle them."

"As acting chairperson," Angel announced, "we'll do it your way, Jack. Just know that neither you nor your accomplice will have a vote in the judgment."

"Have you also taken leave of your senses?" Luther shouted. "You cannot lock us up without first filing the legal claims, and then having the council decide whether the charges have merit. Besides, the green-haired witch used a DES potion on my wife and me, rendering us powerless. Why even keep us in these jails?"

E'tty1 answered, "Because you have powerful allies who might attempt a rescue."

"Luther," the chairwoman began, "if the evidence presented begins to favor you, I will have the fields taken down. But remember, with the DES inside you, I can read events inside your mind which you might otherwise have protected with power or magic. And"—she pointed at the bespeckled man beside her—"Aristede Pre'vost, sitting in for his brother, Alex, can tell lies when they're told. This is why I expect this meeting won't last long."

The Fontenots kept their composure while asking a second time for the reading of the charges against them, hiring a lawyer, and time to prepare a defense.

Renaud shook her head. "You know speedy trials are our tradition. It's not like we hold court very often. Lawyer? Really! I admire your tactical delay strategy. Only Earth has lawyers and how many would defy the ban on associating with us to come here? Very few. I will allow your calling forth witnesses, should you have any." Addressing Jack1, she directed, "You may begin."

Mindful of how his testifier listened in from another room, he called for Susie Drake. She entered the chamber amid much chatter, carrying a remote control and grabbing hold of a small stool, and sat in front of the council. Angel instructed her colleagues to refrain from asking Drake questions unrelated to the case, at least until the hearing ended.

"Susie," Jack1 started, "please show us the holograms which attracted your attention."

A button pressed on the clicker resulted in a beam creating a 3-D hologram in a manner thoroughly viewable by all, no matter where they sat. Via a function in the manmade teleportation gene of every Exile, the spectators could move the holo-outline closer for better viewing, if necessary.

"This chart displays the lineage of Lointain's first one hundred families from the time this world came into existence until now. It's a copy of the same image on display in every Lointainian government office." Another key pushed sent an ostensibly parallel diagram next to the other. "You might think you're seeing the same table twice. Wrong! The new pop-up is from Alt Lointain."

"Is she telling the truth?" a councilmember asked. "From *Alt Lointain*?"

"Yes, she's told the truth," Aristede confirmed.

Scrolling down through the ancestries of both diagrams by use of a pen, Drake stopped at 1856. "Lookie here. I'll highlight the differences in yellow on either surface. Okay, that's done. *Hmm.* 'Luther and Edna Fontenot.' It gives your birth years, parents and family names, maiden name Daigle, blah blah blah. Ah, powers! Teleporting, every Exile has that. Shapeshifting is a predominant ability for the Fontenot and Daigle clans." She yawns. "Nothing off at this point between the opposite worlds and nor should there be until 1953 when the two Lointains steered onto alternate paths. Right, Luthy?"

The reigning leader sneered at the lovely one. "Don't call me 'Luthy!' What you say is true, but I see no proof that these charts are from anywhere but this Lointain."

"You'll get your proof, Luthy. Now … what've we here? On the Alt hologram, check out this additional listing. *'A uniting of their metamorphic powers with magic from the Navajo Indians and the Celtic Púcaí generated a separate being for Luther and Edna. Neither cloneable duplicates nor birth-detached doppelgängers, these other selves live and reproduce without an attachment to the originals but cannot occupy the same space whereas the strongest will push out the breath of the other. Known as the Eaftós, these selves possessed the forms of Abner and Ada Pith. The Piths, members of the Exile community since the 10th century, signed a contract with the Fontenots, assuring their loyalty to the stronger pair in exchange for preferential treatment of their family when possible.'"* After waiting for the committee to digest this data, Drake persisted, "You won't find what I read on the Prime chart. It should be there. Everything is supposed to match up before '53. The reason it doesn't, you can chalk up to Luther traveling back in time and deleting it."

Knuckles rapped against the impenetrable pen. *Rap! Rap!* "This is an outrage! I did not delete anything on the Heritage Hologram!"

"He speaks the truth," Pre'vost revealed.

"Do you deny traveling back in time to 1856?" Susie questioned.

Fontenot's face reddened, feet stomped, and fingers formed fists. "This so-called trial is a sham! Fixed! Boudreaux, E'tatanya, Renaud, Pre'vost … these are people and families long associated with the early Lointain council. They're all friends and would support one another to the death! The stench of bias seeps through this force field and chokes me! I cannot receive a fair hearing."

A rumble of agreement stirred in the council, disheartening Angel. "Luther, there are one hundred and thirteen truth detectors among the population. You say Aristede is prejudiced against you? Select your own verifier. Pick two or three, should it please you. As for myself, I will hand over the temporary leadership role to whomever you want."

"Fine," he said smugly. "I have two cousins I trust as a scrutineer, and replacing you, I—"

"Oh, shut up, Luther!" Edna finally spoke. "No one's going to lie for you. Blood is not thicker than water!"

AT AN AGE SLIGHTLY BEYOND three-hundred and fifty years, Edna didn't look a day over thirty-five. No wrinkles lined her face, and the way she carried herself screamed youthfulness. Staring out of her cosmic confines, all indications leaned toward a negative judgment, leading to banishment from Lointain and the permanent revoking of powers. It was not the sort of future her husband had promised when they had married in 1830.

"I want it placed in the record that there's no need for changing anyone where the hearing is concerned." She couldn't make eye contact with Jack1. "I'm sorry about what happened. It wasn't my idea."

"*You traitor!*" her husband thundered. "You sure didn't complain about all the perks you received from being married to the leader of this world!"

"Shut up, Luthy." Susie snickered. "Let's hear what the lady has to say."

Mrs. Fontenot asked for and received a chair and a bottle of water. "It begins in 2035. Ren Pith is responsible for the blackout in Russia and China via his geomagnetic storm. He's the grandson of our other selves."

"It makes him your and Luther's grandson, too," E'tty1 established.

"Maybe yes, maybe no. I'll get there soon enough. What Ren did angered his parents. They exacted much of the blame on the grandparents, Abner and Ada, over the Monarch bee stinging the boy back in 1974 and the subsequent lack of medical care. It was the prehistoric insect prick which gave him the power for conjuring geomagnetic weather. About the Piths"—she nearly spat out the name—"our sole way of communicating with them *was* telepathy. Luther and Abner communicated quite a bit. Ada and I rarely spoke. We had nothing in common."

"Why are you talking about them in the past tense?" Boudreaux1 asked. "They're not dead."

Impatience showered her tone. "Let me finish, please! The widescale power failure fueled ideas in both Abner and my husband. Pith wanted to be rid of Ren, cruel as it sounds. He'd also received a bee sting in '74. It'd given him a milder case of OCD and a stronger dose of the storm ability. You can probably see where I'm going with this but don't interrupt."

Close by, Ren's loathing of his grandfolks skyrocketed while news of the depth of Abner's ailment beckoned the advance of vindication.

"My partner despised our social status. It never bothered me—no Fontenot on the world council. We both held distinguished positions in businesses and on committees. Luther never missed a chance to forge an enterprising opportunity. He's on the board of many companies, and we own more private land in Lointain than anyone." Standing slowly, she moved toward the side nearer Mr. Fontenot's cube and yelled, "You ruined everything we built! I told you how somebody would see through your scheme! I'm leaving you, Luther!"

His mind told his body, "slump your shoulders, give her the devasted posture." The body revolted, telling the mind it should say these words: "You approved the strategy and made viable suggestions. Quit acting innocent." Eyeballing E'tty1, he added, "I'm taking over the narrative from here."

"BEFORE I BEGIN," LUTHER SAID, re-energized after counter-accusing his wife, "and still not knowing the charges against me, I'll drop the requests for my cousins and a different council leader if you'll be reasonable, Angel, and tell me what I've allegedly done and show me the evidence."

Conferring with E'tty1 and Jack1, Susie favored sticking with Edna as the testifier. "She'll give us what we wanna know," the blonde whispered. "The hubby's gonna pull some tricks."

"Let's show some tricks of our own," Boudreaux1 murmured. "Have our evidence present the charges."

INTO THE CHAMBER WALKED THE accusers, one at a time, each identifying themselves.

"Hi. I'm Winthrop Rodanthe from the 24th century of Alt Earth." Waving, smiling at the jails, he continued, "Hello, Mr. and Mrs. Fontenot. Great seeing both of you again." He bowed to the council. "I loaned them the use of my aerocube in 2035 on Prime Earth. The ship's automatic and tamper-proof log showed they went back in time to 1856, near where Kelowna would one day be. I can't tell you who they met or what they did other than they were very close to Lointain."

After Rodanthe occupied a seat in the small gallery section behind the assembly members, Ren Pith's appearance startled those familiar with him. "Yeah, you know who I am. I never hurt anyone. Can you say the same, Eaftós grandparents? You, Luthy, you and Scab-ner are responsible for the deaths of over three billion people. It sure as hell wasn't me!"

Next, Jack2 and E'tty2 calmly established their distinctiveness. "I attest to the authenticity of the hologram," Boudreaux2 claimed. "In my world, even though the chart links the Fontenots with the Piths, very few people know or care about the connections. Edna is on the world council; Luther runs several successful businesses on Earth and Lointain. Abner and Ada help run a reserve for nearly extinct animals in the planet's southernmost region. I hear tell how this Lointain's Piths have the same jobs. And, um, our Ren is also on the council and is married to Angel Renaud."

Prime Angel winked wickedly at Ren who, cured of the OCD, interpreted the gesture as sweet playfulness instead of a sexual come-on. But then again …

Quietness cocooned Jim-Bob, wondering what he should say. "Um, NYC police Lieutenant Jim Flannagan of Alt Earth. I'm here because of Rodanthe, who admits his bombs destroyed Zeps on Earth below. Uh, well, thanks."

Last but not least, Theresa paraded in, curtseying, obviously being flippant. "I just came along for the ride, kiddos, and when I return home, I wanna bring back a crateload of Dr. Pepper's. Yeah!"

LUTHER STILL FELT CONFIDENT. *I didn't do anything truly bad. Hmm.* A tired excuse. *Rodanthe's attendance is a setback. Pith seems determined to co-blame me for the geo-storm. I'm certain I can cast all the responsibility elsewhere, on a married couple who cannot possibly testify.*

"You should have the Piths in here, Miss Renaud. Their share of the guilt for circumstances involving casualties and injuries rates substantially higher than anything brought about by Edna and me. The inquiry you're conducting will be incomplete without them. Considering we have guests here from a future of Alt Lointain, how hard would it be collecting two local persons who've played pivotal roles in what you seek to uncover?"

Angel stretched her arms across her podium. "You've made an excellent point." Three minutes later, E'tty1 exited the room by teleport, and the chairwoman continued. "She's on her way to the Piths' compound. Before bringing them back, she will remove their powers with DES1. While we wait, please embark on giving us your story."

As his wife did, he requested a chair and water. "Even before the 2035 G-storm, I sought more Lointainian land. The many mountains in this world come loaded with untapped resources, not only for bringing us more wealth but to assist certain of Earth's nations. The council—primarily its environmental and historical committees—blocked every motion I put forth for mining the ores, minerals, and oils. Then the outage in Russia and China reminded me how I needed to sever the Pith connections. Ren's parents adopted a sympathetic approach. It wasn't the first calamity the boy released. First, there was the gigantic crater on the moon in 1980. Abner conveyed absolute hatred for his grandson over the reputation his family received for the Earth incident. So, he and I had a meeting of the minds.

"Before Ren was born, his parents tended to a baby girl, left in their care by a couple having marital difficulties. At one point, a message announced the quarreling pair were going to divorce and put the child up for adoption. The Piths planned on adopting the tot but, to their dismay, her folks reconciled their differences and went on to have more kids. Such was the reason behind Ren's birth—disappointment in losing the girl they loved. I telepathed Abner that we should brainstorm on how to secure a time machine.

"Abner and I both have discreet contacts. One of his connections, an Exile, boasts a power of extraordinary sight and during the '35 G-storm week, spotted Winthrop Rodanthe's aerocube over Vietnam. With the Lointainian's assistance, I met up with the time traveler in Romania. He had traveled here from his world to document the storm and its effects on the two superpowers. It would be much better, I messaged Abner, if I involved myself rather than him, as my emotional ties to the situation were not as complex as his. I'd make certain he and Ada's son and daughter-in-law adopted the girl. Her mother is a good-looking woman, and I'm a handsome man. A little fooling around would seal the divorce and goodbye Ren."

A round of appalled sighs from the council and a whimper from Pith later, Luther resumed, "Rodanthe and I argued over a price and the ship itself. I never told him my plans, but he knew from family history how dicey changing the past can be. I didn't intend to create a new timeline, which meant I had to fly the exosphere runways last traveled by Hugh Rodanthe in the 1970s and repeat his documented route for backward voyages or else risk originating another Alt Lointain and Earth and never returning to this planet again."

"Hold on a sec!" Susie yelled. Scowling at Win, she burst out, "You told us those ramps used by Hugh either needed fixing or weren't there anymore. So, how could Luthy fly through them?"

Theresa came to the rescue. "Sus, dear, remember? He made the statement *before* I generated my truth power on him. The sucker lied."

Asked to start again, Luther related the bickering over the usage of an aerocube. "In the end, Win transported me to his timeline, and there, he let me pilot an older version of the spaceship. You see, during our negotiations, he grasped the notion of how Edna and I would be gone for quite a while because we had to ensure that no casual loops and paradoxes be initiated by our scheme. Rodanthe didn't want to be without his spacecraft for too long a time. We told our family and friends we'd decided on a lengthy tour of Earth. Jack there didn't mind us violating Lointain's terms of length for Earth-bound vacations. He was happy seeing me go. Ha!

"September 2035, we descended back in time for August 1856. Both Edna and I studied the pre-Kelowna region, clothes, customs, money … although we rarely mingled with Earth people. Lointain was still in its infancy. Grandpa Gerard was a mean old cuss. Didn't really seem like your customary educated and refined Exile. But oh, when I proved my identity to him, his attitude and demeanor changed completely. I told him not to do that … how he needed to remain the same and not throw off history. It was the first of many events of the seven-year journey my wife and I synchronized to accurately match known history. Even though we altered a few major happenings, Lointain's future lay mapped out in books and holographic chronicles better than anyone disrupting the past could hope for.

"August 1856, the third week. Your illness, Jack, was a well-kept secret at the time, but not in the future. Everyone reckoned you and your wife were on an African safari. Ha! The old vacation excuse came in handy for my wife and me! No, you had cholera and a viral infection which led to an underactive thyroid, a symptom of which is forgetfulness. E'tatanya was off-world gathering medicinal charms. A perfect storm! So, in front of what I at the time called 'witless witnesses'—meaning, not the brightest observer citizens—I shapeshifted into Jack, and along with Gramps, signed the document."

Jack1 walked in front of Luther's cube. "Those 'witless witnesses' never did learn I was sick. I questioned them, as you know, when you presented the contract. They weren't lying. Gerard couldn't have pulled off an intricate transformation, considering his alcohol addiction. The younger versions of you and Edna worked on a community project in the north country. I double-checked both of your alibis. What a waste of tenacity skills! The document turns over my roles in the community after two hundred years … if I'm still in power. I should have paid more attention to that codicil. Why wait so long for assuming the reigns of command?"

"Up until and including the day we left for the past, there was a multitude of constants for us to cross off the list, confident nothing we did altered the status quo of today."

Nodding his head at Ren, Boudreaux1 said, "He's here. You didn't carry out the venture for Abner."

A drink of water later, Luther said, "I never intended to follow through. In fact, after procuring the paperwork, we set out for the year 1578. There would be no more Eaftós. On the day when the other selves eased into existence as fully born adults, linked with our minds, we severed the cords. Abner and Ada can communicate telepathically with us, and we can sense their presence to a very high degree, but I destroyed the former bridge linking our souls."

E'tty2 commented, "Such a psychic-surgery can prove dangerous, perhaps fatal, especially when it's handled by amateurs."

"Both Piths have shown excellent health since our return," Fontenot countered. "Almost five hundred years they've lived. I don't see any signs of dangerous results."

"We'll find out the extent of their wellbeing when E'tatanya returns," Jack1 stated, "which I expected before now. Excuse me while I contact her." His disposition read calm when sending the psychic call, turning somber within a few moments. Lifting his head beelined at E'tty2's, he stated, "Your diagnosis on the Piths might be correct. Seems they've dissipated into nothingness."

CRANED NECKS AND NON-RESTRAINED questions greeted E'tty1 upon her return. Carrying a shoebox-sized carton, she hushed them all with a finger snap and handed Susie a recording device, consulting with the Exile leaders before making an announcement. During the dialogue, Boudraux1 brought her up to speed on the rest of Luther's discourse.

"Abner and Ada Pith are dead. They—"

"*Yee-haw*!" Ren shouted. "Happy days are here again!"

"As I was trying to say"—when the Prime healer flung back her long green hair, it sounded like a bullwhip cracking—"they had started dissolving over the last few weeks. None of the other workers at the reserve had seen them since early July. Whenever they spoke with the couple, it was either through telepathy or a holograph. Abner left a recorded message on the machine I brought back. Let's play it."

The medicine woman pressed a button and from out the rectangular box, a 3-D-colored image of Abner illuminated the space between the council and the Fontenots. Words came out of the gaunt face, and the sunken eyes stared straight ahead. Luther detected the odds of achieving an acquittal rapidly vanishing.

"Ada and I are not much longer for this world. Much of the fault lies clearly with us. But not all. I will now disclose my business dealings with Luther Fontenot. My wife and I are Eaftós to him and Edna."

E'tty1 hit a pause button, stopping the playback and suspending an open-mouthed Pith. "I'm skipping this part because, while it deals in questionable practices, none of it is relevant in legal terms. I'll restart it … here." Aware of the holograph's settings, she pushed the play button again.

"The Fontenots finally returned in 2047. Luther asked me to meet him on the outer perimeter of the reserve. Was he insane? Being in the same space as him, with Fontenot being the stronger, it would knock my breath out and kill me! I reminded him of this in case time travel had made him forget. He said he'd changed the physics rules governing Eaftós and it would be safe. Trusting him, I reached the designated meeting place first. He teleported in, and as he started walking in my direction, I began choking, losing oxygen! I ran off and telepathed a message, asking him what the hell was he thinking. He apologized, claiming he must've made a mistake in the past.

"He certainly did! I told him how Ren was still alive. 'Our plan didn't work,' he said. 'I tried and failed, sorry.' Instead of elaborating, he dematerialized. I knew he hadn't even tried because I kept comprehensive records of the time when my son and daughter-in-law wanted to adopt the girl they cared for. Nothing had changed in their lives or those of

the child's parents. There should've at least been the most minute alteration in the timeline. There wasn't.

Back at the compound, I drew up a Heritage Hologram. The entirety of the Eaftós clause was gone. Why did Luther delete it? Few people knew, anyway. Or did they? I asked those folks if they knew any Eaftós, and most said they weren't certain such a linkage was possible! Ada and I decided it best to not associate with Fontenots anymore. We had our work, and it was enough.

But, during a necessary business communique in February of 2052, Luther let it slip how he had the bogus change-of-leadership document signed by himself as Boudreaux. I knew about Jack being ill at the time in 1856. It was a perfect ruse. I'd never had any quarrel with Jack, not like I was having with Luther. Revisiting the 2047 incident in my mind, I grasped the intended deception—Fontenot believed he had severed the connection between us! Changing that event failed. Did he personally alter the hologram, or did time do it? Either way, because the holograph was an Exile product, it would show tampering from any source. I dared not trust anyone in Lointain. Not with the other selves' connections.

"Therefore, I hired a freelance worker at Hayalche Incorporated. They're experts at detecting the slightest abnormalities in holo-ware and don't mind if the clients are Exiles. The woman on the case was very talented if not eccentric. She never finished her commission. The first time—"

Ren leaped up, screaming, "He's talking about Isabella! She worked there! She did freelance work! My conniving grandpa employed my girlfriend for a task which got her killed! This is—"

"I know it's hard," Theresa consoled, holding onto Pith's shoulders. "Let's hear what the old geezer had to say. Okay?"

A quick rewind brought the holo-scene back at, "*The first time due to the internet crash when the geomagnetic storm pounded the Earth. Everyone blamed Ren. Why he boasted about committing the horrendous event, well ... I'm sure he meant to act big around the criminal element or impress some girl.*"

"Not just any girl, Gramps! She was a fun-loving, tattooed biker chick!" Ren's interruption brought about silent chuckles and spun eyes.

"*I know it wasn't him,*" holo-Abner continued. "*I know who it was. When I first employed Isabella Raven, I had to be certain I could trust not only her but Fontenot, too. I bugged her apartment—and his house, a little too late, unfortunately. When playing back the recordings of Luther and Edna talking, I overheard him tell her about what I was doing. He had applied a surveillance spell onto my house! The man knew my plans from everything I told Ada. Ending Miss Raven's work meant bringing down the Internet.*"

"Hearsay!" Fontenot roared. "Where's the proof?"

E'tty1 opened a hitherto unseen panel in the box, removing three small, rectangular clips. "Everything Abner recorded from the listening devices is on these, including you, Luther, admitting to the plotting behind and the carrying out of the G-storm. The voice from the grave will settle the matter."

"*Back in 1974, I let it be known that the same prehistoric Monarch bee which stung Ren also nipped me. Not true. My honeybee was smaller. It must've been my age that fended off seizures and only rendered a heaping of OCD which I could live with. The G-storm ability I kept secret until Luther figured it out, us being Eaftós.*

"I never noticed the power was gone until 2048. While I had never used it, I always summoned a tiny bit of its energy up through my chest once every three years for invigorating purposes. Where did it go? I sensed it in Fontenot. On one of my data sticks, he tells Edna how he believes the failure of perfectly disconnecting the Eaftós resulted in a transference of the deadly skill.

"One day in '48, I came home, found it ransacked. Among the missing items were the original recordings of Fontenot. What he didn't know was that I made copies, hidden where he'd never find them, and knowing he kept listening in, I never said a word about them to Ada. I'm filming this holo-message on Earth, far from his reach.

"As you know, on Lointain, most of us didn't keep abreast of the RES-51 virus news until a few weeks into the pandemic. Much as I despise Luther, I know he wouldn't destroy the internet if he realized it would result in the death of billions. What he wanted was Isabella's work destroyed, and all the G-storm did was delay it.

"Luther had gotten rid of the transmitters in his house. It took me a while, but I bribed a competent enough fellow to place a surveillance spell on Fontenot's residence. I learned the date he planned on presenting the phony document to Jack, but why he'd waited since 2047 remained a mystery. Meanwhile, I reconnected with Isabella. She was back to work at Hayalche Incorporated. Obtaining evidence against Luther seemed closer.

"*By eavesdropping on the Fontenots, I discovered Luther's reason for waiting. He couldn't help it—the man has a severe case of OCD! Instead of taking control of Lointain in '47, his disorder compelled him to do it a full ten years later! The things I heard ... his rants ... he barely kept them out of public knowledge. He wouldn't reach out to E'tatanya for help, not risking her finding out the truth behind his condition. What he experienced was revenge for attempting to separate the Eaftós. Unfortunately for Ada and me, he was able to correct his past mistake here in the present.*

"*Once our souls broke apart, tracing my movements became easier for him. Luther gleaned how I worked once more with Isabella. The only way of stopping her permanently was having her killed via a jealous barkeep named Bar T. Ender who, conveniently enough, has ties to Ren. The man owned a second motive for killing the woman. She knew about his ties to the sabotaging of Earth's aerofreight vehicles. On one of my sticks, they argue about whether he can trust her. By the time I had learned Fontenot hired Ender for the dastardly plan, it was too late.*

"*Ada and I slowly began ... evaporating. One final time, I telepathed Fontenot. 'Let's mend fences. You murdered Isabella. But still, I withdraw all investigations of the Heritage Hologram. There's still time for reversing the soul severance.' Instead of showing mercy, he threatened our children. My hope now is someone finds this confession and hands it over to Boudreaux and the council.*"

Three months later...

Excerpt from the journal of Liam Karas, October 2057

SUMMER ... CAN'T BELIEVE HOW fast it breezed by, and I haven't penned a word since returning home. Imene suggested I use today's entry for a wrap-up before recording the memories of my amazing adventures on GNet Discs. As usual, her idea sounds reasonable.

Luther Fontenot. I'm glad he pled guilty when facing the council. Otherwise, we'd have spent way too much time listening to the unimaginable amount of chatter on Abner Pith's memory sticks. For the benefit of Earth, Boudreaux turned the former Exile leader over to the International Court of Justice, along with all the accumulated evidence.

Fontenot's trial is set for February. Both E'ttys came up with DES10Y, a ten-year version of the power Destabilizer. Even if he's not convicted on any of the various charges in an Earth court, he will also have his day before a tribunal on Lointain. Jack wants him depowered before setting foot off Earth.

Has the arrest made a difference in how people view the Exiles? Yes, quite a bit, but for the wrong reason and mostly thanks to narrow-minded conspiracy theorists who reside in two camps. One, people who claim there was never a pandemic (the Old Souls) and others who assert the RES-51 was real, albeit a multi-government creation (Wide-Eyed, or WE). Both societies contend the fault was lain at the Lointainians' feet because the superior race showed a willingness for imparting advanced technologies and magic spells upon the nations of Earth—incantations meant for fighting hunger and bad weather while restoring a cleaner environment. For this reason, both associations declare this planet's colossal industries and many billionaires cited an off-worlder as the catalyst for the virus, whether actual or fake. It's not a bad notion—scapegoating commerce and its wealthy owners who in retaliation denounce a minority. The Old Souls and WE discount all admissions of culpability by Fontenot and decry the DES treatment as "barbaric butchery." Even when the President assembled a panel for studying a normalization of relations with Lointain, a WE spokesperson laughed it off as "propagandistic rhetoric aimed at changing nothing." I say, "We" shall see (pun intended).

Edna Fontenot. She willingly provided evidence against her soon-to-be ex-husband but will still face charges, such as accessory and conspiracy. Jack banned her for life from

Lointain. Last I heard, she's negotiating a part in a reality TV show!

Abner and Ada Pith. A memorial service was held in early August. Ren didn't attend. As I mentioned earlier, Abner's flash drives ended up at the ICJ. Late last month, news broke how someone broke into the court, copied everything on the sticks, and began posting transcripts of the recordings on a GNet site called The Pith Papers. *It's a play on words of The Pentagon Papers (I didn't know what that was until I researched). Already, Hollywood shows interest in developing at least two films on what's already available for reading on the Net. Will the Fontenot's seek a piece of the action? No doubt!*

Bar T. Ender. The Jacks suggested Lointain trackers hunt for the mixologist. But ... surprise, surprise, Jay informed Susie where they could find the killer. How he knew the man's location remains unknown, as does who the hell this Jay character is. Some of us close to Susie believe he's an imaginary friend. Ha! Alt Jack even advanced the hypothesis to her face and received a powerful nose punch in return. Anyway, Ender, who vanished once he ratted out Pith to the Feds, came under Luther's radar when the Exile began keeping an eye on Raven. The barkeep acknowledged he murdered Isabella on behalf of Fontenot and how he supplied Rodanthe the explosives for blowing up the Zeps. He's in prison for quite a long time. Oh, and his real name—Gene N. Tonic. Go figure.

Winthrop Rodanthe. I feel kind of sorry for this guy. He never intended for any loss of life during the explosions he engineered. While coming off arrogant at first, he's very intelligent and witty. Imene interviewed him for The Indianapolis Star, *a scoop that triggered her obtaining the rights for questioning him on national television. When he sought a plea bargain to testify against Fontenot, the U.S. Attorney General (a possible presidential candidate in 2060) nixed the notion, targeting Rodanthe, who he claimed is an example of "a degenerate super-human from a lesser Earth which produces an inferior species of doppelgängers." My wife called the AG a "sub-human racist." She's still receiving hate mail from his supporters.*

There's still hope for Winthrop. Diplomats from the two Earths began extradition discussions and those talks— much to the AG's displeasure—turned into dialogues regarding trade of goods, culture, and ideas. Romantica no longer seeks an arrest of Rodanthe. They have his apprentice in custody and recovered all the property Winthrop had swiped and appear unconcerned about the other charges. Among those items retrieved was a previously unopened diary of the nation's prime minister, detailing how he swindled a ton of money from the pensions of government workers while on his way up the political ranks. Alt New York police and the constable of East Coast Vacationland do have warrants out for W.R., mostly for petty violations.

The Thrusk Brothers met with Rodanthe a month ago while he was in jail awaiting a March trial. They're offering full payment for his legal team if he comes to work for them and turns over all documents leading to the safe creation of aerofreight vehicles and, eventually, flying cars. Winthrop is still mulling it over. The families of those who perished in the Zep bombings don't like the Thrusks' interference. TV and GNet news commentators all agree that Win will probably be in prison for life. In that case, another warden will no doubt request the DES10Y.

The Allgyers. Here's the happy update. Sam is free, reunited with brother Matt. The Thrusks have thrown money their direction from behind the scenes (i.e. rent, legal fees, etc.), knowing the brudres would otherwise refuse any help. They won't hear about it from me.

When asked my price for the investigative work I executed, I said, "We're all good. You guys don't owe a cent." It's not my generosity talking. I'm not hurting for money is all (more on this below). Sam's gonna have a hard enough time assimilating back into the former Amish lifestyle. Both men obtained a major thrill when meeting Susie, the legend of their house when growing up. Neither will likely find themselves welcome among the Amish or their parents ever again. Samuel escaped the electric chair. That oughta win his way back into the hearts of his traditionalist family.

Isabella Raven. Her parents and siblings expressed relief at Ender's capture. Sadly, morons crawled out of the woodwork, condemning her for working for Abner because he's an Exile, proclaiming she deserved to die. **Sheesh!** *When she first began freelancing, the Lointainians were still in favor with Earthlings. She knew what the job truly meant—holding the correct person responsible for the geomagnetic storm. The woman never believed Ren culpable of the crime.* **"An Exile is still guilty,"** *I read one person write on a message board.* **"All that's changed is the name."** *Well, hell yeah! It makes a big difference if you're the innocent one.*

A recent follow-up re: the Heritage Hologram. Isabella's co-workers banded together and completed her work. They found the holo-fingerprints of Fontenot not only in the model which sat untouched after Raven's death, but in other versions of the Hologram. Those types of personal impressions—so I've read—move from graph to graph. Oh, and the boss who sexually harassed her ... he was fired and forced to pay restitution to her family.

The Jacks and the E'ttys. Prime Jack commands his world again. Avoiding any backlash against the Fontenot and Pith families, he dispensed with the normal pomp and circumstance expected over the return to power. He and Alt Jack granted their respective E'ttys permission to journey back and forth from their particular worlds with the provision they don't stray off the current year-path in which they now reside. Any reason for time traveling outside that specified juncture must face approval from the councils of both Lointains. Only the healers and their Jack-approved guests may traverse from Alt to Prime, and vice versa.

Ren Pith. Imene asked me if I thought he truly loved Isabella or if it was the OCD controlling his emotions. I don't know. His reactions demonstrated that he cared for her, but who am I to judge how much ... or why is it even a point of contention? The guy definitely didn't like the paternal grandparents.

Susie and I did watch him reunite with his parents. It was an uneasy moment. They apologized for the treatment he'd received from the elder Piths and also for not reacting more thoughtfully regarding his medical problems.

Susie forgave him for stealing her memories. All the transcripts stolen from the psychiatrist's files are awaiting a claim from the shrink's next of kin. The wealthy and famous persons in NYC whose apartments Pith burglarized reobtained their goods and waived pressing charges on one condition— Ren signs off on a book and movie deal for his story with all earnings going to the collective of those he robbed. When the Suzii heard about this last term, well, a little "arm twisting" (so they told me) altered the deal. Seventy percent of the profits will be divided between foundations for helping sufferers of epilepsy and OCD.

Cleared of any role in the 2052 geomagnetic storm, Russia and China still sought his arrest for the 2035 blackout, despite it being an accident (so Pith claims). During a bargaining session with Jack, both nations declared their intention to forget the capture so long as the Exiles provided them vials of DES for the control of "criminal" Remnants. The Exile leader insists the minor-powered people get a fair trial in a neutral country ... negotiations are still in progress.

Meanwhile, Ren decided against remaining in his home world. "There's a red-haired woman I want as my friend," he told Alt E'tty. "Can you drop me off in Halifax?" He's there now, I suppose. No more seizures, OCD, and the G-storm power is also gone. Alt E'tty will bring him back for the occasional family reunion. No matter the deal over the DES, he won't surrender himself. I wish him well ... despite the trouble he caused!

Theresa Earth. The press nicknamed her "Old Susie." Naturally, she has lived longer than her Prime equivalent. Still, she's quite ravishing. As no one could tie her to the G-storm, she fared quite well with Earthlings. What did she do during her time here? She "borrowed" a considerable amount of money from Susie and bought crate loads of Dr. Pepper and sneakers. During a dinner last week we held for Jack and E'tty, they graced us with a description of how difficult it was transporting Theresa's supplies through time and space. The transfer became stuck between worlds and the crates of soda unloaded; a few hundred cans were left adrift in a middle zone for picking up later. What's worse occurred when word of the arrival of non-durable tennis shoes spread through Alt America. Trouble was definitely "afoot" during the massive Nike-Adidas Riots!

Good news for Theresa surfaced when the E'ttys put their healer heads together (with assistance from their off-world and other-dimension sages), curing the "shit storms." These behavioral fits resulted from the Bahamas hurricane tossing her around like a sack of potatoes back in 2104 (Alt Earth time). Whenever pressure from a tiny mass lodged against her temporal lobe began throbbing, a mental attack ensued. The extraordinary psychic surgeons removed the mound (iced and drained it), bringing long overdue relief. Theresa admitted she had had many more "mini-poop upheavals" than she cared to discuss. "What's gone is past, kiddos," she happily admitted. "Let's only talk about now and later."

Lt. Jim "Jim-Bob" Flannagan. Alt Jack penned a report on the officer's assistance in capturing Winthrop while Prime Jack and the President(!) authored assessments on why Rodanthe should face trial on Prime Earth, crediting Jim not only for the apprehension but for showing competent judgment above and beyond the call of duty, etc., etc. I know the guy well enough by now to know he'll probably turn in his badge no matter who stands up for him, including his obvious girlfriend, Theresa.

She's much more his type than Susie. My theory: the "shit storms" humanized Theresa, whereas Susie still has a chip on her shoulder (God ... please don't let Drake read this!). Flannagan and Earth made eyes at one another long before the cute-teenage-rubbing-arms-signs-of-affection began. Did I type "long?" I did! We weren't even gone any amount of time one could classify as "long." Yet, it sure felt so and in a good way.

As I was saying, kiddos (now Miss Earth has me copping her means of greeting), during the dinner I mentioned above, E'tty said she'd check in on Jim and Theresa and let me know their "status," if any. Late breaking bulletin: the healer popped in tonight and my "probably" is a certainty— Jim quit the force and is shacking up with Alt Susie in Olde Harvard. When he has custody of Jaime, I can imagine how the boy will take to his pop dating "the one and only" while living among a colony of powereds. What does Flannagan do at ex-Harvard? Keeps the peace, assigns guard duties, and investigates mischief. Jimmy's gonna be a Remmie soon if he isn't already. I hope he obtains teleportation. Given the hectic lifestyle he's adopted, he will need a break now and then ... fishing, maybe.

"Theresa, Jim, and Old Man have asked if they might share Thanksgiving with you," the green-haired Exile informed us. "My counterpart and I would love to join in, too."

Imene reluctantly said yes. She's over her dislike of the Exiles but being a veggie, well, turkey baking is on me, kiddos. My wife did meet with Jim and Theresa during their time on Prime. She noted how the lieutenant and I have a rapport not only because of our adventure, but we're both investigators and, apparent to her, we have comparable personalities and viewpoints. I'm not so sure about that last item. So, how did he take to 21ˢᵗ-century America?

"There're advantages and disadvantages," he said. "I like the variety of food choices. and you have much better-quality TV shows and movies. There hasn't been much change in how New York City is laid out. Much as I enjoyed the small-town atmosphere of Mason, I prefer the sliced-up arrangement of my America."

Before leaving for Alt Earth, Jim became the object of a bent-over smooch from Susie, much to the applause of those he'd befriended along the way. When completely vertical, he whispered something into her ear. Later, she confided his words. "Please give Jesus a chance and find a church you can attend."

Imene and I. My adventure triggered a journalistic frenzy for Imene. The woman interviewed everyone involved, Earthling and Exile, imprisoned or not. She talked Susie into sitting for a filmed chat, but no date was set. In her articles, she stressed how her attitude was previously antagonistic toward the Lointainians, a strategy which helped others look kindly upon them again. The limelight didn't spoil her. Both our great-grandparents had wealth thrown upon them; therefore, any accrued money beyond what she considers a normal salary went to charities.

Her handling of various accounts of life on Alt Earth drew the most comments, good and bad. You can't go anywhere these days without hearing debate over Alt America's segregated multi-states and "restrictions on liberties by way of unrestricted AI." It's not really like that. Depending on one's political and social spectrum, Imene's interviews have fallen open to a wide range of interpretations, a sad misunderstanding she never expected.

The best way for clearing matters, so my wife says, is a trip to the Alt planet. A Congressional committee agreed and broadcasted their intention to fund a fact-finding tour of the parallel world to the Exiles' earthly representatives in Kelowna. The Thrusk Brothers, naturally, have offered millions for two tickets! Currently, the junket is not yet finalized.

When the Jacks dispensed credit for Rodanthe's capture to Jim, he insisted I receive half the honors. I said no. The man needs it more for the satisfaction of his superiors not being any more vindictive regarding his leaving NYC with Susie and me. However, Theresa did put a word in for my collecting a gift from the Rennaissance Fair. **Ha!** *She remembered I wanted to bring something back for Imene.*

"She'd like a carved stone outdoor vase," I said. "Medieval-based art has always fascinated her."

So, I figured, at some juncture, Alt E'tty would return with a small, nicely engraved bowl. Coming home one afternoon, I gasped at the sight of seven gigantic planter boxes, carved from stone, stationed an equal distance apart in our horseshoe-shaped garden. Each vase came expertly sculptured with scenes of knights, damsels in distress, kings, queens, English villages, etc., and Imene absolutely loves them.

Unlike her, I haven't succeeded in avoiding the limelight. Freezing when asked personal questions by reporters, my nervous behavior only drags out the embarrassing scenes. Photographs of me with the beautiful Suzii and flashy Exiles precipitated questions which subsisted in the nefarious realm of the absurd. I wasn't about to sink to the paparazzi's level. My responses for almost any inquiry dwelt on the case I felt most proud about— freeing Samuel Allgyer. It may not be what certain cretins wanted to hear, but it sure has landed me a ton of job offers, many of them in other countries.

One last tidbit on us Karases ... once things quiet down a bit more, we're taking Theresa's advice and adopting if we pass all the requirements. Our attorney foresees no problem, especially as neither of us are Remnants. I never slept with a Susie. Honest.

Susie Drake. I saved her for last. "Legend of Legends." "Controller of Charisma." "The Megastar Beyond Compare." "Mythical Maverick." *Just a few of the many headlines describing her these last months. The reception she garnered after Isabella's death was not overwhelmingly in her favor due to associations with the Exile. These days, however, her star shines brighter than ever. Susie's one of those people who cannot acquire oversaturated coverage in the media. People are always wanting to know more about her and, because her life is a lagoon of unknown and/or undisclosed details, your average Joe and Jane can never find satisfaction in learning enough of what's popularly known as "Susie Specifics."*

From the outset, Susie plummeted into the world's focus of attention. There'd be no Ellesmere Island cave, or tent in the Lut Desert, or advertising her talents out as a soldier. "Helping," "rescuing," "redeeming," and "changing" became the most spoken words I heard her speak to the press or people who greeted her ... wherever she went. Change was never ascribed to her personality until now. What happened? I speculate it was Jim's line about Jesus and the church. Susie seldom mentions religion or anything spiritual, but I know from Great-Grandfather Emory's journals how metaphysical matters could push Miss Drake into a vulnerable state (hard as it is to picture). Emory and his wife knew her very well ... worked with her, cared for her. Jim's low-key approach (so I hypothesize) transcended space and time, sending the needed oomph *inside the woman's psyche. How long she remains on the Greater-Good Boulevard is anyone's guess. More power to her!*

Friendship, more than memories, lit the fuel behind Susie's adventure after Sacha passed. Sure, there was no human left with whom she shared common experiences. Unlike most others in an identical situation, Lady Drake is a people magnet. She can pick and choose her family of friends with relative ease, chasing away the vultures and phonies. Already, she informed Imene and me how she'd like to have a once-a-month standing dinner date with us either here in Mason or wherever she might have us flown. When word spread how she was searching for a community setting for a Remnant learning center—such as Old Man made for the Alt Remmies—offers flooded in from the major universities. Susie ... a professor? No, more like a now-and-then administrator (or a disciplinarian!). USC is her top choice at the moment.

Yes, she's going to be okay. It didn't surprise me to hear she's reconnected with the same NYC policeman (now a Remnant) who investigated Isabella's killing. He won't see her too often, not with her newfound enthusiasm for life, but enough for the relationship to last a good while. She's going to be more than okay. She's gonna be the quintessential symbol for hope, and as a comedian who died before my time would say, "Thanks for the memories, Susie."

Intermission (July 2023)

I CALL HER NAME. "SUSIE! Hey! I gotta talk to you."

She doesn't answer immediately. When she does, she screams my name and obscenities (and words I've never before heard, which sound … nasty). I let her rant.

"Oh, good Lord! I thought I was free of you! What do *you* want?"

Not feeling insulted by her tone, I reply, "Just wanted to say goodbye. When you're free of me, you'll sense it in your head, as will I of you in mine. I thought you'd want a forewarning."

"'Kay. Whatever." Not grateful. "How do you know this?"

"Because it's what happened when I first connected with your mind."

Confusion smears itself all over her face.

"You don't remember nor should you. I'm part of the déjà vu package E'tatanya warned you about before removing your memories."

"Is that the reason you showed up in the first place? I still don't remember knowing you were in my head. It was like you were always there."

I explain, "When she severed the recollections, you needed something to fill the gap. Your psyche reached out and yanked me in."

"Why *you*? Why not someone helpful?" she spits. "We spoke less than ten times, and only once were you really of any use, and that was tracking down Bar T. Ender."

I'm used to her criticism. "I doubt anyone else could've assisted you in the way you wanted. You're not exactly the easiest person to get along with. Why me in particular? I think it had something to do with me writing down your adventure."

Exerting my vision, it reached beyond her voice. There … I see her inside a USC dorm undergoing renovation. She's keeping her word about helping the Remmies.

"So, you were a glorified placeholder for what Pith stole. It's all fine now. Thank you for sitting in, hope you enjoyed the show, and oh, hey! I went into a bookstore recently to check out what people have written about me and my friends. I didn't see a single one written by a fellow named Jay. Are you using a pseudonym? Moron, perhaps?"

"Fun-ny! We're on different Earths, Susie, besides being thirty-four years apart."

"Well, ain't that a blessing! Are you still writing your book?"

"Yep. The editing part begins soon. The story—your story—begs for a Hollywood rendition."

Grumbles. "I predict it'll be direct to streaming. Extremely low-budget."

Ignoring her, I go on, "Y'know, being in your head once the memories rushed back, I witnessed it all. Your life story. There's a lot to work with in there."

"Don't you dare!"

Unabated, I continue, "Imagine … you're in the theater watching the film about the Stolen Memories. The credits roll. Up comes a post-credit scene. More kudos. Then, toward the very end … across the screen … the upcoming promise …"

"No! Don't say it!"

Humming a melodramatic movie score of my own making, I envision the final words on the large white canvas. "'Susie Drake will return in …'"

"Argh!"

The End?

Acknowledgements

Many thanks to Kristin Campbell, Todd Hosea, Carol Burkes, Dan Drewes, the Bloomington Writers Group, Gina Griffith Englander, and Rusty Burns.

www.ingramcontent.com/pod-product-compliance
Lightning Source LLC
Chambersburg PA
CBHW070604300726
48975CB00006B/1708